Also available from MIRA Books and
JANET LEIGH

HOUSE OF DESTINY

The Dream Factory

The Dream Factory

JANET LEIGH

MIRA®

ISBN 1-55166-874-2

THE DREAM FACTORY

Copyright © 2002 by Janet Leigh.

Visit us at www.mirabooks.com

Printed in U.S.A.

First Printing: February 2002
10 9 8 7 6 5 4 3 2 1

To
Our Higher Power who blessed me with a lifetime loan
of my beloved husband, Bob, my children, Kelly and Jamie,
my grandchildren, Annie and Tom. They have made my life
rich and full and joyous. And who graced me with family, friends
and associates whose wonderful love, loyalty and support
have been my sustenance through these years.

I am filled with gratitude to:

Laura Archila, who kept me alive and well
and made the household work.

Chelsea Augustine, for a child's enchanting observations.

Jim Gallo, for his colorful contemporary expressions.

Kristi Kittendorf, not only because she translated
my maze of #3 penciled pages into computerese,
but also because she managed to keep our office in order.

Dianne Moggy and my entire MIRA family, for their
publishing/editing expertise and for believing in me.

Dr. Lew Morrill, whose medical knowledge was invaluable.

Lillian Burns Sidney, my mentor since I was eighteen,
whom I miss every single day.

Mr. and Mrs. Saul Turteltaub,
who kept me straight on Hebrew references.

Laura Van Wormer, Loretta Barrett and Shaye Areheart,
who have been guiding lights since my literary career began.

Barry Zwick, a savant who shared with me
his background in business and the military.

"You make a living by what you get.
You make a life by what you give."
—Author unknown

Prologue

Los Angeles, California
Monday, July 3, 1972, 6:30 p.m.

Eve Handel lay quietly on the hospital bed. She was beginning to be able to ignore the intravenous tube that hung haphazardly by her side, attached to the hateful needle that had bruised and invaded her body. Just as the hands of the doctors had probed and poked and jabbed.

The saving grace was the numbing power of their medication. Through the fog of the horrific, crippling pain that had engulfed her right side from her chest to abdomen, clear through to her back and down both arms, Eve had heard the word *morphine* echo against the wall just as she felt the sting of an injection.

She would have liked to have smiled. Finally at age—well almost fifty-four—she was doing drugs. *Cassie will have a good laugh about this,* Eve thought. And then in a moment of clarity, she wondered if she would see Cassie again. *I have to tell her what I've learned. I have to tell her how close we are to the end of our search.*

There were no smiles or laughter in the tiny waiting area of the emergency room at the Randall Burdsey Hospital in downtown Los

Angeles. Six anxious, frightened faces looked up as one of the on-duty doctors pushed open the door.

"I'm Dr. Leonard Westle. We've done everything we can at this time—drawn blood, taken X rays and a cardiograph. And we were able to relieve her suffering somewhat," he said as he scanned the faces of the group before him. "Not completely, because we need to know more about that pain. Ms. Handel's regular physician should be here momentarily and I'm going to wait to make my diagnosis until he arrives. However, I do not believe we are dealing with a heart attack as initially suspected."

A distinguished-looking gentleman with salt-and-pepper hair stood. "Thank you, Dr. Westle. We appreciate the update—we'll wait here for more news."

The doctor nodded and hurried out. It was only six-thirty in the evening and the emergency rooms were already full, meaning he was in for a long night.

The man turned toward the others and attempted to reassure them, but his words fell on deaf ears—each person in the room was too occupied with his or her own thoughts. His own mind was full of apprehensions. Eve had promised that she'd never leave him and he pleaded that it be true. He refused to consider losing the woman he had been seeking all of his life. Fate simply couldn't be that cruel.

Another man sat upright, staring straight across the room. His expression gave his thoughts away—he was incapable of contemplating what might be happening. He could just not endure more pain.

The younger of the two women in the room slumped low in a chair, fighting an inner battle. On one hand she desperately tried not to allow the worst scenario to surface in her mind, while at the same time, the sly sprites of insecurity flashed neon signs inside her head, announcing the worst possible outcome.

Could she survive without her? Everything about her past told her she needed Eve!

A woman around Eve's age stood and began pacing the floor, gnashing her teeth, fervently wishing she hadn't given up smoking.

Silently she berated the gods, the heavens and anyone or anything she could think of for the turn of events. *Why Eve? Why not me? I'm the one who's made the big mistakes, I'm the weak one! All she did was help. Hadn't she suffered enough with that idiot! It isn't fair!*

She stopped roaming as her thoughts suddenly turned to a recent conversation with Eve and to Eve's journal. Even though she had never seen it, she and Eve had made reference to it many times. But Eve had never told her where the book was kept. How could she protect Eve's confidences if she didn't know where the journal was?

No one wanted Eve Handel to die. But not all had the same loving reasons. She was well liked, to be sure. She was respected. But she was also feared. Not because of her demeanor or actual power, despite her importance. But because she knew too much, about everyone. Somehow she exuded a sort of safety net that invited confidences. Friends, family, business associates, all took their worries and problems and secrets to her, wanting to confide, and trusting her capacity to heal, to advise, to comfort, to help. She knew what and how to say what they needed to hear. And, if necessary, she could and would pull some strings to make matters right. Provided the reasons were valid and just.

Through the years as Eve's prominence in Hollywood increased, a rumor had circulated about her appointment book. Hints that it was more than just a date calendar, that it was a diary—with notes. No one could pinpoint where or how this tidbit started and no one knew if it was true. It was a piece of innocent gossip and speculation.

It hadn't mattered until the word of Eve Handel's collapse spread across town.

Some people developed sweaty palms and fluttering hearts when they heard the news. Resentment toward Eve manifested, because some had exposed their naked vulnerability to her, confessed they were not invincible.

And now, more than ever before, everyone wanted to know if the journal existed. And who would be ruined if it was found?

1

Chicago, Illinois
Sunday, July 8, 1934

Arthur Randall Burdsey gazed wistfully into the large backyard of the Handelstein home, where brightly colored balloons waved in the light breeze and the sounds of laughter mixed with music and tinkling glasses and the hum of conversation. A big banner strung across a slightly elevated bandstand was gaily decorated in patriotic red, white and blue. Bold red letters on a white background proclaimed:

Happy Birthday, Ruth—July 9
Happy Birthday, Eve—July 6
Happy Birthday, Little Abe—July 15

Arthur wondered what it would be like to be part of a big family. He was an only child and his mother and father were also only children, so he didn't even have aunts and uncles and cousins around, let alone siblings. Ever since the three Burdseys had moved in nearly a week ago, just two houses down from the Handelsteins, he had been fascinated by all the activity surrounding their home. There seemed to be an almost constant stream of traffic in and out of the house. He thought he had identified the actual residents and there was one girl in particular who had captivated his attention. Naturally he couldn't guess who was who, but he suspected that the extra bodies belonged to relatives and friends. What a lively life they must enjoy, he thought longingly. And Arthur became downcast as he mentally compared his lifestyle with theirs.

Randall Burdsey wed Alicia Goodley in Chicago, January 1, 1917. Fortunately, the World War was drawing to a close, so he just missed being drafted and had not felt the need to enlist. Arthur Randall arrived September 15, 1917. Both sets of parents teased the young couple about the timing of his birth.

"That son of mine!" Randall's father had boasted. "He never wastes time, always gets the job done lickety-split!"

Randall did move at full speed. He was a doer, a workaholic. Arthur didn't see much of his father as he was growing up. Randall usually came home late from the office and he also traveled a great deal. So Alicia, in her loneliness, focused all her attention on the defenseless Arthur. No explanation was ever offered as to why Alicia and Randall hadn't had another child, no one knew if it was by choice or because of a physical condition. Regardless, from day one Alicia treated Arthur as if he were a prize colt. At the least hint of a fever or the slightest sign of a rash, physicians were rushed to the house, no matter what the hour. When Arthur developed asthma in early childhood, it gave his mother an added incentive to continue her possessiveness and protectiveness.

To ease what Randall was beginning to perceive as a dangerous and damaging attachment between his wife and son, Arthur was enrolled in a prestigious prep school and then later into Thatcher, a well known boarding school in Santa Barbara, California. Thatcher was considered the best, especially at keeping well-to-do boys in line.

Arthur was oblivious to the maneuvers of both parents. He was a normal child who, like any other, accepted the doting of his mother because it made life easier. He knew he could pretty well yank any of Alicia's chains he wanted—he was the puppeteer.

But he was equally open and ready for the experience of attend-

ing a facility away from home where he would have many room-
mates and an extended family, so to speak. The machinations of
mother and father had served their own purposes, but had been
ineffective in determining Arthur's behavioral future. He was his
own man.

Now he was ready to start Northwestern University in September
in Evanston, Illinois, and again he would be staying in a dorm on
campus until he was, hopefully, accepted into a fraternity. Evanston
was close enough that he could have lived at home, but once he
had tasted the sweet nectar of freedom and peer companionship,
he was not about to return to captivity. None of Alicia's contrived
grievances had proved sufficient to change her son's mind, so she
had to content herself with making his quarters in their new house
so appealing he wouldn't be able to resist coming home often.

Randall, on the other hand, was delighted with Arthur's new-
found independence. Of course, at this particular time, Randall was
damn well delighted with everything and anything. He had brilliantly navigated his stock brokerage business through the treach-
erous, turbulent waters of the stock market crash.

In the first six months of the Herbert Hoover administration in
1929, the president's attention had been directed toward the wide-
spread disregard for the law, as evidenced by the operations of
bootleggers, highjackers, kidnappers and racketeers and the failure
of the courts to convict and punish such criminals. The United
States had led the world in the sinister statistics of homicide, bur-
glary, holdups and graft.

However, by October 1929, the president was forced to address
a different kind of calamity. Until then, the prosperity of the nation
seemed to be established on a firm and enduring basis; the road to
wealth for all stretched broad and smooth before the American
people. Billions of dollars were drawn from the banks into Wall
Street. And then, the market tumbled like issues of bogus gold
mines. Prime securities dropped violently.

Randall had intuitively felt the upward curve was burgeoning
too rapidly to be healthy. He advised his clients to short their stock
positions, as he was going to do with his personal holdings. ''Short-

ing'' meant betting that the stocks held were going to go down in value. He conducted his transactions in Europe on the wire, and when disaster struck, Randall and those who had followed his lead hit the jackpot. They could cover the shorts at any time, and Randall waited until January 1932 to buy back. He and his associates took unrestrained pleasure in their power and wealth. The recent purchase of the elaborate mansion was only one manifestation of Randall's recently acquired stature.

''Hi!'' called a voice from across the lawn. Arthur jumped, startled out of his reverie, a trifle embarrassed at being caught staring.

''I'm Abe, well, they call me Little Abe because my Grandpa is Big Abe. 'Course, I'm almost as tall as he is already, so I don't know what they'll call us when I grow and pass him. Worry about that later, I guess. You're from the new place, aren't you?''

''Yes, I am.'' Arthur didn't feel apprehensive at all. Strange for him, because he was usually a bit careful with strangers at first. But this young man was so straightforward and natural that he was immediately put at ease.

''My name is Arthur Burdsey. I was just passing by and stopped for a minute to admire the decorations.'' No need to tell him the exact truth, Arthur thought.

''Do you have time? Can you come in? I know the family would like to meet you.'' Abe didn't give him a chance to back out of the invitation, he sort of guided Arthur along as he talked. ''My sisters and I were all born in July, so instead of having three scrabbly parties, Mama and Papa give one whopper. Oh, here's one of the birthday girls—Eve!''

The two had reached a cluster of people, and Eve, who naturally was in the center, excused herself and came toward them when she heard her brother call her name.

Arthur's heart started pounding. This was the one, this was the girl whom he had been drawn to when he was watching the parade of people around their house. She was small, barely five feet, but perfectly proportioned. Flawless skin, dark hair, and her eyes—big dark eyes—intelligent eyes. Eyes that questioned—eyes that looked through you to your inner soul. An aura of mystery walked with her, an ambience of unknowable secrets that made one anxious to find and explore her hidden depths.

"Eve, this is—Arthur Burdsey—did I get it right?"

Arthur nodded nervously.

"Arthur, this is my sister Eve. She's the middle one," Abe rambled on. "Everyone thinks she will be a great actress!"

"Abe, please! How do you do, Mr. Burdsey, welcome to the neighborhood and to our party. Abe, please find a waiter to take Mr. Burdsey's drink order. Meanwhile, why don't we sit at that table over there, under the umbrella. It's beastly hot in the sun."

Arthur barely heard her words, he was already under the spell of her voice, that low, melodious tonality that was so compelling. He could listen forever, he thought, and hoped he would have that option. But he soon realized he was obliged to respond and that he had to concentrate on what she was saying, not just how she said it.

"—in September?" Eve was asking.

Arthur could only guess at what had come before.

"Oh, I, uh, I will be entering Northwestern. As a business major," he added quickly in case that had been part of the question.

"How nice! Will you be living on campus or at home?"

"On campus." And then he hurried to amend the finality of that statement. "Of course, it's so close I can come home whenever, can't I? I mean, to see my folks. Or—whatever," he lamely dwindled off.

Abe arrived with a waiter who carried a heavy Georgian silver tray laden with Viennese crystal glasses filled with champagne and punch.

"You can have anything you like, these were just handy," Abe said.

"This is fine, thank you," Arthur replied, choosing the punch.

Eve and Abe then made the rounds with Arthur, introducing him to the rest of their family and friends.

At seventeen and a half, Arthur's physique was already defined. He was six feet tall, lean but not thin, handsome in an athletic, wholesome way. His hair was brown, highlighted with streaks from the sun, his face glowed with a California tan and his hazel eyes were open and direct. He made a very favorable impression when presented, his demeanor above reproach. What was not always immediately sensed, though, was his wit and humor, qualities that surfaced as a relationship grew.

Arthur stayed as long as he dared, not wanting to be accused of being a party crasher.

"Thank you, Mr. and Mrs. Handelstein, for your kind hospitality. You were gracious to a stranger," he said as he bid his good-bye.

"Not a stranger any longer, now you are a neighbor. We look forward to meeting your parents," Mildred declared warmly, and honestly. Both Mildred and her husband, Samuel, had immediately liked this young man.

The following Wednesday morning, Abe rang the Burdseys' doorbell and asked to see Arthur. Arthur, dressed in tennis clothes, eagerly bounded down the stairs to greet him.

"Hi! Good to see you!"

"I'm the appointed messenger," Abe explained. "We didn't get your telephone number the other day, and Mama and Papa wanted to invite you and your parents for Sunday lunch."

"I accept for me right now," Arthur declared hurriedly. "And I will ask my mother and father tonight. Thank you. By the way, do you play tennis?"

"Some, but it's not my strong suit."

"I'm not exactly pro material myself," admitted Arthur. "I know! I'll arrange for a couple of instructors at the club and we can play doubles. We'll have some laughs, might even learn something!"

"Sure! Sounds great!"

Alicia and Randall had a previous engagement for that Sunday, but the two families did make a plan for another time.

After a hearty midafternoon meal, Arthur asked and received permission to treat the Handelstein siblings to a movie. However, Little Abe was off to see Big Abe and Ruth wanted to finish the book she was reading, *La démocratie en Amérique,* by Alexis de

Tocqueville, the French writer and politician. So that left Eve and Arthur to go see *It Happened One Night,* a Frank Capra romantic comedy starring Clark Gable and Claudette Colbert. The film had received rave reviews, even though it was considered a bit racy. Evidently Gable appeared in one scene wearing only an undershirt and trousers.

"How ridiculous!" scoffed Eve as they were coming out of the theater. "Tarzan, Mr. Ape Man himself, didn't wear *any* shirt and hardly anything for pants. No one seemed to make a big hoo-ha about that! At least everyone had the sense to appreciate the writing in this. And the performances, weren't they wonderful?"

On the way home in Arthur's 1932 Ford V8, they chatted about each other's plans, backgrounds and families. Without any effort, or consciousness, the two fell into a comfortable exchange.

"My gabby brother already told you my ambition," Eve laughed. "What about you?"

"I imagine I will be doing something in the business community, but not just because my father is a stockbroker, that could almost discourage me." Arthur hoped he didn't sound too disrespectful, but Eve gave no particular reaction, so he went on, fueled by his enthusiasm.

"It really interests me. The art of investing, the timing, the knowledge needed to manage money, it's all a tremendous challenge and responsibility, and that excites me."

Eve thought for a moment. "I can relate to that. Each day on Wall Street is different and needs a fast and different response, just like in the theater. No audience reacts the same to every performance so you have to be ready to make instant adjustments."

"Yeah, that's it!" exclaimed Arthur. "Not many people understand that." After a pause he continued. "Maybe my father does, but he never talks about it, not with me, anyway. Of course, he's not home much to talk about anything." Arthur gamely tried to make a joke of it.

Eve immediately sensed the loneliness of this sensitive young man and, as she wrote in her journal later that day, she decided that this summer would be dedicated to giving Arthur a taste of being a part of the sizable Handelstein clan.

I think Arthur is a very nice person. Poor guy! He seemed a bit melancholy this afternoon. I wonder what it would be like to be an only child, with a father who doesn't appear to be too communicative with his small family. And a mother, I suspect, who depends on her son for the companionship she craves and doesn't receive from the father. Wow! That is sad! Someday this might be another layer to add to a characterization. Mmm—I'll just tuck this little tidbit into my storage bin.

But that's for later! Now we have to concentrate on launching him into our varied menagerie.

It was easy to have Arthur included in their activities because everyone enjoyed his company. Arthur thought he had died and gone to heaven. He entered into the family's penchant for discussions, haltingly at first, then with as much gusto as all the others. Eve was taking classes at the Chicago School of Dramatic Art, even through this vacation time, so Little Abe filled in and exposed Arthur to swimming and Grandpa Handelstein. Arthur couldn't keep up with either of them, but even Grandpa had to give him credit for his persistence. And his good nature. Little Abe asked him one day how he managed to keep his cheerful disposition and balanced take on life.

"God, I don't know. Am I like that? Sounds sort of dull!"

"Oh, no!" Abe said quickly. "Not at all. It's just nice to be around you."

"Maybe—" Arthur tried to reason. "Maybe, well, I recollect when I was little there was a girl in class who always seemed to be unhappy and would tear up at almost anything. And the teacher said one day, 'Remember, laugh and the world laughs with you. Cry and you get all wet!' I guess I still don't want to get all wet!"

National and world affairs gave enough ammunition to keep blood pressures high that summer and fall. The Handelsteins' reliable old oak table almost gave way under the emphatic poundings of fists making points.

G-men knocked off Baby Face Nelson and Pretty Boy Floyd. Hitler murdered Austria's Chancellor Dollfuss. Il Duce had begun his Ethiopian massacre and Yugoslavia's King Alexander was assassinated.

Thank God there was also amusement to counter the grimness. Little Orphan Annie, Daddy Warbucks and Sandy gave people a warm glow. Flash Gordon provided excitement and stirred the imagination.

And the motion pictures paved a road to one's own never-never land. You could hoof through *Gay Divorcée* with Fred Astaire and Ginger Rogers. You could suffer with the voice of Greta Garbo as her characters sacrificed themselves for romance, made all the more delicious for being doomed. You could laugh yourself silly with Laurel and Hardy or the Marx Brothers. Or you might be the giddy, glamorous Carole Lombard, who could be stunning while doing a pratfall and look gorgeous with an ice pack on her head.

Ruth, Eve, Abe and Arthur took it all in, resulting in the best summer ever. Then suddenly it was fall. For the first time Arthur regretted his decision to live on campus. He promised his delighted mother—and himself—he would be home *every* weekend. He didn't want to miss any chance of being with Eve. And all the rest of the family, too.

And he kept his word. Eve was usually free on Saturday and Sunday. But full-time at the Chicago School of Dramatic Art meant just that. Every day was jammed with voice lessons, and body-movement and speech-control courses. The students were required to read a play a week and be ready to recite aloud from that play and discuss it intelligently. Through discussion, the students debated whether or not the author had succeeded in the play's intent, the style and the consistency.

On Friday afternoons four or five pupils would prepare a chosen scene and perform it in front of the whole class. Then it would be critiqued by the teacher and the rest of the students, who examined interpretation, understanding, the choices made in the performance of the character, and overall believability.

When a new theater production came to the city, the entire school would attend matinees, one grade level for each Wednesday and Saturday performance. Those afternoons were especially memorable for the students were observing and absorbing the talent of an elite group of professionals. It was the custom of the time that the stars who opened a play in New York would then tour with the project. So Chicago and the whole U.S.A., even Europe at times, were able to appreciate Broadway's best.

Eve flourished, radiant with the joy of her calling. At the end of the fall semester, before Christmas break, the school presented a program for the friends and families of the trainees to show how their budding aspirants were coming along. The headmistress would choose approximately twenty students, from the beginners to the advanced, to perform a scene from one of the classics. Very often scouts from higher-learning theatrical institutions would attend to see if there were any likely candidates worthy of their consideration.

Eve invited Arthur to come with all of the Handelsteins and the maternal side of her family, the Von Blauers.

"I hope you're not going to get bored," Eve mumbled anxiously.

"Of course I won't," Arthur assured her. "But just in case, Little Abe and I brought along our bubble-blowing kits to amuse ourselves."

"Oh, you are so bad!" scolded Eve.

"No," countered Arthur, "just incorrigible!" Then seriously, "All I ever have to do is look at you up there—down here—anywhere, and I'll be content and happy."

She looked into those engaging hazel eyes and her heart skipped a beat. Somewhat flustered, she shooed him away. "You'd better find the others or you won't have a seat—to play with your bubbles."

Eve watched as he loped easily toward the crowd, surprised that she couldn't dismiss him from her mind at will. She had to force her focus into position. Once that was done, however, she was completely engulfed in her mission.

Usually, the scenes were something from Shakespeare or *Little Women* or *Pollyanna*—all good vehicles to showcase the students' blossoming talents.

Eve, however, had boldly decided to go a step further. She took the book *Hans Brinker and the Silver Skates* and actually created a soliloquy from a passage where there was no dialogue, only inward thoughts and description. She played Hans Brinker, who saw the leak in the dike, put his hand in to stop the leak and saved his village from flooding. That was the action. But it was Eve's vocal dramatization that set the tone and mood of the scene.

The audience sat spellbound for the fifteen minutes, then fell silent, allowing this distinctive approach to register. The silence was broken with a tremendous ovation. Grandpa Handelstein was on his feet applauding and Arthur and Abe were whistling and yelling "Bravo! Bravo!"

An unknown gentleman peered closely at the program. With an enigmatic smile he wrote notes in his handy notebook and then closed it with a satisfied thump.

It was the Christmas prom at Northwestern, the school's last event before everyone scattered across the nation for the holidays. Fortunately for Eve and Arthur there would be no sad separation, they would be only a few doors away from each other.

The band played all the favorites, and the young people strutted to the Lambeth Walk and went breathless doing the Charleston and the Big Apple. Eve was quite popular with Arthur's friends and he was bursting with pride that he was the lucky one escorting the belle of the ball.

Arthur had gone out for "rushing," a period in which the fraternities on a college campus invited men who were interested in joining a fraternity to a series of parties. Then each fraternity compiled a list of whom they believed would make a good "brother" and of whom would fit in with their particular group. Finally, a secret ballot was taken on each man to assure that all the active members agreed on the choice of the new "pledge."

The applicant, on the other hand, put down his first three selections on the chance that his name would appear on more than one fraternity's acceptance roster. As was the case with many, Arthur was wanted by almost every house that had hosted him. Because his first preference had been Alpha Chi Tau, he was now a pledge at that fraternity. At the beginning of the next semester he would be formally initiated, but until then he was the apprentice, subject to practical jokes and horseplay.

Arthur was as capable of being the "jokee" as he was of being the "joker," during the hazing time. No heavy duty tricks were allowed on this campus, so everyone just had good fun.

This evening, however, with Eve on his arm, he was one step ahead of his superiors. And he was relishing his position.

The music switched to more romantic tunes as the night progressed. The lights dimmed. Couples swayed to "Star Dust" and "Embraceable You" and "Deep Purple." Eve and Arthur drew closer and closer. She was having stirrings she had never experienced before. When she performed, she had always felt strong emotions—fear had made her break out in a cold sweat, anguish had brought tears and sobs, panic had caused her to nearly collapse. But this, this was different. A tremor went through her body. Some unfamiliar flutters in her groin made her want to be tight against Arthur, to press herself almost into him. She was flushed, euphoric.

Arthur was on the same plateau. His lips brushed against her ear, and he whispered, "Shall we go?"

She nodded, as if in a trance, and quietly they slipped out and went to find his car. They were silent as Arthur drove toward their suburb. When Lake Michigan came into view he pulled aside and stopped the car at one of the numerous lakeside parks. It was dark except for the brilliant reflections of the moon cavorting on the water. Trembling, Arthur leaned over, took Eve's face in his hands and kissed her softly. His hands moved downward to embrace her as they kissed again, this time with more intensity. She reached up and held him firmly, firmer with each touch of their lips. He took off his overcoat and suit coat and gently pulled Eve's cape from her shoulders.

"Are you cold?" he murmured.

She shook her head, almost afraid to talk, afraid this moment, these sensations would disappear. He moved her slowly down on the seat and was above her. Their bodies blended, he could feel her breasts through his shirt, and she could feel a growing hardness caressing her skirt.

They clung to each other, savoring their passion. Kissing, hugging, inherently moving together, reaching higher and higher until they could reach no further. Breathing heavily, the two still gripped each other, still kissed, still hugged.

"Oh, Eve, I love you," Arthur said ardently. "I loved you before I knew your name, before we met. I loved you the first time I saw you."

Eve could not respond, she didn't know how to yet. Her mother had told her daughters about men and women, marriage, how children were conceived, including the necessary knowledge of their body parts and functions. But Mama had never said anything about the charged sensations she had just encountered—feelings she was still dealing with. Mama had never described the longing and the burning energy that were lodged in the innermost core of her being or the exploding shudder that had ripped clear through her.

Arthur studied her, not sure what was going through her mind. He knew she was troubled.

"Dear Eve, I would never intentionally do anything to embarrass you or put you in harm's way. I hope I didn't offend you, I'm afraid my love for you overflowed and overpowered my senses."

He thought a moment before continuing. "Please understand, I don't expect you to return my love in full. You...we...are too young to think about marriage or total commitment, I know that. But I...I felt...tonight that perhaps you do...do care for me a little...and that's all I need. If that is true, that would make me very happy."

His eyes looked toward her, so full of compassion and anxiety and hope. Eve couldn't help herself, she opened her arms and cradled his head to her chest.

"You are so special, Arthur—a gentleman, a friend and...and

even more. I don't know what—more—yet, but we'll find out, together.''

What happened tonight? What did it all mean? Am I in love? Is that it? And if so, what am I supposed to do? I know I can't talk to Mama about this—Ruth, maybe? But I'm not sure I can confide to anyone about what I really fear. I liked having those feelings, and if he had attempted to actually— actually go all the way—would I have had the strength of character to deny him? Or would I have given in to his—and my—desires? I honestly can't say, and that's what's scary! What kind of girl am I—oversexed? Bad? Normal?

Oh, I can still smell him—his arms around me—our bodies touching...

In the spring of 1935, Arthur asked Eve to wear his fraternity pin, a sign that would indicate they were ''going steady,'' and she said yes. This was a move wholeheartedly approved by both sets of parents.

Eve had not shared her questions and apprehensions about that prom night with Ruth, or anyone. Instinctively she understood it was something she would have to figure out for herself. So, during the inevitable dinner discussions, she paid particular attention to any subject that might be related to emotions and emotional reactions. At some point, Ruth was on her soapbox proclaiming the positive effect of psychology on mankind. When Eve actually expressed an interest, she eagerly suggested Eve read John B. Watson's writings about behaviorism.

''Also, Darwin, Pavlov and certainly Freud will be stimulating,'' Ruth added.

''I'm not completely sold on the idea that doctors—strangers, actually—should toy with people's minds. They could do much damage to someone instead of, as you maintain, Ruth, helping that person,'' said Mama Mildred.

''Why, Millie, I'm surprised. I thought you always held to the theory that the more we know, the better off we are,'' chided Papa Samuel.

"I still believe that!" Mildred said hotly. "But I meant regular education, not this mumbo-jumbo talk about the inside of my brain. How do they know anything about my head? It seems to me that behavior and morality are God's business, and we parents are the conduits to our children, not some outsider."

Mildred and Samuel Handelstein were not overly religious, even though Mildred had grown up in a very Orthodox family. They observed the Sabbath and the other major Jewish holidays: Passover; Hanukkah, although they still exchanged gifts with their Christian friends; Rosh Hashanah; and Yom Kippur.

Nothing was solved that evening about the pros and cons of psychology. But something was gained. Eve did go through the material referred by Ruth and found some possible answers.

According to these texts, her involuntary impulses were not unusual, she was not unique, she was not wicked. She discovered that loving and liking are positive emotions, and emotions and feelings are intertwined, generally in connection with sensations that may be weak or strong. Sigmund Freud emphasized the importance of sex in human behavior. "In a normal sex life," he said, "no neurosis is possible."

Eve was relieved but also warned. She learned what being a teenager implied. Not a child, nor an adult. Coping with physical, emotional and intellectual changes, never knowing if the growth patterns of each was in sync.

Eve was convinced that because of her chosen profession, which certainly dealt in raw emotion, her senses were finer tuned than the majority of sixteen and a half year olds. Understanding this made her realize she must exercise more caution than most girls her age or she could lose control. That could mean real trouble. She also recognized how fortunate she was that Arthur was the kind of person he was. That moment of passion could have had an entirely different ending with someone else. Oh, what a sweetheart was Arthur!

Eve discovered that having opened the gates to her sensual self, she found new depths in the plays she read and the scenes she performed. Another layer had been added to her interpretation of a character now, and she soared to new heights in her presentations.

2

Chicago, Illinois
Tuesday, September 3, 1935

Mrs. Leticia Barnum from the Chicago School of Dramatic Art looked up from her desk to face the inquiring eyes of Eve Handelstein. Immediately she jumped up and hurried to greet Eve.

"Oh, my darling Eve, don't look so anxious. I sent for you to tell you something wonderful. Now, sit down and make yourself comfortable."

Mrs. Barnum looked at her protégée fondly. "My dear, I know you were preparing for the fall semester here. But we just received word that you have been awarded a scholarship to the London School of Dramatic Art!"

Eve held her breath, afraid that any motion might frighten away the words that were still hanging in the air. Eve looked at the woman standing before her, fearing she, too, might disappear and make this only an apparition. But the woman didn't go away. The woman was smiling and reassuring her and holding out her arms.

Eve rushed to Mrs. Barnum, crying and laughing, "It's true? It's really true? I can't believe it! I'm so excited I could explode! Oh, excuse me, I don't know what I'm doing!"

"That's all right, I understand."

Eve released her hold on Mrs. Barnum. ''Oh, I must run home to tell Mama and Papa and—the world! Thank you, oh, thank you!''

''I did nothing,'' Mrs. Barnum said. ''One of their representatives attended the program last December and was impressed with your work. You earned this yourself because of your dedication to your talent. Now be off, and share the happy news. We will miss you terribly.''

Eve flew home, bounded up the front steps, burst into the foyer and spotted Mama, Papa and Grandpa Handelstein in the living room. Grandly, she flung the door wide open, paused to make sure she had their full attention and dramatically made her announcement.

''I'd prefer to see you a cripple in a wheelchair for the rest of your life than an actress on the stage!''

Eve Handelstein's body quivered and jerked with each of her grandfather's words. For each word thrust like a knife, delivering death, death to her dream.

Eve was tiny, and as she looked up at the stern, ramrod-straight figure with the graying goatee and mustache, she realized it was as if he was carved in granite. He was a stone monster.

Ever since she could remember, Eve had wanted to become an actress, had wanted to perform. She recalled standing, at the age of five, behind a curtain in a hall and singing in her youthful but quite alto voice, ''Till the sands of the desert grow cold.'' The audience had assumed the singer was a man, and when the tiny figure in the black velvet dress with its starched white collar stepped out, they had gone wild. And in school, when asked to read several verses of a poem, she would recite and dramatize the whole piece. Eve was usually the center of attention with young and old, whether she was singing or mimicking, or playacting in some form. It had always been that way and she thrived on the exhilaration she felt when she heard their applause.

And Eve's family had always supported her. They were proud of her talent and encouraged her to take both singing and piano lessons, where again she excelled. Grandpa, too, had always attended the functions that featured any of his grandchildren, and especially Eve. And when she had finished high school in three years at the age of sixteen and been asked to study at the Chicago School of Dramatic Art, free of tuition, the entire family had been full of praise.

And now, when she had come home triumphantly to announce she had been chosen for a scholarship to the London School of Dramatic Art, Grandpa Handelstein had dropped this deadly bomb. Why? Hadn't he realized all these years where this was heading, what career Eve was pursuing? Obviously not. Obviously it was "acceptable" to dabble in the theater as a pastime, but *never* full-time. In traditional families, "show business" people were still considered to have loose moral values, especially women.

But no one had ever said "You mustn't be an actress!" No one had ever said "It's wrong to be one." The shock of Grandpa's declaration was almost too much to bear.

Abraham Handelstein's statement to Eve was particularly stinging, so incredulously cruel, because *he* was a cripple. His right foot was deformed, his leg withered, and he *knew* what he had had to bear in his time. How could he even think that heartlessly, let alone voice such thoughts!

Eve bolted upstairs, too stunned to cry, a swelling surge of fury almost exploding beneath her skin. Frightened by the intensity enveloping her, she locked her door and ran wildly to her closet, reaching behind the ledge where she hid her journal. She cradled the notebook close to her bosom, eager to transfer this boiling cauldron of poison onto its receptive pages. Throwing herself onto the bed, she began to write ferociously.

I hate him! I hate him so much I wish he was dead. I hate his horrid sick leg. At least he has walked and talked and swum and worked and fathered children. He has lived! He wants me not to live! He wants me to dry up, to be old like him, to have my mind and body shrivel and shrink to nothing—like a petrified wooden puppet. That's it—he thinks I'm a doll on strings. Strings that he manipulates. I would rather die!

Eve was free, free to verbalize, to expose her naked innermost emotions in her journal, no matter how sordid or how foolish or how romantic those thoughts might be! No censor here, no raised eyebrows or smirky side glances, no debates or arguments. She reigned supreme in this one domain.

Eve Lena Handelstein had already been challenged to deal with a physical obstacle of her own. In the spring of 1922, at not quite four years old, she had been diagnosed with Bell's palsy when paralysis struck the left side of her face. With few treatments available, Eve's mother had frantically grabbed at any possible straw. Someone suggested an old-fashioned remedy that put the patient in an oven for up to one minute. So Mama Mildred had fired up the coal on the side of the big black kitchen stove, and when the oven was warm, in went Eve. Mama diligently applied poultices to the afflicted area, but not even the soft, heated cloth and ointment would relax the nerve. When Eve smiled or talked, the left side of her face was frozen, so the right side of her mouth would crease almost to her eye.

Bell's palsy was not an uncommon illness, and her mother was terrified that Eve's adorable, perfect image would be permanently disfigured as so many others' had been. In desperation, Mama Mildred took her daughter to the famed pediatrician, Dr. Pipes. He stood Eve on the examining table and, with two small rubber hammers, hit every spot on her body, down the left side and down the right side. Dr. Pipes concurred with the diagnosis, but was able to offer the only real ray of hope at the time. The Handelsteins were told there was a treatment in Vienna, one that wasn't in the States yet, that could improve Eve's condition.

Eve and her mother spent ten days in Vienna, then the center of advanced medical procedures. Day and night, even while she was asleep, trained doctors massaged her face. And gradually, ever so gradually, the nerves relaxed their viselike grip and began to live again. A miracle was at work.

At home, Mama had a barber come every day to give Eve massages. And the therapists in Vienna had shown Eve daily exercises to do as well. With the thumb and forefinger of her two hands, she would travel all over her skin, pushing up and making hundreds of little pinches, stimulating the muscles and nerves.

Dr. Pipes had also cautioned Mrs. Handelstein against upsetting Eve. He felt that aggravation might cause a relapse and recommended that if the child wanted something, she should have it.

What four-year-old could ask for anything more? Eve ruled the roost, she was queen of the realm, she was spoiled rotten. And it hadn't taken long for her siblings to use her power for themselves. Whatever *they* wanted, they had Eve ask for it.

The Handelstein offspring had never been allowed fireworks on the Fourth of July because they had been considered too dangerous. Eve was persuaded, coached actually, to say, "I wan fiah cwackes." And lo and behold, that year the young ones had the noisy celebrators. They were shaped like canes, with a bit of exploding powder on the tip, and when they bounced on cement, the contact caused sparks to fly. Eve hadn't really been too interested, but the others had great fun.

The constant disciplined facial gymnastics and the methodical rubdowns began to pay off, and it appeared that the effects of the disease would not be permanent.

Ironically, the training for the profession Eve's grandfather now so despised was also beneficial to her recovery. She learned to control speech, to control her tongue. The class would hum—aaaa, eeee, iiiii, oooo, uuuu—for at least a half hour a day. They hummed in the front of their mouths and eventually could talk and do a long speech without moving their lips to any degree.

With all of the elements combined, as time went on, the palsy was barely discernible.

When Eve was around twelve, Mildred and Samuel took their family to visit Samuel's cousin, Moses Handelstein, and his wife, Sarah, in New York. After a dinner party in their town house, Moses asked Eve to do a reading. All the relatives knew about the talent in their midst.

The guest list included Mr. and Mrs. Louis J. Selznick from California. Mr. Selznick was the very successful motion picture producer. When Eve concluded her performance, Mr. Selznick turned to Mildred and said, "Millie, your daughter is better than Mary Pickford!"

Mildred beamed with pride.

Mr. Selznick continued, "She could be even more famous, a bigger star! If only she didn't have that crooked face." His trained eye had seen the minuscule irregularity on Eve's face.

Mildred could have easily killed Louis J. Selznick on the spot.

Eve Handelstein had grown up in an atypical environment. Contrary to the existing adage of that time that "Children should be seen and not heard," Mildred and Samuel believed in involving their children in a diversity of subjects—politics, sports, arts, school activities, attitudes, any current event. Breakfast, and especially the evening meal, were a buzz of conversation and discussion.

The children were invited to initiate topics and express their opinions. If there was a disagreement, and there usually was, each had to present the grounds for their belief, sum up, and all would then weigh the results.

Ruth Lena was the oldest, born July 9, 1917. Then came Eve, born July 6, 1918, and finally, a son, Abraham Vanja, born July 15, 1920. There was almost a fourth, but Mildred had a very difficult labor and Naomi was stillborn, August 8, 1925. Mildred could have no more children.

Ruth's interests leaned toward politics and issues of the day. Eve had always thought her older sister should run for public office, but, of course, that was completely out of the question for a woman. Ruth did write for her school's paper and she was notorious for championing causes through her articles. She majored in journalism in college, not a complete feminine taboo, but also not the expected female vocation of the time.

Eve, quite clearly, steered a straight course toward anything connected to the arts. Her maternal grandmother had had a lovely singing voice, a three-and-a-half-octave range, and had introduced her daughter Mildred to concerts and theater at an early age. Predictably, Mildred, in turn, passed on her artistic appetite to Eve and Ruth, albeit that Ruth preferred to dissect the content or message of an opera or play rather than relish in the emotional experience. Not so Eve! Once, when Eve was nine or ten years old, she attended the matinee of a very adult drama, starring the great Judith Anderson. When the second-act curtain rose, the pregnant heroine learned that her lover had been killed. Eve was so engrossed and involved that she screamed at the news exactly the same time as Judith Anderson.

Years and years later, Eve would have the good fortune of meeting Judith Anderson. When Eve told her the story, the legendary actress looked at her and said, ''So you were the little bastard who screamed that Saturday afternoon!'' She had remembered!

Abraham, Little Abe as he was affectionately called, was gung ho for sports. Grandpa Handelstein, Big Abe, took special interest in him and had been instrumental in promoting the boy's athletic education, inspiring him to take care of his body and to become strong. Despite his own physical handicap, Big Abe had developed the rest of his physique to perfection. He swam every day in Lake Michigan at Lincoln Park beach, and as soon as Little Abe was about five years of age, the boy went with him. They only missed a few of the coldest days of the year. Grandpa Handelstein's older brother, Emanuel, eventually bought a grand estate in the suburb of Winnetka, which housed both an outdoor *and* indoor pool. So the two Abes never again had to bow to inclement weather.

Eve stumbled blindly out of the house, now sobbing hysterically. She had no destination, she just wanted out of that Machiavellian place. Unconsciously her body went toward Arthur's house. He was just about to get into his car when he saw the pitiful figure staggering along the sidewalk.

''Eve! Eve!'' he called.

She looked up, not seeing.

''My God! What's wrong? What's happened?''

Eve shook her head, ''Please, please, take me away from here....''

Arthur bundled her in the car and took off. He just drove, not talking, not asking, only being there for her.

Gradually she stopped crying and sat staring out the window. When they were on the outskirts of the city, he pulled over to a deserted park on the waterfront, turned off the ignition and waited. He so wanted to comfort her but knew she wasn't ready to be approached.

It was a beautiful day, not too warm, not too windy. The water lapped gently against the shore. The sun shone, bouncing highlights off the lake.

Finally Eve turned and stared at him sadly from her tear-stained face.

"Have you ever seen something die? Seen something die right before your eyes?"

Arthur shook his head, very worried.

"I just did. My dream was murdered."

Arthur was able to determine what had happened from the bits and pieces he wheedled from her. But he still didn't really understand.

"I don't get it. How can your grandfather tell you what you can or can't do? Don't your Mom and Dad have the right to decide for their own child?"

Eve sighed. "It's very—complex, Artie. I'm so lost right now, maybe if I try to explain it to you, it might help to make some sense to me."

She drifted off, focusing on unfolding the events that had formed her grandfather's life.

Eve began haltingly. "Abraham Handelstein was born in 1879, in January, in a small village called Esztergom, which is on Balaton Lake about fifty miles southwest of Budapest. The family made a plum brandy called Slivovitz, that was their business.

"Well, one day while he was playing in the orchard, he slid down a tree and a huge sliver stuck in his leg. He was too—manly, I guess—to tell anyone, and, of course, because he neglected it, the wound became infected and gangrene set in. The doctor thought he might have to amputate.

"For therapy he began swimming across the lake and back every day. He strengthened his whole body and saved himself from the surgeon's saw, although his foot looked like a clenched fist and his leg had the circumference of a youngster's wrist.

"But, except for that, he grew to be a perfect specimen of a man. Tall, handsome, muscular, erect. Grandpa married his second cousin, beautiful Arianne, in, yes, in 1896. He was seventeen and she was sixteen. My papa, Samuel David, was born December 6, 1896.

"Arianne was pregnant with their second child when a nobleman, a count of the province, decided he wanted this pretty peasant maiden for himself. Fortunately, the village rabbi was able to convince this minor member of royalty that he couldn't just up and take the girl. He reminded the count that those days were gone, the people might retaliate, that they might balk at paying their levies."

Arthur watched Eve in amazement. As miserable as she had been and—he was positive—still was, she couldn't stop herself from entering into the full dramatization of the story she was telling. Her eyes flashed, her chin lifted in defiance. God she was incredible! And beautiful! And desirable!

"The nobleman hesitated, realizing there had been growing political uneasiness in Hungary. It was then he noticed Grandpa's handicap, saw the lake and had an ingenious idea. He considered himself quite an athlete, so he suggested a 'fair' solution. The two men would race each other, swimming to and from the opposite shore, and the first to touch the bank on the starting side would win Arianne.

"Of course he completely ignored the fact of Grandpa and Arianne's marriage," Eve said disdainfully.

"Grandpa didn't say a word, just removed his shirt and shoes. The count was so taken with his brilliance he didn't notice Grandpa's powerful upper body. The rabbi started them off, and the nobleman did indeed set a fast pace. But Grandpa pulled even, and on the way back, stroked to an unquestionable victory."

Eve quite obviously relished this outcome.

"The loser sputtered and fumed, and rode off muttering vengeance in his humiliation. Arianne glowed with pride and love for her husband, but the rabbi and the villagers were concerned that the defeated nobleman might take further action.

"You see, after the merging of the two cities, Buda and Pest, into the capital of Budapest, there were several factions vying for power. Social unrest had found spokesmen in a social democratic party and a radical party of left-wing intellectuals, mainly Jewish.

"Ruth should be explaining this part to you, she knows about the politics of the situation," Eve said apologetically.

"No, no! You're doing fine, I understand what's going on," Arthur assured her.

"Anyway, the leaders of that tightknit little community feared the count would accuse Grandpa Handelstein, and others along with him, of being part of these rebel groups who were plotting schemes against the government. So they decided he should flee to America where his brother had migrated. Arianne was to go later with the children."

Eve was quiet for a bit. Arthur was somewhat encouraged. Telling him about her grandfather's history took her mind off her own unhappiness, at least momentarily.

"Arianne died in childbirth. Most say she died of a broken heart, she missed Grandpa so much. A while later he married Grandma Hannah—this was in Chicago—and sent for his two sons, my papa, Samuel, and my uncle Louis. Then there were more children, Uncle Jacob and Aunt Sonja."

Eve took a deep breath. "He's quite a man, isn't he? Had some kind of life! You know he learned to speak English without a trace of an accent, he has a really good ear." Sarcastically she added, "He would have made a darn good actor!"

Arthur wanted to ask what she was going to do but was afraid that might send her off again. So he sat and tried not to fidget.

Eve kept probing her tucked-away memories, still hoping, still needing a clue, a hint, anything that could make this afternoon…understandable, reasonable. Still looking for any suggestion of Grandpa's humanity, so she could hate him less.

"I think back," Eve said softly. And Arthur knew, although he was hearing her, that she was speaking to herself, an inner self, of long ago.

"I think back," she repeated, "when Grandma Handelstein died. How old was I—four or five, maybe. I wasn't allowed to go to the funeral, or the cemetery, I was too young, I guess. One day, Mama and my aunts went to visit Grandma's grave, and they left me in the car. But I got bored and climbed out and wandered around, sucking my thumb as usual. Mama found me and asked me why I was sucking my thumb. I remember just saying, 'I don't know what else t'do.'"

Eve paused, lost in the past. "I think sucking my thumb was like my safety net, or haven. And Mama, who was probably wanting to break me of that habit, said, 'We are in Grandma's *garden,* and Grandma, as a special favor, asked you to promise you wouldn't suck your thumb anymore.'"

Again she hesitated, regrouping her thoughts. "There was a night a while later. Mama and Papa were out, but Grandpa Handelstein was sitting—in the same parlor. I couldn't sleep and strayed downstairs. He said, 'Nussie, what is the problem?' Almost everyone called me Nussie, which means 'little one' in Hungarian. 'You should be dreaming of angels by now.'

"'My eyes won't close,' I said.

"'Well why won't your eyes close?'

"''Cause I can't suck my thumb!'

"'And why can't my Nussie suck her thumb?'

"'I promised Gamma.'

"That stopped him for a minute. Then he asked quietly, 'And where did you promise Grandma not to suck your thumb?'

"'In Gamma's *garden.*'

"Grandpa picked me up and carried me back to my room, even with his bad leg, and told me quite solemnly, 'Oh, well then, that is very serious. One must never break a promise, especially to someone in their *garden.*'

"He tucked me in and read to me until I fell asleep."

Arthur saw a tear wind its way down her check.

"How could that man be the same man who talked to me so today?"

Now he could see the combating forces wrestling for supremacy.

"Mama and Papa do manage their own children and have taught us to be independent thinkers as you may have noticed. But Grandpa is a legend, such a confirmed patriarch, it's very difficult to strongly and publicly defy him. Also, unity is important to our whole family."

She paused again, still showing the effects of Abraham Handelstein's brutal edict, but beginning to seem more resolute, surer of her path.

"I will accept the scholarship, I will go to London. And I will learn everything I can about the theater, every element that makes up the whole—acting, directing, writing, set designing. You name it and I'll study it—anything and everything! Grandpa may have put up a stoppage, a block. Maybe I will and maybe I won't be an actress in the true sense of the word. But I'll be a part of the business *in some form!* Because I *have* to be! It's my life! It's my love! It's my passion! It's my *all!*''

3

Over the next nineteen months Arthur was shown the proof of Eve's declarations. Her enthusiasm and excitement practically jumped off the pages of her letters. Even though he knew it was fruitless, he wished he could have inspired her to such devotion, that he could be her goal. He wanted her to be happy, to follow her dream, but he missed her and she was so far away. And so consumed! His only solace was that there didn't seem to be time for anything in her life but work. At least she hadn't found anyone else. So far so good there!

Eve's parents had arranged for her to stay with friends who lived in London, a Hungarian woman married to a painter. They were comfortable with that, and Eve was delighted. The artistic environment was a huge plus for her.

Both Mildred and Samuel had been disturbed and upset by Grandpa Handelstein's arbitrary outburst. Eve and her mother had never completely excused or forgiven him. It had been a terrible thing to say to a young person who had idolized and respected the elder all her life.

Grandma Handelstein had always kept a bowl of fruit in Grandpa's sitting room outside his bedroom. In the morning, if a piece of fruit was missing, it meant he hadn't slept well and had had a bad night. God forbid two pieces were gone! She would then alert the rest of the family. That is how much he was revered and feared.

The family never openly discussed Grandpa Handelstein's manifesto. Samuel and Mildred merely explained that Eve was continuing her education at the London School of Dramatic Art. Put in the context of general learning, her move was normalized and accepted.

At the end of the spring semester in 1937, the Handelsteins decided Eve should return home. Reports from Europe were not good, there were too many potentially explosive arenas. No one knew where the next trouble spot might erupt.

Arthur was ecstatic. Eve was truly glad to see Arthur and her family, and she understood the logic of the recall. But she soon became restless in Chicago. There was no school available that could follow the London School of Dramatic Art. She felt she was running in place, in the middle of a road, going nowhere. It seemed everyone around her was pushing forward, with full support. Even Arthur.

This coming September Arthur would begin his senior year at Northwestern and during the summer he was working part-time in his father's office. His spirits had reached a new high, not only because Eve had come home, but also because he and his father had found a common denominator and had shared more time together than previously in Arthur's entire life.

Sister Ruth was going to be the editor of the newspaper when she entered her junior year at the University of Chicago. So her summer months were geared to lining up her staff and deciding the format and direction of her publication. She started research on some special features she hoped to include in the paper. One thing she knew for sure, there would be a whole page devoted to editorials. She couldn't wait!

Eve's brother, Little Abe, was lifeguard at a local public pool, while training every day for the swim meets he hoped to win that would pave his way to the 1940 Olympics. Naturally, Grandpa Handelstein supervised those sessions.

Mama Mildred saw Eve's growing discontent. She suggested to

her husband that she take Eve to New York to visit Samuel's cousins, Sarah and Moses Handelstein. Mildred thought Eve could look around New York for a school or a job—at least she would be actively pursuing something! Neither Mildred nor Samuel knew what the future would bring for their daughter. They were troubled and confused about what to do, about how much or how little to help. Both realized Eve's talent, but weren't sure where that gift could lead her.

In New York Eve talked to anyone who would listen. Her relatives did know quite a few people in the entertainment field and they were able to open some doors. But it didn't take long to figure out that, because she was a woman, the chances of her gaining acceptance as a director or producer—anything but an actress— were slim. She finally landed a nonpaying position as a second assistant to an off-Broadway producer—in other words, a gofer. That was all right, for a while. She hung around the readings, the rehearsals, the story conferences, she was allowed to stay as long as she was quiet. But eventually she couldn't help herself, she had to interrupt and explain what to her was such an obvious hole in the script, or such an ineffectual approach to a role. The main problem was that she was right most of the time, and that didn't sit well with the author or the performers, especially since no one was salaried yet.

"Gordon Bennett!" Eve said in exasperation. "I'm only trying to help make it better!"

"Gordon what?" the director asked.

"Gordon Bennett!" she repeated. "Oh, I'm sorry, I forgot. I've been in London and picked up some of their sayings, I guess. That means 'Good grief!' You see, there was this American, Gordon Bennett, who lived in Paris and London. He became rather famous for his crazy exploits and that's how that expression came to be."

"And what were *you* doing in London?" the lead actor said, sounding as if the heat had just been turned up to the boiling point.

"I studied at the London School of Dramatic Art on a scholarship for over a year and a half." Eve didn't mean to brag, but she couldn't help but be a little proud.

The director could see a storm developing, so he stepped in. He couldn't afford to lose one of his better known players. "Miss, ah, Handelstein, thank you for your invaluable assistance, but I think it best if you picked up your belongings and went on your way. We'll just have to stumble along without you."

A crestfallen Eve and Mama Mildred returned to Chicago in October 1937. Eve made the rounds of theatrical agents and production companies, but there were no openings unless one had an established reputation in some branch of the industry. She haunted the movie houses and agonized over every role she could have played. *The Good Earth,* starring Luise Rainer, mesmerized her, until Bette Davis as *Jezebel* took command. Her world revolved around films and any touring play that came through Chicago.

One day she was moping around the house when a friend of her father's, Jules Cozakman, telephoned. He explained he had heard from her papa Samuel that she was interested in the entertainment business. And it happened that he knew a very important man, a leader in the field, who had just arrived in town. Mr. Cozakman would be happy to drive Eve to his hotel for a meeting.

Her mind raced. No one was home to ask for permission. It was unusual to go for a ride, unescorted, with someone she barely knew. But she couldn't allow this golden opportunity to slip away. She swallowed hard and recklessly agreed to be ready in half an hour.

What to wear? Was the mogul looking for someone plain? Or glamorous? Or a qualified assistant? What? Frantically she pored through her wardrobe, hangers clicking loudly against one another as she pushed them aside. Finally, still not sure of her choice but knowing time was of the essence, she settled for a royal-blue suit with a deep-vee-neckline white blouse. She thought, hopefully, that the outfit would be neutral enough to fill the bill for all possibilities.

She was dressed and waiting downstairs when she saw the grand white Cord convertible sedan drive up. As soon as she was seated, submerged in the soft red leather, she made mental notes of the appointments of this clearly distinctive car. Not for herself, she really wasn't interested in autos or anything mechanical. But she knew Arthur and Little Abe would be fascinated with her information about Model 810.

The man behind the wheel, Mr. Cozakman, was around her father's age—early forties. But there the similarity ended. He was slightly taller, much heavier, and the balding process was well advanced. Small beady eyes that kept darting in all directions were set in an otherwise unnoticeable face. There was nothing exactly sinister about him, but still Eve was rather uneasy, probably because she'd never done anything like this before.

"Uh, Mr. Cozakman, what is the name of this, ah, gentleman? Is he headquartered in New York or California? Do you know exactly what he's looking for?"

"My, my," Mr. Cozakman chuckled, although it sounded more like he had something caught in his throat. "We're just full of questions, aren't we? All in due time, my little Eve, all in good time. Now, why don't you tell me about yourself."

So for the next fifteen minutes, Eve related the history of her education. They had traveled to another upscale section of Chicago, and as Eve was finishing the episode of the New York disappointment, his car slowed and he parked in front of a relatively new building.

"Oh, is this the hotel where the mystery man is staying?" Eve asked, emphasizing the words *mystery man.*"

Her sarcasm was lost on Mr. Cozakman, however, as he was intent on describing the imposing structure before them.

"What you see here is the latest concept in big city development. Obviously, there are three stories, and each floor has two magnificent spacious apartments. One can enjoy luxury living without landscaping problems, ideal for a bachelor."

Eve thought that this was an odd configuration for a hotel, but then, what did she know about commercial real estate? They took the small elevator to the top floor. Soon after he pushed the buzzer, a woman opened the door. Eve guessed she was about forty, with a kindly face and sturdy body. She wasn't dressed as a housekeeper so Eve assumed she must be a secretary to the "important man." Mr. Cozakman introduced Eve to Mrs. Birshgeld, and silently she led them to an ornate, overfurnished parlor. The massive mahogany pieces, together with the muted brocade upholsteries and heavy dark drapes, were not overly inviting. The woman disappeared after a long, scrutinizing look at Eve.

"Sit down, my dear," said Mr. Cozakman, indicating a large deep couch.

Eve quickly scanned the room and headed for the smallest chair she could see. "This is fine, thank you."

He shrugged, picked up a similar chair and placed it near hers. Neither spoke for the next few minutes. Eve squirmed in her seat, trying to initiate some sort of small talk, but not having any luck. She couldn't dismiss this queasy fluttering in her stomach.

Mr. Cozakman rose abruptly. "How inhospitable of me! What may I offer you to drink? A sherry, perhaps? Or champagne? I do have an excellent selection of champagnes."

"Some water would be nice," Eve answered politely.

He bustled about, getting water from the kitchen, slicing a lemon at the portable bar. She noticed he poured himself a hefty portion of liquor from a decanter.

"There you are, the lemon gives it a little flavor," he said, handing her a glass and sitting down again, moving his chair closer to her in the process. He lifted his tumbler, "A toast! To the beautiful and sexy Eve!"

Was she imagining it, or was that a hint of something—something ominous in his voice? This was getting weird. She'd been there twenty minutes and still no sign of Mr. Important. And this guy seemed very much at home here.

Finally Eve summoned up the courage and asked, "Where is your friend, Mr. Cozakman? You act as if this is *your* apartment, not *his* hotel!"

He hesitated only momentarily. "Actually, this *is* mine. Did I say we were going to his hotel? I'm sorry. I meant to say we were supposed to meet him at my place. My friend evidently has been delayed. But not to worry that pretty head of yours. I'll do my best to entertain you and make you comfortable while we wait." And with that he placed his hand over hers and squeezed it.

Eve jumped up and moved away quickly. She realized she had made a very bad decision and panic was about to set in. "I don't think I should wait any longer. Will you please take me home?"

"Come, come," he said soothingly, "surely you can give him a little more time." He hoisted himself off his chair and moved toward her slowly, "And allow me the pleasure of your company. How can I persuade you?"

Eve would have laughed if she weren't so frightened. This was like a scene in a bad movie. But she felt more like screaming right now, because he was circling around her, stalking as an animal around its prey. She was trapped! Where was that lady? Where was the door?

"Stop! Mr. Cozakman, I will yell so loudly the world will hear me if you take one more step."

Without warning, the door was violently yanked open and a wild-eyed Samuel Handelstein burst into the room, roaring "You son of a bitch! You no-good cur! I'll kill you!"

Samuel lunged toward the bigger man and struck. His fist made a direct hit and sent the man reeling backward, knocking over a table and lamp and landing him solidly on the floor.

Samuel threw himself on top of the downed man and pummeled him with his fists mercilessly, releasing the fury that had fermented on the frenzied drive to the apartment.

"You scum! You bastard! I'll fix it so you won't get close to anyone again!" Samuel screamed.

Mrs. Birshgeld ran in and tried to pry Samuel away from Mr. Cozakman. "Please, Mr. Handelstein, stop! Don't get yourself in trouble." Samuel paid no attention to her.

Eve was visibly terrified. She attempted to help Mrs. Birshgeld pull her father off the man. "Please stop, Papa! Please!" She started to sob. "Take me home, Papa, I'm so afraid!"

Samuel was breathing heavily and both women could see he wanted to finish the job he had started. But Eve's plea had registered and he reluctantly stood, still glaring at the crumpled figure.

Mrs. Birshgeld talked rapidly, wanting to keep Samuel's focus away from her employer. "Normally what Mr. Cozakman does is his business. But your daughter seemed so young—and so vulnerable. Well, I—I recognized the last name and phoned an office. I assume there are other Handelsteins, so I was fortunate to find you on the first call.''

Samuel managed a grim smile. "Yes, there are quite a few of us. But it is we who are fortunate. Without you..." He could not go on.

"Why don't you leave now," Mrs. Birshgeld said gently.

He looked at Eve's anguished face, put his arm around her protectively and slowly nodded his head. "Thank you, madam! We will go. I am forever in your debt. Will you be all right?" He motioned toward the prone, but stirring, Mr. Cozakman.

"Oh, yes." She sighed. "I'll see to him and then gather my things. I've had enough."

"If you need help in finding a position, or in *any* way, please let me know." Samuel handed her his card. "We'll keep in touch," he said as he led Eve out.

Papa Samuel did not chastise Eve on the drive home. He felt she had been through enough and was confident she wouldn't act that rashly again.

What he couldn't get over was what a rotter his so-called friend was. In actuality, Cozakman was only a distant acquaintance.

Samuel shuddered to think what might have happened if Mrs. Birshgeld had not intervened. He made a mental note to keep track of that lady and her circumstances.

Samuel suggested the two of them not discuss the disturbing episode with anyone, except of course, Mama Mildred. That was just fine with Eve. She certainly had no desire for this to be tossed around and dissected over dinner tables, especially Grandpa Handelstein's.

Boy, I really messed up today. How could I have been so stupid? But who knew some creep would try to act like this? What a harrowing experience! I do realize this type of incident could happen to any female. But I have to be honest, I'm troubled about more than just this afternoon—I don't want to think about it, I don't want to face the possibility, but I must.

Did this old codger believe that because I wanted to be a part of the entertainment business he had more freedom to be offensive? That he wasn't required to be morally correct? That I was easy pickings?

And if so, do most men also think that to be true? Is this the norm for women in my chosen profession? Are we due less respect than our counterparts in other fields?

I've never doubted my ability or determination to pursue this career. But, for the first time, I'm questioning the wisdom of my choice. Am I able to meet the challenge of men like Mr. Cozakman?

I can never say this to anyone—but I have to wonder—was Grandpa Handelstein right when he made his declaration? I just don't know!

Inevitably, word trickled out. Ruth had accidentally come into Mildred's sitting room when Mama was attempting to help Eve sort things out. Actually, Eve was glad her sister knew, she felt Ruth might understand more about this than even Mama. After all, Ruth was functioning well in a mostly male environment. And then, of course, Little Abe barged in on another discussion period. But at least it went no further than the immediate family. Except for Arthur.

"I'm sorry, Eve," Abe apologized. "I didn't mean to, but Artie and I were gabbing about some 'man thing,' and I was getting madder and madder at this jughead of yours and blurted it out. Boy, it's a good thing Artie didn't come to rescue you. You should have seen his face, he really would have killed that asshole! Whoops, sorry about that. I got riled up thinking about it again!"

Eve had to chuckle as she reached over to give him a hug.

"My big-little brother is becoming quite the rogue! You just better be sure you don't slip and swear around Mama and Papa or else—" With her finger, she mimed slashing her throat.

"I'm not upset you told Artie, he's such a part of us. I probably would have said something eventually, anyway. However, this—person—you so aptly described is not, I repeat *not, my* jughead. I don't even want to know whose jughead he is!"

The next Saturday night—Eve always would remember the date—November 20, 1937, Arthur picked her up, supposedly to attend a concert of the Chicago Symphony Orchestra under the direction of Frederick Stock. But instead he headed south of the Chicago loop.

"I hope you don't mind, Eve, but I canceled the tickets for this evening's performance, we can go another night. I need some time with you."

Eve was curious, even apprehensive, because Artie seemed so somber. But, respecting his contemplative mood she said little, sure he would reveal his thoughts when he was ready.

About ten miles out of town, he pulled into what seemed to be a large, rambling old farmhouse. There were a few cars in a parking area. No neon sign identified what the interior held, but a well-built durable wooden placard on a sturdy post announced this was the Country Inn.

"A buddy at AXT (Alpha Chi Tau) told me about this place. It's quiet, has good food, and it's a place to relax and talk."

They walked into a hallway and it did look like someone's home. There were some occupied tables in the "living room." A large glowing stone fireplace separated the "dining room," where a few more tables were added.

"I was lucky we got in on such short notice. Usually reservations are made way in advance," explained Arthur as they followed the man who had greeted them at the door. "But there had been a cancellation just before I called. Must be an omen that tonight was meant to be!"

People always took notice when Eve entered a room, and now was no exception. It wasn't that she was the most beautiful girl in the world, there was just a presence about her that demanded, and deserved, attention. Heads carefully turned as they maneuvered through to the "den." There were only tables for two here, and their empty one was in the corner near a smaller fireplace. It was very cozy, very romantic.

As soon as they were seated a waiter brought a wine stand with a bottle of Dom Pérignon champagne chilling in the ice bucket.

"I told a little lie," Arthur confessed. "I said I was surprising you with this on your twenty-first birthday. Naturally, they assumed I was already of age."

He motioned for the steward to open it, which he did with great aplomb and ceremony, pouring a bit for Arthur's approving sip, and then grandly filling both iced glasses.

"To my wonderful Eve, every day with you is a celebration!"

Eve was moved by his words, and toasted him silently with her eyes.

"I probably ordered this more for my fortification than anything else," Arthur said nervously. He emptied his glass, placed it on the table and resolutely took her hands in his.

She knew he was ready now to discuss what was on his mind.

"Will you marry me, Eve?"

She was so startled her mouth opened, but no sound came out. That was not what she had expected. That was the furthest idea from her mind.

"Don't answer yet," he pleaded. "Let me finish! This is my last year in college. I'm already working with my father, and I know I'll be in business with him and will be able to provide for you—and a family. I've loved you from the day I saw you, and I hope you return some of that. I could understand if your love wasn't as all consuming as mine, that would almost be too much to ask."

He paused, poured more champagne, gulped a little.

"Maybe I should have waited a few months more before mentioning this. But when I heard about—the thought of that ape—I just went ballistic, crazy. I couldn't stand the idea of anyone coming near you, touching you, hurting you. I want to take care of you, I want to protect you!" Arthur looked at Eve with tears in his eyes. "I want to make love to you. I want to hold you. I want to love you forever!"

It was Eve's turn to concentrate on her glass. And sip. Her head was in a whirlpool, thoughts tumbling like clothes in a washing machine. She kept telling herself not to get sucked under, to keep above water, to think.

Married? Is that what she should do? She loved Artie, how could anyone not? And she was the lucky one he chose. She would be with him all the time, never be exposed to animals like what's-his-name again. She'd be safe. And when Artie touched her, she did get those feelings. Maybe all this had happened to show her the way!

Arthur was watching her, trying to keep calm, but he couldn't keep his butterflies camouflaged.

Eve leaned toward him and put her quieting hands over his restless fingers. "Dear Artie, remember the night of the Christmas prom? We parked. We kissed. And—we hugged!"

"I'll never forget that night, ever!" Arthur interrupted.

"I said you were a gentleman, a friend and—even more. I think I know what *even more* means now. I do love you. And yes, we can become engaged. I need some time to, to put my thoughts in order, though."

Arthur just sat for a minute, hoping he understood correctly. He looked at Eve with a "Did I hear what I think I just heard?" expression. She nodded, answering his silent question.

Barely able to contain himself, Arthur signaled the waiter for the check. He threw some bills on the tray, gathered Eve from the table and hurried toward the door.

The maître d' was concerned. "Is everything all right? Was the service acceptable? You didn't even order dinner!"

Arthur laughed. "All right? It was perfection! This is the most wonderful place in the world! This is the most beautiful night of my life. And I'm the luckiest and happiest person on this planet." And the two swept off, leaving behind some very perplexed people.

Once outside Arthur took Eve in his arms and squeezed so tightly she could hardly breathe. Then he leaned down and his lips found hers.

"Darling Eve," he began between kisses, "take all the time you want. We have our whole lives...."

They were standing in the freezing air, but neither felt any chill. He lifted her so their faces touched and their bodies could be closer together. The movement against each other created a current that surged through their veins. They were clawing each other, vainly trying to get through the barriers of their clothing. Arthur's mouth caressed her eyes, her cheeks, her throat. His tongue hungered toward her breasts.

"Oh, God, Eve, I love you so. I want you so much I can barely stand it," he panted.

Eve responded by forcing her pelvis even closer to his groin, crushing into him, her arms clasped around his neck. She arched her back and groaned with pleasure as his lips found one escaped nipple and then the other.

"I'm yours, Artie. Please, please take me," Eve pleaded, aroused beyond caring. Still holding Eve off the ground, Arthur stumbled for the car, managed to open the rear door and placed Eve gently on the cushioned seat.

Urgently he spread her blouse, enough to cradle her bare breasts in his hands, burying his face in their softness.

"I don't want to pretend anymore—make it real," she whispered.

His mouth moved upward. "Shh—kiss me! Hold on to me!"

They were moving rapidly, kissing wildly, and lips locked together, they floated to their own private place.

On the drive home, Eve and Arthur couldn't stop touching each other. Or talking.

"My dearest Eve—" Arthur began. Suddenly, he whooped with joy and pulled off the road to hug her.

"I just realized, now I can say 'My dearest Eve,' and it's for real—because you are my dearest Eve. Because you are mine, just as I am yours. We belong to each other, isn't that wonderful!" Arthur laughed and started to drive again, doing figure eights down the highway.

"Lucky for us there is no traffic and no policeman near to see us, or we'd be in big trouble." Eve was attempting to be sensible, but actually she was almost as giddy as Arthur. She had a sense of well-being when she was with Arthur, of completeness. And the emotions he provoked in her sent shivers throughout her body, even now, just thinking about it.

I really said yes, didn't I? Am I right? What about my dream? My goal? Well, what about it? So far it's only brought heartache and trouble and disappointment. No one seems to be knocking at my door with any offers. And when I knock, the door stays closed. Artie is so special. Possibly I should forget about this business and learn how to be a woman!

I am so bad! I wanted him to be inside of me, I did! I wanted to understand what these sensations are all about. I still do! If this is being a woman then I want to know it all. I know we're supposed to wait for marriage, but I can't help what I feel! Maybe, now that I'm going to be engaged, Mama would take me to the doctor for that—I can't remember the name— oh, a diaphragm. But then, what would Artie think of me?

Arthur officially asked Samuel Handelstein for his daughter's hand in marriage the night before Thanksgiving. The Handelsteins and Burdseys were already planning to share Thanksgiving dinner, so the engagement was announced at the table. Arthur slipped a three-carat square-cut diamond—carefully selected, this was his first major investment—on Eve's ring finger and the two were bombarded with congratulations and tears and questions and toasts.

Randall and Alicia Burdsey were overjoyed with this development. To Randall it meant Arthur would be even more dedicated to their work. And for Alicia it was the answer to her dream. Now she would have a daughter, and soon grandchildren. Her life would be full again.

Everyone quieted down when Grandpa Handelstein stood. "We thank you, Lord, for the gifts you have bestowed upon us. For our full table, our healthy bodies, our spirituality." He paused and looked directly at Eve. "And now you have blessed us in yet another manner. Since you know all, you were aware of our concern about Eve's future plans. And now you have favored us by bringing pride to this house with my granddaughter Eve's choice to be the wife of this fine young man. *L' chayim!*"

The message Grandpa Handelstein sent was loud and clear. Eve, Mildred, Samuel and Arthur, too, knew what he was saying.

"That is just not fair," Eve complained to her mother and father after everyone had gone. "He had no right to pass judgment on my career, even if it has been unsuccessful, in front of Arthur's family. He embarrassed me and made me out to be a stupid fool for having goals of my own, other than being a wife." She paced the room nervously, agitated.

Mildred and Samuel exchanged worried glances. "Now, now, Eve darling," Mildred said soothingly. "We must remember Grandpa Handelstein is thinking in terms of the 'old school.' His reasoning is just the way, and time, he was raised. He meant well."

Eve still didn't look satisfied, so Samuel carried on.

"Mama and I wish he hadn't made any reference to your—profession, even though the remarks were slight. But, Grandpa is—Grandpa. You know we are both proud of your accomplishments, of you. And we all are very fond of Arthur, as you are aware. I think Grandpa was just trying to convey that in his own inimitable fashion."

Eve paused and contemplated her parents. She understood they didn't condone what the older man had said, they simply wouldn't openly oppose him. Again the streak of defiance that was always beneath the surface peeked out from its hiding place. She had the urge to tell everyone, to hell with what you think, I'll go out and make it on my own yet!

But no sooner had she thought it than she quashed it. She had no place to go, no place to even start. Anyway, she didn't want to blame or hurt Mama and Papa. And God knows she didn't want to upset Arthur because of her fanciful need for recognition. No, she would submerge that notion. But it did still rankle her.

4

Chicago, Illinois
1938

Eve was to be a June bride, just before her twentieth birthday. Ruth would be maid of honor. Little Abe was to be Arthur's best man, and he was already strutting like a peacock. More thought went into his outfit than Eve directed toward her own wedding gown.

Arthur asked a couple of his fraternity brothers to be ushers. Eve had been gone for so long her girlfriends had wandered off, following their own pursuits. But she asked her Chicago School of Dramatic Art teacher, Mrs. Leticia Barnum, to be one bridesmaid. Eve's hostess while in England, Delia Latvinick, was delighted to have an excuse to come to the States to be her second bridesmaid. Her husband Sergio was off in the country working on new canvasses for his next exhibition.

The holidays were over and the planning and the details began in earnest. Guest lists. Where to have the wedding and the rehearsal dinner and the reception and the showers. Color themes for all the events. China patterns to be registered. Along with the crystal and flatware and linens. Eve's head, like a toy top, was spun in too many directions. Even Samuel had suggestions, especially in regard to the invitations. Eve agreed wholeheartedly with one name he added, Mrs. Yvonne Birshgeld, the lady who helped save her from the ogre Cozakman.

But something was wrong. The sabotaging undertones crept in ever so slowly, eroding the comfort zone that had glazed over Eve's inner being. From afar, almost detached from herself, she began to see two simple caring souls being gradually buried alive with—"things." Who, what, when and where took precedence over the why. Just being together. Enjoying each other. Touching each other.

Eve didn't believe either Arthur or she had consciously fallen into this materialistic trap, it just seemed to evolve. Arthur and the fathers huddled over housing, should they build, buy, rent? Should they borrow? Accept an outright gift, as Randall Burdsey suggested? Arthur felt as if he were in the eye of a cyclone as he faced the challenges of adult responsibility.

Eve and the mothers were engrossed with the immediate particulars. But they also discussed the question of when to start a family. Mildred felt they should wait a bit, Alicia Burdsey wanted them to start right away and the more the merrier. One positive result from this conversation was that Mildred took Eve to their doctor to be fitted for a diaphragm.

Eve bet Mama wouldn't have been so quick to get this contraption if she knew how Eve had longed for one a few weeks ago.

To escape the seemingly endless preparations and talk, Eve took to dropping by her old alma mater, the School of Dramatic Art. Just to kibitz and observe. The teachers were all fond of Eve, also appreciative of her talents, and they welcomed an unbiased point of view regarding some of their pupils' work, especially the Friday afternoon sessions when scenes were performed before the class.

Eve's perspective on these amateur offerings was keen, she had an innate ability to go right to the core, to show where the focus had strayed, or why the choice of action was weak or unclear. In explaining her reasons, she unconsciously showed them how to approach a role or a scene honestly, how to give a character a background and life. Some of the students asked her to meet privately, if she could spare the time. Eve did so gladly, paying no heed to her orchestrated schedule. This was much more appetizing.

None of this went unnoticed by the headmistress.

The letter was dated Monday, March 7, 1938

Dear Miss Handelstein,

Allow me to introduce myself. My name is Peter Padon, partner of John Darius, owners of the film studio Pad-Dar Pictures. I originate from Chicago, actually owned some nickelodeons there and then theaters prior to my involvement with Hollywood. I only mention this because it explains why I called the Chicago School of Dramatic Art for information and assistance.

We at Pad-Dar have decided to begin a department, similar to the program at MGM, for training possible and existing contract players. Mrs. Leticia Barnum could only recommend one person to head such a division, and that was you, Miss Handelstein.

We would very much like to meet with you and discuss this possibility, if you are remotely interested. Mrs. Barnum did mention you were about to be married, perhaps you already are, so this prospect may not appeal to you at all. Or maybe you and your husband would enjoy a visit to California.

We hope to hear from you in the near future. In any case, please accept our best wishes.

Sincerely,
Peter Padon

Mildred was positive Eve had not left the house, but she hadn't heard a sound from her daughter in at least two hours. That was odd! But then, maybe she had just been too busy. Frankly, Mildred hadn't even given it a second thought when Eve didn't come down for lunch. It seemed everyone was going in all directions these days.

The upstairs was quiet. She rapped gently on Eve's door. There was no answer, so she opened the door slightly and peeked inside. The room appeared to be empty at first glance. Then her eye caught the small figure that was almost hidden behind the drapes of the window seat alcove.

"Eve?" asked Mildred.

No response.

Now her voice was louder. "What is it? What's the matter? Are you ill, honey?"

Eve's swollen, tear-stained face looked sadly up at her mother when the drapes were pulled aside.

"Oh, Mama," cried Eve, burying her head in the comforting arms. "What am I going to do? I'm an awful person, I'm not the same as you and Papa and Arthur and—everyone else!"

Mildred just soothed Eve until between sobs she could explain what was wrong.

"I—I know...now...for sure I know, I can never be good like you. I tried—I tried so hard—and I love Artie! But I'm not normal! I don't want to be a married lady and talk about—about lunches and decorating and clothes and...babies! I want children, I love children! Just—not yet."

Even though the words started out somewhat muffled, Mildred heard distinctly. And she understood. And her heart was heavy.

Eve went on. "I thought I could sink my hopes, drown my ambition—I did my darnedest! But lately, I've been going to my old school and working with the young ones. And I feel alive again! Completely vitalized again!"

Jumping up she hurried to the nightstand and grabbed the letter, waving it at her mother.

"It was easy at first. No one wanted me, anyway, no one believed I had anything to offer, there was no future for me in the entertainment world. In any capacity."

Eve stopped long enough to hand the letter to her mother, then continued her laps around the room.

"When Arthur proposed, I thought—because I cherish him deeply—marriage was my answer. And I hold him dear now. But all the hullabaloo of a wedding was driving me crazy. I really don't care about showers—or *any* of that stuff!''

Eve knelt and focused on her mother's sweet face. Mildred had provided Eve with those lustrous dark eyes, which she had inherited from her Polish father. But her other features were more in keeping with her mother's German ancestry, blond hair and fair skin, a straight, perfect nose. Eve traced the outline with her fingers.

''Mama, I am so sorry I can't be the kind of daughter you have every right to expect. I don't want to be a disappointment to you. But I would cause more damage if I weren't honest now, if I waited until after the ceremony to explain what is in my heart. This is the first concrete job interest I've had since I left London. And what happened? My whole being quivered with excitement, there was no room for anything else in my mind.''

A new batch of tears started rolling down Eve's cheeks.

''I may never meet anyone like Arthur again. He is an extraordinary person, and he deserves someone who will give him all of herself. I can't do that right now.''

Eve's eyes pleaded with her mother for approval. Or even understanding.

''I realize what I'm giving up, and maybe for nothing. Pad-Dar may not like me. Or they may worry about my lack of professional experience. Who knows? But they did ask for me. And I know I have to try.''

Mildred sighed deeply. Then tilted her daughter's chin upward.

''I can't pretend that I'm not—affected by this. I can't say, either, that I am totally surprised. When you and Arthur told us of your engagement, I was delighted, as you know. However, the announcement was unexpected. I wasn't sure you had reconciled yourself to—letting go of your childhood dream.''

She studied Eve for a long moment. ''You have to face the fact that this decision is final. You can't come back in a month and say, I made a mistake, let's just act like nothing's changed. You can't play games with people's lives and emotions. You do know that?''

Eve nodded and answered solemnly in a tiny voice, ''Yes, Mama.''

She looked so young, so innocent. Mildred gathered Eve in her arms, "Honey, I fear for you. It is not going to be easy, not the leaving here, not the going there. You don't know anyone, you are dabbling in a—a very different profession, in a strange city. You are not sophisticated in 'their' ways. Look what happened with that terrible man, Mr.— The one who said he was your father's friend! I'm afraid there are many of his type in Hollywood."

"I'll be good, Mama. And I'll be very careful."

"Dear child, it's not you who has to behave. It's them!"

They hugged, each lost in her own thoughts. Mildred rose finally. "I will speak to your father about how best to handle the situation. You are right about one thing, it is better now than later, for everyone. I can be the messenger to all—except Arthur, of course. He is your responsibility. And I don't envy you."

She saw Eve wince and slump against the wall.

"I will pray for our guidance, my darling."

April, 1938

The wheels of the locomotive whirred, taking Eve and Mama Mildred further and further west from Chicago. Eve's parents had insisted she not travel alone, so Mildred accompanied her daughter on the trip.

Their drawing room was roomy and comfortable. The movement of the speeding train had lulled Mildred into a peaceful nap.

Eve looked at her mother, envious of her serenity. She wondered if she would ever sleep soundly again. Or if she would ever have an unclouded mind again.

Repeatedly those days, those awful days that would be etched on her soul for eternity, began their insidious attack. She could feel the wretchedness begin to well up inside of her now. Afraid she might boil over and wake Mother, she reached in her bag for her journal, hoping to quell this pending outburst.

I keep seeing everyone's shock, bafflement, resentment. I can't even describe Grandpa Handelstein's reaction! He thinks I'm a disgrace, a pariah. I don't think he'll ever spare me. But it's Artie who haunts me, his forsaken, lost look at me and then at the ring in his hand and then back to me. If only he had been furious, yelled at me, thrown something, cursed me—something—anything! I keep envisioning those wonderful hazel eyes wide with disbelief, then gradually narrowing as reality registered. I can picture a light dimming as if a curtain had been drawn across his face. When I live that afternoon over (oh please God, don't make me go through that again), I start to choke and can barely breathe thinking about Artie and the pain I've caused. But wasn't I right? I mean, I did do the honorable thing for Artie's sake. Somehow tell me—tell me I did! Maybe that would ease these tons of bricks that are pressing against my heart. Here I go, fantasizing again, all the festivities at Artie's university, all the gaiety surrounding the graduation, everyone looking forward to a summer of fun and frolic. I could have been a partner in that inner circle of joy. But no—smart me—I chose to bow out, to leave that scene, because I'm so...so what? I might as well feel sorry for myself, no one else is going to. I can just hear the gossip! "Well, she made her bed, now she can sleep in it. Alone! How dumb can a person be!" I wish you were a thing I could hit and kick but I can't hurt a piece of paper, can I? Thank God I have you—my outlet—the place I let go of my anger, my frustrations, my anguish, my fears. I wish, oh how I wish, you could tell me why! Why am I cursed with this burning inside of me? I know you can't answer—there is no answer—I know I can't ignore what so damnably exists. Life is so weird, such a paradox! How can each stage, each step, bring such euphoria and such despair at the same time? Why? Why?

Los Angeles, California
Monday, April 18, 1938

Peter Padon was in his mid-forties—short in stature, leaning toward the plump side, a little rough around the edges. But the hairy-bear look masked a gentle nature. He settled comfortably in his chair, satisfied with the decision that had been made.

"Welcome to Pad-Dar, Miss Handelstein. You're now part of our little family."

Eve swallowed, trying to find her voice. "Th-thank you, Mr. Padon. And please tell Mr. Darius how much I appreciate your confidence."

"I guess you'll need time to move from Chicago. We're ready to start when you are. Ha-ha! That reminds me of the old show-biz joke, ha-ha. Third cameraman— 'Ready when you are, C.B.!' Ha-ha! You know, Cecil B. DeMille? Thousands of extras? First cameraman— 'Hair in the aperture, sir!' Second cameraman— 'Out of focus, sir!' Well, anyway, uh, you probably already heard that many times. Uh, your husband comin' back to California with you when you're all packed up?"

Eve was flustered. First, she didn't know what on earth he was talking about. And second, she didn't realize he wasn't aware of the developments in her personal life.

"Ah, I—rather we—postponed the wedding. Actually, we changed our minds."

Mr. Padon was instantly solicitous. "I'm sorry, I didn't know." He obviously was ill at ease. "Well, uh, then goin' to work will be good for you. We'll keep you plenty busy!"

He observed his new employee carefully. "You're just a kid, Miss Handelstein. You come on so strong when you talk about your job, it's easy to forget just how young you are. Your whole life is before you, there's no rush to settle down. Now, if you're goin' to be alone, me and the missus would be happy to put you up till you get settled."

"Oh, that's so nice, Mr. Padon, but my mother is with me for the moment, and we are both staying with relatives. I will call you as soon as I've made my plans. Again, I am grateful and will try very hard to justify your trust."

She walked on a cloud, keeping her composure until she was safely tucked in a taxi. And then she let out a war whoop! "Ya-hoo! I work for a *movie company!*"

The driver was startled, swerved to avoid a car that pulled out, and began to get hot under the collar. But then he took a good look at his buoyant, bright-eyed passenger and relented, caught up in her enthusiasm in spite of himself.

"Whaddya do fer this movie company?"

"I am going to teach acting," Eve announced proudly. "No! No! That's not right! I hate when people say that."

Very deliberately, she rephrased her sentence. "I am going to guide actors and actresses, help them develop and expand the talent they have been given, show them the tools of their craft."

Much better description! Much better!

"You're awful little to do all that!" The cab driver's voice brought her back to the present.

"Good things come in small packages!" she said gaily.

It was nice to feel happy, for a bit, anyway. And it would be a relief to bring her mother some glad tidings. The last month or so had been anything but easy or pleasant.

Eve and Mama Mildred were staying with Samuel's sister, Sonja Arianna, and her husband, Saul Rosennavitch. Their son, Joshua, was about the same age as Eve. A few years ago he had persuaded Aunt Sonja and Uncle Saul to shorten Rosennavitch to Rosen, and he advised Eve to do the same—to shorten Handelstein to Handel.

"Why would I want to do that?" Eve had asked.

"It's just simpler," Joshua explained. "Everyone has a hard time with the spelling and pronunciation. And think of the time you'd save signing your name."

"I'll see," she answered. "First things first!"

There were many decisions to be made. She didn't want to go to Chicago to gather up her things, there was no way she could go through the goodbyes again so soon. Anyway, Arthur shouldn't have to deal with her presence yet. He was getting ready to graduate and certainly didn't need her to mess him up anymore right now. Hopefully time would make the inevitable return trip more bearable.

So, Mildred would see to the packing without her. Eve also wasn't inclined to keep living with her relations, even though they had graciously offered. But she also knew neither Mama nor Papa would consent to her staying in Los Angeles by herself.

Oddly, it was Samuel who came up with the solution. He had tracked down Yvonne Birshgeld's address, mainly to send a wedding invitation. Obviously, that was no longer necessary. However, where she was living was extremely pertinent. When her husband died, she had moved to Los Angeles to be near her sister. She had no children. Samuel contacted Mrs. Birshgeld, who was both surprised to hear from him and delighted with the nature of the call. Evidently the sister had decided to live with her daughter so Mrs. Birshgeld was now free.

This arrangement proved to be advantageous for all. Eve would stay with her aunt and uncle until she found an apartment, and then Mrs. Birshgeld and she would move in at the same time. Mildred was reluctant to leave her daughter but was somewhat mollified knowing Eve would not be unattended at any time. Mildred still harbored the belief that behind every male lurked a potential monster. And the fact that Birshgeld had a car and knew her way around also gave Mildred peace of mind. True, it wasn't a fancy car, but it was good enough to get the job done. Actually, any kind of car was a real plus in a city the size of Los Angeles. So, Mrs. Birshgeld was able to chauffeur Eve around to various parts of the city to see what rentals were available.

The Rosens lived in Hancock Park, located between downtown Los Angeles and the fledgling development of Beverly Hills. It was quite a fashionable neighborhood, even though many of the rich, especially the movie-industry rich, had moved west toward the ocean, beyond Beverly Hills to Bel-Air, Holmby Hills and Santa Monica. But these areas were far too expensive for Eve. Pad-Dar Pictures was roughly between Universal Studios to the east and Warner Brothers to the northwest on the valley side of the Hollywood Hills. That is where the two women concentrated their search.

Eve's starting salary was eighty-five dollars a week. She figured she could spend up to one hundred a month on a lease. Mrs. Birshgeld would live with her and do light housekeeping for room and board. She'd really be more of a companion than anything else, and if she wished could find another position to supplement her income. Samuel, however, unbeknownst to Eve, had offered Mrs. Birshgeld a monthly support allowance, just to insure that she would always be around to watch over Eve.

"Don't fret, Mr. Handelstein. I will take good care of your daughter." Samuel believed her and was somewhat relieved. Eve was the most difficult of his children to comprehend. Not just because she was strong-willed, although she was that! But she had always seemed focused on this—vision—of hers and that made her old beyond her years.

She had never really enjoyed playing the normal childhood games, seldom had friends of her own age. Maybe it was due to the Bell's palsy she'd had when so young and the discipline she'd had to learn to overcome the paralysis. Samuel had never completely understood her. He had hoped the engagement to Arthur was her step toward conventionalism. Then, sadly, he had to acknowledge that it was not meant to be. It was good this job of Eve's was not in Chicago, that would have been too trying for everyone. It was also good Mrs. Birshgeld was available in California.

Mildred had finally left for home. Aunt Sonja and Uncle Saul and Joshua were out for the evening. And Eve was alone in the big house, packing her few belongings, getting ready for the move the next day. They had found a nicely furnished two-bedroom duplex on Valleyheart Street, a few blocks off Ventura Boulevard. Convenient, within the budget, and surprisingly clean and comfortable. It even had a small walled outside patio.

Eve turned on the radio for company. All of a sudden, she felt so—alone—so terribly alone. The music station was playing the popular songs of the day, "This Can't Be Love," "I'll Be Seeing You," "Love Is Here to Stay," all the sentimental love songs.

Eve tried to control her emotions, but finally lost the battle. Tears, then sobs racked her body. She ran for the journal, needing her sanctuary desperately.

I can't make these images go away, they keep floating around me, driving me mad—I'm dancing with Artie, his strong arms holding me close and then closer. We're laughing over some shared private joke...kissing...hugging! I miss him so, miss having him near, miss talking to him, miss loving and being loved....

Los Angeles, California
Monday, August 1, 1938

There was a tap at the door of Eve's office. Matilda Carliss, her secretary, had not buzzed on the intercom, so she assumed it must be one of the bosses.

"Yes?" she called.

"Knock-knock!"

Eve smiled, it was Peter Padon with his newest knock-knock joke.

"Who's there?"

"Cantaloupe!" he answered.

"Cantaloupe who?"

"Cantaloupe without a gal!"

"Good one!" Eve laughed. "Come in."

"Knock-knock!"

Oh-oh, another. "Who's there?"

"Amsterdam!"

"Amsterdam who?"

"Amsterdam tired I can't stand up!"

Eve giggled and walked to the door. "Well you had better come in and sit down, then."

Peter entered jovially. "Not too bad, huh? At least I only tell you the clean ones."

"I thank you for that," she said warmly. "Even though I've been here three months and I am now twenty years old, I still don't believe I'm ready for the down and dirty yet."

Peter looked at her fondly. "And I don't think you'll ever be, you're a real lady. A spitfire, but a lady."

Eve blushed and changed the subject quickly. "So, what is on your agenda today?"

"A couple of things. First off, John and I are very happy with what you're doin' here. We've noticed, even in this short time, how the contractees have gotten better when they do the small parts we give them. And we like those afternoons—I know, only a few so far—where you let them do different scenes. Helps us see them in new ways."

Eve just glowed, she was so pleased.

"Now, I've a favor to ask."

"Peter, you know if it is within my power, I would be honored," Eve said earnestly.

"Well, this sure is up your alley. A good pal, Mo Jeddu, he owns Status Films, has a—friend—and he wants her to have a screen test. But they don't have no one like you there so he asked if you would, you know, work with her and do a test. With a complete camera crew of course. All the trimmings, anything you need. You would be in charge. It's okay with us, and he'll pay you extra, I made sure of that. But I said to Mo, I said it's up to the little lady."

Peter was suddenly embarrassed. "I—honest—I didn't mean that as a smart-ass remark. Nothin' to do with your size, I swear. Or a crack about—you know—the lady bit."

Eve went over to the older man and took both his big hands in her little ones and looked him straight in the eyes.

"Please, Peter, believe me! I know you meant no disrespect. You, the entire organization, have only shown me kindness. And I am not sensitive about being petite, that's how God made me."

She felt him relax somewhat.

"Now, even though I may not choose to use strong language in my personal life, trust me, if the role called for it, I could and would use any four-letter word in the book. Plus, I would know what they meant. I think. At least most of them. And I do understand about men and women. And mistresses! All right?"

He nodded and hugged her, "You're somethin,' you know that?"

"So—" Eve was all business "—when do we start with this young woman? By the way, what's her name?"

June Islen glided slowly into Eve's modest office and simply took Eve's breath away. Eve had been told she was sixteen, but the aura that flowed from her was beyond age. It was as ancient as Cleopatra and as recent as Jean Harlow. Eve sensed immediately the walk and her air were not affectations, they were real. June Islen was sensuality personified. About five feet six inches in height, a voluptuously rounded 120 pounds, with the weight in all the right places. Her hair was dark and shiny and hung straight to her shoulders, framing translucent, shell-like skin. Smoky gray feline-shaped eyes, chiseled nose and generous carnal lips completed her striking appearance.

The girl didn't appear frightened, she had an open, unsheltered way about her. Eve began with casual conversation, asking about her family, her background. It didn't take long to discover there wasn't much of either.

She was born on June 17, 1922, in Ely, a town in eastern Nevada. Her parents moved to Las Vegas when her young brother died at birth. They felt the baby might have had a chance of survival in a more sophisticated and skilled facility. June indicated she thought they were looking for someone to blame, but valid claim or not, the change couldn't bring the child back, and somehow their lives went downhill from there. Both started drinking heavily and both fell into the gambling trap. So many locals in a gambling environment ended up forced to stay and work off their debts, leaving escape almost out of the question. Although she never said it, Eve got the impression June's father had either abused her, molested her, or both. Eve had a fleeting idea—if the girl did stay around—that she needed to research a good therapist. But that was a big "if" and a long way down the road

June had run off to Los Angeles about a year ago when the situation at home had become unbearable. She lied about her age and got a job as a cigarette girl at Ciro's, a popular nightclub on Sunset Strip. And that is where she met Mo Jeddu.

"He's been so kind to me. Almost like a dad." She hesitated and then said quite honestly, "Well, not exactly—you know! But he's not mean or bossy and doesn't hit me or get mad at me. Always bringing me something, it's like Christmas most every day. His wife left him for a tennis player or something like that and I guess he's sort of lonely."

She looked at Eve in surprise. "I haven't known you ten minutes and I already told you my life story. I don't do that."

Eve smiled reassuringly. "I'm flattered you trusted me. I promise you, whatever you should say to me in private will never go any further."

June eyed Eve closely. "How old are you, anyway? You're not much older than me, are you?"

Eve realized this was an important moment to gain June's confidence. "You're absolutely right. I'm only twenty. But I have had a lot of experience in theater and in working with undeveloped talent. And I have had success. Have faith in me. Let me guide you, cultivate the qualities you have. Let me put on film what I see in you!"

The wariness, any hint of suspicion, vanished from June's mind. She completely believed Eve.

A scene from *Libeled Lady,* a 1936 film starring Spencer Tracy and Jean Harlow, was chosen for the screen test. Eve was determined that sexuality not be the center of concentration, that would be clearly evident to anyone who had half a brain. What she wanted was to have the viewer, who would already be interested because of the obvious, become involved in the girl's naturalness and vulnerability. She kept stressing to June, "Don't try to *act,* that is a dangerous verb. Just speak the words that explain what is going on, as you, June Islen, would say them. Think what your character is trying to get across to the other person and don't let anything get you sidetracked.''

Fortunately June's voice didn't have a western twang; it almost sounded like a soft, mild, slow Southern drawl.

''There was this lady who waitressed at a diner in Ely, she was from North—or was it South—anyway, one of the Carolinas. We became friends and I'd hang out with her when I wanted to get out of the house. Maybe I just picked it up from her,'' she explained when Eve had wondered about her voice.

''It sounds delightful and fits you perfectly. It adds to your realness, your honesty. Don't ever lose that, June. Or try to change it. Or listen to anyone who tries to change you.'' Eve was adamant. Because tampering with her down-to-earth quality would be disastrous. As June was, Eve believed men would want to love her but also protect her, and women would want to look like her and identify with her because she seemed like one of them.

Eve knew if she could get this on film, if what she saw came off on that screen, June Islen would be a blockbuster star!

Los Angeles, California
Monday, September 19, 1938

Eve Handel cautiously and nervously drove to Pad-Dar Pictures.

Today was a milestone in her young life, for several reasons. One, this was her maiden voyage, first time solo in her new black Ford convertible. She had taken her cousin's advice and shortened her name to Handel when she applied for her driver's license and found that it really had simplified matters. Peter Padon had a friend who owned a Ford dealership, and he had given her a great deal on the car. For the past few months Yvonne Birshgeld had patiently taught her how to drive. So, today was the day, the day of freedom, the day she really felt as if she belonged in California.

It was also the day she was to hear how Mo Jeddu liked June Islen's screen test. Landmark number two. Eve had rehearsed with her, then with the help of the cameraman in regard to shot angles, the test had been done. An editor on the lot had assisted Eve in putting the film together, and the music department had even supplied some background music.

Eve had enlisted the aid of Michael Flanders, a contract player at Pad-Dar, to play the Spencer Tracy role. He was from the New York stage, about twenty-four, and very intense. He had sandy, reddish hair, piercing eyes and a sensitive face—and Michael was talented. He wasn't the typical leading man, but then, neither was Spencer Tracy. He willingly agreed to do the test, especially when he saw June Islen. He might be married with two children, but he wasn't dead yet. And, if the test turned out well, he would have some good footage of his own work to show.

Eve hesitated at the door to Peter Padon's office, full of apprehension. The result of that test could determine her future. But there was no one to hide behind, nowhere to go at this point. Except through those portals. She swallowed, her mouth dry, but she forced herself to walk in, showing as much confidence as she could muster.

Peter was at his desk, John Darius sat in one of the armchairs, and a stranger was in a second one. Eve assumed, correctly, that the gentleman was Mo Jeddu.

''Come in, Eve, come in.'' Peter rose quickly and escorted her farther into the room. ''You know John, and this is Mo Jeddu, owner and CEO of Status Films.''

Mo Jeddu stood to greet her. He was taller than Peter by three or four inches, and leaner. Eve guessed he was also older than Peter. The image of a hawk crossed her mind—sharp eyes, thin face, curved nose.

''So you are Eve Handel! I heard you were young, but no one mentioned how striking you were!'' He kissed her hand gallantly. His voice was surprisingly soft; she would have expected it to be harder, in keeping with his appearance.

Peter pulled another chair closer to the group. ''I think you'd better take a load off your feet, we've got lots to talk about.''

Eve tried to read the atmosphere in the office. Something was up, that much she knew, but what she couldn't tell. They seemed too congenial for the news to be all bad, at least that was somewhat comforting.

Mo Jeddu rose. ''Miss Handel, the test you shot of my fr—of June Islen is dynamite. She's going to be a huge star. Not only has Status signed her to a seven-year contract, but Jenine Jasmine—

that's June's new name—will be starting a film as soon as the script is finished.''

Eve clapped her hands with joy. "I just *knew* she had something special! I am so happy for her."

"Yes, you certainly *did* know what you saw, and you also knew how to get what you saw on the screen. Ju—Jenine knows that, too, and—" a sigh escaped from Mo Jeddu "—and she is already giving orders that she won't work with anyone but you."

Eve looked confused. "But she has to! How can I...? I don't understand."

The men laughed, not unkindly, only in amusement at her reaction.

"Don't worry your pretty head," John Darius broke in. "The details have already been worked out, providing you agree, of course. Pad-Dar and Status are going to share you. Jenine will go over everything with you before she ever goes on a set, and then the director will do his usual thing, but Jenine will already know how to play the scene. They may send other actors of theirs to you, too. Oh, and Pad-Dar is loaning Michael Flanders to Status as Jenine's co-star, they had such good chemistry. 'Course, Status will loan us Jenine for a flick, so everybody's happy. Well, what do you think?"

Peter added quickly, "Don't forget to tell her that the $85 a week goes to $100 a week—from each of us. That's two hundred big greens."

Eve was flabbergasted. She couldn't have dreamed of a better scenario. Finally, at last, a few people believed in her ability.

"I honestly don't know what to say. I'm simply—overwhelmed," she managed to get out. "My family will never believe I am speechless."

"Just say yes," Mo said. "It's good for you, it's good for us."

"Then yes! Oh yes!"

Mo exclaimed, "It's settled! Congratulations! Now, I want you to read the pages so far of *Wicked Eyes*—that's the new movie. You might have some ideas about the dialogue. You know, will it be right for Ju—damn it, I can't get used to Jenine—anyway, if it would be right for her. You got her nailed, and I don't want anything phony. Know what I mean?''

''Exactly, Mr. Jeddu. I wouldn't want that, either. Part of her appeal is that true-to-life quality, no frills, just a real woman.''

''We call that a good broad! And it's a compliment!'' Peter explained.

''All right, Peter. I'll make sure Jenine Jasmine remains a—good broad,'' Eve promised.

That evening, after Yvonne and Eve had toasted the events of the day with a bottle of champagne, and after Eve had called Chicago to share the good news, Eve lay in her bed staring at the ceiling, unable to sleep. She gave up the pretense, went to the window to catch a bit of the gentle night breeze. It had been a hot day in sunny California and the cooler air felt good. She slipped on a light robe and walked out to a chaise lounge in the enclosed patio, bringing her large appointment book with her. Sometimes, especially if it was work-related—like now—she would jot down impressions in her appointment book instead of her journal.

> *I like Mr. Jeddu, "the hawk." And he's absolutely right— keep June, alias Jenine—a good broad. Men do come up with odd expressions, don't they?*
>
> *Isn't it amazing! The lightning-quick chance that can change our lives in just twenty four hours?*

Eve's mind wandered, reviewing the responses of the family. Mama still worried about the male bosses taking advantage of her. Papa'd been proud, but she knew he wouldn't tell Grandpa Handelstein. Ruth was thrilled, and also excited about her senior year and the fact she knew now for sure she was going to be a writer. Abe gave the biggest yell and immediately wanted to come visit. Except he couldn't right away because he was in serious training for the 1940 Olympics, and oh yes, starting college. He seemed more at ease with her than he had since the breakup with Arthur. She knew he had been upset about that, but maybe he had forgiven her by now. She wondered if Arthur had forgiven her, if he would ever forgive her...if he could ever forgive her.

Chicago, Illinois
Monday, September 19, 1938

A tanned, relaxed Arthur Burdsey sauntered up to the reception desk in front of Randall Burdsey's office.

"Anyone in there, Betty?"

The pretty dark-haired girl quickly spun her seat around at the sound of his voice.

"You're back! Did you have a good time?" she asked wistfully, already sure of the answer. What she wouldn't give to spend a month tooling all over Europe, especially with *him*. Arthur was on every female's wish list since he had become a free man.

"Just great, thank you. I'll tell you all about it when I have a chance," he said politely. "So it's okay?" He indicated the closed door.

"Oh, sure!" She followed him with hungry eyes as he disappeared into the room beyond.

The elder Burdsey looked up when he heard the click of the latch, and his eyes sparkled when he saw his son.

"Well, well! You look good, I can tell the outing was worthwhile. Sorry I wasn't home last night when you came by—big meeting—you understand."

"No problem! I was so out of it, I just wanted to get to my place and be horizontal. But now that I'm back, maybe I can relieve you of some of those meetings."

"I'm fine! I'm fine!" Randall said. "You know me, I thrive on this stuff. Now, tell me all about your trip."

For the remaining days of March and most of this past April, Arthur had been in limbo. The trauma of Eve's decision hovered over him like a possessive shroud. He couldn't escape from the cavity in which he had been thrown. Yet, even in his own haze of grief, he could also find room in his heart for Eve's despair. Arthur trusted that she had fully intended to honor their love. He understood what the letter from Hollywood signified to her. Hadn't he been with her the day her grandfather almost destroyed her! And hadn't he waited all those months when she had been in London! He had to surmise it was almost inevitable that her talent would be noticed, because he, too, believed she had a gift. In a way he blamed himself. If that ass of a man hadn't threatened her, he probably wouldn't have proposed so quickly and she would have had a chance to try her hand at working before settling down. All the timing had worked against them. But, damn it, it hurt! And, damn it, he loved her so!

Graduation activities helped fill some of the void. He was much in demand, and that was fine with Arthur. "Variety Is the Spice of Life" became his motto. "Hooking Arthur Burdsey" became the goal of Chicago's mothers and daughters.

The aborted marriage had been a terrible blow to Arthur's mother. In her head, Alicia Burdsey had already pictured her days filled with shopping and planning, already knew exactly how she would furnish Eve and Arthur's home, the nursery especially. Now she felt lost and alone again. Arthur was becoming more like his father every day, business, business, business! Or, out on the town.

Arthur grappled with the sensation of being smothered. And finally, he allowed himself to identify the source of the reason. True, his mother's countenance was a continual dampener. But, additionally, the setting of the Burdsey house and the Handelstein house, so close together, was a constant remembrance of what had been. He had to get away. An ingenious idea came to him. He pleaded with his mother to help him. Because only *she* could find the right apartment for her rejected son. Only *she* could furnish it the way he would be comfortable. Only *she* knew him well enough to make this move palatable.

It had worked. Alicia had a mission. And she devoted herself to the cause. And Arthur was delighted with the results. Alicia buzzed around like a contented bee. She found an ideal co-op, despite the fact it was probably too large. She *did* have taste and decorating skills. Once it was completed she arranged for a housekeeper so that Arthur had nothing to worry about. All he had to do was call and say if he would be in for dinner, and if so, how many would join him! Alicia had a genuine flair, and gradually other people wanted to consult with her. Arthur inadvertently had shown her a way.

The rationale for the European jaunt had been two-fold. Randall thought it would be good for Arthur to have some time to play before coming into the office full-time. And he wanted to initiate his son into the social angle of his business. His intuition, which had a high percentage of accuracy, told him Arthur would be an excellent liaison between his clients and himself, and would certainly be a lure for new investors, as well. Arthur related to people extremely well, men and women alike took to him. His guileless friendliness was an open door to trust.

"What did you think of the Sardos family?" Randall asked Arthur.

"Very nice. And so hospitable. Beryl and Nicholas—they insisted I call them by their first names—wanted me to stay on their yacht and cancel the rest of my arrangements. I couldn't, but I did promise a full visit one of these years. Not that that would be a chore. My God, it's a magnificent ship, 190 feet, four decks, twelve in the crew, including two Cordon Bleu chefs. Quite unbelievable."

"Did you meet any other people?" Randall asked.

"There was another family on board. Sofia and Bruno Morellini and their five-year-old daughter, Maria—beautiful child. From New York. Nicholas suggested I give Mr. Morellini our card, so I did."

Randall nodded in satisfaction. Morellini would be a welcome addition.

"Follow up on that one when you go to New York. Good work." Randall leaned toward his son conspiratorially. "Now, did you have any fun yourself? Did you get lucky?"

"Well, ah, I did meet some attractive young women. They—their—bathing suits, ah, not much to them, you know? There was this beach on St. Tropez, and I swear, each girl was prettier than the one before. Anyway, they're very—friendly—there. To be perfectly frank, Dad, it's hard not to walk around with a perpetual hard-on."

Betty, in the outer office, heard Randall's hearty laugh and wondered what the joke was. One good thing, the old boy should be in a better mood now that his son was back.

There had been one girl in particular who stood out from the sea of beautiful bodies. Arthur had traveled on the Sardos's yacht, *The Swan,* from St. Tropez to Cannes. The ship anchored at a lovely inlet, Cap Camarat, where the guests took motorboats to an open-air restaurant, Chez Camille, for a lunch of lobster and bouillabaisse. Launches kept popping in and out; obviously this was *the* spot for the rich and famous on break from water skiing and swimming.

Beryl and Nicholas knew everyone, it seemed, and each new group of arrivals would greet them with hugs and kisses. Nicholas always asked them to join his table. A striking nineteen-year-old ended up sitting next to Arthur as the seating arrangements shifted with the latest additions.

"Bonjour!" she said gaily. *"Comment allez vous?"*

Arthur had used very little of his high school French on the trip. He had learned that most French—at least those he'd met—spoke English fairly well and really took offense when a foreigner, especially an American, butchered their language.

"Tres bien, merci, but I'm afraid that is the extent of my French," Arthur apologized.

"Oh, but that ees okay, I speak English very good," she replied quickly. "My name ees Nicole de Garsolette."

He brought her extended hand almost to his lips as he had seen the European men do. "I am Arthur Burdsey."

Nicole was petite, her measurements perfectly balanced. Short bobbed black hair, dark luminous eyes, full, pouty lips. He could see flashes of white skin peeking out from the wisp of cloth she wore that the sun had missed; otherwise she was a golden brown. A thin gold chain dangled carelessly from her little waist, the knobbed ends brushing back and forth across her flat tummy and the top of her scant bikini bottom. There was something very sensuous about those swinging baubles, taunting yet protecting the territory they patrolled. Arthur could feel his reaction.

She was vacationing in Cannes—apparently *no one* stayed in Paris during August except the tourists. Her family had known the Sardoses for many years. She modeled occasionally for fun but had no serious goal in her future at the moment.

"Life ees for pleasure, no?" she declared in an adorable, almost childlike voice.

"No!" Arthur agreed fervently. "I mean—yes!"

At this point, Nicholas Sardos tapped his glass for attention. "I have decided to have a party when *The Swan* docks in Cannes this evening. That is, if we are given a slot large enough to tie up this Goliath. Last time it took our captain over two hours. Hopefully, we'll see you all there at nine."

Everyone began to go to their separate boats. Nicole rose to leave. "Weel you be there tonight?"

"I'm checking into the Carlton when we land, but I'll come back for dinner."

"Tres bien! A tout à l'heure!"

"I guess that means I'll see you tonight," Arthur laughed. He was glad, and excited. He wanted to see her again.

It was a picture-perfect night, and everyone on board the ship looked as if they had stepped out from a page in a fashion magazine. The men were handsome in their white dinner jackets. And the women were in full bloom, wearing a colorful assortment of couture "cruise line" fashions.

Nicole was particularly fetching in a white chiffon, ankle-length gown with a crisscross halter-neck. She fit comfortably in his arms as they joined the revelers, who barely allowed the band to take a break. The layers of the sheer material of her full skirt swirled wildly as they danced the jitterbug, the fox-trot, the rumba, even the new craze, "truckin." Arthur marveled at the European endurance—water sports all afternoon and celebrations all night. And he wondered at their ability to isolate their frivolity, their fun, from some of the grim realities that engulfed so many countries. There was not one discussion the entire evening about Britain's Neville Chamberlain, or Hitler's annexing of Austria, or of Stalin, or Spain's Civil War. He knew in the States this evasion would be an impossibility.

When guests began to leave, Arthur suggested he see Nicole home. She agreed, but only if they went along the beach path. They took off their shoes and walked along the sea's edge. The moon smiled on the water and the stars shone like precious gems. He asked her about his curious observation, if in her experience tonight was the norm, or possibly an exception.

Nicole turned to him, her eyes wide. "You mean because we do not talk politics? Or about the ills of the world?"

She tossed her head in annoyance. "Europeans know war. We have had to endure more than Americans. Eef troubles come, we weel take care of them. But why spoil joyous times by worry ahead? We must leev while we can!"

With that she laughed and ran ahead in a billowy cloud of white. Arthur caught her easily and pulled her to him, kissing her. Nicole drew back slightly and whispered, "Come. Our cabana ees near."

Inside the shelter she lay back on a chaise lounge. "There ees room for two," she beckoned.

Arthur shed his coat and slid in beside her and kissed her again. She responded warmly. He brought his hand around the nape of her neck to bring her closer and touched the fastener of her top. Gently he undid the hook, exposing her milky white breasts, the nipples already hard to his touch. Nicole sighed and reached to discard his tie and open his shirt. Her hands wandered over his chest, feeling his muscles, and playing with his hair. They kept moving, slowly going downward. His belt was loosened, his zipper pushed down. Her hands found him and encircled him.

Arthur did away with her dress. There was the gold chain, the spangles now pointing to where the treasure was buried, just waiting to be found. He rolled over, his arm supporting her, their desire mounting. She guided him to her and he found she was already moist and ready for him. Their rhythm was tentative at first, but gradually the pace increased until the moment came.

At his highest peak, Arthur cried out, "Oh, Eve! Eve, my darling!" But it wasn't until both had quieted down and were relaxing against the pillows that his mind actually registered what had happened. Had he said those words out loud? Or had he just voiced them in his subconscious? He glanced surreptitiously at Nicole. She didn't seem unduly perturbed, as she rightly would have been if she had heard another woman's name at such a delicate time.

But why would he do such a thing? One didn't have to be a genius to figure the answer. Nicole and Eve were similar in appearance—small, dark hair, dark eyes—and even slightly alike in personality. Both were independent and spirited women. He had been attracted to Nicole because he was easily able to substitute her for Eve. Arthur faced the truth, he was a long way from forgetting Eve.

Arthur was embarrassed, even mortified. It was inexcusable that he place someone in such a position, even though it had not been intended. He was very respectful toward Nicole on their walk to her hotel. And regretful he was leaving, assuring her they would meet again, but knowing that was not possible, or wise. Arthur had the impression that she wouldn't be too bothered one way or another. She might only be nineteen, but she was quite sophisticated and evidently satisfied with the results of the evening. Mentally, he gave himself a little pat on the back, he must have done something right. He tenderly kissed her goodbye. On the way to the Carlton he decided that it might be more appropriate and safer for him to date blondes for a while.

Los Angeles, California
Monday, July 10, 1939

Peter Padon, John Darius and Mo Jeddu practically knocked Eve's office door down in their rush to get in.

"We did it! You did it! We did it!" they yelled, overlapping one another excitedly. They were waving newspapers in the air as if they were banners at a football game.

"Did what? What are—" asked Eve, completely bewildered.

"It's, well, we were pretty sure we had a winner when the preview cards turned out so terrific. Those audiences went ape over Jenine, the picture, Michael, Jenine. But you never know until the big guns come out—that's the critics—and they *loved* it. They loved her, him, them, everything! The advance public relations got everyone's attention, the previews showed the public was with us, and now these reviews put the icing on the cake. We'll take out ads all over the place, this is hot! I can hear the sound of money falling—falling—falling!" Mo Jeddu was sputtering in his enthusiasm.

Peter grabbed Eve and danced her all over the room, singing "We got a bonanza! We got a bonanza! We got a bonanza!"

John and Mo stood and clapped their hands in time to Peter's chant.

"All right already," gasped Eve. "Sit down before we all have heart attacks. My birthday was last week, but it sounds as if I may be celebrating tonight. Now, explain all this slowly and carefully."

When Eve had read the rough draft of *Wicked Eyes* last September, she certainly did have some suggestions. Her finely honed sense of storytelling uncovered the flaws in the script, as well as defined the female role to best suit Jenine. Fortunately, she had the support of the two studios, because writers, and especially seasoned ones, rarely took kindly to the thoughts of a young newcomer. But this writer recognized the merit of Eve's proposals even without the head office, so it turned out to be a happy meeting of the minds.

Eve never went on the set, but she rehearsed the scenes with Jenine each night before the next day's shooting. With Eve's guidance and her own native talent and street smarts, Jenine had given a dazzling performance. The gamble had paid big dividends.

Even before the fan mail began pouring in, other studios wanted to borrow Jenine for their projects, the newspapers and magazines wanted interviews and photo sessions. But Status Films knew they had a gold mine and were very selective about what publicity she would and would not do, which just put her more in demand. And, of course, only Pad-Dar Pictures had rights for loan-outs. No doubt, Jenine had made a vivid impression on Hollywood.

With the attention, of course, the town's bachelors hovered over her like vultures, ready to swoop and pounce. She didn't stop seeing her benefactor, but Mo was smart enough to realize he couldn't keep her bound to him alone; she was far too young and too full of a zest for life. And love.

"For Christ's sake," he complained ruefully to Peter, "she had to have a damn schoolteacher on the set when she was working. It's the law!"

Peter consoled him, "Well, that won't last for much longer. Think of it this way. It's good she's seen at openings with the big stars. Gives her more importance, stature. Just be grateful you don't have to do the boogie-woogie! And don't worry, she can take care of herself.''

But as Eve was just beginning to discover, the question really was, could the men take care of themselves? Some nights Michael Flanders would join Jenine at Eve's rehearsal sessions, and he got in the habit of driving Jenine home to her apartment. It seemed like the two had begun to practice more than the dialogue.

Michael had come to Eve's office one lunch hour toward the end of the film. ''I need your help, Eve'' had been his opening words.

She sat calmly, waiting for him to continue. ''Uh, I have a problem. Mmm, I guess I have two problems.''

He stood up and paced. ''First, I—I have a tendency to drink too much. I don't mean to, but if I start, I just keep going.''

''What can I do?'' she asked.

''About that? Nothing, really. Except not tell anyone, especially the brass.''

''Fine. Your secret's safe with me. But I wish you would see someone. Aren't there clinics?''

''Yes, yes! I'll do that.'' Michael sat down beside Eve. ''But, it's the second thing.'' He jumped up again. ''I've—been having an affair with Jenine.'' Now he rushed on. ''I'd take her to her door, and she'd say, 'Why don't you come in for a drink?' And, of course, I would, and she would down a couple of shots, too. The first night I actually started to leave, but then she said, 'How about one more for the road?' Well, a kiss led to holding, and we were all fired up from the booze, and, well, you know…''

Eve had just nodded in understanding.

Michael looked sheepishly toward Eve. ''I shouldn't be telling you all this, you're barely older than she is, but you seem so— together—I felt I could trust you.''

''You can, Michael,'' Eve assured him. ''Four years may not sound like a lot, but believe me, it really puts Jenine and me miles apart.''

''Jenine is…quite a lover. We would be together every night you needed me for rehearsals. And sometimes—it's happened more and more—she'll suggest we have lunch in her dressing room to go over our lines. I'm not trying to cop out and put it all on her, don't get me wrong! She's very—enjoyable! As a matter of fact, she turned me on even when we did the test. And she doesn't put any demands on me or expect anything. But, I'm not a good two-timer, and I'm afraid my wife will find out and I really do love my wife and kids and don't want to lose them—"

"How can I help?" Eve asked gently.

"Maybe if you explained to Jenine, about me and the family—you see, I don't want her to be mad at me and not work with me or be hurt or something."

Eve felt sorry for him; he really was a decent guy and wasn't meant to be a Don Juan. But, he was human.

"Try not to worry, Michael. I'll have a chat with Jenine. I'm sure she will appreciate your situation."

"Oh, thank you, Eve. You're the best!" He gave her a quick hug and was on his way, a much relieved man.

Eve had sent a message to the set, asking if Jenine would mind stopping by after work.

"Whew!" Jenine exclaimed when she walked into Eve's office about six-thirty that evening. "I'm glad this flick is about over. I'm beat. Got anything to drink?"

Eve did have a small portable bar so she fixed them both a cocktail, a very mild cocktail. When Jenine was relaxed in the comfortable armchair, Eve carefully relayed the gist of the conversation with Michael.

Jenine had looked at Eve in amazement. "Is he for real? I mean, he's honestly upset about him and me?"

Eve nodded solemnly.

"Pu-leese tell him everything is fine! Don't bother me in the least! And I adore working with him, he's damn good. So there is *no problem.*" She mischievously added, "He's good in bed, too! But I got my eye on a guy on the set—a grip—with a body that has muscles out the kazoo. I hope *all* his muscles are in good shape!"

Eve had been surprised, and even a little shocked. But then she realized that Jenine would be candid with her because she had already proved her friendship, and in Jenine's mind, Eve was totally dependable. And, of course, Jenine's assumption was right, Eve would never betray her confidences. But Eve did hope Jenine would be cautious. Studios liked their stars to be morally correct— sexy, yes—but "nice" sexy. She hoped this young girl's obvious appetite for love wouldn't cut short what could be a long and successful career. Eve wasn't clear, either, about Jenine's relationship with Mo Jeddu. She knew what it *had* been, but wondered if something had changed. In any case, Eve wasn't about to open that Pandora's box. She smiled inwardly. Somehow, despite her concerns, she had a hunch her ward was shrewd enough to land on her feet.

Jenine had interrupted Eve's thoughts. "You know who's been sniffing around? Johnny 'Pick Up the Check' Meyers! And you know who he fronts for, don't you?"

Eve shook her head.

"Howard Hughes, that's who! He does all of Mr. H's—arranging. I think I'll play real dumb and not take the bait. That'll drive him crazy. What do you think?"

"I have absolutely, positively no idea. This is out of my league, dear. You don't want my advice."

Jenine had laughed. "Maybe *you* need *my* advice. I should take you under my wing. You're so serious about work, I bet you never go out and let yourself go—dance and kiss and be romantic and just...get loose! Do you?"

All of a sudden, Eve felt on the defensive. The roles had been reversed, and now she was the pupil, not the teacher.

"Of, of course I see people—men—out of the office. I just haven't found someone I want to be with."

The intercom saved Eve from further discussion. "I'm leaving, Miss Handel. Do you need me for anything before I go?" Matilda Carliss asked.

"No, thank you. Actually, I think we're all about ready to call it a day. Have a nice evening!"

My emotional state swung like a pendulum today as diagnosed by first Michael and then Jenine. He thinks I'm "so together," and she feels I'm a workaholic and sexually repressed. Poor Michael! I can easily empathize with his weakness in not being able to resist Jenine. How many times did I wish Arthur hadn't been such a gentleman with me! How can I be so together and mess up as I did with Arthur?

I honestly told Jenine the truth. I have been approached by several men at both studios and I have gone on dates. But these guys seem to have one goal in mind—drinks, dinner and bed! Now, we know I'm not so darn puritanical! Truly, I haven't been attracted enough to anyone to pursue a—well— a closeness. There's nothing more disgusting to me than some jerk trying to stick his tongue down your throat when you don't want him to.

Los Angeles, California
Monday, August 14, 1939

Nick Larrington asked Eve's secretary if Miss Handel was free.

Matilda Carliss knew the next appointment hadn't arrived, but she would make sure her boss wanted to be disturbed. She was always very protective.

"Let me check. Who may I say is calling?"

"Nick Larrington, head of casting at Status."

Matilda spoke into the intercom and immediately said, "Please go right in, Mr. Larrington."

They had met briefly a few times at studio functions and Eve rose to greet him. "Such a nice surprise! What brings you to Pad-Dar?"

"Quite frankly, to ask you for a favor. I know, well, everyone knows, how you spotted and developed Jenine's t—"

Eve cut in. "Please! Jenine did the work and had the talent."

"Okay! I understand." Nick liked her for that. Rare for someone not to claim all the credit for a success. "However, be that as it may, I would still be grateful if you would attend a play with me at the Pasadena Playhouse and give me your input on one young actress in particular. Mr. Jeddu told me that you were associated with both studios and that it would be all right for me to call upon you.''

Eve laughed. ''Yes, of course, I'll come. I'm realizing I'm in an odd position around here. Anyway, I'm delighted you asked and am eager to see some theater. I've missed it.''

The evening at the Pasadena Playhouse was the beginning of a healthy friendship between Eve and Nick Larrington. After seeing Heidi Graham in *Once in a Lifetime,* they both agreed she should be tested. Eve would coach her in the basics for the test, and then the heads of the studios would determine what, if anything, came off on the screen.

That first outing had spawned the development of a very special coupling. They saw every little theater group in Los Angeles and its neighboring communities. They went to every movie—big ones, small ones, foreign ones, documentaries. Always learning. Always looking for talent, raw or experienced. Always talking. Together they were responsible for several additions to both studio's rosters. Heidi Graham included.

It was wonderful for Eve. She had the companionship of an intelligent, witty and pleasant man who shared her interests and never put sexual pressures on her. A perfect combination. For both. Nick likewise enjoyed the camaraderie. Plus, for the first time he had someone who could help him professionally with delicate issues at the studio.

Status, at Nick's suggestion, had put a famous English stage actress under contract. A test was made to see how she looked and sounded on film, but they'd discovered a problem. The lady in question, Cynthia Cellac, photographed beautifully, but when she spoke she projected her voice as one does in a theater. And because the camera was able to get in so close, the lens saw her Adam's apple bob up and down. It was very unappealing.

Nick asked Eve to view the test and she was quickly able to deal with the problem. She just sat and talked with the actress in her small office and went over the lines. Then she explained to Cynthia that she didn't need to be any louder on the set. The two became personal friends as well as business associates. At one point, Cynthia sought Eve's professional advice. She had been asked to do a picture and wasn't sure if she should because her role ended after the second act. Eve read the script and told her that if she played the role the way Eve knew she could play it, the audience would only be thinking of Cynthia.

Cynthia heeded Eve's counsel, and was nominated for an Academy Award the next year.

Los Angeles, California
Monday, February 5, 1940

Joseph Hassal leaned back against his chocolate-colored leather chair in his elegantly appointed office and gazed at Peter Padon, John Darius and Mo Jeddu. He was an imposing man and his frame filled the chair—not overweight necessarily, just big. Because of his size people often assumed that he held a physical profession, but his keen mind made him one of the best investment bankers in the state. Hassel's bushy crop of graying hair outlined a tanned, strong face with shaggy eyebrows, piercing dark eyes and a nose that looked as if it had been broken many times. He showed his German-Jewish heritage despite the name. Like so many immigrants who arrived at Ellis Island, his father had simplified his surname of Hassalstroud to Hassal.

"Well, gentlemen, I don't foresee any problem with your proposal to merge. Pad-Dar Pictures and Status Films are independently owned studios, both financially stable. And, contrary to the norm, both extremely compatible. I would still recommend, however, that you be represented by separate counsel, which will just insure a continuance of your harmonious relationship.

"The procedure will follow the established course. The value, earnings power, history of earnings, plus any forecast of future earnings that could affect the share price, will all be determined. That ratio will decide the number of shares allotted to each company, with each one's approval, of course. Do you plan to go public?''

The usually quiet John Darius answered for the group. ''Yes, we do, Mr. Hassal—''

''Please,'' Joseph Hassal interrupted, ''if we are going to be working together, let's drop the formality. I'm Joe.''

''Uh, thank you, Joe.'' John Darius was not used to being so vocal. ''I'm sort of the silent partner, I guess you call it. Peter ordinarily does the talking. But, well, when this merger business got started, I realized it was a way for me to get out and—''

Peter Padon broke in. ''Understand Mr.—Joe—this was not my doing. John's the best partner a guy could have. I hoped we could make this next step together. But—'' Peter gazed fondly at the older John ''—but, I respect his wishes and am glad he can go out with a bang. If you'll pardon the expression!''

The men chuckled and John Darius continued. ''The merger should have happened a long time ago. We practically are one already, sharing the girl—don't get me wrong—not that kind of girl, a very talented young lady who guides the actors and actresses at both studios. Plus, we loan our people only to each other. And— oh, never mind—I'm rambling on like an old fool. Anyway, by going public, I can let Peter buy me out and I'll retire with hopefully, a little bundle.''

Joseph Hassal smiled. ''I can practically guarantee a handsome profit. But, first things first. After the initial steps I mentioned are taken, you will then have to settle upon the officers and appoint a board. The board must have a chairman, or it can be co-chaired and have a number of vice presidents. The size is optional, but my advice would be to keep it on the small side, otherwise it becomes unwieldy. And I would have the board appointees be an even number, so the chairman is required to break a tied vote. All information must appear in the prepared prospectus so the public is aware of everything. Any questions so far?''

Peter Padon and Mo Jeddu exchanged looks, nodded, and Mo gestured for Peter to speak.

"Mo and I would like to co-chair the board and we would ask John Darius to be first vice president. Now, don't say nothing yet, John, hear me out. A board meets—once a month?" Peter glanced at Joseph Hassal.

"That's correct. Unless, of course, there is an emergency," answered Joseph Hassal. "Don't forget, there are committees that function as well."

"Okay. So, even though you're not financially involved, John, it don't mean we can't have your input, your savvy. But you wouldn't have the day-to-day crap to deal with."

Joseph Hassal broke in. "There is no need to make a commitment at this time. Much work must be done before that part is due. I do believe, for what it's worth, that the suggestion is an excellent one."

The truth was that John Darius was privately delighted at the plan offered. He knew he would go mad if he became completely detached from the company he helped establish. But his doctor had warned him that too much work would kill him. He had never divulged this bit of information to Peter or Mo, he had only said he was tired and wanted to travel and relax and spend time with his long-neglected wife and children and grandchildren. This would allow him to keep a little finger in the pie without risking his health.

"To go on," Joseph Hassal said. "Do you have a name for the new company?"

"Utopia Studios," the three men said, almost in unison.

"I like that," exclaimed Joseph Hassal, "unity and decisiveness! So, Utopia Studios will go on the market at the price agreed upon after all the preliminary studies are over. It could open at four-times earnings, or more, or less. At that time, you will determine what percentage you want to open to the public. The standard amount is anywhere from five to twenty percent. Often, a gesture is made to special people, allowing them options to buy a small amount of shares at the opening price. Because once the shares are on the market, the price could soar. Or, it could go down, which, in this case, I think is highly unlikely. So, shall I proceed?''

''Absolutely!'' all three men said emphatically.

Pad-Dar Pictures and Status Films were appraised at equal net worth after all taxes and all assets were accounted. This meant the new company, Utopia Studios, would begin with $50 million earnings and each share would be worth five dollars.

The two former companies each owned fifty percent of the stock. John Darius sold Peter Padon his twenty-five percent, so indeed, John would have quite a nice nest egg of $12,500,000.

Both Padon and Jeddu gave five percent or five hundred thousand shares to be offered to the public at five-times earnings. The underwriter, investment banker Joseph Hassal, allowed two and a half percent or 250,000 shares, to be available for options at initial opening price to a few handpicked colleagues.

Mo Jeddu and Peter Padon co-chaired the board of directors; John Darius was assigned first vice president. The remaining members of the board would have the right to buy the stock options. Joseph Hassal became second vice president. Chester Chaucer, head accountant of Status, and Keith Kartonia, chief accountant of Pad-Dar, were installed as treasurer-secretaries. Members at large included Sidney Markvitch, lawyer for Status; Angelo Westini, Pad-Dar's lawyer; Nick Larrington, continuing as casting head of Utopia; and Eve Handel, in charge of talent at Utopia.

Status Films had been located a few miles north of Warner Brothers in the San Fernando Valley, and because it had more office space, it became the headquarters of Utopia. The Pad-Dar property continued to be used for sound stages. Both locations would now boast the banner Utopia Studios.

On Monday, April 29, Joseph Hassal called his friend, Randall Burdsey, in Chicago.

''Randy, how are you? How's Alicia and that good-looking son of yours?''

''Fine, fine!'' Burdsey replied. ''And you? Esther and Douglas all right?''

"Couldn't be better! Douglas is very excited, he's going to be working for Utopia Studios. I just became an officer on the board and bought a small percentage of the company. When I mentioned my son was interested in the film business the bosses thought they might use Douglas in the production end. Start him off doing tests, maybe shorts and documentaries, see if he can cut the mustard.''

"I can tell you, it's wonderful having your son involved in your business," Burdsey said proudly. "Arthur is going great guns, really bringing in new clients and pleasing the old ones. And is he a cocksman with the ladies! A real chip off the old block!''

Hassal smiled. "Sounds as if the apple didn't fall far from the tree, congratulations!'' His voice took on a serious tone. "You have always been helpful to me with your guidance in stocks, and I wanted to do the same for you, if I could. On May 1, 750,000 shares of Utopia Studios will go public. Now, I'm not telling you anything that is not in the prospectus, except to give you my personal opinion. These are solid people, the outfit solvent, beyond reproach and reliable.''

"It's odd you should call regarding this today. I did receive the material, and even though show business is not my forte, I made a note to look into it more thoroughly. It looks promising, the figures look good.'' Burdsey was beginning to be piqued.

Hassal continued. "It's opening at five-times earnings, but my gut feeling is that it will climb steadily higher.''

"I do appreciate your input. Thanks. I'll get on it right away. Hope to see you soon, but in any case, we'll keep in touch.'' Burdsey was eager to get moving.

"Oh, my God, I don't know what to say—or do!'' Eve was beside herself. Peter Padon, John Darius and Mo Jeddu had just told her that not only was she on the board of Utopia Studios, but she was to receive a substantial salary increase. Plus, she had the opportunity to exercise options on ten thousand shares.

"At five dollars a share, you say? That's $50,000 dollars! Oh, dear!''

The three men were pleased that they were able to give Eve her just reward. She had certainly earned it. But then it dawned on them—$50,000 was probably a huge sum for her to come up with.

John Darius had a solution. "This is a tremendous opportunity. If the stock goes as Hassal thinks it will, you could end up with a nice security blanket. I now have more dough than I need. I want to loan you whatever you—"

"Oh, Mr. Darius, I couldn't! Papa said we should never borrow. That we should only buy what we could afford or do without."

"I know, I know," John said soothingly. "And he's right. But this isn't quite the same thing. I'm not talking about a fancy house or a big car or a pretty dress. This is for your future! These chances don't happen often. You're gonna pull down $600 dollars a week. Now, you know you can pay me back out of that. No sweat, either."

Eve's mind was racing. She understood the logic of what he was saying. But it was against everything she had been taught. She had budgeted her salary carefully and had actually saved ten thousand dollars in the two years she had been in California.

No one—not Mama, not Papa—had ever thought of making so much money. But the film business was different. Where else would she have this kind of stepping-stone to financial security?

"I do have some money tucked away. If I should be indebted to you for—" it was difficult for Eve to even say the amount "—$40,000, I could begin to repay you with my $400-a-week wage increase. Then, if the shares should become more valuable, I could sell some and pay off whatever was left. Would that be all right?" she asked, her voice dwindling to a whisper, showing the effort this decision had taken.

"Whatever makes you comfortable, little lady," John answered gently.

Peter Padon interrupted. "Good! That's settled then, everybody's happy!"

Eve gave a weak smile, hoping she had done the right thing.

"Now," Peter went on, "to other matters. Joseph Hassal has been extremely helpful to all of us. Of course, he has come off pretty good, too. Still, it couldn't hurt us to give his son a whack at the business. That's where you come in, Eve.''

''Me? How can I help?'' Eve was surprised.

''Mo and I thought we'd start him off producing tests—for contracts or for parts in a flick. Natch, that falls in your department. Check out his concept of the scene, how and what he hopes to do with the material, see if he has a spark. Okay with you?''

''Certainly! I'm flattered you would value my judgment!'' Eve replied happily.

Mo Jeddu spoke. ''Honey, this meeting and your job wouldn't have happened if we didn't believe in you!''

Douglas Hassal sauntered casually into Eve's office after being announced. He wasn't cocky in his manner, yet he moved deliberately, confidently, as a man used to having his own way. The navy blazer and the gray gabardine slacks were perfectly tailored, flattering his sizable physique. Like his father, he had a tendency to be on the heavy side, so the two always had to watch their diet. Thick dark blond hair hovered over slanting brown eyes and full pouting lips.

When he was born, April 10, 1917, his mother Esther had named him after an up-and-coming leading man, Douglas Fairbanks. If she had had a girl, she had planned to name the baby Mary, for Mary Pickford. Esther was a good soul and she granted her son his every desire. She'd dreamed of having another child and often asked Douglas if he'd like to have a little brother or sister.

But despite his age, Douglas quickly realized that having a sibling would negatively affect him—he would have to share what he now had in full and he didn't like that one bit! He howled, had such a tantrum that he scared the wits out of Esther.

''No baby! Me baby!'' he had screamed.

''There, my sweetheart! Don't fret, don't cry! Yes, you are my baby, my only baby. Just you, my darling!''

Esther never had a second child. She couldn't bear to disappoint Douglas, so she made sure that either she or Joseph used a form of birth control. And their only son grew up believing he could do or have anything he wanted.

And right now he wanted to be in the movie business and he knew Eve Handel could help him. But he'd been unprepared for her appearance. His father and Peter Padon had explained about her talent but had not mentioned how young and beautiful she was.

"Mr. Hassal, a pleasure to meet you," Eve exclaimed, rising from her desk.

With a grandiose move, he brought her hand to his lips. "It is my pleasure and delight to see you, Miss Handel." His eyes caught and held hers in a steady gaze. "I had not expected someone so— lovely and delicate."

Eve became somewhat flustered. She withdrew her captive hand and said rather brusquely, "Mr. Padon suggested we collaborate on a project and I thought a contract test would be a good start. A promising new actress, Heidi Graham, is due for her yearly option. The bosses like to see recent film on their people before picking up another year. Are you familiar with Heidi's work?"

"I'm afraid not, Miss Handel."

"She's done a few bit parts, but Nick—Nick Larrington in casting—and I think she is ready to do more. And please call me Eve— Douglas. What do you think of the scene from *A Star Is Born* when Esther Blodgett, now Vicki Lester, comes home with good news about her career, Norman Maine's drunk, she doesn't say a word about her news and only tries to encourage him?"

"One of my favorite films!" Douglas said excitedly. "If this Heidi has an ounce of appeal, it will show here! Who can we get to play Fredric March's role? We have to be sure—"

The two huddled in discussion until Eve's next appointment arrived. They set a time for the following day, each promising to do some homework and come with a list of leading men.

Douglas Hassal walked out of the building wearing a wide grin. This was going to be a cinch! He liked the work already. And he was going to stick like glue to this uniquely artistic Eve Handel. She was the key! He was intrigued, there was an emanation of something undefinable about her. Yes, she was clearly a find!

12

Los Angeles, California
Saturday, August 3, 1940

"Big Abe was great!" exclaimed Little Abe. "Mama and Papa weren't sure, even though I'm twenty now, but you know them—always worrying. But Grandpa convinced them, mainly because you're here! Everyone figured you and Mrs. B could keep me in line."

Eve smiled and walked over to give her baby brother a peck on the cheek. He was so open—so boyishly excited—so irresistible. Yvonne Birshgeld and she were going to have their hands full keeping the girls at bay. She was happy he was going to stay with her. Odd how all of a sudden, Grandpa Handelstein was citing her as the reliable one to watch over Little Abe. Whatever happened to the hussy who left her home for Hollywood and the fast life? Because of that dispute, she hadn't allowed herself to acknowledge being homesick before. But seeing a member of her family again made her admit that there had been something missing in her life. A sense of wholeness, of kinship, filled her with joy. Maybe she could go home this Christmas with Abe, maybe it was time.

Abe had been crushed when the 1940 Olympic Games had been canceled because of the war in Europe. But, typical of the young, once that dream had ended, he immediately began to construct a new one. The University of California was obviously a better place to pursue his choice of profession, physical education. The climate was plainly better suited for bodybuilding and swimming. Grandpa Handelstein agreed and the blitz was put in action. Papa Samuel and Mama Mildred didn't have a chance. Especially with Eve living in California and Yvonne Birshgeld there to look after both. With no valid objections it had quickly become a done deal.

Eve's financial situation had resolved itself quite well. Utopia Studios' stock had doubled its opening value within two weeks. Eve immediately sold four thousand of her ten thousand shares at ten dollars a share and repaid her loan from John Darius. She put the remaining six thousand shares in a safety deposit box and planned to leave them there, hopefully to grow in value. When she heard there was a chance Abe might come out, she looked for and found a four-bedroom house, with a fenced yard and a swimming pool. She could afford the rent now with her new salary.

Abe was ecstatic. "I can practice here! Right in our own place. Unbelievable! And maybe we could get a dog? Could we, please?"

Eve hadn't had time to think about pets. All of her attention and energy had gone into work. But, sure, why not? A dog would make them a family.

"Oh, and Eve, I forgot to tell you. I applied under the name of Handel at USC. I kept thinking, it really is simpler."

The test with Heidi Graham had gone well. Douglas Hassal did have a flair for producing. He saw a scene as a painting and was inventive in bringing together the pieces of the canvas and the colors to best enhance the parts. Eve did the groundwork and preparation with the actors. The outcome was quite effective. Heidi Graham was signed for another year without hesitation.

Utopia contracted Douglas Hassal as an associate producer, giving him the opportunity to work under an established professional for a year. He wasn't too thrilled about that, he wanted to be *the* producer with Eve doing what he couldn't. But he knew he had to bide his time. He continued to meet with Eve on any ideas he had, and when the right one was ready he would spring it on the big boys. He was sure his confederacy with Eve was going to be fruit-ful and successful. The long-range plan was to move closer and closer to Eve, not too fast—she was very smart, and also gun-shy around men—until gradually their bond would seem so natural, so comfortable, that their union would be inevitable.

It was just after six in the evening and Eve and Jenine Jasmine had settled down with their cocktails in Eve's small study. Jenine seemed a bit on edge, not her usual unflappable self. She pulled a package of cigarettes from her bag, offered one to Eve, who de-clined, and started puffing nervously.

"I don't remember you smoking," Eve said quizzically.

"I just started, I'm trying not to look like a beginner because, well you know, in the next pic the gal uses a cigarette case to hide info and pass it along."

"Oh, that's right! It read so well I just didn't think about you having to actually smoke. Of course, it would look stupid and sus-picious if she never had a cigarette. Do you mind? We could change the prop, maybe." Eve was upset with herself for forget-ting.

"Not at all," Jenine answered. "Everybody else smokes, and I kinda wanted to learn. Makes me look grown up and—"

"—sophisticated?" Eve filled in.

"Yeah, sophisticated!" Jenine repeated.

There were some moments of silence, and then Jenine blurted out what was on her mind. "Eve, I'm pregnant. I must have had too much to drink one night and got careless. So dumb! The guy don't know and I don't want him to. I have a doctor who's going to fix me up, but I can't stay at my place. It's too risky. And I was wondering if I could stay with you. I'll be okay in a couple of days the doc says, just a little weak and some bad cramps. Like I was having a hard time with my period. That's what I could tell every-one! You have an extra room and that nice lady who lives here, and that way we could also work on the script! Whaddya say?"

Eve was stunned. She knew what her answer would be, but she wasn't exactly sure what her emotions were.

Eve finally spoke, slowly, trying to assure those anxious beautiful cat eyes. "You are absolutely welcome here for as long as you want. And your—situation—is safe with me, I would never betray you."

Jenine grabbed Eve's hand, her eyes filling and overflowing. "I knew I could count on you. Oh, thank you so much."

She hugged Eve, sobbing. "Please don't hate me or think I'm bad. I wouldn't hurt a baby, or anyone, if I could help it. This—this—thing is not easy for me. But it's the only way out. I wouldn't be right for the kid, I know it! This business is all I can do, and whoever I am and whatever it is I do, the audience likes me. And I like them. I'd screw a kid up for sure! And I'd fuck up the one thing I *can* do for sure! But, I'm sorry. I'm so sorry. I wish I could be normal like you and everybody else. But I'm just stuck with—me!"

Eve held the younger woman in her arms, comforting her. And she remembered when Mama Mildred had held her in her arms in Chicago. When Eve had berated herself because she couldn't be good and normal as Mama was, she couldn't marry a wonderful man because she was different, she didn't want the trappings of being a wife and mother, because she had a burning desire deep in her heart!

No, she could not judge Jenine. For she would be judging herself as well.

Today was a tough one! First I had to confront the fact that maybe I was spending too much time on Douglas Hassal and his story. How could I have neglected that cigarette case for Jenine? I should have been the one who suggested she actually smoke—plain carelessness. Was I so concentrated on the characterization that I missed an obvious prop? Boy, that won't happen again, she is top priority at Utopia.

And then Jenine dropped the bombshell! I am so sorry my friend, not just the studio's star, but my friend, is in trouble. I'm grateful she trusted me to confide in. I'm glad she found a doctor who will perform the operation. But an abortion? I just don't know what to think! Birth is so precious a gift—such a miracle—how can I understand ending a life?

But I must be a realist, musn't I? I want to be a woman! And I want to be fair! My heart is torn apart. There's no doubt in my mind that having the baby would destroy her career, she would be crucified and I honestly don't believe she would make a good mother—but I can't be the one to decide! I can't be sure either way.

I don't know—I don't know! Of course I chose to help her and keep her secret. What else could I do?

CHAPTER

13

Los Angeles, California
Friday, December 20, 1940

Eve Handel looked curiously at all the people scurrying around the Los Angeles airport. They made her think of a long column of ants that had been disrupted and forced to scatter for safety in all directions. It was fascinating to watch the diverse emotions playing on the faces, covering all spectrums. She watched a teenage girl come through the arrival door, her eyes glowing with excitement, searching for loved ones. Her steps suddenly quickened as she dashed to the waiting arms of her family. A young man lurked behind until she was ready to greet him. And then a tender kiss was his reward. How sweet and joyful!

Eve's eyes shifted to another couple. At a departure gate. The boy was in an army private's uniform, his sweetheart—no, his wife, oh, they were so young!—clung to him tearfully, hanging on until the last possible moment. And then, forced to let go, her eyes traveled with him, and she stood on tiptoe to get the final glance as he turned to wave before disappearing down the corridor.

Eve had to restrain herself from going over to console the poor soul. If the war in Europe spread, she could imagine this scene happening over and over and over. How tragic and sad!

The pageantry was endless. A mother, father and their three children were enveloped by grandparents. The way the grandmother took the baby in her arms, Eve had the impression it was the woman's first sight of her new grandchild. Eve wondered what that must feel like.

Where did she fit? Eve wondered. She definitely knew where she and Abe were going. She peeked over at Abe, who was engrossed in the latest *Life* magazine, unaware of the dramas unfolding around him. Eve hoped he could keep his naiveté for a long, long time.

So she knew where. And why. But she wasn't rushing to get there. Would everyone and everything just fall into place, like before? But how could it? So much had changed in her life, as it must have with the rest of the family. Would they have anything in common? Telephone calls could never really take the place of one-on-one, heart-to-heart talks.

And would Arthur be at home? She had been too embarrassed to ask Mama, or even Abe. And she had no idea how she would handle that!

And Grandpa Handelstein. Would she have to endure his constant barrage against her business? Or had he lost ground since he had endorsed Little Abe's move?

The whole flight was a series of ifs and ands, whys and whats, ups and downs. Until she was exhausted from battling the unknowns.

Eve stepped tentatively through the terminal door. A smiling, waving Mama Mildred, Papa Samuel and Ruth allayed Eve's fears. Her pace accelerated and she ran into their welcoming embraces like a small child. She was passed along from one to another and then it was Little Abe's turn.

There was no letup in chatter driving in the car. The sight of her home affected her more than she would have imagined. And being in her old room again really choked her up. The memories flowed in like torrential floodwaters. But strangely, she almost felt she was remembering another—person. Another life.

Ruth ventured in. "You okay? Want to be alone?"

"No, no!" Eve said. "Gosh no! I want to see you as much as I can and hear all about you and—and everybody."

"Well 'everybody' isn't in town! I'm not sure if that's good or bad for you." Ruth peered into Eve's eyes and saw the relief. "Good! It's good for you! I have no idea if Artie heard you were coming in or not. But the word is that he went to Sun Valley, Idaho, to stay with his friend, get this, *the* Wade Colby! You dig? *The* heartthrob of the world!"

Ruth had a flash. "Hey, do *you* know Wade Colby?"

Eve smiled. "No, I'm afraid I don't. Contrary to public opinion, everyone does *not* know everyone in Hollywood. I do like his work, though. He's a natural."

"Well, I had to ask. If you did, I thought we could sort of— keep him in the family, so to speak!"

Eve laughed and put her arms around her sister. "Oh, I have missed you and your outrageous sense of humor. Now, what's up with you?"

"Not a lot!" Ruth stated matter-of-factly. "Since I graduated I've been hanging around newspaper offices. I'm kind of in the apprentice stage. They give me the soft stories to cover—women things like teas or fashion shows or similar boring stuff. You know me, I'd like to get into the nitty-gritty, the political cesspool or undercover crime, something exciting. It may be I'll have to do some digging and research, find an angle and write a spec article."

Eve had a thought. "Didn't Papa tell us when we were little that he had met gangsters and federal officers because Grandpa Handelstein made liquor? Or something like that? Prohibition or…?"

"Oh, yeah, that's right! Bet he has some stories, if he'll tell me. I'll work on him after the holidays."

"And how about romance?" Eve teased. "Anyone special?"

"The ones who like me don't interest me. And the one I have eyes for doesn't know I exist. So, I'm fairly dull in that department. Now, about you! Who is this Douglas you keep mentioning? Sounds as if you spend a great deal of time with him!" Ruth had turned the tables.

"Douglas Hassal is a new producer, and my bosses asked me

to help initiate him into the film industry. I think he's bright, and I do enjoy working with him, he's so receptive. We've had dinner several times, but it's really because of business.''

If Douglas Hassal had been a fly on the wall right then, he would have been very pleased. His objective was progressing right on schedule.

The dinner table was full of lively conversation, the topics had no limits. Only Grandpa Handelstein had been included for this night. All of the uncles and aunts and cousins would congregate for the Christmas Day celebration on Wednesday.

Everyone concurred with the reelection of Franklin Delano Roosevelt. Samuel even took umbrage with *Life* magazine's endorsement of Wendell Wilkie. But he did agree with the editorial that indignantly illustrated the barrage of ''items'' hurled at Wilkie, a candidate for president of the United States of America, during his tour of the nation.

''Vote as you will,'' he declared. ''But show respect!''

Of course, the state of Europe monopolized much of the talk. Hitler's campaign continued—Norway, Denmark, Finland, France had fallen. Mussolini had entered the war against Britain and France. The air blitz on London had taken a terrible toll, but the RAF retaliated. Still, Britain stiffened for invasion. Italy went into Greece. Britain and Italy battled in Africa. How could the United States stay at peace? How long did the U.S. have? All eyes turned to Little Abe. Would he be called?

Films did not escape this exchange. Mildred and Samuel had both enjoyed *Abe Lincoln in Illinois,* although Ruth had preferred the injustice and suffering portrayed in *The Grapes of Wrath.* Little Abe loved *Boomtown* with its action and he-men, Clark Gable and Spencer Tracy.

Grandpa Handelstein turned to Eve during this discussion. ''I haven't seen a movie this year. But now I'm interested in what our 'professional' representative thinks.''

Eve looked at him cautiously. Was he mocking her? Or was he genuinely curious? Maybe because she hadn't become an actress but was successful in another capacity, he felt he had won and was showing some form of approval. Then again, perhaps it was his way of turning the knife one more time, only deeper.

She experienced an odd sensation. She found she wasn't afraid of what he thought, one way or another. The confidence of having proved herself in just two and a half years in a complicated environment, the knowledge that she was fiscally responsible, gave her the self-assurance to answer him with complete control.

"I thought all of your choices were excellent and for the right reasons. It boils down to one's tastes and which movie answers the needs or preferences of an individual, doesn't it. *Rebecca* was at the top of my list. Mr. Hitchcock is a master of storytelling, of suspense, of luring the audience into a maze and then making you, the viewers, participate with him as he leads you out."

Grandpa Handelstein contemplated his granddaughter. He then stood.

"I would like to make a toast for this evening's homecoming dinner. 'May we never forget what is worth remembering or remember what is best forgotten.'"

Little Abe stayed in Chicago until after the New Year, but Eve had to leave on Sunday, December 29. She needed to be at work on Monday, and Douglas Hassal had persuaded her to attend the New Year's Eve party at his parents' home. Actually, it was his home, too, as he still lived with his mother and father. Most of the staff of Utopia would be there, so she was looking forward to a pleasant evening.

The solitude on the trip back to Los Angeles gave Eve an opportunity to evaluate the happenings of the last nine days in her journal. She had imagined so many scenarios, anticipated such a variety of reactions, and ended up being practically totally surprised and unprepared. But the relationships had weathered the distance and differences. She was grateful and relieved.

Grandpa Handelstein had given her the most dramatic shock. Her own revelation that she no longer feared him was awesome. Then his almost conceding acceptance of her profession was also very welcome. Deep down, however, she would always harbor that unanswerable question, could she have been successful as an actress? And that would always be between them.

The only flaw on her holiday was gazing at the Burdsey house. It was the only time she felt the outsider, the unwanted, the intruder. She ached for what was lost to her.

Alicia and Randall Burdsey had stopped by to wish the Handelsteins a happy holiday on Christmas Day. They had been unaware that Eve was in town, and despite an initial awkwardness, had been happy to see her. Randall Burdsey was especially interested once he made the connection between Eve and Utopia Studios. He owned the largest block of stock in the company that had been offered to the public. Randall made a mental note that he or Arthur should visit Hollywood and their investment sometime soon.

CHAPTER

14

Los Angeles, California
Tuesday, December 31, 1940

Douglas Hassal drew in a deep breath and exhaled slowly. He was stunned as he looked at Eve standing in her doorway. Behind, the soft light from the living room lamps framed her body like a halo. Her ebony hair, which normally hung straight and turned under slightly at the nape of her neck, was pulled back into a French twist, emphasizing her milky-pearl skin and huge dark eyes. She seldom wore makeup except for lipstick and a touch of blush. But tonight her eyes had been enhanced by shadow and mascara. Her lips were the same scarlet as her gown.

The strapless flaming red jersey clung to her figure until it flared out at the knees, the calf-length front cascading longer in back, flamenco style.

"You're so—so—beautiful!" he stammered.

Eve was pleased with the effect. She had to admit, Jenine knew her stuff. When Jenine Jasmine had heard Eve was attending the Hassals' New Year's Eve party, she had insisted she be in charge of wardrobe. The head costume designer at Utopia would do anything for the studio's pet, so together they came up with tonight's creation. Jenine supervised the hairdo and the makeup, too. She

was going to be there with Mo and she couldn't wait to see everyone's reaction to Eve's new look. She bet it would set some people
back on their heels! This was fun! It also was a very small way to
repay Eve for a very big favor.

Eve had not protested, but went along with it, even enjoyed the
preparation. True, if left on her own, she doubted she would have
chosen the style or color. Why was she so careful, so reserved?

She knew the answer. It was because of the incident in Chicago
with that horrible man, Mr. Cozakman. His lack of respect toward
her, and then her own fears that all men thought "actresses" or
"movie people" were fair game—except Arthur, of course—had
caused her to retreat into a comfortable cocoon. She couldn't alter
her physicality. But she found herself opting for plain colors, simple textures and shapes. She tried to melt into the background, not
be noticed because of her appearance. Only in her work did she
want to stand out. The emotional residue had changed her attitude
in general. She grew tougher, wasn't as trusting. But this facade
was alien to her true nature. She had always been fun loving and
adventurous, to the point of being daring. She had never been the
shrinking violet type!

Eve wondered if Jenine, in her basic gut wisdom, had sensed
this side of Eve.

Esther and Joseph Hassal lived in a posh section of Beverly
Hills, very near Pickfair, the estate Mary Pickford and Douglas
Fairbanks had built. They had tented the sprawling backyard, built
a dance floor over the pool, constructed tiers on the grounds to
ensure balanced tables, and then covered the plywood with fake
lawn. The motif centered around the glowing ball that dropped in
New York City's Times Square at midnight every December 31 to
herald in the New Year.

There were a hundred sparkling balls hung from the top of the
tent, poised for their moment of glory, the countdown to
12:00 a.m. The sides of the large tent were lined with a painted
backdrop of the New York City skyline of tall buildings. Included
in the mural were theaters with actual neon lights outlining names
of the current productions appearing in each. *Johnny Belinda, The*

Corn is Green, My Sister Eileen, Pal Joey, Panama Hattie—all blazed out at the revelers. Movie houses were featured as well, again with the titles in colorful bulbs. *Our Town, The Philadelphia Story, Kitty Foyle, Fantasia* and *Tin Pan Alley* shone conspicuously.

"What an ingenious idea!" Eve complemented Esther Hassal when Douglas introduced Eve to his mother. "I actually feel I'm at the top of the Empire State Building looking down on New York."

Esther was flattered but wary. She had been anxious to meet this young lady Douglas had talked so much about. Joseph had met her at the studio and had a positive reaction. But she wanted to see for herself, men can be easily fooled by an attractive woman. She wasn't about to allow someone unworthy to get too close to her Douglas. She would be the fly in the ointment if some temptress tried to get her hooks into her son. He was too young to be seriously involved, anyway, only twenty-three. Esther had to concede one thing, this Eve Handel was a looker. Not in the conventional idea of beauty, but rather in a uniquely compelling manner. Esther planned to stay nearby and keep a sharp eye on Eve.

She had seated Douglas and Eve at her table. She noticed Eve was quite comfortable with the other guests, male and female, able to join in a conversation or just listen politely. Esther's intuition told her this was not an act but normal behavior, genuine. At least that was one good quality. And Eve didn't attempt to monopolize Douglas, she shared her attention with everyone at the table. If anything, Douglas seemed to want to appropriate Eve's time.

It was a wonderful night. Eve felt on top of the world. When she saw Jenine Jasmine and Mo Jeddu, Jenine had given her the thumbs-up sign, signaling success. The band played all the popular tunes and the dance floor was consistently crowded. Douglas was quite accomplished as a dancer and Eve was so light and easy to lead they glided effortlessly around the floor.

"This is one of my favorites," Douglas said gently when the orchestra began "The Nearness of You." He held her even tighter, their bodies pressed closer. "We fit well together, as one," he murmured in her ear.

Eve could feel his excitement. Her own senses were stirring, awakened after the long dormancy. She surprised herself.

"Ten, nine, eight—" the resplendent one hundred balls had begun their descent and the partygoers were yelling the countdown "—seven, six, five, four, three, two, one. Happy New Year!"

People kissed their partners and then everyone else. Except Douglas. He wouldn't let Eve go. It was a long, intense kiss, one that was finally interrupted by Esther and Joseph Hassal.

"Aren't you going to wish your mother a Happy New Year?" Esther asked her son.

Joseph was a little drunk. "Come here, you pretty thing, and give the old guy a kiss," and he pulled Eve toward him and bent her back à la Valentino and planted a smooch right on her lips.

"Careful you don't drop her, you old goat," warned a crony of Joseph's, laughing as he helped Eve straighten up.

"Aren't you the Romeo!" Esther said dryly to her husband. Then she gave Eve a peck on the cheek. "Happy New Year, dear. We didn't have an opportunity to talk much. Maybe we can persuade you to come for a quiet dinner so we can become better acquainted." She pointed to Joseph. "I promise you, he will not do that exhibition next time."

"I would very much like to come again. Thank you for including me in tonight's celebration. It has easily been the most pleasant evening I've had since I arrived in California," Eve said sincerely.

Esther concluded that Eve had passed the first inspection. She couldn't find fault so far, but time would tell.

Douglas Hassal was smart. He knew Eve had reacted to their closeness and their kiss. There was a possibility he could make it with her tonight. But he didn't want to rush it, to chance it. She would be really ready in the not too distant future. He could wait.

My red flag went up tonight, I have to be careful! I guess I thought I wouldn't have to deal with those pangs of emotion again, those flashes of passion. Did I really believe I could go through life without love, punish myself forever because I hurt Arthur? No, my mind worked more like Scarlett's, "I'll think about that tomorrow!" Just put off what I don't want to face. Actually, to be honest, no one has interested me enough—until now. Down girl, down—don't jump to conclusions!

Los Angeles, California
Thursday, February 27, 1941

"This is so exciting! If I'm nervous, can you imagine how the nominees feel?" Eve whispered to Douglas.

It was the thirteenth Academy Awards banquet and they were two of the 1,500 guests crunched together at the Biltmore Bowl of the Los Angeles Biltmore Hotel. There were two "firsts" happening that night. President Franklin D. Roosevelt would give a six-minute direct-line radio address from the White House, recognizing the industry for its contributions toward national defense and solidarity. And, unlike the previous Oscar nights, the names of all the evening's winners had been kept *secret,* thanks to Price, Waterhouse & Co. The winners would be announced when the sealed envelopes containing the results were opened and read. It meant the air was thick with suspense.

Bob Hope started the program and was hysterically funny as master of ceremonies. The audience went wild when he received a silver plaque for "his unselfish services to the motion picture industry." Eve was also thrilled to see Alfred Lunt and Lynn Fontanne, theater's grand couple, onstage to present the acting awards.

Jimmy Stewart won Best Actor in *The Philadelphia Story.* Eve was sure Ruth would be upset that Henry Fonda didn't get the gold statuette for his work in *The Grapes of Wrath.*

Eve was surprised when Ginger Rogers in *Kitty Foyle* beat out the favorites, Joan Fontaine in *Rebecca* and Bette Davis in *The Letter.* But both the Supporting Actor and Supporting Actress awards went to favorites: Walter Brennan in *The Westerner* and Jane Darwell in *The Grapes of Wrath.*

Eve was disappointed that John Ford was chosen Best Director over Alfred Hitchcock, but she felt vindicated when Hitchcock's *Rebecca* was selected as Best Picture of 1940.

To Love Is to Hate was the title of the first feature Douglas Hassal hoped to produce. And he wanted Jenine Jasmine to play the lead. The problem was, *everyone* wanted Jenine Jasmine in their next project. But he had an ace up his sleeve. Eve Handel! Now that she was collaborating with him on the script and becoming more and more excited about the prospect of Jenine doing such a dramatic role, he knew his chances were looking better and better.

The story was about a man who loved a woman so deeply, he could not get enough of her. He wanted all of her, every minute of the day and night. And when she rebelled, claiming pieces of herself and her life, his love turned to hate. At last she was forced to fight for her life, finally killing him in her desperation to get away. It was a perfect part for Jenine, the audience would understand how a man could go crazy over a goddess such as she and would believe her need to have independence and her determination to get it.

It was the Friday after the Academy Awards. Eve had been busy all week, and Douglas was champing at the bit, wanting her undivided attention. He barely waited until her last appointment had left the outer office before charging into her inner sanctum.

"Sorry, Doug," Eve apologized, "everyone seemed to need something right away this week. There were panic buttons all over the place."

"Ah, my poor little bird. Maybe we should forget working tonight," Douglas said, not meaning a word of it.

"No, no! Tell you what—Yvonne left to spend the weekend with her sister, but she made dinner. Abe went skiing at Lake Tahoe with his buddies. Anyway, the house will be quiet, we could relax and have a bite—nothing fancy—and then get cracking on the script. I would really like to get away from this office. So, how does that sound?''

''Sounds like a bit of all right!'' Douglas happily answered.

A boisterous, barking bundle of fur greeted Eve and Douglas at her front door.

''I don't think you've met Rosie, she was probably with Yvonne when you picked me up at New Year's. Abe wanted a dog, so we went to the pound and there she was. How could anyone abandon this darling!'' Eve knelt and let the pup give her doggy licks. ''She's a mix, Irish setter and golden retriever, we think. The vet figured she was about four months old then, which makes her almost eleven months. Abe named her Rose—as in 'Abie's Irish Rose'—and she is already hopelessly spoiled. Why don't you fix us a cocktail while I feed her? If I know Yvonne, the ice bucket is probably full and Rosie's dinner all ready.''

''Oh, this feels good,'' Eve sighed a few minutes later as she sat back in the sofa, kicking her shoes off and curling her feet under her, sipping her drink.

''I fixed you my specialty,'' Douglas said, sitting next to her. Rosie, her tummy full, snoozed on her pillow. ''A vodka martini with, not one, but two olives. You like?''

''Mmm, yes, I like. But I'd better not have too many, or my head won't be clear for our 'labor of love.' Hey, not a bad pun! Maybe I should have said 'labor of love and hate!'''

They discussed *To Love Is to Hate,* starting at the beginning and examining each scene progressively. Dinner was forgotten, the second martini was almost gone, and they'd reached the point where the man has the initial inkling that the woman is beginning to drift away from him, ever so slightly.

''He has to have this wrenching ache in his gut, it has to trigger his obsessiveness into the first hint of violence.'' Douglas paced the room, clenching his fist and pushing it into his stomach to demonstrate. He threw himself down on the couch and leaned toward her.

"It's you! That woman is you, and I am the man. I have the ache, I want you so bad I hurt." His lips were on Eve's before she had time to say anything, demanding lips, penetrating lips. She responded unconsciously, reacting to his insistence. He lifted her effortlessly from the couch, still in command of her mouth, and carried her to the first bedroom he saw, which by chance was Abe's. She was trancelike, knowing what was happening, not fighting, not participating fully, just letting it happen. He undressed her, fondling and kissing every part of her body as it was revealed. Then he removed his own clothes and stood over her, his eyes showing his desire, his manhood showing his need. Slowly he climbed on the bed and started to rub himself over her brow, past her eyes, into her throat. Now she was alive, her blood on fire. Now she gave vent to the fervor that had been under lock and key. She writhed with pleasure as he traced her contour, ran his hands over her full, upright breasts, to her soft abdomen, down her hips, along the inside of her leg clear to her toes. Moans escaped from her. She reached for him and he let her look and touch, almost with wonder. He felt her tremors. It was time. He reached quickly into his pants, which were carelessly draped on the bedpost, and found a condom that he quickly slipped over his erection.

Douglas lowered himself onto her, his own hands guiding him to her opening. Eve arched her back and wrapped her legs around his middle, trying to bring him closer and even further inside. She was beyond reasoning, abandon ruled. She matched him movement for movement, never wanting this to end, yet rushing to reach the apex. They were gasping, not breathing now. And then, oh yes, and then came the explosion as they reached the culminating point. Spasm upon spasm swept over them, leaving no room for anything but sheer sexual passion. Douglas kept tight within her, neither willing to let go. Their bodies glistened with sweat.

Gradually the panting returned to breathing, and they relaxed their grips on each other. Eve didn't attempt to analyze their actions. But she did articulate one thought to herself. She had finally experienced being a woman. And she was glad!

There would be a lot to write about later that night!

Los Angeles, California
Saturday, March 22, 1941

Eve was excited. Ruth had called on Monday to ask if Eve planned to be in town for a while and if so, would it be a convenient time to visit. Eve had enthusiastically said yes to both questions, and she and Abe were now on their way to pick their older sister up at Union Station in downtown Los Angeles. Ruth wasn't thrilled about flying yet and the train had given her a chance to read and relax.

Eve was grateful now she had the four bedrooms. What a kick for all of them to be together. She wondered if Mama and Papa were lonely with the three of them away, or if they welcomed the privacy after so many years.

"Honestly? I think Mama and Papa were relieved. Grandpa Handelstein caught the flu in January and hasn't been able to shake it. They insisted he move into Abe's old room until he's better. So, they won't be missing me for a while," Ruth explained when Eve had asked.

"Well, you look wonderful! Positively glowing!" Eve said as she and Yvonne Birshgeld bustled around, getting Ruth settled. "How long can you stay?"

Ruth hesitated before answering. "I'm not sure. That depends on a few things."

Eve sensed an uneasiness in Ruth; she wasn't her usual "in command" self. She didn't push, as she reasoned Ruth would talk about whatever it was when she was ready. During dinner, Ruth volunteered one motivation for coming west. She thought there might be more opportunities for female journalists and writers in California.

"People out here seem more liberal toward women, more accepting. Look at you, Eve. You were very young and inexperienced, yet they gave you a chance," Ruth pointed out.

Eve mulled this over. "That's true. There's no doubt I was out-of-my-head lucky. But my work is so specialized, there isn't the competition that exists in your field. However, I do believe you're right about the attitude toward women in general. Anyway, you're so good I'm sure you will have no problem, here or wherever."

"From your mouth to God's ears!" Ruth said hopefully. "Of course, like all writers, I also think I could write a book. After you left, as you suggested, I did ask Papa about his childhood experiences and about both Grandma's and Grandpa's backgrounds. I was toying with an idea—perhaps a book about our family history, disguised naturally, would be interesting. There are some colorful characters! I thought you might help to jog my memory because I remember when you learned to write, you always jotted down the day's events in a journal. Do you still?"

"Yes, I guess it just became kind of a habit. My old ones are boxed up at home in Chicago, probably in the attic. You're welcome to dig them up."

Abe interrupted. "Wouldn't it be neat! All of us here! If you do move, you should shorten your name like we did. Otherwise people wouldn't know we're related."

Ruth laughed, "One step at a time, my not so little brother. We'll see how things go."

Abe left for a night class. He had his own wheels now, so he was released from bondage. In January, Eve had given him her Ford convertible as a combination Christmas and upcoming twenty-

first birthday present. She knew how difficult it was not to have a
car in Los Angeles, everything was so spread out one was at the
mercy of buses or trains or other people's schedules. She was grateful she was able to do that for him.

Eve had treated herself to a red Mercury. Normally she would
have settled for a more conservative auto, but in defiance to—
whom? Herself, maybe?—she boldly chose a flamboyant model.
She was making a statement, mainly for her own edification, but
at least she was making it. *I'm not hiding anymore, world! Look
at me all you want! I am not afraid!*

Yvonne Birshgeld retired to her room and the two sisters were
left alone in the living room. Neither spoke for a bit, both lost in
their own thoughts.

Ruth broke the silence. "This is a nice house, Eve. Very homey,
very comfortable and easy."

Rosie had jumped up on the couch and was snuggled closely
against Eve.

"Thanks. I like it, too. If I ever buy, I would hope to create the
same atmosphere. Like Rosie here—what's the sense of having a
pet if it can't be near you? The furnishings shouldn't dictate to
you, they should be the background for—actual living."

"That's what I feel here." Ruth sighed. She gathered her
thoughts—and courage—and faced Eve. "I didn't come to you
only because of the work. There's—something else."

Eve waited patiently, letting Ruth set her own pace.

"Remember I told you at Christmas that the one guy I have eyes
for doesn't know I exist?"

Eve nodded.

"New Year's Eve I went to a party at the Burdseys', and he was
there. I think he's remotely connected to Arthur's father's business,
I'm not sure how, but he has been at their home before. He's
always been pleasant enough to me, just—distant."

Eve could see Ruth's mind going back to that night, that place.

"I guess I looked nice, better than usual, I mean. Mama and I
found a blue chiffon gown that, well, Mama said it matched my
eyes and complimented my blond hair."

''You must have looked beautiful,'' Eve said softly.

Ruth blushed. ''Anyway, he paid particular attention to me, danced almost every dance with me. And then, at midnight, he kissed me—kissed me so romantically I trembled down to my toes.'' Her eyes were tender with the memory.

''We both were light-headed from the champagne, and when he steered me away from the music, into the empty library and into the darkened office beyond—I—didn't object. I was so thrilled and happy and, in my head, in love. He stopped dancing and encircled me in both arms and kissed me long and hard. Again and again. And when he guided me to a deep leather couch, I—didn't resist. The room was lit only by the moonlight coming through the window, I felt completely in his power, willingly so.''

Ruth started to cry. ''I'm—I'm—s-sorry, Eve. And so ashamed.''

''It's all right, Ruthie, it's all right. I understand, sweetheart, believe me. If you are haunted by this, you must get it out or it will fester inside. Let it go, let it fly away in the air, or it will destroy you. You can't tell me anything I haven't felt or experienced myself.'' Eve's eyes were filled with moisture.

Ruth looked at Eve through her own tears, and realized she had just heard something that no one else knew. Except for one. Eve had confided in her without hesitation. She hugged Eve, knowing she could tell her secret now without fear of being damned.

''He moved his hand over my body and massaged here...'' Ruth looked down at her ample breasts. ''No one had ever touched me there before. I was hypnotized, frozen. He kept going, to my ankles, and he took off my heels. I did protest then but he smothered me with kisses and I was swept away. Oh, Eve, it was wonderful. I can't help it, I'll never forget that feeling.''

Eve squeezed Ruth's hand supportively.

''He walked me home, filling the night air and my head with promises, before he kissed me good-night. I waltzed upstairs to my room and dreamed of love and marriage.'' Ruth gazed into empty air, completely dejected. ''What a fool I was! I never heard from him again. And I would not call him, even when I found out—I was pregnant!''

Eve was stunned. She had thought Ruth was only relieving the burden of guilt because she had had an affair.

''I don't want to have an—an abortion. I'll carry the baby to term and then put it up for adoption.'' Ruth turned away. ''I didn't mean to dump this mess on you, and I won't bother you for long. I just didn't know where to go or what to do, all I wanted was to get away from Chicago and the family. This would kill Mama and Papa and for Grandpa Handelstein...'' Ruth finally broke down in complete despair and huddled into the corner of the sofa.

Eve shook herself loose from her shock and took charge. She made Ruth face her and put her hands on her sister's shoulders to hold her firmly. ''Now, let's not talk any more nonsense. You will stay here at this house. I will convince Mama and Papa that you can find a good position here and how happy we will be together. You go back to collect your things right away, don't forget your typewriter. I will find a doctor, and a trustworthy lawyer. No one will know anything except Yvonne, Abe and me. And you don't have to worry about us.''

My poor Ruthie! Why did this have to happen to her? She's always been so self-reliant, so sure and capable. I wonder, is there any way I could have helped prevent this? That first time I had all those questions about sex and feelings—maybe if I had shared that with her we could have read about it together and discussed it more. But no, that's not right, she already had read, even recommended what books I should study. I know, I know the trouble. She was aware academically, not physically—that has to be the answer! Oh, Ruthie—

It all worked. Mildred and Samuel were satisfied, pleased that at least the children were safely under one roof with a competent guardian. Yvonne Birshgeld immediately became the mother hen. Abe was surprisingly mature. His first reaction was to go to Chicago and punch the guy out. When that appeared highly implausible, he assumed the role of man of the house. Which of course, he was. He was solicitous, protective of his charges, took more of the chores around the house—especially anything that involved strength. And he made sure that his three women did proper exercises, setting up a regimen that best suited each one's needs.

He had joined a health club near their house soon after he arrived in California. Initially he was only involved with his own training, but when the manager saw how he had arranged his workout so that it was in proper balance for the desired result, he asked Abe to suggest a program for him. Abe had questioned him extensively—diet, habits, measurements, medications, medical problems—and then prescribed a schedule. Abe was thorough and knowledgeable, and it wasn't too long before Abe was hired as a consultant for a number of members at the club. He was as happy as a lark, right in his element. Grandpa Handelstein had been so proud when Abe told him the news.

Yvonne Birshgeld's sister led Ruth to a woman obstetrician, Dr. Angel Roberts, who came highly recommended. Dr. Roberts practiced in Tarzana, a suburb northwest of where they lived, far from the prying eyes of Hollywood. Ruth registered under the name of "Mrs. Martin Morse," explaining her husband was overseas and Aunt Yvonne was taking care of her.

Eve, through casual conversation with their aunt and uncle, the Rosens, had discovered an attorney who handled adoptions. Mr. Sam Gershe's offices were in downtown Los Angeles, and his clientele leaned more toward the business community and the San Marino district. Few, if any, entertainment people came his way. That was a requirement in this case, because in dealing with a lawyer, Eve would have to disclose the real names involved. Otherwise there could be legal ramifications regarding the adoption. Mr. Gershe assured Eve he had never had any problem in all his cases and that he could promise complete confidentiality.

Using the yellow pages, Ruth called a secretarial service that served her purposes. Yvonne drove to their location in the morning, picked up the work to be done and delivered it back finished in the afternoon. Until the baby came, Ruth could earn a living, and in her spare time, she could begin an outline of her book.

Los Angeles, California
Monday, June 2, 1941

Douglas Hassal walked back and forth nervously in Eve's office, waiting for her to return from the meeting with Peter Padon and Mo Jeddu. Douglas had submitted the script of *To Love Is to Hate* last week and now they had called Eve in for a discussion.

Douglas had been out of sorts lately, fate had not cooperated with his planned agenda. Everything had been progressing so well, beyond his expectations. Who would have guessed that inside the young, virginal Eve Handel lurked a sensual tornado? His goal had been to marry her brain, but her ardor was icing on the cake, making him more eager than ever to close the deal.

But then the sister came to visit and took ill. He was put on the back burner and he didn't like it there one bit. Eve still worked on the script with him, but only at the studio. He had not been invited back to her home, and their dates had been confined to a measly number. The only positive note was the dinners with his parents had been particularly successful. Esther and Joseph were favorably impressed. But generally Eve seemed distracted, her mind obviously not on him. Damn that sister.

He heard someone enter the anteroom, then the inner door

opened. Douglas could tell by her walk, even before he saw Eve's face, that it was good news.

"You've got the green light!" she yelled. "It's a go!"

Douglas picked her up and whirled her around the room. "Tell me, tell me all, my lovely."

"I will, but I can't talk up in the air. Put me down," Eve laughed.

He lowered her, brushing her body against his as she slid. For a moment, their spark ignited. But it wasn't the time or the place. Eve collected her composure. "You and a writer should start polishing the script. At the same time you can begin preproduction— getting a director, casting and so on. I am to work with you in any way you need, testing players, whatever. As usual, I will prepare Jenine for all of her scenes. Shooting should commence no later than the first of the year. That gives Jenine a little rest after she finishes her current film. Congratulations! You did it!"

"No," Douglas said solemnly. "*We* did it. I told you New Year's Eve that we fit well together, as one. It's true, we are a great team. I think we should make us a permanent partnership. What do you think?"

Eve was not ready for this. She was so caught up in Ruth's situation, she had put her whole life on hold for the time being.

"Doug, please try to understand. I'm not registering what you just said, or implied. Right now it's difficult for me to evaluate or sort out what I think. Nothing is clear for me, nothing makes complete sense. When my family recovers from the, from this crisis, I will try to get back on track again. I hope we can just stay status quo for now. Can you be patient?"

Douglas had no choice but to acquiesce. But he was heartened. He knew she reacted to him emotionally. He knew, too, she relished the creative challenges he brought to her. If he had to sit tight, he could do that. Because he believed he would prevail. Anyhow, the first step had been accomplished. He was a full producer!

Ruth had no idea what a toll pregnancy would take on her. Eve found her completely undone when she came home from the studio one day in early June.

"What is it? What happened?" Eve asked anxiously.

"I, I felt, I felt its little foot kick—" Ruth gulped. "I felt a life! It's my baby, mine! I can't just give it up."

"There, there, Ruthie," Eve soothed. Eve was concerned. Ruth was having these anxiety attacks regularly now. She had talked to Sam Gershe about it, because he had found a suitable couple, and she worried Ruth might change her mind. This couple lived in a small town in Northern California. They had been closely scrutinized and had met all the qualifications.

"It's a normal reaction," Sam Gershe had explained. "The more the fetus moves, the closer it comes to being a real human being. If your sister had been impregnated by a longtime boyfriend and there was a hope of them getting together to raise the child, this would be a different story. But in this case the man does not know, there is no relationship whatsoever, and no chance there ever will be. That presents a problem. She would have to bring up the baby by herself, the baby would bear the stigma of being a bastard—I don't have to go on. As sophisticated as we think we are in 1941, society still does not look kindly on unwed mothers and the children are the ones who suffer."

Eve understood all of this and tried her best to relay it to Ruth, who subsequently realized the validity of the lawyer's statements. Until she felt movement again. It was a dramatic roller coaster!

Ruth's dilemma forced Eve to examine her own beliefs. Without a doubt, she had no desire to face the suffering poor Ruth was experiencing. For the first time, the institution of marriage took on a whole new significance. For a woman, and especially for a child. Before, she hadn't been mature enough, but now she could reason. If Arthur had not been able to control himself and she had become pregnant, she would not have been in Ruth's chaotic state. Because Arthur and she would have married immediately. To hell with her dreams! So, that was then! But here she was today—more than three years later—employed and having made a good start in her profession. She wanted children at some point—was the time approaching for commitment?

Eve's secretary never interrupted her sessions, but Abe sounded hysterical. Matilda buzzed the intercom. "Excuse me, Miss Handel, but your brother is on the phone, and he sounds—well—wild!''

Eve quickly pressed the blinking red light. ''Yes? What? Okay, okay, calm down! I'll be right there!'' She ran for her purse, shouting orders. ''Reschedule Heidi—my sister is having a, uh, an attack! Cancel the rest of the day! Call Mr. Hassal—tell him I'll talk to him tomorrow! I have to get her to the—to the doctor. Sorry, everyone!''

Abe was a wreck. He had come home before going to his health club and found Ruth bent over with cramps. Mrs. Birshgeld had left to bring Ruth's work back and then stopped at the market. He had panicked and called Eve. Now he was trying to soothe Ruth.

''Ooh, there's another—one,'' she exclaimed in anguish. ''It's too early! Only the fifteenth—only August—too early!''

Abe was hopping around, mumbling aloud. ''What's she need? Where's her pocketbook?'' He rushed to get it. ''Where's her robe?''

Eve bolted in the door. ''Leave a note for Yvonne while I get Ruth in the car,'' she barked at Abe. ''Call Dr. Roberts, tell her we're leaving now. Then grab some— Oh, you did, atta boy. Bring her things and follow me in your car.''

Rosie was all excited, going around in circles, wondering what the fuss was about. ''No, Rosie, you can't come with us this time. Be a good girl! And Abe, for God's sake, drive carefully!''

Dr. Angel Roberts was waiting at the emergency entrance of the Tarzana Medical Center. She was in her mid-fifties, small framed, had a kind face and graying hair pulled back into a bun. There was an air of quiet solidity about her, exuding confidence with compassion.

Ruth was moaning, reacting to each wave of pain, but her main concern was the date. ''Too soon, too soon, baby too soon...'' she kept repeating.

''Mrs. Morse—'' Dr. Roberts voice was soft, but stern ''—you must stop fretting or you will make this more difficult for you and for your child. There is no cause for alarm. Six weeks premature is not that unusual. But you can't waste your energy worrying. We need your strength now.

"I'll take her to the examining room, and then probably to Delivery soon," she said to Eve. "The contractions are quite close together, so I don't predict a long labor. All should go well, barring unexpected complications. The baby will be in an incubator at first, how long depends on the condition at time of birth and progress thereafter." Dr. Roberts smiled knowingly as she walked away. "Don't despair. You won't have to wait too long before you can both hold the baby."

Eve flinched. How could she explain, neither Ruth nor she would be able to even see the baby, let alone hold or cuddle it. She had witnessed the torment that racked Ruth these past weeks, and even she had wrestled with her emotions, the maternal instinct was so indelibly etched. She had to be the unyielding one for them both. One look, one touch and they would be lost. Eve promised Ruth, herself and the baby, that she would be strong!

Mrs. Birshgeld, Abe and Eve were in the waiting room. It was about 8:00 p.m., roughly four hours later, when Dr. Roberts came to them. "Congratulations! You have a beautiful little girl in the family. And Mom is fine, tired but all right. I would suggest only one of you come in to say good-night. Oh, on your way to her room, you may get a glimpse of the newborn in the nursery. You won't see much because of the incubator."

Eve made up her mind, she had to trust Dr. Roberts. She told Yvonne and Abe to start for home, then followed the doctor out into the hall. Hesitantly, she explained the circumstances, without using actual names.

Dr. Roberts studied Eve carefully. Then put her hand on Eve's shoulder. "I understand. I expected as much. Your sister is very brave, she chose the difficult path. Be prepared, she is going to be deeply depressed and will need everyone's help." She sighed. "I will put on her chart that she has a slight cold and cannot be exposed to the baby until completely germ-free. Your sister will be released before then. When the time comes, perhaps Mrs. Birshgeld can pick the child up and deliver her to the lawyer, who will introduce her to the parents. Ruth made the right decision and your family will weather this storm. Don't hesitate to call me if I can ever be of any help.''

Eve dragged herself in the direction Dr. Roberts had pointed out. She was exhausted, physically and mentally. She couldn't begin to imagine how Ruth must feel. Looming ahead was the sign that read Nursery. Several people were standing in front of the large glass window, ''oohing and aahing,'' making silly faces, waving, needing to demonstrate in some way to the bundle inside how happy and proud they were to welcome the newcomer. Eve's legs seemed to have lead in them, making her move snail-like past the never-ending, ever-lengthening window. Her eyes took on a will of their own and turned defiantly to look into the large chamber. Tiny cribs were lined up in rows and toward the back were a few machines that must be incubators, bearing no identification that her betraying eyes could see.

Eve retrieved her control, and then determinedly walked into Ruth's room with difficulty.

I am barely able to see, but if I don't talk, my whole body will weep tears, not just my eyes. Walking past that nursery tonight was sheer torture. I wanted to bang on the cursed window and yell out which one of you is our little girl—I don't even know. I'll—we'll never know you. Never be able to soothe your cries or patch up scraped knees or comfort wounded pride. Never gaze at you sleeping, touch your innocent skin, hug you, cuddle you. Never, never see the first step or save a lock from the first haircut—bronze your first shoes.

Thank you, God, for making her well. Let her know she is loved. I have to send this out through you, dear Lord, because you know how impossible it would be for her mom to form these words. I beg you, please let her understand her mom did what had to be done, did what was best for the child.

So I say goodbye, goodbye, sweet niece. Goodbye from all

of us—your mom, your aunt, your uncle. You will be in our hearts forever.

We pray our Heavenly Father will watch over you.

Los Angeles, California
Sunday, December 7, 1941

The telephone ring broke the quiet, peaceful Sunday morning brunch that Eve, Ruth, Abe and Yvonne were enjoying. It noisily clanged several times before Yvonne could reach it to answer.

"Good morning—excuse me, good afternoon! Yes, Mr. Hassal, Miss Handel is in, one moment."

Eve walked lazily to the telephone. "Hello, Doug. How are you this fine day? Yes, of course I'm all right, why wouldn't I be? *What?* No, we haven't heard— Abe, turn the radio on, quickly!"

Eve was attentive for a minute, then said, "Let me call you back after I hear what's happening. Thank you—yes, yes—I'll call you!"

The four of them huddled around the RCA console, listening to unbelievable, unacceptable words. Pearl Harbor on the Hawaiian island of Oahu had been attacked by Japan. There had been no warning, no ultimatum such as Hitler sent when his legions poured across some new border. Indeed, two Japanese envoys were at that moment in Secretary Cordell Hull's office at the State Department, making bland protestations of their peaceful intent.

Abe went to the bookshelves for an atlas so they could follow the path of the assault. The planes, anywhere from seventy-five to one hundred and fifty, came in from the southeast over Diamond Head, whined over Waikiki, over the candy-pink bulk of the Royal Hawaiian Hotel. Torpedoes tore into Pearl Harbor, dive-bombers swooped down on the Army's Hickham and Wheeler Fields. From Pacific Heights through the town they soared, leaving a wake of destruction.

Douglas couldn't wait for Eve's return call; he rushed over and arrived unannounced at her home. He had finally met the sister and the brother and the housekeeper, after the sister had recovered from her "illness." But, in his opinion, Eve was still spending too much time doting on her family. Thankfully she hadn't shorted him on his project—he relied on her uncanny grasp of a scene or a script more than he liked to admit. But he would have preferred more personal hours to bolster his confidence and take care of his needs.

Douglas burst into Eve's house like a bull charging into a bull-ring. "It's very bad! There are rumors of spies, possible air attacks along the West Coast from San Francisco to Los Angeles. Safety precautions have begun already."

He clobbered the dining room table with his fists in frustration; the cups of coffee, now cold and forgotten, clattered in protest and the liquid sloshed onto the saucer and tablecloth. "Wouldn't you know this would happen right when I'm ready to start the film in four weeks? *Now* what's going to happen?"

Everyone had their personal laundry list to work out. No one knew for sure how this national disaster would affect their lives. But no one doubted for a second that it would.

Eve was to have an early Sunday dinner with Douglas, his parents, Peter Padon and his wife Helene, Mo Jeddu and Jenine Jasmine. Douglas decided to wait for Eve to dress, as his early arrival had thrown off their schedule.

He apologized. "I'm sorry to have barged in like I did. I just wanted to make sure E—all of you were all right. I needed to see."

Ruth smiled. "Your concern is appreciated. Also, your call. We may have sat here all day in ignorance. Usually we listen to records and read and don't turn the radio on."

Mrs. Birshgeld had gone to see her sister, Abe had an appointment at the health club, so Ruth was left to make small talk while Eve got ready. "From what I've read, during times of war, entertainment is more in demand than in regular or peaceful times. Obviously the people, the public, need an outlet for their anxieties and/or a boost in morale. I imagine your business will be booming if we go to war."

Douglas was paying attention. The sister was not a dumbbell.

Ruth thought for a moment before continuing. "I'm not in your profession, but it occurs to me as well that the motion picture industry could provide invaluable assistance by making documentaries for the armed services and the government. Recruiting—selling war bonds—general information about the dos and don'ts for service personnel and also civilians."

Douglas's mind was going a mile a minute. This would build on the industry's contributions that President Roosevelt had mentioned in his speech at the last Academy Awards. He could register big points by suggesting this to the studio. He could begin after he finished *To Love Is to Hate.* And, as an extra bonus, producing these documentaries would more than likely keep him out of the draft!

Another idea hit him. "Didn't Eve tell me you were a writer?"

"Yes, that's right," Ruth answered, somewhat puzzled.

"Are you on a project now?" he demanded.

"Ah—not exactly—I'm working on an outline."

"Would you be interested in doing research on the kind of material that would be useful in the war effort, and in writing treatments on the assorted subject matters?"

Now Ruth's brain was whirring. Interesting idea—good experience and exposure here as a writer. Why not? She certainly felt qualified. "Well, yes, I guess I could be interested. How long are documentaries ordinarily?"

"It varies. But I'm sure a few calls will tell us the optimum number of minutes a short should run. This is getting exciting. Can you start right away?"

"Not until tomorrow, I'm afraid," Ruth laughed.

"What are you two plotting?" Eve asked when she walked into the living room.

"Oh, nothing," Douglas said elusively. "Just a little business talk." He winked at Ruth. "We'd better get moving or we'll be late."

"Are you sure you're okay?" Eve asked solicitously.

"Of course!" Ruth answered. "I can take care of myself. Remember, I'm older than you! Now, be off so I can have some peace and quiet."

Not surprisingly, the evening was spent discussing the day's horrible news. The attack took on even worse consequences as the amount of actual damage and the number of casualties started to trickle in.

Douglas seized the opportunity. It was the perfect time to mention "his" plan of producing informative and beneficial short films for the armed forces and the general public. Everyone jumped on the bandwagon.

"The studio will do it as a public service and we can deduct the cost," said Mo Jeddu.

"I know quite a few brass in D.C. I'll find out exactly what they need and want," offered Joseph Hassal.

"I can tour with each print as it's ready and make appearances along with the film." Jenine Jasmine *knew* what the boys needed and wanted, and she was ready to make her own personal contribution to the war effort.

And Eve added, "I will help with the actors and with putting the pieces of the scripts together."

"Doug, you better get someone else on this so we're ready to roll. Don't forget, you got a flick to deliver first. Charity begins at home, you know!" reminded Peter Padon

"Already workin' on it, boss!" Douglas gave Eve a smug, that's-my-surprise look. Eve caught on immediately that it was Ruth and flashed him a thank you with her eyes.

"That was extremely kind of you," Eve told Douglas on the drive home.

"Not at all," he said modestly. "She strikes me as a smart lady, guess it runs in the family, and I have a hunch she can write."

"Oh, she can write," Eve assured him. "She was the editor of the school paper in college and she has done articles for magazines and newspapers since she graduated. She won't disappoint you."

Doug maneuvered the car over to the shoulder of Mulholland Drive. They were at the top of the mountain, and behind them was the climbing, curvy road that had taken them from Beverly Hills. Ahead was the vista of the San Fernando Valley; sparkling diamond lights stretched as far as the eye could see.

"It's so beautiful," she marveled. "I never stop just to look."

"I'm looking at the brightest jewel of all," he said softly as he slipped his arm around her and pulled her close to him. He kissed her gently, and then cupped her face in his hands and gazed into the deep wells of her eyes, the wells that had no bottom, the wells that had mysteries no one could imagine.

"And I want your sister to be busy and happy because I want to take you away. I want us to get married so I never have to leave you at a door again, my whole being throbbing, yearning for you. I want to close our bedroom door and take you to heavens you've never known. Marry me, Eve. Marry me!"

Eve was very moved. She did feel for this ambitious young man. She hadn't felt this emotion for anyone else—since Arthur. It wasn't the same as she'd felt for Arthur, maybe nothing ever would be—oh, why couldn't she just say yes!

Instead, she tenderly kissed his hands and took them in hers. "I promise I will give you an answer when I return from Chicago. Bear with me for just a little longer, please!"

Eve, Ruth and Abe had decided to spend part of the holidays in Chicago with the family. Grandpa Handelstein was not very well and they thought Mama and Papa needed their presence. And now with the country officially at war, who knew what travel conditions would be in the future?

There was quite a stir around the Handelsteins' neighborhood when they arrived. Alicia and Randall Burdsey were having a grand holiday gala and Arthur was bringing Wade Colby as guest of honor. It seemed Arthur and Wade had attended some big charity affair in New York and planned to take the train to Chicago, stay a couple of days and then train it to Sun Valley, Idaho. A last fling before Arthur entered primary training for the Army Air Corps. He had enlisted immediately after Pearl Harbor.

"We are all invited," Mama Mildred enthused. She stopped suddenly and looked at Eve. "That is—that is—if you want to go."

"It's all right, Mama. Don't think about it now, we'll see." Eve took her mother by the arm and with Ruth walked upstairs toward their old rooms. "Tell us about Grandpa, dear Mama. We'll let Papa and Abe—can't call him little anymore—talk their men talk."

The night of the ball, Eve determined she simply could not attend. It would be too awkward for all concerned and might spoil the whole evening. But she insisted adamantly that everyone else must go. "How else am I going to know all the inside scoops! I want to know what the ladies wore, and who likes who, and—and whatever else!"

Reluctantly, they did her bidding. Ruth whispered as she left, "I'll find out everything and tell you straight!"

Alone, Eve had herself a good cry. And after a time of feeling sorry for herself, she knew she had to have at least a glimpse of Arthur once more. Quickly, she slipped on a pair of black slacks, the newest fashion, and pulled on a black turtleneck sweater. Black boots, a long black coat and a black scarf wrapped around her head completed her camouflage. She would blend easily into the dark night.

The guests were all inside by the time she walked noiselessly to the Burdsey house. How many times, she wondered, had she taken this same path? Too many to count, that's for sure. A couple of windows had been opened slightly to allow for fresh air, so she could even hear bits and pieces of conversation.

She drew in a sharp breath when she caught sight of Arthur. He had filled out some, seemed bigger than she remembered. Or maybe it was that he exuded a self-confidence, a command of himself and his surroundings that made him loom larger than life. But he still had that boyish vulnerability and openness that was so endearing.

Eve prayed that God would keep him safe and not let anything happen to him.

Wade Colby was standing next to Arthur. What fine specimens those two were! She had heard that some sort of accident a while back had made Wade Colby ineligible for the services, causing him grief but pleasing his studio no end. She knew that Utopia Studios had already discussed trying to borrow him for a picture, but Twentieth-Century Fox was being very coy with their hotter-than-ever star.

An attractive blond girl, tall and athletic looking, joined the two men. Arthur kissed her and then obviously introduced her to Wade Colby. Eve felt a stab of jealousy run through her whole body. Was this the girlfriend she'd been told about? What was the name? Oh, yes, Gwen Clarke, a socialite from the Chicago elite. Rumor had it that she and Arthur were to announce their engagement, but that the war interrupted.

Eve hoped she would make him happy, he deserved the best.

She saw Arthur talking to Ruth. He glanced in the direction of the Handel house and a cloud passed across his face. And then he was back to being Arthur again.

A bit later, when Abe and Arthur sauntered toward her direction, she hurriedly ducked. But they stopped at one of the makeshift bars that was near her hiding place.

"So you like California?" she heard Arthur ask Abe.

"A lot!" Abe replied. "The weather is really super, and that makes it better for my work. I'm a health consultant at the club now." Eve could hear how proud he was.

"Good for you! When do you finish college? I forget."

"I graduate this coming June. Then, if I haven't been drafted and the war is still on, I think I'll enlist in the marines. I know that would suit me better than the army."

Eve shuddered. Her little brother shouldn't have to think about things like war and enlisting and which branch of the armed services to go to. But she knew the truth was that all the "little brothers" in the country were facing the same challenge.

Arthur's voice overrode her thoughts. "I hope that isn't necessary, I hope with all my heart! Now, you say you'd like a beer?"

"Yep!"

"You know the theory of turning the glass sideways as you pour the beer to keep the foam down? Well, that's hogwash! The truth is, pour it straight in and let the bubbles rule. And the reason? Wouldn't you rather have the gas out than in? Voila!"

With a flourish, Arthur handed Abe his foamy beer and toasted Abe with his champagne. "To you, my friend!"

Abe said quietly, "To us all!"

Eve silently echoed Abe's words. How typical of Arthur, his humor and his caring, almost in the same breath. Arthur had been so close she could have touched him. Touched him to say goodbye. She was glad she had been able to observe tonight. Because whatever was between Arthur and her was in the past. She saw he had moved on with his life. And now—so must she. She would marry Douglas. They were compatible, they were in the same business, they were a good team. It was right!

Los Angeles, California
February 14, 1942

"I now pronounce you man and wife. You may kiss the bride."

Douglas Hassal bent and kissed Eve Handel Hassal sweetly on the lips. The string quartet played Mendelssohn's Wedding March and the newlyweds turned to face the hundred or so gathered guests. They walked down the few steps from the raised platform and were immediately surrounded by well-wishers.

Esther and Joseph Hassal had insisted on having the wedding at their house, especially since Eve's home base was so far away and the bride and groom could not leave work in the middle of a film. The honeymoon would also have to wait. A weekend at the swanky Del Mar Hotel in Santa Monica would have to suffice for now.

Esther had been in her romantic dream world. It was she who suggested Valentine's Day as the date. "It will be so poetic, and the decor will practically do itself—ideal for a wedding. Neither family is Orthodox, so we'll have the rabbi perform the regular ceremony, not the traditional. Now, you two decided not to have a large affair, so I think we can keep it around a hundred, give or take a few. Oh, I saw the most beautiful material for the tables at Shaxted's in Beverly Hills...."

Esther wasn't being overbearing or intrusive. She genuinely loved Eve and thought of her as a daughter and wanted to relieve her of all the burdens of arrangements. Mama Mildred and Esther had met via the telephone and had been in constant touch since their children had delivered the joyful news. Mildred and Samuel couldn't come earlier as Grandpa Handelstein had taken a turn for the worse.

The question of where to live solved itself conveniently, if a bit unconventionally. The third floor of the Hassal estate was where Douglas had set up his bachelor quarters. It was as large as the entire ground floor with a kitchen, dining room, living room, study, his and her baths and dressing rooms. Completely independent. Eve could redo the interior to suit her tastes whenever she wished, or had the time, whichever came first. They had their seclusion, but also could take advantage of the handiness of prepared meals and daily services.

Eve was actually relieved, because to try to set up housekeeping and decorate a new place would be extremely taxing at this particular time. *To Love Is to Hate* was progressing well, but her workload was quite demanding. She was preparing scenes, not only with Jenine, but with other key characters. And Douglas ran every question by her before he made a final decision. It was exciting to be so involved, but there weren't many free hours.

Fortunately, she did adore her new in-laws. Esther even had a dog, a shih tzu named Scarlett, and expressed the hope that Eve might want a pet, too, then the two "babies" would have company.

"I would love to have a puppy. No way I could take Rosie from Ruth and Abe and Yvonne. I was wondering what I would do. So now I'll have my own to hold me until my two legged 'baby' comes along. I'll get a male, call him Rhett, and maybe we'll have more little furry things running around."

The costume designer at Utopia had whipped together a stunning yet classic bridal outfit. Luscious cream-colored satin clung to Eve's silhouette, flaring slightly from the hips to her ankles. A deep vee neckline was trimmed with double rows of seed pearls, as were the wrists of the long tight sleeves. Flowing tulle was fastened to a tiara made of the same gems. Dainty satin high-heeled pumps completed the picture. Douglas added a three-carat solitaire diamond engagement ring and a wedding band of diamond baguettes.

Ruth as maid of honor wore a simpler version of the bride's gown, but in a very pale, almost ice-blue color. She glowed with the happiness she felt for her sister. Ruth knew how deeply the break with Arthur had affected Eve and feared she might be forever leery of another commitment. But now, she could let go of that worry.

"You look absolutely incandescent," Nick Larrington said to Eve as he embraced her. "You've turned me in for a permanent theater partner, and it obviously agrees with you. I'm going to miss being able to whisk you off at a moment's notice to the local theaters to scout for talent."

"But I have two replacements ready and willing to take my place," Eve assured the studio's head of casting. "I don't believe you've met my sister, Ruth, or my brother, Abraham, better known as—"

"If you say Little Abe I'll take you over my knee and spank you. And I'm now big enough to do just that!" Abe threatened, shaking Nick's hand.

"Eve has talked quite often about the pleasant evenings she's enjoyed with you," Ruth said politely.

"I like theater, too," Abe said.

"Then maybe both of you will join me as I continue on my quest for talent. I lose one and gain two. Not a bad trade!"

Eve and Douglas kept circling to be sure they greeted everyone. The two sets of parents were mixing extremely well. The Hassals had the Handelsteins in tow and were taking them around, introducing everyone. Mildred and Samuel had never met any of Eve's friends or co-workers. Eve heaved a sigh of relief; one could never be sure how in-laws were going to react to each other. She felt very grateful.

"Jenine, you look so lovely. But why are you crying?" Eve asked in concern.

"I—I always cry a-at weddings!" Jenine managed to say.

Mo Jeddu took Eve by the shoulders. "Congratulations, little lady! You've come a long way in only four years. I'm proud of you." Peter Padon and John Darius echoed Mo's remarks.

Yvonne Birshgeld was sitting at a table with her sister, Beatrice Adams, when Eve found her. She looked sad. "It's going to be so strange, not to have you living with us."

Eve hugged her hard. "I'll miss not being with you, too. But we're so close, it's not as if I was going to another state. You'll have plenty to do keeping track of Abe and Ruth."

Eve hadn't yet revealed what she had done. At the first of the year, Joseph Hassal had helped Eve negotiate a deal so that she could buy their rental home. Now everyone would be secure, even though Eve wasn't actually there. By doing this, Eve felt she would always have somewhere to go—it wasn't a complete severing of her ties. She would continue to pay Yvonne's salary as caretaker of her investment. Samuel supported Abe's room and board until he finished school in June. Plus Abe was building his clientele at the club. Ruth was on the payroll of Utopia as Douglas's assistant in the war documentary department. She still worked at home because Douglas wanted her to be in the background for now. He presented the material and ideas she brought to him to Peter Padon and Mo Jeddu. Which was fine with Ruth; she wasn't particularly anxious to be involved with the studio, she just relished the opportunity for writing credits. Mr. Hassal's contacts in D.C. had given her a long list of their "needs." Ruth had bought a car from someone going in the service and was completely autonomous. So Eve felt comfortable that everyone was taken care of—that she hadn't abandoned them or left anyone hanging.

The evening was coming to an end and Eve slipped upstairs to change into a suit. Ruth and Mildred joined her to share a last few moments together. Mildred and Samuel were leaving the next day. They wept together, tears of joy for the union, tears of sorrow for the separation, tears for the years of the past, tears for the unknown years of the future. Tears for each one's private innermost thoughts.

On the way down the staircase, Eve turned her back and threw her bridal bouquet into the crowd. There was a loud scream and then applause—Jenine Jasmine had caught the bouquet.

"Oh—my—me a bride?" Jenine looked around in bewilderment, full of sentimentality and champagne.

"Don't look at me, I'm too old," Mo Jeddu laughed, kidding her out of a mood. "Why not you? Only not until the movie is in the can!"

Eve came from the bedroom of their suite—an angel floating down from a cloud. A billowy white chiffon peignoir barely veiled the chiffon gown underneath. Douglas was in a Sulka silk robe, sitting by the bay window overlooking the ocean.

"Nothing quite as alluring as simple nature, is there?" Eve murmured softly, putting her arms around him from behind.

Douglas rose and turned. He was bedazzled by this vision that was now his, his very own. "That's true. Because Mother Nature made you and there couldn't be anything more exquisite." He reached down and uncorked the bottle of iced champagne. He took the chilled glasses and filled them. "A toast to us! This is a night to savor the taste of fine wine—and of love. This is a night to explore and satiate the appetite of desire."

They clinked their glasses and drained the contents. He poured again. "Leave them for a minute. Let me look at you." He untied the ribbon at her neck and the negligee slithered to the floor. Then the spaghetti shoulder straps were slipped off her shoulders and pulled slowly down her body until she was standing naked before him. He loosened the belt of his robe and allowed it to fall, revealing his own nudity. She was trembling, sensing something different, but not knowing what it was or why she felt that way.

Douglas lifted Eve and placed her on the floor. He reached for his champagne and began to drip it over her body until the glass was empty and she was covered with droplets. He lay beside her and started to lick each drop. "Oh, it is good, it is like nectar from my goddess."

His tongue lingered as he reached her pelvis, prying into every groove, every chasm, every crevasse. She shivered as his tongue investigated every inch, her entirety charged with electricity. He drove on mercilessly to the soles of her feet and then returned to her mouth.

"Oh, Douglas..." she was almost crying in her craving. "Make love to me, make love to me now."

He moved to straddle her, thrusting forward, embedding himself deep in her, almost harshly.

"Yes, Douglas, yes," she called out, ignoring the pain. "Oh, come to me, fill me—"

He continued to thrust fiercely, punishingly, until the inevitable and coveted zenith arrived.

Exhausted, they curled against each other until finally Eve brought the pillows from the bed and they lay looking at the sky, sipping champagne. She had never imagined that making love could take so many different turns. They were married, so she had to assume that it was all right to be so completely free, to stray from the conventional. Was this real love, she wondered? Or was it simply sexual? Whatever the answer, it didn't matter, because this was her life now.

Soon, Douglas took the bottle of Dom Pérignon and handed it to Eve. "Now it's your turn to drink of me."

Los Angeles, California
Sunday, July 5, 1942

"Mama and Papa tried not to get emotional, but they didn't quite make it. Heck, I didn't do so well, either." Abe was telling Eve, Ruth and Yvonne about his trip home to Chicago to say goodbye before leaving for boot camp. His parents had come to Los Angeles only briefly for his graduation in June. He had then enlisted in the marines and had received his orders to report to San Diego on Monday, July 6.

"At least for the moment you're close to one home," Eve said, attempting to make everyone feel better. But it was a lost cause. The war had finally engulfed their very own family. Food rationing? Gas rationing? Didn't matter! But this—this was their flesh and blood, who would be just twenty-two years old in ten days.

"I'm sure I did the right thing, though," Abe explained. "Maybe I wouldn't have been drafted as soon as this, but the water is better for me—that's for sure!"

There was a contemplative silence. Abe was the one to break the quietness. "I know, Ruth! I'll jot down notes on my days as a new recruit—more ideas for your book."

Ruth laughed. "Between you and Eve, I just might actually write a book one of these years."

Tuesday, July 7
Happy birthday to us all! Some celebration! Had my head shaved and gear was handed out. Talk about routines to learn—idea is to take everything out of your head you think you know, then teach you their way to be a marine!

Friday, July 17
Too damn tired to write much this week. Drilling gets tougher and tougher and a few guys have already flunked out. Got in trouble when I grinned after a guy's fatigues caught on barbed wire. DI says, "Think it's funny?" And he threw me a twenty-pound weight. Told me to hold it over my thick skull—up in the air. Thought my arms would fall off.

Sunday, July 26
They showed a lot of training films today—like you're writing, Ruthie, but these are old ones. Couple of us called our rifles guns by mistake. To show respect for the rifle we had to march around a track for an hour singing "this is my rifle," holding our MIs high over our heads and then "this is my gun," grabbing our crotch—so embarrassing!

Friday, July 31
Not sure I'm cut out for the military—guess I've been allowed to be an individual all my life—hard to conform. Tomorrow we head out to "the range" for a week—it's toward Laguna Beach—for target practice. They say it's a slight letup in the rigorous exercises.

Wednesday, August 6
They were right—not as intensely physical—still bad enough. Found out I'm a pretty good shot—coordinated—if I could just adapt to being treated like I'm a number, not a person. Tell Nick I'd sure rather be seeing theater than shooting paper

dummies—can't imagine how it'll be when the paper becomes a human being. Actual combat footage is almost too much to watch—but need to—have to harden our hearts as well as our bodies.

Los Angeles, California
Friday, August 21, 1942

"Is Mr. Hassal in?" Eve asked Douglas's secretary, Nell Brewster.

"Mrs. Hassal? Thought it was you. I'm afraid not. He's out of the office and didn't say when he would be back."

"Please tell him to call as soon as you hear from him!" Eve slammed down the phone. "Damn!" she muttered. Then she clutched her stomach. The pains were not excruciating, but she shouldn't be having any pains at all.

Eve dialed Dr. Angel Roberts. When she thought she might be pregnant, Eve had decided to go to Dr. Roberts. She felt comfortable with her and trusted her, personally and professionally. It had been such a happy day when the tests confirmed the pregnancy. Everyone had been thrilled, although Douglas had been quieter than Eve had expected. But Mildred and Esther had both assured her that it often took the man a little time to get used to the idea of becoming a father.

"Just as a precaution, why don't you come to the hospital?" suggested Dr. Roberts after listening to Eve's concerns. "Are you able to drive or is there someone who could bring you?'' Dr. Roberts spoke calmly and quietly, subduing Eve's fear.

"Oh, I can drive. Maybe I'll stop by Ruth's. Someone should be there to go with me."

Eve, Ruth and Yvonne looked anxiously at the doctor. "After my examination, I think it would be wise for Eve to remain in the hospital, at least overnight, so I can monitor her condition. I'm hoping this flare-up will subside, but I can't promise anything for sure. I'm going to give Eve a sedative, she needs rest, so there's no reason for anyone to stay."

"I'll find Doug, just don't worry," Ruth said as she and Yvonne hugged Eve goodbye.

The injection did allow Eve to doze off, but fretfully. She tossed and turned, and the contractions were growing stronger and occurring more frequently. Groggy, Eve rang for the nurse, who helped her to the bathroom.

"Oh, my God, I'm bleeding!" Eve screamed.

The nurse quickly called for the doctor. "I'm sorry, I'm going to have to put you under. You're aborting," Dr. Roberts gently explained.

"No! Oh, no! Please no!" Eve sobbed hysterically, thrashing about.

"Keep her still so I can give her another shot," ordered Dr. Roberts. "Don't fight me, Eve. You'll feel better soon now."

"Don't take my baby!" Eve was still crying and yelling, but gradually the effect of the medication took control. "Please, d-don't—don't take my—"

Eve struggled to open her eyes, mumbling the last thought she could remember, "Don't take my baby!" She looked about wildly, trying to focus, trying to get through the foggy vision.

There was a hazy outline standing by the bed. "Easy does it," the figure's voice said. "Just be quiet now. Everything's going to be okay."

The cloud was clearing and Eve recognized Ruth. "The— baby?"

Ruth gravely shook her head. "There was nothing Dr. Roberts could do. But that doesn't mean you can't try again, honey." Ruth felt so badly. Why did it have to happen to Eve and not to her? "I talked to Doug. He desperately wanted to come but there was some crisis with the editor. He sends his love and will see you as soon as possible, either here or home, depending how long you have to stay."

She didn't repeat the whole conversation she'd had with her brother-in-law. Somehow Douglas's response hadn't set right with her. "Oh, no! Not now—not when I need her here!" were the first words out of his mouth. Ruth shrugged off her qualms, more than likely she had called when he was caught up in his problem and hadn't realized how his reaction had sounded. She was entirely too sensitive, that's all there was to it! And there was certainly no reason to mention this to Eve.

Eve was able to go home that Sunday but only if she promised to rest for a few days. She had no intention of keeping her promise, however, because she knew the best cure for her deep depression was to lose herself in work. That way she wouldn't have time to think. Plus, Douglas needed her. At least she would be good for something.

Los Angeles, California
Saturday, September 5, 1942

"Why didn't you tell me you were sick?" Abe demanded.

"Because it wasn't necessary!" Eve explained, somewhat hotly. "There wasn't anything you could have done, and I'm fine, and I don't want to talk about it anymore!"

Ruth surreptitiously put her finger to her mouth. Abe got the message and switched topics.

"I never appreciated being at home before. I never even thought about it—it was a given, something I took for granted. But now— I love your home." He ran around kissing the walls, hugging the furniture. "I'm home! I'm home! And I love it!"

Everyone laughed at his antics. But the moment also had a plaintive note. Abe would only have two days of leave before reporting for the next phase of training, four weeks at Camp Pendelton near San Onofre Beach. And after that—who knew?

Eve, Ruth, Yvonne and Nick Larrington were gathered at Eve's old house as Abe's welcoming committee. Douglas was in the final stages of post-production on the film and was needed at the studio. Actually, he could have freed himself, but he thought spending

Sunday with Abe would be enough. He liked Abe but didn't feel the same tug of family ties as Eve.

The change in Abe was remarkable. His body had always been well-proportioned, but now it appeared stronger, more mature—harder. His face also reflected the experience of growth over the last eight weeks. There was an inner current of understanding, of awareness that was new; perhaps he was showing the dent in his innocence about life. But thank God he could still run around the house like a nutty kid.

The phone rang. Yvonne answered and called to Eve, "It's Douglas."

"I'll take it in the den, something to do with the mixing, no doubt. The technical side of this business is the least exciting but so important." To Abe she said, "No fair telling them anything I want to hear. I'll make you say it all over again if you do!"

When Eve had finished Douglas's call, she quietly opened the den door and overheard Abe say "Tell her about Arthur," before he saw her and abruptly stopped.

Eve felt a heavy lump in her chest. Was something wrong with Arthur? Had anything happened to him?

She tried to keep her voice casual and light-hearted. "What about Arthur? How's he doing?"

Abe blushed and stammered. "Well, uh, I got a letter from Arthur, and I—" He looked helplessly at Ruth.

Ruth came to Abe's rescue. "Quite frankly, dear, Abe didn't want to distress you. And he wasn't sure if he should mention Arthur at all."

"Of course he should talk about Arthur," Eve declared strongly. "He's our friend and always will be."

"But you and Artie, I mean—" Poor Abe was wrestling with his embarrassment.

"Abe, I'm married, remember? And even if Arthur doesn't want to talk to me, his welfare is still important to all of us. Is he all right?"

"Oh, yeah, he's okay. He just told me about his flying schools and all that stuff." Abe was uncertain if he should continue.

Ruth could tell Eve was relieved about Arthur's safe condition, but also unwilling to ask further about his activities. But she could.

"So, tell us about 'all that stuff.'"

"Let's see, he started in January in a civilian pilot training program, right at the local airfield in Chicago. Pretty neat, being so close to home. He was there for, wait a minute, let me get the letter so I don't mess anything up. It's in my duffel bag."

Abe jumped up and ran to his room. Eve, Ruth, Yvonne and Nick looked knowingly at one another. Ruth said what all were thinking. "He's such a wonderful human being, I've missed him terribly. Damn stinking war!"

Abe hurried back into the room, scanning the pages he carried.

"He had sixty hours of flying time in nine weeks. Then he went to basic flight training at Randolph Field, Texas, just outside of San Antonio."

Abe read silently for a minute.

"Well...?" Ruth asked.

"I'll—I'll—skip through some of this," Abe said, flustered.

"Probably about a girl!" Ruth teased.

"None of your business!" Abe retorted. "Oh, here's a laugh! Evidently the cadets listened to the radio station out of Del Rio, Texas. And ads such as 'pay $2.75 for a photo, autographed, of Jesus Christ coming out of the sky' were common. Isn't that a hoot?"

"How long was—Arthur, is it?—there?" Nick inquired. "I don't know him, of course, but it's interesting to hear about the program. I'll be thirty-two in November, and I've been thinking about joining the air force. That is, if I can qualify and if I'm not too old."

Abe returned to the letter. "He received seventy hours in the air during a nine-week period. Then the next and final phase before transition training, which is just the squaring away for actual duty, was advanced flying school. Again, it was seventy hours flying in nine weeks. Artie went to single-engine school and flew AT-6s."

Quite obviously, Abe was very impressed with this part. "They learned aerial gunnery, combat maneuvers, navigational skills—you know, like formation and instrument flying.''

Abe looked up at his rapt audience. ''Artie didn't tell me this. I asked someone at the base, and they said only the *best* out of basic went into single-engine instruction, because that was for the 'fighters.' ''

The room was very still. Abe continued. ''Artie is in Chicago now and celebrating his twenty-fifth birthday with his folks.''

After a long pause, Abe finished his news. ''Before he leaves for England and active combat.''

There it was! The war was brought right into their living room, brutally attacking their heartstrings. No more practicing, this was for real. No more ''soon,'' tomorrow was already here.

I haven't had the desire or the courage to even get near these pages of late. Odd, this had always been my first stop in times of crisis, I never thought the day would come when I didn't want to—or wasn't able to—put down a word. But everything has seemed so futile, so unimportant. Life's gone on, just not inside me.

And then the real world intruded on my hoarded private hell and forced me to look outside of myself. My little—Abe would be so mad at me if he saw this—Abe is soon to be sent somewhere. Only God knows for sure! And my Artie—my best friend—is already fighting overseas. Oh, Lord, keep them both safe!

I realize I had to let go of my personal self-centeredness and be grateful I am here where I can be of help to others—where I can use what was given to me in so many good ways, where there are countless roads to travel that lead toward contributing to life. Maybe I can even, hopefully, have another chance for a baby, if it's meant to be.

So I must have faith that everyone—and that includes me—will forgive my indulgence and welcome me back into some state of normalcy.

On a ship somewhere in the Pacific Ocean
Sunday, October 11, 1942

Sunday, October 11
I'm on my way. Finished Camp Pendelton on October 3 and
orders came right away. Can't say where to or what kind of
ship I'm on. Guys are listening to all these sad songs, makes
me lonesome. But I've got three girls to come home to, got
them beat all to hell.

Tuesday, October 13
Thirteen turned out to be my lucky number. Almost got caught
screwing off on guard duty. Had the 12:00 to 4:00 a.m. watch.
Rocking on ship made me sleepy and I curled up in back of
some sandbags on deck. Couple of officers came along. I
woke up and heard them wondering where the guard was. I
jumped up, ran around the other way and met them. Could
have been *big* trouble.

Sunday, October 18
Now I can tell you where I am because I'm here—at Camp
Catlin near Honolulu on the island of Oahu. This is sort of a
R and R place. Guys come here from the battlefront to get
their bodies and heads healed. Must be awful—some of these
poor bastards are almost crazy. What they've seen and experienced is just too much to cope with. I sort of backed into
an assignment the first day here. We were given a few hours
off so, no surprise, I went to the beach for a swim. One of
the sailors got careless and went out too far and was too weak
to get back. Lucky I noticed. Anyway, I think I broke a record
getting to him and it was a cinch to bring him in—no big deal.
But everyone was patting me on the back and thanking me.
The officer in charge called me in and I'm now the official
lifeguard at the camp. For a while, at least. I wrote Grandpa
about it—figured that might cheer him up. Be sure to write
and tell me how everyone is doing.

Los Angeles, California
Friday, December 25, 1942

The strident ring of the telephone jarred Eve to consciousness.
She glanced at the clock, 2:15 a.m. Who could it be at this hour?

"Hello."

"Eve?" bellowed a woman's voice. "It's me, Jenine Jasmine—
wait a minute—" Eve heard her speak to someone. "What's my
name? I forget!" There was a muffled sound, and then Jenine came
back on the line. "Oh, yeah! It's Jenine Jasmine Smith—Mrs.
Claude Smith! We just got married!"

Eve bolted upright. "You what? Where are you?" She tried to
keep her voice low so Douglas wouldn't be disturbed.

"You know, in Las Vegas, on the bond tour. I wanted you to
be the first to hear."

Eve thought Jenine sounded drunk. Somebody from the studio
should have been with her. "Oh—thank you. I'm just not quite
awake yet. Are you all right?"

"Sure am. We gave the caretaker the slip and here we are—all
hitched up. Cla-Claude—we've got to fix that name—Honey Buns
is sooo cute. And he just reeks hormones, if you get what I mean.
Will you tell the studio for me, pretty please with sugar on it?"

Eve sighed, worried about what Mo Jeddu and Peter Padon would say. "Of course I will, dear. Now, what are your plans? Oh, my! It just dawned on me—the opening of the picture is tomorrow night."

"Shit!" Jenine exclaimed. To her husband she said, "We'll have to go to L.A. tomorrow." To Eve, "Don't worry, we'll be there. This'll give the reporters something to talk about! See ya—bye!"

And it did! The publicity department sent out a bulletin about the elopement, and no newsperson wanted to miss seeing the "mystery man." Every premiere automatically received good coverage by the press. But Jenine Jasmine's announcement caused a stampede as everyone wanted the most advantageous position from which to photograph or interview the happy couple.

Mo Jeddu took the news philosophically. He knew it had to happen sooner or later. He genuinely liked June, as he fondly liked to think of her, and hoped she would be happy. But he doubted this union would last, she was too much for one man to handle.

Jenine Jasmine stepped out of the limousine and into a barrage of cameras and microphones. She wore a tight, clinging gown of shimmering silver bugle beads on nude chiffon—and that was all. Except for silver pumps and long diamond earrings. The beads caught the lights from the flash bulbs and she almost glowed like neon.

Claude Smith from Boise, Idaho, tried to retreat back into the car when he saw the horde of madmen racing toward them. Douglas and Eve were still inside, however, and Douglas gave him a little goose to propel him into the open beside Jenine. Claude was tall, blond, pleasant-looking and a very young, unsophisticated twenty-four. He was on leave, having just graduated from a midshipman school before shipping out. His eyes had practically bulged out when he saw Jenine Jasmine at the bond rally. And his mouth had dropped open when she spotted him in the audience and called him up on the platform. The crowd had loved seeing a serviceman with her. She made him go with her on every stop. Then they'd had drinks. Then dinner. Then drinks. Then they'd gone back to her suite. Then drinks. Then the twenty-four hour chapel. He was still trying to digest what had happened to him, events had moved too rapidly to make much sense. He wasn't sure if he was in love or just enamored, but he did know the last forty-eight hours had been a blast. An unbelievable adventure filled with lust and passion and excitement. The future was an unknown factor at this point in his life, so he had decided to ride this wave as long as it lasted and see what the next one washed ashore.

The public embraced the rash romantic marriage; its urgency expressed the emotional boomerang of war. The reviewers went wild over *To Love Is to Hate,* citing the growth and depth of Jenine Jasmine as an actress. The film was a complete success in all ways, and Douglas Hassal had established his position at the studio.

Los Angeles, California
Monday, August 30, 1943

"I have Heidi Graham on the line for you, Miss Handel," reported Eve's secretary. Eve still used her maiden name at work.

"Hello, Heidi! I have good news. Utopia is exercising its yearly option. And no test. Your work has been consistently excellent and the next picture could put your billing above the title. Can you believe it's been four years since Nick and I saw you at the Pasadena Playhouse? I'm very proud of you."

Eve listened for a moment. "Of course you can come in for an appointment. Let me transfer you to Matilda to make a time."

Eve sat quietly as Heidi Graham poured out her problem. "I know this is personal, not business related, but I don't have anyone else to talk to about this."

"You can come to me at any time about anything. You are like family to me."

"Oh, thank you, Miss Handel." Heidi fidgeted a bit, then began. "Remember when I did the picture for the producer Lawrence Wenmueler?"

Eve nodded.

"Well, he was very kind and seemed to take an interest in my welfare. He mentioned other projects he thought I would be right for. And then, because of gas rationing, he offered to have his driver pick me up and bring me home after work. Sometimes he would leave the studio—at the same time."

Eve had a hunch what was coming.

"One night he put his arm around me, just gently, and said how much he liked talking to me. I knew he was married, and I wasn't sure what he meant. And I was nervous."

"I understand."

"I kind of slipped away and made light of what he had said. I told him I was grateful for his interest and would try hard to justify his belief in me."

"You did exactly right!"

"Since the film was finished, he has called a few times, suggesting we have a meeting to discuss other roles. I want to work, but I don't want to—to—"

"I know what you're saying. And I completely agree with you. We'll find a way to approach this situation." Eve sounded more confident than she felt. The image of Mr. Cozakman and her enraged father loomed large in her mind. She couldn't settle Mr. Wenmueler as Papa had settled Mr. Cozakman. What could she do?

Heidi continued. "I want to ask your advice. I have been seeing a man, a nice man, Rodney Powers. He's in the publicity department and has accompanied me on interviews and escorted me to openings and other functions, almost since I first signed. He asked me to marry him. I like him a lot. But I don't know if I love him. I want to say yes because I know I would feel protected and safe and secure."

She looked earnestly at Eve, her big brown eyes wet with moisture. "Would it be fair to him? Would I be—betraying him in some way? I would be a good wife, a loyal wife, a supportive wife! I promise that! Is that enough?"

Eve comforted her, holding her like a child, even though—like Jenine—she was only four years her senior. "My sweet Heidi, I can't be absolute. But it seems to me, your evaluation of your feelings toward Rodney would qualify you to make an excellent wife. What is the definition of love? Of a 'good' marriage? If you like each other, respect each other, honor each other, what else could you hope for? Prince Charming doesn't always ride up on a white horse. Sometimes he chugs up in an old rattletrap car. But he's still Prince Charming! There are some questions that can't be answered before one marries, only afterward.''

Heidi pulled away, and now her eyes were shining. ''What would I do without you? I appreciate you so much.''

Eve was relieved she wouldn't have to confront Lawrence Wenmueler, although she would have done something if Heidi hadn't solved her own problem. She had met Rodney Powers on several occasions and was impressed with his demeanor. Eve believed the two would complement each other.

Well, well! Two of my ''girls'' will be married off now! It's interesting how some of these so-called business associates have become like ''family'' to me. I am pleased that they trust me, depend on me—and I feel good if I am able to console in any way, or when asked, to offer advice. Thank you, Lord, for my extended family.

25

Los Angeles, California
Saturday, January 22, 1944

Eve picked up the January 24, 1944, issue of *Life* magazine. This was the first somewhat relaxing day she'd had in months. Not only had she been doing her regular duties at the studio, but she was once again deeply enmeshed with Douglas on his next feature, *Lost Women*. It would star Jenine Jasmine and Heidi Graham. Eve had gone to bat for Heidi and had prepared a spectacular test. The powers that be took one look and were convinced Heidi was ready for this very dramatic role. Contrary to what the title might suggest, it was the story of nurses who were flown behind front lines to tend to the wounded as they were airlifted to hospitals in England and the U.S. Loosely based on a true story, these nurses were away from their regular unit, in Istres, France. While bringing some patients to the village, their lorry was strafed, killing all but the two women and disabling the open motor truck. The film would show their struggles to reach safety and their adventures along the way.

Whenever Eve had a little time off, she would acknowledge again how fortunate she was not to have to spend it dealing with the household arrangements. She could indulge her thirst for reading, or whatever else pleased her. She didn't even have to worry about Rhett, her year-old shih tzu. All she had to do was love him. Like right now. Rhett was nuzzled close to her on the chaise lounge. He was gloriously happy and contented when "Mommy" was home. Of course, he didn't have a bad time when she had to leave because he had Scarlett to tease and bother.

The *Life* editorial discussed the fact 1944 would be the last year on earth for many of America's fine young men. Eve shuddered, allowing this dark but unfortunately true statement to register. She sent up a prayer for Abe and Arthur, and for all those she didn't know. And then she realized how important *Lost Women* could be. It would give laymen such as she an idea of the hell of war, using a theatrical, graphic media. She would have Jenine and Heidi watch every news footage available no matter how raw—plus the documentaries that Douglas had made. She would insist they visit the hospitals and get firsthand information from the patients, study procedures and techniques, attitudes and body language. She hoped she could make them understand what a significant service they could perform with this film.

Eve reached for the telephone, excitement mounting for the project. But the ring of an incoming call came first.

"Hello. Yes, this is Eve Handelstein Hassal." She knew right away it was Mama or Papa, no one else used her full maiden name.

"Hello, sweetheart!" It was Papa, but his voice was different. "I'm sorry to bother—"

Eve interrupted. "Papa, you never, never bother me. It's a joy for me to talk to you, I wish we did it more often."

"I hope I don't have to make this kind of call too many times—it's hard!"

"Papa, what is it?" Apprehension filled her body, she couldn't remember him sounding this way.

"My father—Grandpa Handelstein—died during the night. In his sleep." His voice was low and heavy with sorrow.

"Oh, Papa, I'm so sorry, so very sorry!"

The magazine lay open on her lap, and the editorial stared at her, daring her to question its prophecy of death. But, of course, she couldn't. It made only one mistake, limiting its prediction to young men.

Eve and Samuel spoke at length. Mildred came on the line as well, and Eve offered the comfort they craved. She understood what they needed to know, that they needed to know what were her feelings for her grandfather.

Without guile, Eve was able to say she fully accepted Grandpa's toast he made at Christmas in 1940. ''May we all never forget what is worth remembering or remember what is best forgotten.'' She had grown enough to allow the healing of the scar. She *was* an actress, only the multi performances came from different bodies. Actually, her impact was far more than if she had become the actress.

Grandpa Handelstein could rest in peace.

Camp Catlin, Oahu
Sunday, February 6, 1944

Sunday, February 6
Got Mama and Papa's letter about Grandpa Handelstein—I feel bad I couldn't be with him more in the last few years. At least he knew I listened to him and followed his lead in regards to physical education. I'll miss him.

Abe added a P.S. on his note to Ruth.

Heard from Artie—flying lots of missions over Europe and okay so far. He can't say much about where or when, but scuttlebutt here is it's hot and heavy over there. I worry about him. Oh, had a nice letter from Nick Larrington a while back. He was disappointed he didn't make it into the air force. I wrote him and told him he was doing his part by finding people who entertain all the guys. And it's true! Movies mean a lot—they're the link to home. Every single dude here has a pinup! Betty Grable, Jane Russell, Rita Hayworth. Except me. I couldn't make up my mind on which one. I should get a picture of Esther Williams, you know, swimming and me—ha-ha!

London, England
Tuesday, July 18, 1944

First Lieutenant Arthur Burdsey gazed out the window of his hospital room in London. It was pleasant to be able to see the sky and the sun, almost like a regular day in life. Because at night, with the blackout curtains, it felt like a tomb or a dark cave. He had been told these bombings weren't nearly as bad as the blitz in 1940. How had they endured the terror night after night?

Arthur had had his own share of terror. He had reported for duty in time to be one of the fighter plane escorts for B-17s on the first all-American bombing hits into northern France.

In 1943 Arthur made continuous trips over France and into Germany, running interference for the B-17s. The Ruhr cities, among others, had been targeted for round-the-clock bombings. The Allies were retaliating.

He didn't relish trying to take out another plane, but he knew without a doubt it was either him or someone else. He preferred the enemy to remain nameless and faceless.

Then came D-Day, June 6, 1944. More than one and a half million troops, land and sea and air combined, joined in the climactic push—the invasion of France on the Normandy beaches.

Arthur could not single out any one impression of that day. It had been such a tangled web, such a cacophony of sounds and sights and emotions. First the rush of excitement, the anticipation of participating in such a monumental endeavor, being a part of history. He would never forget the barrage of artillery fire, the whine of bombs, the thunder of their explosions, the roar of aircraft, the staccato bark of machine guns, the yells and screams of the victors and victims on both sides.

He relived the nightmare of seeing smoke pouring from his engine, the shock of realizing he had been hit. Instinct took over; he couldn't remember a conscious train of thought. He hadn't wanted to bail, he'd be a sitting duck for enemy bullets. Better to battle his plane down to a crash landing, not an easy task when the controls were haywire. His mind remembered spotting a fairly open field and aiming to set down there, a huge jolt followed by several more hard thumps, a butt as his craft plowed into something—and then nothing.

Arthur had slowly come around, rattled into consciousness by a rolling, bumpy sensation. Through the haze, he realized he was on a makeshift stretcher, carried by two dark figures. He could see other outlines ahead and he assumed there were more in the rear. But who were they?

Someone jogged up from behind. A man with a raspy, hoarse voice whispered, "So, you're awake!" He spoke English quite well, but with a decidedly French accent.

"Keep very quiet! We think the Germans have been pushed back, but we cannot be certain. We're taking you to a nearby farm and tomorrow to St. Lo—we know the Allies will be in control by then. We couldn't take time to treat you, are you all right with the pain?"

Arthur nodded, not even sure yet where he hurt. He must be in some kind of shock. Carefully he went through a body roll call. His head ached; they had roughly tied a bandanna around it, probably to stop the bleeding. Everything seemed okay until he came to his chest. Bruised or broken rib, or ribs, no doubt. The next noticeable damage, beyond scratches and scrapes, was his right leg.

It must have jammed against the wall of the cockpit on impact. He had no idea the extent of that injury. All in all he appeared to have gotten off pretty easy. Without these guys, however, no telling how he might have fared.

He drifted in and out of consciousness. During one alert moment, he thought he was in a bed and that Eve was bending over him, washing his wounds.

Was he dreaming or losing his mind?

The image persisted. Now he was aware again, and he *was* in a bed, with clean linen, in a quaint, cozy room, and a dark-haired girl *was* tending to him. But it wasn't Eve.

Why couldn't he forget? Would he ever be free?

Arthur was airlifted to England that same day. There were far more casualties than the limited medical personnel in the field could handle, so any patient that could be moved was sent immediately to the facilities in London.

It was there that the extent of Arthur's injuries were determined. He had suffered a concussion and lacerations on his head, two cracked ribs, a compound fracture of the right leg, plus minor contusions and abrasions. He would recover fully, but would probably not see active duty for some time. Perhaps never again if the war would just end!

Arthur had spoken to his parents a week after his arrival at the hospital. He had not been reported M.I.A. because he had been rescued so promptly, which meant Alicia and Randall Burdsey had been spared the anxiety of a long, torturous wait for news of their son. By the time they set eyes on him, his hair would have grown out where it had been shaved for the stitches, his ribs would have mended, only his leg would still show the effects of the crash.

His brain might have been jarred, but it had not stopped functioning. He had so much time to think. Since December 7, 1941, his life had been consumed by his dedication to serving his country. Now that he was on the disabled list for a while, and heading for home soon, his mind kept asking, "What next?" Until now, he and everyone else in uniform hadn't counted on having a future. And he damn well came close to proving that was true. He knew he had been pursuing the right profession before he enlisted, he liked it and it liked him. But he was beginning to question the locale and decided a change might be stimulating and challenging. Maybe California? Abe was there, Wade Colby was there.

And Eve was there! Did he have to see her in her new environment to fully accept that she was lost to him? Maybe that was the only way he could really close the door on that chapter of his life.

Los Angeles, California
Monday, May 7, 1945

Jenine Jasmine's secretary, Myra Jones, burst into the reception area of Eve Handel's office. "I need to see Miss Handel right away."

Matilda Carliss could see the woman was quite agitated. "Now, now, be calm—what is the problem?"

Myra Jones held up a telegram. "This came for Miss Jasmine. It's from the government—the delivery boy said it was the war department or something like that—"

Matilda quickly buzzed the inner office. "Miss Handel, I think you should come out here."

Eve hesitated only slightly before ripping the envelope open. "If this is what I'm afraid it is—oh, my God—it is. Claude Smith has been killed—his ship was sunk. Oh, dear, what a horrible shame!"

Jenine Jasmine and Heidi Graham were on a sound stage, dubbing a few scenes that had been shot on location under conditions where it was impossible to get a clear sound track. "Looping," as this process was called, was extremely difficult, especially in such a highly charged impassioned script as *Lost Women*. The two stars had to re-create the intensity of the drama in a completely sterile setting, without benefit of the excitement of the live, on-set action.

Eve violated the movie code of honor and entered through the heavy stage door when the red light was blinking.

"Who in the hell—oh, it's you, Eve." Jenine was showing the strain. "This is so fucking tough, trying to get it up again—"

"I know, dear, I know." Eve led Jenine aside. "Excuse us for a moment, Heidi."

Heidi sensed something was wrong and nodded silently.

Eve spoke quietly, holding Jenine by the shoulders. Suddenly a high-pitched scream filled the room. It was eerie, not quite human. Heidi ran to Jenine, who was sobbing now and lashing out at the world, the war, life.

"Sweet son of a bitch! Why him? Why Claude? Never got around to fixing that name. Never got around to even know him, really. I think I might have liked him—a lot. So damn young— and innocent."

Heidi was weeping with Jenine and comforting her; they had become very close during the filming. The microphone was still live when Eve had interrupted the session and the engineer hadn't thought to turn it off. And then he deliberately left it on, not to be crass, but these sounds of raw, ardent, agonizing pain could never be duplicated or manufactured. The girls wouldn't have to do any more, he could make this fit the picture. It would be what it was— powerfully real.

Just as the public had approved of her elopement, it rallied around Jenine in this time of tragedy. Her loss symbolized every-one's loss. What made his death even worse, if possible, was that the very next day, May 8, 1945, Germany signed the papers for an unconditional surrender.

Jenine called Claude's family. She had met them briefly on Claude's only leave after the marriage. They were heartbroken, but they thanked her for giving their son such happiness. "He wrote to us often, and in every letter he told us he had never been happier. We're grateful for that, and for you."

"I'll be!" Jenine said to Eve, dumbfounded. "You mean I ac-tually did something right?"

Camp Catlin, Oahu
Wednesday, July 4, 1945

Wednesday, July 4
Happy Fourth! And is it ever! For me, anyway, and for Artie!
Artie first. As you probably know, he'd gone back to England
again after his wounds healed. But now he's out for good, and
he may come to California to open a branch of his old man's
business. Wouldn't that be neat?

Thursday, July 5
Had to run off yesterday, no one was patrolling the beach.
Are you ready? It looks like I may get off this damn island.
I'll let you know as soon as I know.

Monday, July 9
Glad I didn't mail this yet. One of these days, sooner than
later, I am going to wish us happy birthday in person. Just
got my present—I'm on my way to Oak Knoll Hospital in
Oakland, California! I don't need a hospital—I repeat—nothing is wrong with me. It's an automatic destination from the
Pacific, before next assignment or discharge. Everyone smells
victory around here, atmosphere is very upbeat.

Eve had not celebrated the Fourth of July or her birthday, for
that matter. She had been in the hospital again because of her

second miscarriage. What was wrong with her? The doctors didn't have the answer. She so desperately wanted a baby and yet no one could tell her why she couldn't carry a child to term. Eve was grateful Douglas had been so supportive. He hadn't shown his disappointment in front of her once, not once!

Ruth Handel was restless. She was bored writing the war documentaries. Besides, she hoped there soon wouldn't be a need for them anymore. The outline for "the great American novel" had been put on hold, and no inspiration was forthcoming. Actually, Ruth felt her life had been put on hold, that she wasn't focused on much of anything. Certainly not a social life. She had gone out some, but there wasn't anyone she cared about enough to pursue a relationship. It was probably her fault, it was difficult for her to relax on a date. Any hint of kissing or touching and her alarm system sent up the red flag. Pretty hard for anyone to get past that barrier.

Ruth did enjoy accompanying Nick Larrington on his talent scout journeys. She didn't feel threatened by him, and he was witty and stimulating and fun to be around. The status of his personal life never came up, and like Eve, she didn't ask and didn't care. He was a cherished friend.

Absentmindedly, she picked up a current issue of *Photoplay,* a popular movie magazine. In thumbing through she happened to glimpse a still of Jenine Jasmine. There were several glamour shots and a picture of Jenine and her husband, Claude Smith. The text recounted their romantic elopement. Obviously, this edition had been sent to the printers before Claude was killed.

Ruth read the article, critiquing as she went along, mumbling to herself, "Jeez, I can write better than that." And then, "Damn it, Jenine's not like that, you dumbbell. I bet you took that line out of context!" Ruth finished and threw it aside in disgust. "What gibberish," she muttered, "that writer doesn't know her ass from a hole in the ground!"

Yvonne Birshgeld came from the kitchen. "Were you talking to me, Ruth?"

"No, sorry. I was just commenting on a stupid story in the July *Photoplay.* I could beat that with my eyes closed."

"Then why don't you?" Yvonne asked.

"What?"

"Why don't you write a piece that is suitable?" Yvonne repeated.

"Me?" Ruth was surprised.

"Why not? You know all those stars in the magazines. Or could know them if you wanted to with your connections. And then, because you're talented, the articles would have depth and understanding and quality. I think the editors would jump at that."

Ruth contemplated Yvonne. "I never thought of that. But wouldn't I be cashing in on Eve's position? Using her success to gain access? I'd die if anyone thought that!"

"If you weren't able to deliver, after a while that assumption would certainly surface." Yvonne was adamant. "But you can deliver! You are able to write and write well. I've read all of your work, and it's good. Even though most of it has been abstract, on subjects you don't really know except through research, you managed to infuse humanity and compassion into your pieces. To breathe life into inanimate objects. Think how rich you could make a story when you knew the people or came to know them! If I were a personality who was to be profiled or interviewed, I would insist on speaking with someone like you. Someone intelligent, with warmth and wit. People like Jenine are at the mercy of these leeches!"

Ruth had never heard Yvonne talk so fervently. She was pleased by the positive attitude toward her work. She did believe in herself enough to think she was capable of doing something like Yvonne suggested, but she wasn't convinced it was the proper thing to do.

"But what a wonderful idea!" Eve was jubilant and excited when Ruth broached the subject. "Yvonne is absolutely on target. You should hear the complaints from Jenine and Heidi—even me! Some of the questions are so asinine and vacuous and—uninteresting. Go see Harvey Hill right now, he's the head of public relations here at Utopia. Oh, this is so perfect."

Chicago, Illinois
Monday, August 20, 1945

"May I speak to Wade Colby, please? It's Arthur Burdsey. Hello, Wade! Yeah, I'm really back for good and in one piece, just dented a little. Hey, congrats on your nomination for *Seek and Destroy*—I know you didn't win, but I wanted to say you deserved the recognition. I saw the film and thought you were extremely good. Studio keeping you busy? Whew, I'm tired just listening to your schedule. I guess Sun Valley won't be open this year? Well, you might get lucky and see me before the next ski season. I think I may be your way early next year, Dad is considering opening a branch. I know, I know, it's true, California *is* allowing all sorts of riffraff into the state these days. You'll just have to grin and bear it, and put up with me...."

Now that the war was officially over on all fronts, Arthur was trying to get his life back on track. He was definitely going to California, for a year at least. If he liked it, maybe he'd stay longer. At the moment, however, he only wanted to be free.

Arthur had caught up with Abe Handel when Abe arrived in Chicago on the tenth of August to spend the second week of leave with his parents. After Oakland, Abe had gone directly to Los

Angeles for the first week. Arthur had to chuckle every time he thought of Abe trying to explain his latest orders.

"You're assigned *where?*" Arthur had been incredulous!

Abe had blushed sheepishly. "I have been positioned as lifeguard at the Women's Marine Corps Swimming Pool, across the street from the Navy Annex in Arlington, Virginia."

Arthur wasn't about to let him off the hook. "How many women are there in this particular place?"

"Roughly 3,700."

"And how many men are there to make out—I mean, look out—for these poor little darlings?"

Abe was squirming with embarrassment. "I think about six!"

"Six? My goodness!" Arthur exclaimed in feigned horror. "We'll have to send you extra bottles of vitamins, to keep up your strength. Wouldn't want you to simply waste away."

"Aw, Artie—"

"Is this by chance the unit that men call 'BAMS'?" Arthur was in his glory.

"How do you know that?" Abe retorted. "You were in the air force, and nowhere near any marines!"

"True! But word travels far in the service. The rumor is that the men don't last long, the BAMS are too much for them."

"Shit! Why me?" poor Abe asked. "First, a male 'nurse' on a beach, and now a watchdog for 'Broad Ass Marines'!"

"Because you're a lucky son of a bitch!" Arthur became serious. "And everyone, including me, is damn glad you are!" He slapped Abe on the back. "Don't pay any attention to the ribbing! It's just envy and jealousy. Because every single guy I know would jump at the chance to be in your place."

No doubt, Abe was in a unique situation. He and the five other fortunate young men received their regular pay, plus per diem, since they lived off base and were only given lunch. Abe opted for a room in a boardinghouse—he was tired of sleeping on a cot with twenty to forty guys in a barracks. The privacy was welcome.

The duty was quite pleasant. He was personally able to work out and train regularly. And he organized fitness programs for the women, had several swimming classes a day separated according to ability. He'd even pulled a few floundering swimmers out of the pool. For the most part, the ladies were okay, although there would always be some bellyachers in any group.

Invitations for dinner were endless. And he accepted a few each week. It was a delightful change to have pleasant conversations and share a movie or theater or a concert with a friend. And that was as far as it went. Sometimes the gals would come on strong, but he managed to exit as tactfully as possible. He wasn't interested in a romantic involvement.

Abe had never had a need before to question his sexual prowess. Athletics had always been his highest priority. And friends, both male and female, were also very important to him. He had been on dates during his school years, even kissed girls good-night, but it hadn't registered—hadn't meant anything. Now it seemed he was expected to make a move. It wasn't enough anymore to be pals or buddies, one had to be a lover. If this state defined maturity, he didn't think much of it. He believed his existence was rich and enlightened and would become more so as he lived and experienced new things. He felt he was doing what he knew how to do to benefit humanity. Helping people to keep their bodies healthy and fit maybe didn't warrant a Nobel Prize, but neither could it be dismissed, it was a worthy contribution.

Abe mulled over this shift in attitude at great length. He decided on a course of action, at least until he was discharged, which should be fairly soon. He would indicate he had someone waiting for him in California and wouldn't cheat for anything. Probably most of the guys had a sweetie or even a wife at home and still played around, but he would explain that wasn't his style. And he wouldn't be totally lying. His closest confidants *were* in Los Angeles—Eve and Ruth and Yvonne. He definitely needed their input to help him sort this problem out. Why did everyone work so hard to make life complex?

31

Los Angeles, California
Saturday, March 9, 1946

"**J**esus, the 'Who's Who' of Hollywood is here!" Randall Burdsey exclaimed to his friend and host, Joseph Hassal.

"I figured most of the heavy hitters would still be in town tonight since the Academy Awards was just last Thursday. And it made the wife happy because she could piggyback the Oscar theme. Every party has to have a theme, you see!" Joseph rolled his eyes toward the heavens. "Complete bullshit, but don't tell Esther I said so. If this is what she likes, so be it!"

Esther Hassal beamed proudly at the milling throng. This was her best gala to date. There hadn't been one regret in the RSVPs, which had almost presented a problem. A hostess always overbooks, counting on a few no-shows. But the wonderful Dave Chasen of Chasen's Restaurant and his magical elves handled the logistics with complete aplomb.

The motif had been carried out spectacularly. The standards supporting the massive tent were shaped like old Oscar himself and sprayed gold. Miniature golden Oscars in beds of simulated reels of film were the centerpieces for the tables. Gold-plated china and crystal place settings shone brilliantly on white lace over gold tablecloths.

Huge posters of the Best Picture nominees for 1945 lined one side of the tent: *Anchors Aweigh; The Bells of St. Mary's; The Lost Weekend; Mildred Pierce* and *Spellbound.* A star indicated that *The Lost Weekend* had won the award.

Blown-up stills of the nominated actors and actresses—and the winners—were displayed on two other walls of the tent.

Ray Milland had won for Best Actor in *The Lost Weekend* and Joan Crawford had taken home the Oscar for her performance in *Mildred Pierce.*

Keeping to the theme of the evening, the orchestra played all of the nominated songs and movie scores. The menu was displayed in the form of an Academy ballot at each setting, and the place cards were small certificates of nomination. Conversation was lively, a large percentage of which addressed the pros and cons of the Awards show itself and the choices of the Academy members. The majority agreed that the event's co-hosts, Bob Hope and Jimmy Stewart, were terrific together. Everyone lauded the return of the glamour, the finery, the searchlights, the red carpet—a celebration of the beginning of postwar Hollywood.

Randall Burdsey surveyed this assembly of the rich and famous and was satisfied with his newest expansion. He had had the idea of opening a branch in Los Angeles a few years back. But the war had intervened and most plans had been shelved, some never to resurface. Actually, it had been Arthur who reintroduced the idea when he was discharged from the service.

Joseph Hassal had met Randall Burdsey in 1930 when an acquaintance recommended him as a smart and reliable stockbroker. Joseph had tested the waters with a nominal investment at first. He had followed Randall's advice, which was to short his stock positions. When Randall said to buy back in January 1932, he had, and, of course, made a killing. Convinced then of the man's ability, Joseph increased the amount of his account quite substantially. Subsequently, over the years both men, and eventually their wives, established a long-distance friendship. Each son had met their father's friend once or twice, but not each other.

When Joseph heard Randall was opening a branch of Burdsey & Co., in Los Angeles, he thought it would be a nice gesture to have a reception. "It will give Esther something to plan! And you, and your son as well, since you say he will be managing this office, will meet most of the important people in the territory."

So now Esther and Joseph Hassal, Alicia and Randall Burdsey and Arthur Burdsey stood by the door to greet the guests.

Eve had been flabbergasted when her in-laws told her about the event. She'd swallowed hard when Joseph had mentioned, "Randall said you and your family were actually neighbors in Chicago. So you must know Arthur, the son?"

"Ah, yes. We were, I mean I was— our house was near theirs." She was uncharacteristically flustered. "I—did, uh, do know the son."

If only the floor could have opened up and swallowed her!

Later, with Ruth, she confessed, "I don't know what to do! Or how to react! Or how much to tell Doug! Maybe I could get sick! Is 'cold feet' a disease? Oh, dear, I'm sounding like some kind of nutcase."

Ruth hadn't seen Eve that undone before, certainly not about a social affair. She wondered if her sister had been completely honest about her feelings for Arthur. Honest with Ruth—and honest with herself?

Aloud she said, "Now, Eve, listen to me. You are married, it's been almost eight years since you broke off with Artie. It might be a little awkward at the very first, which would be quite normal, but then I'm sure it will be a cinch to fall right back into the old friendship pattern."

Eve was skeptical, and in a small voice said, "I—hope so. Oh, God, I hope so!"

"And," Ruth continued, "I think at some opportune time, you should casually say to Doug something like, 'Oh, Artie and the three of us were good pals! At one point, Artie and I even had a case of puppy love, you know, kid stuff! But that was long ago!'

Believe me, there won't be a problem. If Artie is going to be in this town, it's better to face him sooner than later so you can both get on with it.''

Ruth soothed some of Eve's anxiety. But then she had another thought—what should she wear? Eve had called Jenine Jasmine and asked for help.

''You got it! I wasn't sure if I'd even go or not, too stiff for me. But if you're getting all gussied up, I don't want to miss that. I'll drag my newest millionaire along—invite said something about a stockbroker? Maybe I'll bring in some business!''

Jenine had wangled the color scheme of the party from Esther Hassal's personal assistant. She and the trusty head designer at Utopia had decided on fine white satin, sprinkled delicately with gold flecks. High neck, tight long sleeves, form-fitting to Eve's hips, where the bias-cut material gently fell away. But when she walked, one could see the contour of her body. An interesting feature of the gown was its open back. From the band of the collar to below her waistline, bare skin was exposed, startling and very inviting. Jenine's makeup and hair people had once again taken excellent care of Eve.

Eve was a vision as she glided down the winding stairway. No one would have guessed her knees were wobbly. Eve was grateful Jenine had such a flair for fashion, because she felt good about the way she looked. And that always bolstered a lady's nervousness and apprehension.

''Ah, there you are, Eve,'' Joseph Hassal exclaimed. ''You look like a million bucks—no—make that two million!''

He brought her to the three Burdseys. ''I guess I don't have to present my daughter-in-law to her old friends, right?''

Arthur Burdsey had been dreading, and anticipating, this moment for weeks, maybe for years. His heart was thumping so loudly he was sure everyone could hear. He couldn't speak, his throat constricted. Dear God, this wasn't fair! How could she be more dazzling and appetizing than he even remembered?

And then Eve spoke. Each word was like the thrust of a knife to Arthur. It was that voice, the voice he had loved from their first meeting nearly twelve years ago.

"Welcome to Los Angeles, Mr. and Mrs. Burdsey. Arthur—it's so nice to see you again. I—we—were relieved to hear of your safe return from the war."

Eve thought maybe that sounded too personal. "Abe kept us all up to date on his chums." Why couldn't she say anything right?

Arthur finally was able to get out a few words. "Uh, thank you. I was lucky."

She searched Arthur's face and could see, behind those hazel eyes, obvious effects of painful experiences he must have had in Europe. He had matured faster than need be, lost a touch of the childlike sensitivity since her brief glimpse of him outside his house that December night in 1941.

Douglas arrived at the group, his interruption saving further clumsy conversation. Introductions were made, idle chitchat exchanged. And that's when a slight commotion and a buzz of excitement suddenly filled the air. Arthur looked toward the entrance. "Excuse me. I believe a friend of mine is here." And he escaped to greet Wade Colby, who couldn't help causing a fuss wherever he went.

Tall, well-proportioned, handsome with dark brown sun-streaked hair and bright blue eyes, Wade Colby was the most important star in Hollywood. And to top it off, one of the nicest people on the planet. And charming!

Arthur brought Wade around to each cluster of guests, after the initial perfunctory meeting of his host and hostess and their family. Wade tarried as he kissed Eve's hand, registering his distinct approval. He glanced at Arthur as much as to say, how did you let this one get away? And Esther Hassal, of course, was all atwitter. But Wade seemed capable of handling every situation—nothing daunted him.

Jenine Jasmine enjoyed seeing Eve shine out of the office. She was also intuitive enough to recognize that there was something special about tonight. When she saw Arthur, and then Arthur and Eve, she immediately knew they had been in love, perhaps lovers, perhaps still were! But she couldn't figure out why Eve had married Douglas instead of Arthur. It would be interesting to find out. Meanwhile, Arthur was definitely worth looking into, once she knew she wouldn't be stepping on Eve's toes.

When Jenine met Wade Colby, fireworks nearly exploded on the spot. There was going to be a "hot time in the old town" the night of their inevitable date. She was certainly glad she had decided to come this evening! Two winners right off the bat!

"I've got to hand it to Eve," Ruth said quietly to Abe. "She is one hell of an actress, because I *know* how scared she was!"

"True," Abe replied, just as softly. "Poor Artie didn't cover it quite as well. Can you believe he's still hurting?"

"Who's hurting? What are you two whispering about?" Nick Larrington asked.

Ruth laughed. "Eavesdroppers get no info."

"All right then, I'll fix you! Come dance with me. Excuse us, Abe?"

"Oh, sure!" Abe sipped his champagne, watching Nick and Ruth join the other couples. He was content to be alone for a bit. Seeing Arthur's lingering feelings only highlighted the difference between the two friends. When Abe had finished his service and returned home, he had tentatively discussed the disturbing question of his dormant sexuality with Eve. Somehow he felt Ruth wouldn't be as objective because of her own unhappy history.

Eve was grateful her brother was able to air his uncertainty with her; instinctively she knew this was a good sign. Obviously, she did not know much about this sort of problem. Her first objective was to convince Abe not to worry unduly, not to dwell on suppositions until everything got twisted out of proportion, not to let confusion reign. It could simply be that he hadn't found *the* person to stimulate his emotions.

Eve's most important contribution was to find a qualified psychiatrist so that Abe could be counseled by the best. Without divulging any whos or whys, Eve tracked down Dr. Philip Canfield, recommended by Dr. Angel Roberts. He practiced in Encino, so like Dr. Roberts, he was conveniently located away from the main-stream of Hollywood.

Abe had only just begun seeing Dr. Canfield. He liked the doctor and was comfortable with him. It was too soon for any explanations or even interpretations. Abe wasn't trying to rush any conclusion, he was going about his life as he always had. Just sometimes, situations like tonight's party bothered him.

Nick came back, shaking his head in mock disgust. "That Harvey Hill from publicity pulled rank on me. I think he has eyes for Ruth."

"Don't you?" Abe kidded.

"No, not exactly." Seeing Abe's surprised reaction, Nick hastened to explain. "Don't get me wrong! I adore Ruth, consider her to be my best friend, like Eve. But I don't 'have eyes' for her, not that way."

Douglas hadn't been in a very good mood lately. He was consumed with the disappointment that *Lost Women* had received no Academy Award nominations.

"What is *wrong* with those dumb asses? It opened to great reviews, big box office..." he continued as he twirled Eve around the dance floor.

Eve had been hearing these complaints since the nominations had been announced in early February. "Doug, dear, no one can explain the whims of the members of the Academy. Maybe they just think of the last few films they saw."

"My name should be up there on the wall!"

"It will be—soon, I bet." She tried to switch subjects. "Look at Heidi and her Rodney. They've been married about two and a half years now. Don't they look happy?"

"I guess."

"Oh, there's Michael Flanders, how pretty his wife is!" Eve was hoping she wouldn't see any signs of his drinking. This was not the time, or the place, or the crowd in which to act foolishly. So far he appeared in control.

"We've got to find a blockbuster script. Or book. Something

that will set this town on fire!'' Douglas returned to his priority topic.

Eve sighed, ''I've been reading everything within reach.''

Douglas suddenly had a thought. ''You know, Dad told me Burdsey is really loaded. I might want him to help finance one of my pictures some day if I should ever do an independent. I'll go kiss up to the wife, even ask her to dance—the supreme sacrifice! You nail the old guy and, yeah, the son, too. It's great you know them!''

Eve looked at him in dismay. Where was this labyrinth leading?

New York City, New York
Saturday, January 7, 1950

"Hold on, man! Shit, hold on or you'll fall off!" Marcello Savilini yelled to his friend Salvadore Traconi. The two nineteen-year-
olds were lying facedown with arms stretched forward, fingers dug
deep into the frost-covered grass, clutching the hard ground.

"It's spinning, the earth's fucking spinning, it's gonna toss us
out, toss us into friggin' space," Salvadore cried.

It was eleven o' clock at night in Central Park. Passersby barely
paid attention, just a couple of crazy kids, probably drunk. In truth,
they were stoned, higher than a kite on four shared marijuana
joints.

"It can't do this t'me, I'll blow my big chance," Marcello
wailed.

Both were part of the Actors Studio—the evolution from the
Mercury Theater Company and the Group Theater—that had cul-
tivated the "method," derived from Stanislavsky's system. Marcello's "big chance" was being brought about by Eve Handel and
Nick Larrington, who'd just made a New York talent scout trip.
They had seen him in one of the Actors Studio sessions and had
been impressed with his work and his raw animalistic appeal. Ar-

rangements had been made for him to fly to California and make a test. The boys were celebrating Marcello's last night in the city.

Salvadore's head suddenly jerked up. "I think it's stoppin, the spinnin' is lettin' up!"

Slowly, cautiously, Marcello raised his head. "Yeah, you're right. Wow, lucky fer us. We coulda been floatin' in the air with them stars." He rolled over on his back and gazed at the sky. It was a clear, cold January night and the heavens glowed brilliantly. "I'm gonna be a star, too! But in Hollywood!"

Salvadore propped himself up on one elbow and looked wistfully at his buddy. "Will ya come back t'see us? You won't get no 'big head,' will ya?"

"'Course not, Brillo-head! You're my *amico!* I'll even send fer ya, I mean if I stay!"

Salvadore settled down, content with the answer. They both knew that if anyone else called Salvadore "Brillo-head," he'd end up with a shiv in him. But Marcello was allowed because he said it with love in his heart.

The two young men had grown up together in the section of New York known as Little Italy. Not a large area, it was located in Lower Manhattan, near Chinatown. Their parents were friends and had arrived in New York on the same boat from Naples, Italy, in 1925. The boys had been born in 1930: Marcello on December 26, the youngest of four; Salvadore on November 11, the third child of five. Their walk-up apartments were on Mulberry Street a few doors apart.

They had played in the streets, attended school sporadically, fought their rivals, dated, lost their virginity early in life, participated in a few petty larceny episodes. They were too young to be in the war, but they had battled their own enemies. The other ethnic neighborhoods ganged up on kids from Little Italy and Germantown during the hostilities. Those youngsters, and their families, had to defend themselves constantly. No one dared leave home alone, you had to move in packs. Fortunately, this pair had survived with only some black eyes, bumps and bruises and one broken hand (somebody's jaw had been too hard). Not everyone was that lucky.

After the war, their mutual interest in theater had probably saved them from getting involved in really serious conflicts with the law. Many of their peers had chosen, or had no other choice but to follow, the wrong road.

And look what had happened—Marcello was on the road to California!

Marcello Savilini had walked into Eve Handel's office a bit more subdued than his usual cocky self. He was still recovering from the shock of his first plane trip, his first ride in a chauffeur-driven limousine, his first stay at a fancy hotel, the Beverly Hills, to be exact. Then Levis Greene, the representative from MCA, the Music Corporation of America, his newly signed talent agency, had picked Marcello up in his Lincoln Continental convertible and delivered him to Utopia. Mr. Greene had explained the studio would pay his expenses, plus a per diem, until the test was completed.

Eve made small talk with the young man while she tried to decide what scene to use. The reaction of her secretary, Matilda, when Marcello came in the door had not been lost on Eve. Matilda had seen a lot of good-looking men go through that door, but she had really ogled this one.

Eve studied him carefully. Thick unruly blond hair fell every which way, but didn't cover intense blue eyes. Eyes that mocked you, dared you, and if you were a woman, undressed you. He was average height, about five foot eleven, with a strong, wiry physique. Eve sensed the presence of a jungle creature, one who would tread cunningly soft, but could attack brutally. One with crafty awareness, and on the other side, one with gentle love. Definitely one with a zest for living.

At that moment Jenine Jasmine burst into the room as she usually did, started to talk to Eve, and then caught sight of Marcello.

"Oh, oh, oh, what have we here?"

Eve started to introduce them, but Marcello suddenly overcame his bout of angst and beat her to the punch. "I'm Marcello Savilini. Who are you?"

He was deliberately taunting Jenine, Eve realized, and enjoying it. She saw Jenine's back straighten and her eyes narrow, she knew how to cross swords, too. Then it dawned on Eve! Jenine should do the test with him—sparks would fly, for sure. And the scene should come from *The Postman Always Rings Twice,* the John Garfield and Lana Turner movie.

The lights went on in the projection room, and Peter Padon, Mo Jeddu, Eve Handel and Nick Larrington grinned at one another.

"You two did it again!" said a pleased Peter. "Jesus, I thought we were gonna have to call the fire department! Whew, did they sizzle! He comes off that screen like a young Clark Gable. Name's got to go, but that's easy. Now, to find the right launching property."

"Doug and I read so much, always looking for stories, as you know. Well, a couple of years ago, after Doug had decided on the film he's now readying for release, I found something else I liked, and sort of set it aside until Doug was free." Eve sounded excited. "It was a first draft from a new writer, Mickey Moralis, titled *Slightly Crooked.* I think it's a possibility for Marcello."

"What's the gist?" Mo asked.

"A young prizefighter, rough guy obviously, known to take a dive if the price was right, but actually he's a fairly good boxer. A wealthy widow sees a match that he throws. She sends for him, confronts him, challenges him to become a real fighter with her backing. Of course they fall for each other, interesting combination because they are both strong and tough. The Mob factors in, will he or won't he betray her—that's a very bare outline."

Peter and Mo nodded in unison, then Peter spoke. "Let's see it, like *now.* Sounds perfect. Lots of bare hunk for the females to get horny about and fists and tits for the males." He didn't even hesitate anymore—the men had accepted Eve so completely they no longer felt the need to watch how they expressed themselves. And Eve was not bothered at all, really never had been. "Love scenes, action, suits him to a T!"

He stood up, the meeting was over. "Good work! Eve, could you stay a minute, please?"

Now alone, Peter sat on the edge of his desk and contemplated

Eve. "The majority of the studios are beginning to cut back on their contract lists. Mo and I think it's a time to beef ours up, kind of like buying in when the stocks are at a low. We don't want to overload, just add the really good finds. That's why we sent you and Nick to New York and why it's important that you were successful. But you contribute so much more. We've hinted and beat around the bush about this but now I'm saying it straight out. We would like you to be to us what Irving Thalberg was to Louis B. Mayer. And with that, to increase your stock holdings."

Eve started to say something, but Peter quickly cut her off. "Don't say nothin' yet. Give it some time."

She looked at Peter with tears in her eyes, thinking of the first time she ever saw him. How long ago, almost twelve years! Eve went to him and hugged him tenderly. He held her gently, each silently exchanging the friendship and affection they felt. Peter's eyes were now dewy, too.

"Dear wonderful Peter, I truly cherish you. And your proposal is the nicest, most rewarding, gratifying present ever offered to me. I don't even think I have to try to tell you what this means to me, you must know!"

Eve took his face in her hands and scrutinized him deeply. "Yes, you do!" She continued softly, almost sadly. "In my wildest ambitious dreams I never thought this could happen, and I am so grateful, and proud."

She wandered about the office, searching for the words. "I relish my work, my position. I feel so blessed to use what was given to me to further creativity, to guide talent. I just can't give up the actual contact. I can't lose the thrill of steering someone to really connect to a role, to breathe life into a soulless character. I am nourished and fulfilled when I see a person with potential develop and grow."

Eve knelt before him. "I'll gladly take on new responsibilities. I'll always be searching for material. And if I spot a weakness or a hole in any script, you know I'll open my big mouth. So, I don't need a new title—it's more important that I be able to keep in touch with my people." Her voice pleaded with him to understand.

Peter exhaled slowly, realizing this was a lost cause. He smiled at her. "Okay, have it your way. But at least make an old man happy and let him win one point. You will accept a bonus, won't you?"

Eve laughed, "As my Papa always says, 'I may have been born at night, but not last night.' I would be most appreciative of your generosity."

Eve kept rerunning the test scene and came to the same conclusion each time—Jenine should play opposite Marcello in *Slightly Crooked,* which had been given the green light the day it was read. The writer, Mickey Moralis, now considered Eve to be his guardian angel, and was eager to begin polishing the script as soon as the casting was done. Doug would produce, but Eve, as expected, would orchestrate the creative end from her office.

"But will Jenine do it?" Peter and Mo asked. "No question they would make the audiences cream their pants, but how about his part being so big? And he's younger!"

"I dare say Mickey can fix the role size problem. It could begin with her, show the boredom with her life and how much more she has to offer—switch to him, set up his character—and then the rest is really their story. He can handle it." Eve deliberated. "In my opinion, the age doesn't enter into the equation. No one thinks of how old Jenine Jasmine is, she's beyond that. Anyway, she doesn't look twenty-eight and Marcello seems older than, what, twenty? But it just doesn't matter. It's what's happening between their wills and in their heads—and in their groins—that counts. Quite frankly, there is such passion lurking, and I for one don't give a damn if it's lust or hate or both—I want to see it erupt. I guarantee you it will. And I have to imagine Jenine is smart enough to recognize everything I've said."

Indeed, Eve was correct! Jenine couldn't wait to match wits— and whatever else—with this arrogant street urchin. She sensed an inferno raging inside, waiting to unleash its fury on the world. And she wanted to be around, to provoke it, to clash with it, to use it, and to enjoy it.

Marcello Savilini was now Marc Saville. He had signed all the contracts, and with help had found a comfortable, furnished two-bedroom apartment not too far from the studio. His starting salary was $500 a week—he had tried not to show them how stunned, and tickled, he was.

However, he was no shrinking violet! As soon as the assistants started to brief him, explaining about the need for a similar-looking guy to act as a stand-in and another to be a stunt double, he thought of his friend.

"Do these dudes get paid enough?"

"Of course, within reason, naturally."

"Well, no use to fiddle-fuck around! I won't okay nobody 'cept my b—'cept my regular one from New York. He looks like my brother," Marc said boldly.

Oh, shit, he thought, I gotta call and tell Sal t'dye his hair—*rapido.*

"Does this—person—know how to box? Take falls? The production can't afford to have you do the hard stuff, you might get hurt!"

"Fer Christ's sake, we been fighting since we was born! He's been on his back more than a two-bit humper! His moniker's Salvadore Traconi. He can hang with me, he's sort of like my personal secretary."

Marcello Savilini was beginning to like being Marc Saville—a lot! As soon as Salvadore arrived, the two went looking for a car. Marcello had never owned an automobile, but Marc would. Fortunately, Marcello and Salvadore had learned to drive in New York when they had tried a turn as cabbies, which just hadn't worked out. The money was, well, barely okay, but it was so boring. Like many aspiring and broke young actors, they had gone to waiting on tables. The tips were good, especially from hungry females, and you could pocket the cash, no records.

"Find Beverly Drive on the map," Marc ordered, driving merrily along in his used 1948 yellow Buick convertible.

"Where do I look?" Salvadore was still travel weary and very confused.

"In Beverly Hills, you jerk-off!" Marc jabbed his finger at a general area on the map. "Jeez, Sal, get with it. Oh, that's your name now, Sal—uh—Tracy, yeah, Sal Tracy! Anyways, this guy at the studio said I oughta go to a store called Sy Devore's to buy some new duds. Can't go around lookin' like a hick, have t'look like a star! And you need somethin'.''

"Hey, easy, I ain't got enough moola. You better watch it, too, you're spendin' like it's goin' outta style."

"Relax, man, got it covered. Studio advanced some money, this MCA knows their stuff, I tell ya. I had t'join the actors union, the Screen Actors Guild. And that ain't cheap! I had t'have a car, only way t'get around out here. And I have t'dress good. They can always take it outta my salary. MCA thinks Utopia will redo my contract 'cause like I told ya, they already have a job fer me. How's about them apples?"

"Wow!"

"Did ya hear the salesman say this was Janet Leigh's car, and she hardly drove it, that's why it was such a steal. He said she bought it 'cause her boyfriend at the time, Arthur Loew Jr., had one. And get this, when they broke up, she sold it. I'd sure like t'put the wood to her!"

"You already worked with the sexiest skirt in town, that Jenine Jasmine. Whatta pair of hooters on that one!" Sal was almost drooling.

"Yeah, gotta admit, they came through loud and clear when we did that test. And she's doin' the flick, too! I know I turned her on. But she thinks she's such hot shit, I'm gonna make her beg fer it!"

The making of *Slightly Crooked* was an ocean of contention and required a degree in psychology to boot. The actual arena fight episodes were physically exacting, but those proved to be the easiest scenes for everyone to deal with. It was the regular scenes, the dialogue and dramatic scenes that were the battlefronts. The more formidable, the more cussed they became, the more exciting they were to see. Eve ended up being on the set more than she wanted, but the director was simply unable to cope with his two strong-minded stars.

Eve hoped to manipulate Jenine and Marc's rivalry, so perfect for the characters, keeping it alive and festering, until the resolution at the end. At that moment, when they actually came together, she expected the passion to detonate. And when the director said "cut, print," she had no doubt Marc would pick Jenine up, lips still locked and carry her to her trailer where they would consummate what had been incubating these many weeks.

Eve's imagination didn't stop there. She figured after the initial combustion the two would regroup at Jenine's place and continue to explore their—differences—far into the night.

Eve did know her people.

Chicago, Illinois
Saturday, July 8, 1950

Eve sat on the floor, her head on Mildred's lap. "I've been going round and round in my head, Mama, trying to put a perspective on this—development—in my life. You have been understanding, especially with me and my different approach to being a woman. But when any one of us had a problem, you would always be there, explaining about keeping a balance in our lives, weighing the good and the bad." Eve had recently endured her last miscarriage. Last because this was her third and Dr. Roberts had been forced to tie her fallopian tubes.

Mildred stroked Eve's forehead and listened.

"I've been trying to do like you said, Mama. So, on the plus side I'm in my chosen profession and succeeding—did you know Peter Padon told me if I were a man I could be head of the studio? It doesn't get any better than that!"

"I'm, we're so proud of you sweetheart."

"Two, my husband and I respect each other and work beautifully as teammates. And, now, don't be embarrassed, Mama, I know it's not a subject we've discussed much, but I think my generation is a little more open about it, sexually we are very compatible."

Eve glanced up and saw Mildred's face redden. "Oh, you are so sweet, Mama. You're blushing!" Eve had to hug her before continuing.

"It's all good stuff! Money is not a problem, our social life is full—" Eve's voice faltered. "I know this, I say it to myself, I say it to you, yet why do I feel like such a failure? Why do I seem so empty?"

"Has Douglas mentioned anything about any disappointment to you? Or acted differently toward you since, since you were ill?"

Eve went backward in time, searching for a hint of a change in Douglas's attitude. "No, not really," she said slowly. "Strange, sometimes I sense almost a feeling of relief from him. Oh, hell, I don't know, I don't know anything anymore. I'm so mixed up."

"Come here, my little girl." Mildred gathered Eve in her arms. "It's so good to hold you close again."

"Oh, Mama," Eve sobbed, "I'll never know that joy. I'll never be able to cuddle my baby!"

"Nonsense!" Mildred said adamantly. She had been rehearsing in her mind how she would deal with her daughter's dilemma. "There are hundreds, probably thousands, of children in this country, not to mention the world, who have no family. Think of what you could bring to a child who is alone. Think of a child, for whatever reason, surely not of its own doing, who has no one to give love to, or to be loved by."

Eve's thoughts immediately focused on a day almost nine years ago, when she had looked into a hospital nursery and said goodbye to an unknown newborn. Certainly the lives of the couple who had been denied their own baby had been gloriously blessed with the birth and adoption of—Eve didn't even know her name. And in return, their tiny gift would be surrounded with love and laughter and two adoring parents.

The message was crystal clear. Mama was absolutely right, though of course she didn't realize how closely her reasoning identified with her very own family. Mildred took a paper from her pocket. "I ran across this excerpt, I'm not sure if it's from a book or an article, but the poem moved me so, I saved it. I guess the good Lord had today in mind when he guided me to keep it.''

Eve read aloud.

"Not flesh of my flesh
Or bone of my bone,
But still the same,
My very own.
Now don't you forget
For just one minute
You didn't grow under my heart,
But in it!

The Adopted Family''

Eve's eyes were brimming. "Thank you, Mama. Thank you for listening. And thank you for making me realize that even if I don't have my own special someone, right now, I'll have my studio charges. God knows they do come to me for everything. And, Mama, I mean everything!''

Los Angeles, California
Saturday, July 5, 1950

"Remember the first day we met?'' Arthur asked Abe, between huffs and puffs. "Your folks—were having a three-way birthday party—''

"Breathe in, then expel the air as you make the effort, or it doesn't do you as much good,'' Abe scolded. "And, of course I remember.''

They were in the gym of Arthur's Bel-Air home. Abe had branched out from the health club and was now a personal trainer. Most everyone in the film industry wanted to keep in shape whether they were in front of the camera, behind it or in an office. There was an obsession in this city about being thin and staying trim.

Abe wasn't the only private workout instructor, Thad Thornton had been around for some time. Thad liked to mix a bit of gossip into his sessions, and some people enjoyed that exchange. Fortunately there was ample business for both. Abe appealed more to the younger set, he was the one who had made sure both Marc Saville and his double/stand-in Sal Tracy were muscle perfect for *Slightly Crooked.*

Arthur had started workouts with Abe as soon as he arrived in Los Angeles. When he decided to stay after a year, he had bought a large but tasteful estate in exclusive Bel-Air, complete with the obligatory Olympic-size swimming pool, north-south tennis court and gym. To keep his mother happy, he had asked her to come to California and decorate for him. That plan had appeased her when he'd moved into his apartment in Chicago and now it helped her get over his move to the West.

He had become noticeably social, entertaining often at his new home, and dating most of the eligible and attractive ladies in Los Angeles. And when a single gentleman was needed to round out a seating plan, he accommodated many of the city's hostesses. As his father had predicted, he was a favorite among females and males, and Burdsey & Co. prospered.

Arthur had spread his interests to include community matters as well. Burdsey & Co. made generous donations to charities and to cultural institutions. At the moment, Arthur was considering building a hospital in East Los Angeles, where there was a critical lack of medical facilities, and naming it to honor his father.

He had been quite selective and discreet with his sexual affairs. Arthur had no desire to become a second Howard Hughes, whose pursuits had become legendary, also infamous. Arthur didn't have a need to keep a scorecard of his conquests, that sort of encounter didn't turn him on. On the other hand, he certainly hadn't taken a vow of celibacy. Usually intimacies happened when both felt the same attractions stirring, when neither were looking for or expecting a commitment, when it was mostly a physical impulse, desired and enjoyed by two adults. Sometimes the pairing lasted for months. For the most part, when they went their separate ways, it was amicable and friendships remained intact. Once in a while, the breakup was literally a breakup—and some antique vases paid the price for the misunderstandings. Those few ladies had become caught up in their own interpretation of the relationship.

There had been only one public altercation and Arthur had been humiliated beyond belief. Notoriety was not his style. This particular young female had gone after him at Ciro's with a broken glass.

She'd probably had a bit too much champagne, or whatever, but something had obviously provoked her. The piece of glass did graze his forehead but hadn't penetrated deeply enough to require stitches or leave a scar. He had felt like a complete ass.

Naturally his buddy, Wade Colby, and Wade's friend, Jude Abavas, wouldn't let up on him. They kidded him unmercifully. One night Arthur was to go to Wade's house for dinner, the dates having been arranged for by Wade. That afternoon a gift was delivered to Arthur. When he opened the package, there was a set of boxing gloves with a note. "For your protection in case the girls get too tough tonight!"

Arthur arrived at Wade's with a leather whip, explaining, "This should keep me safe and keep everyone else on their good behavior!"

Maybe twice he had met someone who made him think this might be the end of his search for his soul mate. But nothing had ever materialized. Something always went awry, disappointing traits seemed to inevitably surface or wrong signals were sent or the ardor turned superficial. He was beginning to wonder if he was destined to remain a bachelor all of his life.

"So who is the lucky lady tonight?" Abe asked Arthur during a break from their routine.

"Gwen Somset. You met her as Gwen Clarke in Chicago at the Christmas party in '41, you remember—when we were still young and innocent!"

Abe thought a minute. "Oh, I think I know, tall, blond, kinda beanpole-like—no boobs?"

"That's the one! She married Harold Somset III, around '44. He wasn't in the war, bad eyes or something. But he was killed in a car accident sometime in '47. Too bad, nice guy. I saw Gwen briefly the last time I was home, and a week or so ago she called to say she had rented a beach house in Santa Monica for a month. Actually it's not too far from Wade's home."

Arthur seemed hesitant, scrounging around for the right words, then decided to just be forthright. "Is Eve feeling better? I heard she was pretty sick." His concern was obvious.

"Yeah, she's doing fine now physically. But she's been really down in the dumps. Although she's been a little brighter since she came back from seeing Mama."

"Are you sure she's okay about—my coming tonight? I don't want to have her upset in any way."

"Hell yes, she's okay about you coming!" Abe was quick to say. "You're family, you ought to know that by now, you dumb shit. And family can't miss our triple birthday celebration."

"Phil, should I bring Nick?" Abe had asked his psychiatrist as soon as the date for the party had been settled.

"What do you think?" Dr. Canfield preferred to let his patients try to reason out the answers to their questions. Then his input would guide them if they were completely or only partially off base.

Abe was quiet for a bit. "I'd say yes. One, he's been a friend of all of ours practically since we came here. It would be odd not to have him there."

Dr. Canfield nodded in agreement. "And…?"

"And," Abe continued, "even though Nick and I have been— sensible—about our relationship, and neither of us are overt in manner or conduct in any way, I have the feeling those dearest to us—know. Eve does for sure, I told her!"

"Does that bother you, about the others?"

Again Abe deliberated. "I don't think so, not the close ones. Mainly because I haven't noticed any change in their disposition toward me. We're like we've always been."

"What about acquaintances as opposed to family and real chums?"

"I wouldn't be wild about thcm knowing, their reactions could hurt, even affect our jobs. But somehow I don't believe they have a clue. First off, most are too wrapped up in themselves, and also both Nick and I haven't given anyone anything to notice."

Dr. Canfield laughed. "You don't need me, Abe. You are re- markably adjusted, and also, very insightful."

"Oh yes, I do, Phil! I was so confused and ignorant, even afraid when I came to you. You've helped me to understand and accept who I am."

It was true. Abe had gone along, sort of in limbo, for the first couple of years after Eve had found Dr. Canfield. Then a series of events combined to change the course of Abe's life.

On October 23, 1947, Congress had begun its hearings into

Communist influence in the movies. It was a devastating time; a time of loyalty oaths and McCarthyism; a chilling time in which free speech and the First Amendment were tossed out the window; a time when anti-Communist hysteria swept through Hollywood, the State Department, labor unions, academia and the armed forces.

Friendly witnesses like Gary Cooper and Ronald Reagan testified. Nineteen so-called unfriendly witnesses were subpoenaed, ten eventually testified but refused to discuss party affiliations or name party members. They became known as the Hollywood Ten and were found in contempt of Congress, fired from their jobs and sent to prison. But the contamination penetrated further. The disease had taken on diverse symptoms, one of which was thinly veiled anti-Semitism.

In November 1947, the film industry's leaders met at the Waldorf Astoria Hotel in New York. Their heritage was being attacked. But they had to survive. They condemned the actions of the Ten and said the studios would no longer knowingly employ any communists.

Michael Flanders had called Eve's office Monday, January 5, 1948, urgently requesting an appointment.

"Eve, I don't know what to do." Michael was distraught, pacing the floor, wringing his hands. His eyes burned red, his cheeks were hollowed.

"My God, what's happened?"

He flung himself on the couch and buried his head in his hands. "Eve, you're the only one I can talk to, the only one I can trust."

"What *is it,* Michael?"

"My contract renewal time is January 15."

"Yes, I know. You have nothing to worry about, it's already been approved." Eve was relieved, thinking that was the problem.

"My agent sent me a copy to sign, and—and—there was this affidavit attached."

"Oh, it's that stupid declaration! Everyone's acting like they're nuts, not just here, all over. Not much we can do, so just sign it and hope people regain their sanity soon."

"That's just it." Michael looked at Eve with tortured eyes. "I can't!"

"I don't understand."

Michael jumped up nervously and began roving around the room again. "When I came to New York City from a small suburb, just after the Depression, all I wanted to be was an actor. I hung out with other young hopefuls—writers, actors, would-be directors. None of us had any money, we only had our dreams. And none of us were political. We didn't give a damn about the left or right or middle."

Eve watched him intently.

"Some guy—or guys—came along and talked to us about an organization or something that believed things would be better if money and jobs were sort of spread around a little more equally. Hell, sounded good to us! Anything sounded good to us, couldn't be any worse! So we joined!"

"Oh, Michael!" Eve sighed sadly.

"I honest to God forgot about it. I started to get work, got married, came out here and lived happily ever after. Until now!"

He sat down dejectedly. "So much for Matthias Sigismeir! He now goes back to not having a pot to piss in. Maybe worse! Maybe prison!"

Eve straightened up sharply. "Who did you say?"

It was supposed to be a laugh, but it came out more like a strangled gasp. "Matthias Sigismeir, my real name! Isn't that a hoot? I legally changed it before I left New York. It didn't matter there, I barely had billing, anyway. But I thought if I got lucky out here, something like Michael Flanders would look better on the marquee."

Eve's mind was grinding feverishly.

Michael was lost in thoughts about his fallen castles in the air. "Funny, my wife came up with the name of Flanders. She had been reading some historical book and had been touched how the Flanders field poppy became the symbol of those who were killed in World War I." He snorted. "Now it can be the symbol of those killed in—the Purge of the Communists!"

"What signature did you use when you enlisted in this—this group?"

"Matthias Sigismeir, naturally. What else would I put down?"

"I think we might be able to squeak out of this." Eve jumped up excitedly.

Michael was completely bewildered.

"What name is on your driver's license, your voter registration and your passport?" Eve asked.

"Michael Flanders."

"So you can truthfully sign that non-Communist pledge because the man called Michael Flanders never belonged to the Communist party, never committed to any foreign doctrine, never participated in any unlawful assemblage. Isn't that correct?" Eve was relishing playing the lawyer now.

"Yes, but—"

"As long as you can put your John Henry on that slip of paper, you are in the clear. They're not going to go back and research the validity of every single person's background. They're after the ones who won't or really can't put their name on that dotted line. The ones whose documents prove their given identity, which the investigators already know. Yours prove that Michael Flanders is Michael Flanders—a name that is on no one's list!"

He was afraid to hope that this might work. "You really think I could—I mean—it would be acceptable?"

Eve chuckled. "We may be—stretching semantics a bit. But it's true. You *are* Michael Flanders! One thing in your favor, too, is that you've never been a political activist, and by God you better not start being one now! I understand they have pictures of a few people under suspicion attending union rallies, allegedly arousing the members against the studios. They could have been innocently asking a question on an issue, or wanting clarification of a clause in a contract—who knows? But in today's climate, I'm afraid they'll be sent to the lions."

"Christ, I've never even been to a union meeting," he muttered. "All that stuff was boring to me. I don't vote in their elections because I don't know who the candidates are!"

"Thank your lucky stars for that! Because if they had one little clue, any hint at all, linking you to some movement, they would seek and find and destroy Matthias Sigismeir!"

Michael looked at Eve with complete adoration. "I don't know what to say, how to thank you! You've just given me my life back, and saved my family from ruin. I'm forever in your debt."

I hope I didn't go too far today. But I had to do something. I couldn't just stand by and see a man's life shattered for no

good reason. And it isn't as if I protected some horrific mon-
ster. Michael wouldn't knowingly hurt a fly—he was just
caught up in a rotten time in our country. I'm truly glad the
idea came to me. I don't feel guilty at all about my partici-
pation. I just want it to work.

Unfortunately, most of the accused were not able to escape.
Their names were indelibly etched in the archives of HUAC, the
House Un-American Activities Committee, and in the headlines of
the print media. The biggest stars and directors in Hollywood—
Danny Kaye, Humphrey Bogart, Gene Kelly, John Huston, among
others—attempted to curb the threatening pandemonium, but were
ineffectual. They were babes-in-the-woods, naive political neo-
phytes, unprepared for the barrage of hostile queries from cold-
eyed seasoned reporters.

In June 1948, Abe arrived at Nick Larrington's house at the usual
exercise time, 6:30 p.m. Nick liked to work off the tension of the
day before a light supper and bed. Instead of greeting Abe in his
sweats and sneakers as he normally did, ready and eager to begin,
Nick was still in his office suit. His tie had been loosened, his shirt
looked wrinkled and messy, and he moved from the door slug-
gishly, almost shuffling.

Abe hesitated, wondering for a quick moment if he had somehow
mixed up the day. But he knew that wasn't the case. Then he
thought maybe he should just leave and not intrude, because obviously something was very wrong.

Nick saw his indecision and motioned for him to come in. As
Abe walked into the room, Nick slumped to the couch, his arms
dangling uselessly at his side.

Abe approached gingerly and sat in a chair facing Nick. That's
when he saw Nick's face. It had been a long time since Abe had
seen such pain.

They sat in silence. Finally, without raising his bowed head,
Nick mumbled in a hoarse whisper, "They killed my friend.
They—those bastards—they killed Saul. Those dirty sons of
bitches killed Saul."

Abe had heard Nick mention someone named Saul. Saul...?
Then he remembered, Saul Liberstein. Nick and Saul had been
school chums in San Francisco. Saul was a writer, started selling

stories to magazines, then segued to script writing. Nick came to Los Angeles and found his niche as a talent scout and Saul went back to his native New York and had become quite successful. They had stayed in touch and remained close. Abe was stunned! Some guys killed Saul? How terrible!

Abe wasn't sure if Nick wanted to talk. He decided to follow Nick's lead, so he quietly waited.

"Same as if they pulled the trigger," Nick growled eventually. "His wife—poor, poor Hannah—can you imagine? She found him...."

Nick began to sob. Abe didn't know what to do. He hurried to the kitchen and brought some ice water and Kleenex, then sat next to him on the couch.

Nick sipped, took the Kleenex Abe offered and got hold of himself somewhat. "I'm sorry—to behave like this. It's, it's such a shame—and a shock. Hannah called me, the phone was ringing when I drove into the garage."

He put the water down. "You know, I'm not a big drinker, but I think—I want a real drink now."

Abe quickly stood up. "I'll get it. What would you like?"

"I don't know, vodka maybe, and tonic."

"I'll join you. We both could use a little something."

Nick took a gulp when Abe handed him the glass, and made a face. "Whoever said vodka had no taste lied. No matter, as long as it dulls the heartache." He shook his head in disbelief. "How could anyone, *anyone,* do that?"

Nick saw Abe's bewilderment. "Forgive me, I'm not making any sense, am I?" He drew a deep breath and exhaled slowly. "A friend—what a joke—an ex-friend of Saul's, testified at one of the HUAC hearings, admitted to having been a Communist, and named eight other party members, including Saul Liberstein. Hell, it was years ago, he never did anything subversive, he was a young idealistic liberal."

Nick fortified himself with another swig. "Saul was not only fired, he was blacklisted from all work. His options were to go to jail or leave the country." He paused, thinking about his buddy. "Saul never was a—a fighter. He didn't like confrontation, just wanted everyone to get along and be nice and do his job. This had to cut his guts out. The family he loved so much—he must have felt he had disgraced, even betrayed them all. If only I had known about it sooner, if only I'd been there, maybe I could have st-stopped him!'' Nick beat the couch with his fist.

Alarmed, Abe put his arm around him to comfort him.

''He had a large life insurance policy. In his desperation—and craziness—he thought it would be better for his loved ones if, if he were dead. That's what the note said. 'I do this for you because I love you more than life and I can't bring any more shame to you. Now you will have enough to be comfortable. Please don't hate me too much, try to remember the good times, the happy years.' Oh, God—then he shot himself.''

Nick buried his head on Abe's shoulder and wept. And Abe wept with him, feeling his anguish, sharing his suffering. For the first time, Abe experienced a sense of oneness with someone other than family, a total involvement and immersion with someone, a loss of self and the discovery of a unity with someone. Abe knew, he would always be there for Nick.

I just reread what I wrote when Abe came home from the service and talked to me, worried and confused about his seemingly passive sexuality. I sounded as if I was quite sure of myself and of how to go about fixing this little problem. It's so simple to define one's answers regarding difficult questions when the subject is still abstract. And it's an unrelenting hurdle when the issue surfaces for real and in one's own backyard.

This afternoon Abe confided in me, he now is certain of his emotional direction. I have to be frank, my instinctive reaction was—denial. I didn't want to deal with his sexual preference. Then I saw his eyes—looking for the okay, searching for any sign of disapproval or withdrawal. But there was something else I saw—a serenity, a sense of security, of self. And I just knew he had found his soul mate and was very happy. How could I ask or want anything more from my dearest brother? Do I understand exactly? No, I don't. But why do I have to? What Abe and Ruth and I share hasn't been changed in any way, our love and caring have not been affected, and in the final analysis those are the only feelings that actually matter.

We didn't discuss this, but I'm sure Abe has spent many

*heartrending and complex hours with Dr. Canfield. I'm just
as positive he came to his discovery through honesty and clarity. And I'm proud of him, proud of his courage and strength,
proud of his dignity in meeting this challenge.*

Ruth plopped on her bed. "Come on up here, old girl!" she
called to Rosie. Rosie was almost ten but she still had a lot of
bounce. Ruth and Rosie settled down for a rest. "Oh, Rosie,
Mama's pooped, but the setup looks great, don't you think?"

Rosie answered by snuggling closer. "You'll see the whole tribe
tonight, babe," Ruth said, turning on her side so Rosie could curl
up in the curves of her tummy.

Ruth had the house to herself now. Yvonne still came daily, but
since there was no longer the need to watch over anyone, she had
gone to live with her sister. Abe had decided to get his own place
around the fall of 1948. She understood, and agreed, a young man
needed his own space, needed privacy. He hadn't taken Rosie with
him because he was away most of the day on appointments and
didn't think it was fair to leave a dog alone so much. But he popped
back often to get in some playtime.

For a while, after the war, she had been worried about Abe. He
didn't socialize as much as she thought someone his age should.
But then she let up. He wasn't moody, or brooding. He seemed
content to be wrapped up in his work and hang out with friends or
family or both. She guessed it was the difference in years, plus the
disparate outlooks of a woman and a man.

In all honesty, she was forced to admit, her attitude didn't vary
that much from Abe's. She had clung to the safety net as well. She
always knew her reason, but she had wondered what his was.

But the last, say three years, had seen a change for the better in
Ruth's life. Her articles about the people of Hollywood, the industry itself, the product generated, were accepted not only by the
movie magazines, but gradually by the newspapers and quality pe-
riodicals. She wrote at home—her old room became her office,
Abe's remained a guest room, and she took over Eve's bedroom.
Her novel hadn't found its way to pen and paper yet, it would have
to wait. It wasn't possible to do justice to both projects simultaneously, each demanded her total focus. She enjoyed the direction
her writing had taken now. An author's life was usually a solitary

one, but with this, she was meeting all sorts of interesting people and going to new and different places. It was fun and stimulating.

Harvey Hill had really helped her get started. He had introduced her to contacts at all the magazines and the other studios' publicity departments. Naturally he had been pleased when Ruth's pieces were accepted so well. In the beginning she had brought the material to him before submitting it, to be sure she was on the right track. He had few suggestions, her work was excellent and had its own distinctive style.

Sometimes their meetings had continued into the dinner hour. They were comfortable with that and with each other and appreciated their budding friendship. Harvey still nursed the wounds from an ugly divorce and wasn't looking for an entanglement. Which was very much in keeping with Ruth's frame of mind.

Harvey was forty-three, ten years older than Ruth, with salt-and-pepper hair and glasses. He stood five feet eleven inches and weighed 170 pounds. And he was very bright!

The telephone jangled in Ruth's ear. "Wh—oh—must have dozed off." The ringing persisted. "All right—wait a sec. Hello?"

Rosie inched her way up right under Ruth's chin. "Oh, hi, Harv! You won't believe this, I think Rosie is trying to talk to you, she's panting into the receiver."

She listened for a bit. "Sure, bring Kane with you. He and Rosie can hang out together. Don't leave him alone. See you soon." Kane was a seven-year-old black Labrador who was Rosie's best friend.

Ruth smiled and hugged Rosie. "You are having company tonight, too, old girl. Now each of us will have our boyfriend here."

Harvey and Ruth had settled into a happy, contented relationship. Each had gradually eased away from their barricade of fear and slowly, slowly begun to build a wall of trust. Neither felt the need yet to take the ultimate step of marriage. They were adults who could live with the way life was for now. Time would tell them if and when.

The growing belief in Harvey's personal integrity had chipped away at Ruth's nervous armor about physical closeness. With each passing month she felt less and less a captive, until finally, she was free. Free to be a whole woman again. Free to unleash the passion that had been enslaved all this time.

They had been at a screening of *Easter Parade* and were in a really happy mood. Ruth asked him in for a nightcap. Harvey played with Rosie while Ruth fixed their cocktails, and when they raised their glasses in a mock salute, their eyes met and each felt a connection—something! They had drawn close and kissed gently. Then their drinks were put aside and they held each other, their hands hesitantly investigating, roving. The touching sharpened. Ruth suddenly realized she wasn't putting her automatic sexual brakes on, and happily at last gave way to complete abandon. She pulled away reluctantly, with a promise to return quickly, and hurried to her room. The protective diaphragm had been bought after Ruth had her baby, but it had never been used. Until now. She undressed and slipped into the most alluring robe she had, which wasn't great but would have to do. She would go shopping soon, like tomorrow. She dimmed the lights, opened her door and called to him. Harvey walked, then ran to her.

"I've been so afraid," he whispered in her ear. "But I've wanted to love you for so long."

"Shh," Ruth breathed. "We've both served our time."

She slowly undressed him and led him to her bed. He opened her dressing gown and joined their bodies. The feel of him, the smell of him made Ruth shiver with delight. When he made them one she was in ecstasy, she never wanted him away from her. Even after they had reached their climax, she held him tight, until she felt him grow once more.

Both could trust again. And love again.

The Saturday evening of July 15, 1950, was a happy experience for everyone, even the birthday honorees.

Los Angeles, California
Sunday, July 27, 1958

Marc Saville was hot and tired and didn't feel too well. He knew better than to mix booze and pot, it was his own damn fault. He motioned to someone behind him, and presto, Sal Tracy was at his side.

"Ya okay?" Sal asked.

"My head hurts, my gut's out of whack, I got trouble with my 'roids, sure everything is fucking great!" Marc growled.

"I dint know."

"Get me some aspirin and a beer, would you?"

"Yeah, right away!" And Sal was off and running.

Marc sighed. Here he was, on a beautiful summer afternoon that should have been spent lounging around a pool or on the deck of some yacht, stuck in the Beverly Hilton Hotel's International Ballroom judging the finals of a California "Miss Teen" Beauty Pageant.

Then he thought of the young hopefuls anxiously awaiting their fate, not having a clue what was ahead for them even if they should come out the lucky winner. How many would have the talent, and/or the courage to see the opportunity through? Marc had to admit, his wasn't such a bad lot. Doing public appearances such as today was a small price to pay for the celebrity he had received!

The success of *Slightly Crooked,* released in 1951, had propelled Marc Saville into fame and fortune. The next project, *Time Bomb,* had the same blitzkrieg effect on the movie-going population. He wasn't only the teeny-boppers' heartthrob, women from age twenty to forty thought he would be nice to have around the house, too! And the guys didn't mind him because he was a "macho" kind of guy.

Everything had come up roses for Marc. And he had brought Sal right along with him. His contract had been rewritten three times; he was now earning ten thousand a week. And Sal earned five hundred a week from the studio, plus Marc paid him extra to be his permanent assistant.

All this had occurred despite the fact that times were changing in Hollywood. The legendary Louis B. Mayer, head of the biggest studio, Metro Goldwyn Mayer, was the first of the entertainment moguls to fall. Dore Schary replaced him. Television had already made its entrance, but each year it was progressively making deeper dents in the film industry's pocketbook.

So Marc Saville's rise in the last seven years was exceptionally remarkable. Marc and Sal shared a luxurious four-bedroom apartment, which allowed for privacy. They were happily lapping up the good life. Marc and Jenine Jasmine had indeed indulged their carnality. It was sort of an on-again, off-again relationship. They would take a break, the studio would reteam them, and that combative confrontation would reassert itself. Between each other, they hit on the biggest players in town, in the country, even in the world.

As hard as Marc played, however, that's how hard he worked. He liked what he did and he knew he was good. He also knew he had to keep growing, keep getting better if he was to have longevity in this business. And that's why he hung around Eve so much. Why he went to her classes when he wasn't actually shooting, why he watched how she carried herself, why he listened to everything she said not just to him, but to others as well. His street-smart shrewdness sensed Eve's talent, her awesome insight and clarity in regard to a role or a script, her gift as a born teacher. He was aware his wanting to learn had to be sincere; Eve could spot a phony in a flash. Fortunately for him, his was an honest desire.

Marc's attention was brought back to the present as the orchestra heralded the beginning of the event. These contestants had won their city competition, then the county, and now were vying for the state title of "Miss Teen." The county level had offered a small cash prize, but the state winner received a larger amount of money, and a screen test at Utopia Studios.

The girls paraded to the platform, walked out and back on the runway, and formed a column across the stage. Then individually, one by one, stepped to the microphone and introduced themselves to the audience and judges.

All of them were attractive and had nice figures. The crowd was loud and noisy in showing their appreciation of these particular attributes. A choice really boiled down to the balance of beauty and shape and—poise. Composure, personality, carriage all played an important factor in the final decision.

After a few, the lovelies were starting to blend into one, until about halfway through the line. Marc and the other three judges almost simultaneously straightened up and leaned forward when the next entry made her way to the microphone. The young woman's voice was alive and energetic.

"My name is Cassandra Hollister and I am from San Jose. I will be seventeen next month, but I finished my senior year of high school this past June." She shrugged and sort of laughed. "I guess the teachers wanted to get rid of me early, so they kept skipping me to the next grade."

The audience chuckled with her. Before she left, she added, "Thank you. Your warmth made me feel very much at ease."

Cassandra Hollister had strawberry-blond hair, a fresh, healthy face with extraordinary hazel eyes and a perfect nose, a very developed body and a wonderfully happy, innocent, open countenance. She exuded an aura of natural grace. Some of the other competitors might have been prettier, but they didn't have that certain indefinable—something.

The judges were unanimous, none of the others had come close to Cassandra Hollister. Marc kissed her softly in congratulating her, and surprisingly, felt a flutter in his groin. She definitely must have something, he thought.

Cassandra was dumbfounded by the turn of events. She hadn't particularly wanted to participate. But the school had selected her, and when she won the city contest, she went on to the county level, feeling a sense of responsibility. No one could have been more stunned than she at her county victory. Just for fun she had taken drama classes, and did sing in the school and church choir, but she hadn't entertained a thought of this as a career. If she could save enough money she had hoped to go to a state college, and maybe become a teacher. The award money would help toward that goal.

The pageant committee had agreed to put the winner up at the Hollywood Roosevelt Hotel until the promised screen test was done. The appointed chaperone of the committee brought her to Eve. For starters, Eve chose a scene that Eva Marie Saint did in *On the Waterfront.* Cassandra had seen the movie and identified with the character. Eve couldn't believe it, this girl was a natural— real, no affectations, just simple understanding. She was excited and decided to do the screen test right away, working only three days with her. Marc Saville had volunteered to do the test with her. Eve smiled to herself, sure that Marc's motives were not completely altruistic.

The result was better than Eve's highest expectation. The two of them jumped off the screen at you, they lit up the whole screening room. Cassandra Hollister was signed to a contract on Monday, August 11, 1958, four days before her seventeenth birthday.

Now came a problem. The committee chaperone was to stay until the test was done. The pageant extended this time until the outcome had been decided, but now their responsibility for Cassandra was over. Eve came up with the solution. The studio lured Yvonne Birshgeld out of semiretirement to be Cassandra's "companion." Yvonne would accompany her on the trip home, to help her pack her things, but mainly to assure her parents she would be in good hands and well protected.

Eve enlisted Ruth's help and found a small place between the studio and Ruth's. Yvonne would live in, cook and take care of the house, drive her until she became familiar with the surroundings and just generally watch over Cassandra, much as she had done when Eve first arrived in town.

Kathleen and Jim Hollister were flabbergasted. Their daughter was going to be an actress in Hollywood? Who would have ever guessed? Kathleen and Jim had no objections at all, they were just surprised. And very proud. They found themselves in the community limelight, too. There was even talk that when her first picture played in San Jose the city would declare a Cassandra Hollister Day and honor the three of them.

Cassandra was an only child and always a princess in her parents' eyes. They had little security, Jim was a car salesman whose salary was based strictly on commissions, so it could be feast or famine. Kathleen kept house and helped out by working part-time in a local restaurant. The youngster loved school, her classmates became her siblings. And homework and reading were her companions when she was alone at home.

Theirs was a fairly normal, lower-middle-class family. Cassandra went to Sunday school, another source for friends. She visited her grandparents for a week in the summertime. The three of them usually spent Christmas with one or the other set of grandparents. Both Kathleen and Jim came from large families, so Cassandra was in her glory with all the aunts and uncles and cousins.

The biggest fly in the ointment came during the "feast" part of Jim's job. If he'd had a good week, that could mean a celebration. Now and then it could be with the guys at work, in which case he might come home late with a load on, and then Jim and Kathleen would argue about that. Or, he might come home, pick up his wife, and together they would get high, then come home and would argue about—something. It always seemed to end with a fight. Cassandra could hear them and hated it. She'd pull the covers over her head to block out the words, and sometimes the sounds of blows and crying. More than once she heard the word *divorce!* Followed by "can't because of Cassie!"

No doubt Cassandra was adored. And despite the traumas that occasionally happened, she managed to emerge relatively unscathed. Maybe bruised a little, but her spirit seemed indestructible.

Marc Saville was very attracted to Cassandra, but he moved slowly, not his customary ''wham-bam-thank-you-ma'am'' style. He was intrigued by her, honestly ''turned on,'' and he didn't want to scare her away.

At Eve's suggestion, Utopia cast Cassandra in a supporting ingenue role, and she scored heavily. Marc kept pushing the studio to put them together in a movie. After one more fine performance by Cassandra, again in a secondary role, the studio, and Eve, gave the green light to star Marc Saville and Cassandra Hollister in a love story, *Fly With Love*. Shooting was to begin on Monday, February 16, 1959.

Los Angeles, California
Saturday, February 14, 1959

"Happy Anniversary" echoed in the beautiful Crystal Room of the Beverly Hills Hotel as a multitiered cake was wheeled toward Eve and Douglas Hassal's table. The two hundred guests raised their champagne glasses to toast the couple's seventeen years of marriage.

Eve looked magnificent in a black velvet gown that had long sleeves, a deep vee neckline with a straight, slim outline that highlighted her anniversary gift, a lustrous triple-strand pearl necklace and matching earrings from Tiffany's. She looked out at the sea of familiar faces. As her eyes wandered around the room, her keen perception saw the reflection of each person's unique bond to the couple, and she sensed the substance of those who were mainly linked to her. How full life was! She knew tonight was more than a celebration of one marriage, it was an anniversary of all their relationships. When she lifted her goblet in acknowledgment, she tried to embrace everyone, hoping they understood what she was implying and how she felt.

Peter Paddon and Mo Jeddu shook their heads in wonder. "Who woulda thought? Whatta gal!" Peter said.

"I know," Mo agreed. "Too bad John Darius hadn't waited a little longer to kick the bucket, he really liked Eve, and this is special."

"Yeah! But he saw enough, he knew she was a winner!"

Jenine Jasmine blew Mo a kiss as she danced by in the arms of Wade Colby. Wade and she had had their blanket drill and were now just good friends. Jenine liked Wade's beautiful wife and ex co-star, Penelope. She also liked his best friend and partner, Jude Abavas, a real hunk. But then Jude had gone and married that scuzzy bitch, Madge Moore. Jenine's gut instinct told her there was something weird going on in that one's head, even though God knows it was gorgeous.

At thirty-six, Jenine was still the hottest box office draw in town. She'd been married a few more times: a musician, a sports star, an author, even a business tycoon. The latter had given her some stock in one of his companies for a wedding present. But soon after, he was investigated by the Securities Exchange Commission for fraud and she had to testify in court. In the end, her stock was worth nothing.

"The fucking I got ain't worth the *fucking* I got!" Somehow she always managed to muddle through with the ever-present help of Eve and the studio. Eve was used to getting calls at three in the morning and talking Jenine out of suicide, or killing her then husband, or calling reporters with dirt on whoever had wronged her. Eve had great compassion for this endearing, talented, but troubled spirit.

In the thirteen years since moving to Los Angeles, Arthur Burdsey had perfected the cloak of concealment when around Eve. His mind had told him over and over and over that their lives had gone in different directions and that there was absolutely no connection except as family friends. But his heart was weak and skipped a beat every time he and Eve met. Which seemed to happen more often now than in the first few years. Douglas appeared to be the instigator, especially when Arthur's parents visited Los Angeles and more frequently after Arthur's marriage to Gwen Clark in 1954.

Tonight had been a particular challenge for Arthur, because when Eve's eyes had swept over the crowd, it struck him that those wondrous mirrors to her soul lingered and said something to him. But then he forced himself to shake off his obvious delusion and accept reality. Eve and Douglas had been married for seventeen years and were evidently on solid ground. He and Gwen had been husband and wife for five years, together for seven, and were very compatible. What in the hell was he thinking?

Ruth and Harvey Hill—yes, they had up and done it—had gotten married. And on New Year's Eve! Ruth's sometimes bizarre notions decided this timing was the ultimate purge of her one New Year's Eve fiasco. She could finally thumb her nose at that bastard and declare victory. It had taken a while, a long while, twelve years to be exact, before she and Harvey went to Las Vegas on December 31, 1952. She had struggled hard to forgive herself for the baby, to believe she even deserved a chance to live again. Eventually, with nurturing, she came to the realization there was nothing more she could do about the child, it was a loss she could never replace or repair and would have to endure. She could only hope and pray that the Lord had taken care of her little girl, and that she was loved and happy and protected.

Harvey had been quite wonderful when she had bared her past. He had understood her inner war, had been completely supportive. He assured her, and honestly so, that the question of being parents would be hers to answer. He was grateful his previous marriage had produced no offspring. "What a disaster that would have been for those poor kids!" he had ruefully laughed. But he would abide by Ruth's wishes. He just wanted to be with her, to love her, to share the rest of his life with her. Tonight they celebrated the love between Ruth's sister and brother-in-law.

"Who's that dancing with Mrs. Birshgeld?" Cassandra Hollister asked.

Marc Saville swiveled his head. "Oh, that's Abe, Eve's little— well, not so little—younger brother. Nice guy."

He held her closer as he spun her around. "I don't want to talk about anyone right now but you and me. God, you look so beautiful! Not that it's a surprise, you're more beautiful every time I see you."

Marc bent and nuzzled against her neck. "How I would love to see you when you wake up in the morning next to me. No makeup, just your soft skin to touch and—"

Cassandra was flustered. She pulled back a bit. "Uh, wasn't it nice of the studio to—to loan me this dress? Wardrobe made it for the last picture, and when I mentioned I wasn't sure what to wear tonight, they—they just said—"

"Oh, Cassie, I want you so bad," he whispered, brushing his lips gently from the back of her ear, along her throat. He felt her tremble.

"Let me take you away right now—to your place or mine. We could always say we were rehearsing our scenes for Monday's shoot."

Cassandra felt her control slipping and was frightened. She was a virgin, but she wasn't without emotion. She had necked and petted before, and had been aroused, but she was always able to be master of the situation. Now she wasn't so much in command, and she worried about what would probably happen. It was just over six months since that unprecedented day of the contest. Her life had done a complete 180-degree turn and Marc had been there every step of the way. It was impossible not to be infatuated with him, and she believed she was falling in love with him. Or had already fallen.

Marc's reputation was not exactly a secret. And Cassandra could not reconcile being "one of his girls." Because she knew she did care for him, it would hurt too much when this particular bee went on to suck another flower's ambrosia. But it was so hard to deny him, especially when her body was urging her to say yes.

Yvonne Birshgeld saved the day. As she and Abe glided by, she said quietly, "Cassie dear, I'm rather tired, and Abe offered to drive me home. I might suggest that you make it a fairly early night as well." She smiled warmly. "It's a big week coming up, for both of you."

That little break allowed Cassandra the opportunity to regain her composure, and Marc knew the moment was gone. He also knew Cassandra had almost caved in. His time would come—soon.

Marc was so worked up that as soon as he dropped Cassandra at her apartment, after a long and heated good-night kiss, he rushed home. Sal usually had a couple of "friends" around and tonight was no exception. Marc barely said hello. His need was great and he grabbed the nearest girl, who happened to be Gigi, and hurried her to his suite of rooms.

The shooting of *Fly With Love* was sheer enchantment, the easiest filming Eve and Douglas had ever undertaken. If a stranger walked on the set, he could immediately sense the ambience. The two leads set the tone and the crew participated. There were no egos, no tenseness. Just the joy of doing good work with gifted actors, accomplished craftsmen, and with the aura of love hovering in the air.

Utopia Studios was so excited by what they were seeing every night in the dailies, they decided to push for a holiday release. The two weeks of Christmas and New Year's were always big box office—children out of school, parents on vacation, family outings.

The preview ratings on *Fly With Love* were all excellent; the critics liked it, even though it was considered a "soft" movie; and the public embraced Hollywood's newest "young lovers."

There was a premiere and gala party for the opening on Friday, December 18, 1959. Cassandra could barely contain herself.

"Hold still, sweetheart!" Yvonne Birshgeld scolded. "How can I zip you up when you're prancing around like one of Santa's reindeer?"

"Oh, I'm sorry, Yvonne," Cassandra gushed. "It's—it's like a dream! I used to read in the movie magazines about these affairs, look at the pictures of the glamorous ladies in their gorgeous gowns and the handsome men in tuxedos. Now *I'm* going—and it's a film I'm *in*—and with a wonderful man!" She flounced about the room singing, "I've got the whole world in my hands, I've got the whole world in my hands."

Yvonne ran to catch her, finally zipped the dress, and then twirled her around. "Let me look at you." Yvonne's eyes were misty. "You look like a princess, Cassie, just exquisite."

The studio designer had found a bolt of chiffon and a bit of matching taffeta that were the color of Cassandra's hazel eyes. The folds of the copious chiffon skirt and the off-the-shoulder bodice of the gown were sprinkled with tiny gold beads that caught the light every time she moved. The taffeta was used as a broad sash, a cummerbund that accentuated her tiny waist and full round breasts. Eve had loaned her long yellow diamond earrings to complete the vision.

"Now, are you positive you are all right about being alone tonight?" Yvonne brought herself back to business.

"Of course! I am a big girl of eighteen and I am capable of taking care of myself."

"Well, I've warned the building's security to be alert. Ring them if you need anything. Oh, and don't forget to turn the Christmas tree lights off, lots of fires start that way."

Cassandra gave her a mocking glare. Yvonne sighed. "I know I'm a worrywart, I just feel badly about leaving you. But my sister isn't well and she does need me."

Cassandra went to Yvonne and gave her a hug. "Go and don't think about anything here! My folks went off a lot and I was able to fend for myself even then. Actually, this will be good for me, you spoil me too much. Now that I think about it, I don't want to see you until Monday morning—no, no, not a word! Monday morning and that is final! I'll tell security myself, so go—scoot!"

It was indeed a night of wonders for Cassandra Hollister. Marc was dazzled when he came for her, the big limousine arrived in front of the Egyptian Theater on Hollywood Boulevard and she was startled by the battery of lights and cameras, surprised by the cheering crowds. Marc held her arm tightly, guiding her through the maze of microphones and people. They sat next to Eve and Douglas, who were strutting like proud parents.

When the film started, Eve squeezed Cassandra's hand reassuringly, aware of how awesome it must be for someone to see themselves up there on a huge screen for the first time. No one had wanted Cassandra to see rushes, she was so natural they feared in her inexperience she might start thinking about how she looked or moved rather than just letting her actions flow honestly. In truth, she was mesmerized. She'd had no clue that what she had done on a stage on a small set would look anything like what she was seeing. It was as if she was watching someone else, someone in the movies, someone who was like a relative, but wasn't Cassandra Hollister. And she was having fun, going along in that make-believe world the same way she always had done before when she saw a film.

The after-dinner party was truly a gala event. The audience had been thoroughly entertained and expressed their feelings by their response. And all present sensed the magic, the chemistry of the film's two leading stars.

Cassandra and Marc were on top of the world. Congratulated, kissed, hugged, exhalted—they were Cinderella and Prince Charming.

"I think I'm tipsy, or else just high on the whole night!" Cassandra said giddily.

"Me, too!" Marc agreed. "But I know why I could jump over the moon."

He looked at her with adoration in his eyes. "It's because of you. It's because—Cassie I can't believe I'm saying this—I love you! I love you! I love you!"

He leaned toward her and kissed her softly. "The party's almost over. Why don't we split while we're still ahead."

In a trance, she nodded.

Neither spoke on the ride to Cassandra's apartment. Their hands touched and they could feel the electric current flowing through their veins. Quietly she opened her door, the guard must have been making his rounds on another floor since they didn't see him.

She dialed the in-house phone. "This is Cassandra Hollister. I am home and safe.'' A pause. "Yes, it was a wonderful evening. Thank you, good night.''

Cassandra didn't quite know what to do or say. Awkwardly she asked, "Would you like a drink? Or—''

Marc didn't let her finish. " I don't need nothing. Except you.''

He went to her and took her in his arms. "We'll dance to the beat of our hearts.'' Marc moved her slowly around the room, their bodies drawing nearer and nearer, melding into each other. He managed to lose his coat one sleeve at a time, shed his patent pumps, and loosen his tie and shirt, always keeping in motion. She yielded to his every lead as he guided them to the bedroom. Once inside, still swaying, he began to imperceptibly unzip her gown. Bit by bit she was revealed to him. He gazed, captivated by her beauty, and astounded by himself. His behavior had been so unusual. He had waited a year and a half for this moment. That had never ever happened to Marc Saville *or* Marcello Savilini.

Cassandra was in a dreamlike state, not knowing, not afraid, just floating with her feelings. Marc placed her cautiously on the bed and quickly undressed, almost shy to show himself fully yet. He carefully pulled off her stockings.

It was ridiculous, but he was actually nervous. He couldn't remember if he had ever made love to a virgin. She had never mentioned whether she was or wasn't, but he knew. He just knew!

Cassandra looked at him with her trusting eyes, and he was overcome with emotion. He lay beside her and began to touch her, starting at the top and continuing downward. Then his lips followed his fingers, leisurely, savoring each fresh discovery. He could feel her responding, uncoiling lazily like an awakening snake. They rubbed skin against skin, breast against breast, their flesh glistening now with the heat. Finally he lifted himself above her and probed. Very delicately he introduced himself and he was welcomed warmly. There was one point of resistance and she gasped in pain. But then he was embraced again, and he searched further. And further. Each breakthrough bringing spasms of quivering delight.

Marc had not experienced this style of passion before. This

wasn't merely the satisfying of a physical need. There was more here, fulfillment, compassion, sentiment—responsibility?

Both wanted to remain in the euphoric state they found themselves. But the energy strengthened and the glorious consummation arrived. They lay spent.

Gradually, he rolled on his side. "Do you need a blanket?" All of a sudden, he was very protective.

She nodded and he hurriedly undid the bed, and they slid beneath the covers. Cassandra hadn't said a word. She was deliriously happy and complete and didn't want anything to interfere with her fantasy world. She wanted only to be closeted with him, to hold and be held, to caress and be caressed.

Marc propped himself up on one elbow, and stared at her intensely. "Cassie, I've never said this to anyone before. I don't know if I've got the right stuff or not. I'm not sure I even know what it really means. I'm probably half-cocked and I don't care! What the hell, if you're willing to take a risk with me, I'm asking—will you marry me?"

Cassandra didn't hesitate for a second. "Of course I will, my darling."

"You're gonna what?" Sal Tracy yelled, his mouth drooping in disbelief. "What did the broad do to ya? That's a bad deal—like puttin' an umbrella up your ass and then openin' it!"

"Watch your mouth, Sal," Marc growled. "Or you can take a flying fuck pill and get out!" He paced the floor. "I know it's a shock, for me, too! But she's different. She's sweet and innocent and decent. She has class and maybe some of that'll rub off on me. Maybe she'll help me clean up my act—shit, she don't even know I got an act to clean up! And you know what? I bet it wouldn't matter to her if she did!"

Marc threw himself down on the couch. "Fix me a drink," he ordered. "I'm a better person when I'm with her. I talk better, I even think better. And she makes me feel better, in all ways."

Sal sat next to him, "I gave ya a double. Me, too!" He sighed. "So this is the end of us, huh? No more Marcello Savilini and Salvadore Traconi. *Finito!*"

"Don't be an *asino!* You're my *amico!* These will be your digs, you'll still be my right hand, we'll still hang out together. So don't sweat it!" Marc assured him.

"Fuck me blue! One virgin *shtup* and my buddy's gettin' hitched!"

CHAPTER

36

Los Angeles, California
Friday, June 17, 1960

"This is the damnedest idea, no one does costume parties anymore," Douglas protested. "That went out when the Hollywood Foreign Press stopped giving them and switched to the Golden Globe Awards instead. Only Jenine would think to bring them back!"

"You don't have much to complain about," Eve said wryly. "All you have to do is get into a bodysuit with fig leaves and hold your tummy in!" She laughed. "Adam and Eve wasn't such a bad idea of yours, no one will have trouble remembering my name, and the outfit is very comfortable. I wonder what they wore when it was cold."

Eve looked in the Bible. "Here it is, 'The Lord made them skins to clothe them.' Okay, I can wear my leopard cape. Looks like you're out of luck or out of character!"

He thought for a minute. "Oh, no, I'm not. Remember that poncho-type thing I bought in Argentina? It's leather. Now, where did I put that?"

The thought of going to Jenine's costume ball—actually she was giving herself a birthday party—as Adam and Eve had come to

Douglas when he was viewing the latest film of some possible new starlet. Between pictures he liked to experiment with these screen tests as he could do pretty much what he wanted. They weren't actual dialogue scenes, because Eve would then have been involved. Instead he would put the prospect in different costumes and settings to see what kind of excitement she could generate. Sometimes these vignettes became quite risqué and Douglas would share them with the studio executives. There was no censorship board to contend with since it was not for public release, so as producer Douglas could be more revealing, more provocative, more sexual. As a matter of fact, he and the others would more often than not end up with very itchy pants.

There were many grumblings and groans around town that night.

Cassandra had found an elegant empire gown, a replica of the early nineteenth-century French style, in the studio's vast wardrobe department.

''Do I look too fat?'' she asked Marc anxiously.

''You are so slendiferous, it wouldn't matter if you did. But you don't!''

Cassandra and Marc had been married January 1, 1960, at Eve and Douglas Hassal's home, with the blessings of everyone. The movie-going populace had adopted them as their own. When it was announced Cassandra was pregnant, the baby became their baby, the union was theirs. The women lived through Cassandra, picturing themselves Marc Saville's wife, the men were muscle-flexing Marc who was Cassandra Hollister's lord and master.

Fortunately, during the first picture when it was clear the two were gangbusters on the screen, Eve had found a book perfect for the reteaming of the couple. The studio had immediately put a writer on the story so it was ready to begin at the first of the year. Good timing! They finished *Only for You* before Cassandra started to show at all.

Marc looked dashing as Lady Cassandra's counterpart. With his *tonnelet,* stockings, high boots, flaring cape and rakish hat he was every inch the intrepid adventurer and nobleman.

Always on the alert, the powers that be made mental notes—a

historical swashbuckler saga should be put on the agenda for their two stars.

The affair actually turned out better than expected. Once there the guests cut loose and entered into the spirit of the theme with full and hardy participation. People's ingenuity had been put to the test, and it was surprising and interesting to see how imagination flourished.

Ruth and Harvey were hysterical as an aging Romeo and Juliet who had survived. Nick had rummaged around Western Costume and found a gargantuan monster costume, so he was Goliath to Abe's sandaled, toga-clad David, complete with slingshot. Which he used to good advantage during the evening, shooting little paper pellets.

Arthur and his wife Gwen were the Cowardly Lion and Dorothy, with dog Toto. Western Costume had provided many costumes for this particular soiree, but not the dog. He was real and kept getting loose and misbehaving, lifting his leg on everything or trying to mate with everyone's foot and ankle. It was hilarious, unless you were Gwen.

Wade Colby played King Arthur and fair Penelope his Lady Guinevere. "We should have made this film together before you retired, my darling," he said softly. "But I would have had to change the ending, I couldn't stand the thought of you having a Sir Lancelot!" She reached up to kiss him lovingly as he whirled her away.

The hostess was the betrayer Delilah. She had hired an actor from Central Casting to follow her around as her slave, carrying Samson's "head" on a large silver platter. Impressive, if a bit wicked. But that was Jenine.

Douglas had forgotten his earlier criticism and was having a good time. The two-olive vodka martinis were leaving their mark on him, making him more amorous than usual. He began to dwell on the segment he had seen that inspired the Adam and Eve garb for the party. The more he envisioned, the more lustful he became.

"Let's go home," Douglas urged Eve.

It was unexpected, he seemed to be enjoying himself, but it really didn't matter to her, so they left.

Eve and Douglas still occupied the third floor of the Hassal estate. Every time Eve had become pregnant, they had begun the search for their own home. But then, after the miscarriages, Eve had abandoned that dream. She redecorated their entire space and decided it was foolish to move. As they grew older, his parents had come to rely on them being there, especially Eve. For Eve had relieved Esther of most of the responsibilities of running the household.

They had complete seclusion and freedom, so there was never really any problem on that front. They understood it was comforting for Joseph and Esther to feel family were close by.

As soon as they were inside their domain, Douglas prepared his potent potion. "Now, woman, drink, as I order you." Obediently she bottomed up, wondering what game he was playing tonight.

"Before you ate the forbidden fruit and made me do the same, we wore no clothes at all and weren't even aware we were naked."

He undid their outfits and lead her to the oversize four-poster bed. "You are the serpent. You must tempt me if you can." He put a grape in her mouth and laid himself flat on the duvet.

Douglas's penchant for the erotic appealed to Eve's dramatic disposition, so she willingly joined in his ribald fantasies. Because she was petite she was able to slither along the top rail and then, head first, glide down the post nearest his face. She wormed her way lower, slowly, tantalizing him as her body passed over his eyes, his mouth, his chest, his stomach, toward his groin, thigh, legs. She pivoted and wiggled her way up, retracing her journey. He was hungering for her, but she eluded him until her lips reached his and she dropped the grape into his mouth.

"Now I am in command of your soul," she whispered with undisguised deviltry. She sat, trapping him inside of her, and bent her knees back like a jockey's. "I will ride you, my bucking bronco, you cannot throw me off."

He lurched, he plunged, every attempt feeding their frenzy. Until they both couldn't hold out any longer and tumbled into their own place of rapture.

Kent Cass Saville, soon to be nicknamed K.C., arrived at 6:06 a.m., Monday, October 10, 1960. He favored his mom, fair with strawberry-blonde hair. Eve and Douglas, quite appropriately, became his godparents. Cassandra saw how Eve cradled the baby so longingly and made a silent promise—to involve Eve with K.C. as much as was possible.

One of the many gifts Eve bestowed upon Kent Cass Saville was a puppy. "Every boy should have his own dog. And every family as well!"

Ruth and Harvey had been looking for a replacement for Kane and Rosie, both had been gone for a while, and it was time. A neighbor friend's bitch had whelped on September 18, a litter of five, two males and three females. No one was positive if she was a purebred yellow Labrador, and no one really cared because all the pups were the spitting image of mom. Absolutely adorable. Possession would take place October 30 when the puppy was six weeks old.

Ruth and Harvey picked a male, Jay for JFK. Eve chose a male for K.C., who became Spartacus. And then she couldn't resist, and besides, their house was empty now, too—she picked a female for her mother-in-law. Esther was ecstatic and gave it the name Lucy, after her favorite comedienne Lucille Ball. But Eve was not finished. She, too, felt the need for a cold little nose again and Lucy needed company, so Eve picked a female, too. So, Molly, as in *The Unsinkable Molly Brown,* joined the Hassal clan.

Cassandra and Marc were in the midst of their first interview session, with Prince K.C. reigning. Before they were married, they had found a charming French country-style house on San Ysidro Drive, northeast of Sunset Boulevard and Benedict Canyon. A low stone wall enclosed the property, with flagstone paving in the driveway and on the walkways. There was a small pool and pool house in the backyard surrounded by an expanse of lawn and a border of elm trees.

The inside was spacious but not lavishly large, very warm and cozy. It wasn't completely furnished yet, which suited the television camera crew and press photographers—more room for them.

"How does it feel to be a mom?" "Turn a bit to the right, please, Marc, I'm losing your eyes!" "What is the next project for you, Cassandra?" "Have *you* changed a diaper yet, Daddy?"

Cassandra and Marc took all the questions and posing in stride. She glowed with happiness, cherishing being a mother and wife, and grateful for being accepted and rewarded in her relatively new profession.

"I truly am at a loss for words to describe my joy. To love, and be loved, is the greatest gift a woman could have."

"I'm sorry, Cassandra," the television sound man interrupted. "We have to start again. I'm hearing a strange sound, almost like—snoring?"

K.C. was wide awake, his head bobbing around as he looked at all the people, so obviously it wasn't him. The room went quiet, trying to determine the source. This time everyone heard, "Ugh, ugh, phew, ugh, ugh, phew—"

Cassandra suddenly broke out laughing. She reached under her skirt, which had spread out on the couch, and disclosed Spartacus. He had snuggled down between the sofa pillows to be close to Cassandra and K.C. and then he'd drifted off to sleep.

The cameraman was beside himself. "I got it! I got it! I didn't turn the camera off. Oh, this is wonderful stuff!"

Utopia wasted no time. By January 1961, Cassandra and Marc were cast in a romantic comedy because the costume adventure tale wasn't quite ready. The studio had read the signs. The public was enthralled with idealistic attractive couples. For sure, John F. Kennedy was much more than a handsome face. But there was no denying, the people also pressed his lovely Jacqueline and then Caroline and John Jr. to their bosoms.

Marc and Cassandra and now K.C. had become Hollywood's "first family." So *A Ring for Her Finger* was rushed into production. Not a moment too soon! In mid-April, Cassandra told Eve she was two months pregnant again.

"Would you tell Mr. Padon and Mr. Jeddu for me? I'm scared they'll be mad at me!" Cassandra pleaded.

"Nonsense! How could anyone be mad at you, sweetheart," Eve told her troubled young protégée.

"Jesus Christ!" Mo Jeddu exploded. "Haven't those two ever heard of a diaphragm or a rubber or—or—something!"

Eve was trying to be diplomatic. She wanted to say it was none of his damn business so shut up! Instead, "But, Mo, they're young and in love and they want a family. You'll have this picture to release in the fall and by February or so, the script *and* Cassie will be ready to begin our colossal epic."

He looked a little mellower, so she continued. "Between *A Ring for Her Finger* and the big one, why don't we put Marc with Jenine again, but add a third element. She develops a serious disease and falls for the older more secure doctor, maybe Michael Flanders, and it becomes the battle between the wild young rogue and the safe, dependable man when—or if—she recovers."

"Who does she choose?" He was interested.

Eve laughed. "How should I know? Get someone cracking on it! And yes, I'll work with—you know what? There is a talented new writer I've been hearing about, Dorothy Scott is her name—"

"A woman?" Mo was startled.

"Why the hell not?" she retorted. "I'm a woman, and you don't seem to mind having me around."

"You're—you're different," he stammered, realizing his mistake.

"Hogwash! Margaret Booth is one of the most coveted editors at MGM. And she happens to be a *woman!*"

Mo knew he had already lost. "Okay—okay! See if she's available and/or interested."

Eve leaned over, satisfied, and kissed the top of his balding head. "Whatever you say, boss!"

As she was leaving, he yelled, "And find out how much she costs!" When the door was closed, he muttered to himself, "Probably thinks she's hot stuff and will try to rob us blind."

"Why does this shit always have to happen in the middle of the night? Don't they never come in the daytime? Having babies is a pain in the ass!'' Marc said, pacing the floor in the hospital waiting room. ''Oh, I apologize, Eve, my brain's on vacation, I guess.''

''I've heard it all before,'' Eve assured him. ''And you're right. Giving birth can be a very distressing experience.'' She paused, remembering Ruth, remembering her own heartaches. ''But worth every second of it. Look what your reward is!''

Marc had called Eve when Cassandra started having the pains, and she and Douglas met him at St. John's Hospital in Santa Monica. It seemed they had been there for days, but actually her labor was mercifully short. Four hours after arriving, the doctor came in to bring the latest bulletin.

''You have a healthy baby girl, six pounds ten ounces, and I believe she is going to take after her daddy, not quite as fair-skinned as Kent. You can all come and say a quick hello to Cassie and then she should rest. The nursery is on the way, if you just happen to want a peek.''

Dianne Eve Saville had come into the world at 7:04 a.m., Saturday, November 11, 1961.

''Sal, I'll stop by your place after we finish shooting. Okay?'' Marc quietly told his pal. ''You know what to do!''

Sal knowingly nodded his head and gave the ''gotcha'' signal.

Marc Saville was a happy man. He loved his wife, he enjoyed having the children, and he was extremely pleased with the way both of their careers were progressing. But he was also a thirty-year-old hot-blooded Italian. He had not known that toward the last two to three months of a woman's pregnancy it was difficult, and sometimes risky, for her to have intercourse. Also then for the first six weeks, at least, after the birth sex was not advised.

The first time around he was unpleasantly surprised by this discovery, but he abided by the rules. As long as he could. Then, he began to drop over to Sal's apartment on his way home from work. ''To just hang with the guys,'' Marc explained to Cassandra.

Naturally Sal had both guys—and dolls—as friends. And plenty of rooms in which to ''relax.'' Marijuana was in abundance as well.

With baby number two, Marc was prepared. When the time

came, he resumed his frequent visits to Sal's. Only now something new had been added, the latest fad, cocaine.

"This is hot shit!" Marc exclaimed as he snorted his first line on the initial night he returned.

"Sure beats cold diarrhea!" Sal laughed, glad to have his buddy back. He had instructed Marc on the procedure. He'd dumped the white powder on a flat mirrored surface, chopped the rock crystals as fine as possible with a razor blade, separated them into thin lines, and then taken a small straw and sniffed the powder from each track into alternating nostrils. It hadn't taken Marc long to catch on.

Marc's former "regular" was also pleased to see him again. Gigi was already high when he arrived that designated evening.

"Now that you're primed, Marc baby, let's party," she said seductively.

"Yeah, let's do that!"

Los Angeles, California
Monday, November 13, 1961

The old adage "It never rains but it pours" certainly proved itself once again. The Monday after Dianne Eve Saville was born, Joseph Hassal collapsed in his office and was rushed to the hospital. He had suffered a heart attack.

Douglas hurried immediately to his father's bedside while Eve raced home to get Esther. The doctor didn't want Esther to be alone, as she was a bit frail herself. The three of them waited anxiously while the emergency crew worked over the elder Hassal. He had already been hooked up to their complex machines and tests had begun to determine the extent of the damage.

"I'll try to explain what we know at this point in simple language," Dr. Grant Gaitworth began when he was finally able to see them. "First of all, *heart attack* is unfortunately a commonly used term, unfortunate because of its ambiguity. It doesn't specify the actual problem or the degree of severity."

He saw his small audience stiffen, preparing for the worst. "Clinically, Mr. Hassal's condition is known as coronary thrombosis. Treatment of practically all forms of heart disease has improved greatly in recent years, and the outlook for an active life afterward can be excellent. So if he responds well, and if he follows our guidelines, I am confident he will be home in roughly two weeks and will resume limited activity in a month. Remember the magic word—*if!*'' There was a collective sigh of relief.

He turned to Eve and Esther. ''I'm afraid you two will have the most difficult job. Once patients, especially men, start feeling better, they get the urge to return to their normal routines too soon. The male ego shifts into gear! And you have to be the heavies!''

Eve ran herself ragged getting the house readied. Wisely she decided to put in an elevator, which would ease the wear and tear from climbing the stairs. This would be helpful for Esther, too. She turned part of the basement into an exercise room when the doctor recommended supervised rhythmic workouts. And who better to orchestrate the regimen than Abe!

The studio also demanded Eve's energy and attention. They had liked what Dorothy Scott had written, so she was assigned to polish the epic film being readied for Cassandra and Marc. Naturally Eve was needed to oversee the project.

Plus she had to keep working with Jenine Jasmine on her current picture with Marc Saville, *A Woman's Choice.* Even though Jenine had all these years of experience now, Utopia still wanted Eve's proven instinct to make sure she stayed on track. And then there were the other projects and talent to be considered. The days were not long enough.

''What do you mean you're not coming with me?'' Arthur Burdsey asked his wife Gwen incredulously.

''I mean, I'm not going on a boring visit to sick old Mr. Hassal and then to a boring dinner with your mother and father.''

Arthur's voice was cold and flat. ''I see. And where *are* you going?''

''Patricia Kennedy Lawford asked me to a dinner party, I believe her brother Robert is in town. You could have come, but I told her you were busy. You always seem to be busy doing dull things with dull people.'' She looked at him defiantly.

Arthur finished tying his tie and putting his coat on in silence. He then turned and unemotionally confronted her. ''Gwen, you are a rich, spoiled brat. In the beginning of our relationship and marriage we seemed to be somewhat on the same wavelength, maybe because we played the roles well. Or perhaps Los Angeles was new to you and you liked meeting the varied circles I moved in, some of which included celebrities.''

She started to interrupt, ''I don't need—''

''Let me finish!'' Arthur said firmly. Gwen had never heard him use that tone of voice.

''You probably weren't married to Harold long enough—what was it, three years before he was killed—for reality to settle in. You're like the bouncing Ping-Pong ball in a singalong, you only want to hit the high points. Anytime a problem arises, or even when meeting a responsibility is required, suddenly you can't be bothered.''

Arthur sighed sadly. ''We don't share a common bond on—on anything, really. I knew it, I just didn't want to face it. It's my fault as well as yours, it was just too much trouble to upset the status quo.''

He went to her, kissed her lightly on the forehead. ''I'll bunk at Abe's place tonight. Tomorrow I'll go to a hotel, send for a few things until—''

Gwen cut him short. ''No! No, Arthur! I, I don't want to stay here. Tonight, of course. I mean—I mean—I don't want to live here.''

She walked away, unable to meet his eyes. ''I am going to try for once—believe it or not—to deal with the truth. You're right! I don't like unpleasant situations or negatives, never have. Why should I have to cope with trouble if I don't want to?''

''But that is called life and—''

''Now let me have my say!'' Gwen said sharply. ''I am who and what I am. Maybe it's shallow, so what? You say life has to have pain and sorrow along with joy. Well, I say it doesn't! I choose to ignore the darkness and go along my merry way.''

She whirled, showing no pretense. ''I don't like this house. I don't have fun in it, or with you anymore. I actually have been thinking about moving to Washington D.C. There's always something exciting happening there. I'm sorry I'm not what you need! And that you're not what I need. You're too normal for me, Arthur."

At the door, with bravado, she waved. *"Ciao!"*

Joseph Hassal was holding court in the sitting room off his bedroom. Abe had dropped by to discuss the exercise program he had worked out with the doctor. Alicia and Randall Burdsey and Arthur were escorted in by Douglas. Eve was still at the studio.

Greetings were exchanged, and Abe, unknowingly of course, asked, "Where's Gwen?" And before Arthur could say anything he innocently continued, "Heh, isn't your anniversary coming up soon? How are you planning to celebrate? I bet you have a special wingding planned!"

Arthur grimaced. Then, at least until he had time to explain, he turned his answer into a joke. "Oh, we'll probably make a date with Clarence Darrow or one of his lawyer descendants and discuss a property settlement."

Everyone chuckled at Arthur's sense of humor. But Douglas, in his canny way, sensed an underlying implication and made a mental note to check this out. He knew the wife was independently wealthy, and if there was trouble in paradise, he wanted to keep both sides open as options for future financing. More and more he was feeling his oats, and if the time came that Utopia didn't want to back one of his ideas, he wanted to be ready with his own financiers. Consoling a divorcée, if that should be the case, would not be too difficult to manage.

Los Angeles, California
Tuesday, December 26, 1961

"Hey, everybody! Guess what?" Sal said loudly, pretty much in his cups. "My boss, my *amico,* is thirty-one years young today. How about them apples? And because of that I got some extra special goods. My treat. I'm makin' up, 'case I forgot ya at Christmas!"

There had been a little celebration on the set for Marc's birthday, and he had stopped by Sal's for a pick-me-up before heading home. He finished work a bit earlier than usual, so he wasn't rushed. This was a hell of a lot more fun than that cake-and-coffee crap.

Marc arrived home about six and saw the message light on the telephone blinking. Because he was coming off a high, he was somewhat put out. "Everyone's so goddamn busy with the kids, can't even answer the fuckin' phone. Gotta get me a secretary in here!" he muttered.

It was Sal's voice. "Come right away, urgent!"

Marc had let himself in the front door. He figured Cassandra was upstairs nursing the baby or something and the nanny was probably in K.C.'s room. It was a cinch to go out quietly, with no one realizing he had even been home. He hurried back to Sal's.

He wondered what in the hell could be eating at that nitwit now? He hadn't left more than forty-five minutes ago, what kind of a jam could Sal have gotten into in that time?

Sal opened the door cautiously, making sure who it was first, and Marc slid inside.

"I—I—come back after I thought you'd be done. I was kinda flyin'—got some air." Sal was shaking and pale and Marc could barely hear him.

"She was layin' there—not movin', not talkin'—nothin'. I, I got closer and—and fer God's sake—she's dead." He began to cry. "I didn't know what t'do. I jus' called you."

Sal slumped into a chair and Marc looked to where he had pointed. Gigi was sprawled on the couch, vacant eyes staring at the ceiling. She had put her clothes back on, and a hypodermic needle was beside her with a rubber cord nearby.

Marc was stunned and suddenly very sober and straight.

He knew he had to think and act fast. Gigi had been fine when he left, stoned, but not in a stupor. This wasn't coke, this had to be the hard stuff, heroin. He cursed her, hell, he didn't know she was mainlining. *That* was something he had never done. But no one would believe him if he didn't have an alibi. It was perfectly logical his fingerprints would be all over, he often came by after work for a drink with his best friend and ex-roommate.

"Sal, listen t'me. You gotta get a hold of yourself. We know we didn't do this, so we gotta stand by each other. You covered?"

"Yeah, I walked to a joint couple blocks away. The bartender knows me, we chewed the fat, more people came in and we all were gabbing. He definitely saw me and wouldn't know the exact time I left, it got busy."

"Good!" Marc was forming a plan. "Go back there, slip in and mingle like you'd never left—you went to take a leak if they missed seeing you for a minute. Give me half an hour, then come home and call the police. Tell them you walked in and found her like that. Say she had a key because you hung out together. Remember, I left your place about four-forty-five. That's very important, *capiche?*"

Marc sped to Eve's house. "You have to be home, Eve, you just gotta be home!" he prayed out loud.

She was. "What a nice surprise! Doug is still at work, you know they had those night shots to get. You look as if you could use a drink, are you all right?"

Once they had their cocktails and were seated, he blurted out the whole story. Or almost the whole story.

"This was the first time I cheated, I don't know what came over me. I do stop by Sal's a lot, just to have a few laughs with the guys and a drink or two. Check up on him, you know. Sometimes he had girls there, but tonight, for some crazy reason, maybe my birthday and getting older, I don't know. It just happened. I didn't know anyone was into drugs. When my pal called for help, of course I came."

Marc stood up and nervously stamped around the room. "The problem is I was there when Sal left to go meet someone or something. When I walked into my house and got his message, no one saw me, no one. The police will figure out why they'll find my fingerprints on glasses, et cetera. But they will never believe I didn't have something to do with that poor girl's death, because no one saw me anywhere else around that time."

He knelt before Eve. "Unless I had been with you!"

She stared at him in disbelief.

"I swear I didn't kill her or cause her to die, I swear on my life. I just can't bear the thought of Cassie having to go through this nightmare."

Now it was Eve's turn to roam. She had listened in horror, wishing she could have turned the radio or television off because it was such a bad show. But this wasn't make believe, it was real. Her mind had gone in so many directions, down the paths of disgust, disappointment, denial, hatred, pity. At the boundary of each road, she would end up at the same place. What should she do?

Eve went to one of the bookshelves in the den and pulled out a Bible. "Swear on your children's lives you are not responsible in any way for what happened to that unfortunate young woman!"

Marc could do that in all honesty. She was convinced, at least about the tragic circumstances. Whether this was the first time he strayed, she wasn't sure. But regardless, she couldn't allow her sweet Cassandra to be hurt any more than was necessary. Even this way, it was going to be a calamitous blow.

"What time were you dismissed from the set?" Eve and Marc now had to concoct their story.

"Around three-thirty."

"And when did you leave your—friend's apartment?"

"About four-forty-five. And Gigi, that's her name, *was* her name—oh, shit—"

"Stop it! We have to think clearly!" Eve scolded. "She was alive then?"

Marc nodded. "Sal said he got back at five-forty-five and called me when he found her."

Eve was reconstructing her timing. "My last appointment was over a few minutes before five. Let me see, when I came in the house from the garage, the staff were on their break in their quarters, Esther and Joseph were in their rooms, so no one actually saw me, except my Molly, and she didn't bark, just jumped and wiggled."

She was creating the scenario, and this one could not afford any holes for someone to find.

"So," she continued, "you could have gone to your dressing room on the lot, showered, made a few calls—no—no calls. They could be checked. I know, you started to read the rough draft of *In Shining Armor*. You did get the papers?"

"Oh, yes!"

"Okay. Just before five you—wait a minute—you *have* to have gone by his apartment because your prints will be *fresh*."

The room was silent, heavy with suppositions.

Eve started again. "You didn't begin to read, you had already read it but did want to discuss your ideas. You, ah, know I never finish until five, so you dropped by to see your friend. About four-forty-five you drove back to the studio and caught me as I was getting into my car. That would explain why my secretary and the gate guard didn't see you. We decided you would follow me to my house and talk there. I let you in, so no one had to hear a doorbell—oh dear…''

''What?'' Marc asked in a panic.

''Everyone heard the chimes when you came in just now even though I did go to the door.''

He thought for a second. ''I only picked up, in my haste, part of the script and—and didn't realize it until we were halfway through our powwow. So I ran out to the car to get the rest and the door closed behind me. I had to ring to get back in. How's that?''

''It should work, I can't think of anything else that would be a problem.''

The two went over the details again and decided the strategy was sound.

''Now,'' Eve said, ''you should call Cassie and apologize. I'll get on the line, too, and tell her I'm sorry, but time got away from us when we started dissecting the story. She knows how involved I get. We even forgot it was your birthday—hope dinner was not spoiled—et cetera.''

Somberly, Eve faced Marc. ''You need to understand some things. I am not proud of my participation in this charade. And I am bitterly disappointed in your conduct. But I trust you didn't hurt that girl, and without an alibi the police would be forced to consider you a serious suspect thanks to circumstantial evidence. That would do no one any good, and only bring disgrace and humiliation upon your family and your profession.''

He bowed his head and quietly spoke. ''I have made some bad moves in my life. Certainly tonight was the worst. I am ashamed.'' His moist eyes sought hers. ''I don't know how to thank you. Not just for your help, but for believing in me. I'll try my damnedest not to let you down again.''

Eve sighed. The pages would be full tonight.

Cassandra and Marc were just finishing dinner when the sharp peal of the front doorbell echoed through the house. Marc stiffened.

''Who in the world could that be?'' Cassandra puzzled.

Margaret, their cook-housekeeper, walked hurriedly into the dining room. "A Detective Crow is here to see you, Mr. Saville."

"A detective? What's wrong, what's happened?" Cassandra was instantly apprehensive.

"I'm sure it's nothing to worry about, Cassie. I'll just go find out."

"I'm coming, too," she insisted.

A short, slight man in his forties was waiting in the living room. "Sorry to bother you, Mr. Saville—excuse me—and Mrs. Saville. I know it's late, but I need to ask you some questions. Routine—you know."

Marc was playing the scene perfectly.

"Sure, sit down. Would you like somethin' to drink?"

"No, no thank you. This shouldn't take long." Phil Crow eyed this beautiful couple and hoped to God he was right about that. They looked so young and happy. Sometimes this job stank.

"Do you know Sal Tracy, aka Salvadore Traconi?"

"Of course! He's my best friend, we—my God, is he all right?" Cassandra paled.

"He's fine, just fine!" the detective affirmed. "But there's been an accident at his apartment."

Marc was ready. "What kind of accident?"

Phil Crow wasn't in a hurry. "Were you at his place today?"

"Yes," Marc answered without hesitation. "I stopped by to have a birthday drink with my buddy and kill some time before seeing Eve. Eve Handel is an executive at Utopia."

"And what time would you say you got to his apartment and how long were you there?" Phil Crow asked.

Marc pretended to try to remember. "Ah—I finished at the studio around three-thirty, cleaned up. I knew it was too early for Eve, so I went to Sal's, stayed until, oh, quarter to five."

"Where can I find this Eve Handel?"

"At the studio. Unless you have to talk to her tonight?"

Cassandra spoke up. "Miss Handel's in-laws are not well. I think it could be a problem if you disturbed the house at this hour." She was beginning to be annoyed. "Don't you think it's about time you explained what is going on here?"

The detective continued at his own pace despite her outburst. "Were there other people at his place when you got there?"

"Yes, Sal always has a lot of people around—coming and going. Especially now, holidays and all!"

"Did that include women?"

Marc looked at Cassandra, then back to Phil Crow. "There were—girls—sometimes. Sal had several—lady friends—and so did the other guys."

"What about today?"

"There were one or two."

Phil Crow then became specific. "Was someone named Gigi present?"

Marc had thought out his answer carefully. "I saw Gigi for a little while, but she left before I did. I think I heard her say she had to meet someone and would be back later, something like that."

Cassandra kept looking at her husband intently. She was hearing some things that were new to her, and she wasn't sure she liked them.

"How often do you visit your friend?"

"It varies. He's my stand-in/double, so when we're working I might go by—maybe two or three times a week when we're done shooting. And sometimes I might not be there for days."

Cassandra was coming undone. "Why are you asking all these questions? What's wrong?"

"I'm sorry, Mrs. Saville—" Crow's voice was gentle "—I'm only doing my job. Just a few more minutes."

Now came the big one. "Are you into drugs, Mr. Saville?"

Marc knew he had to admit to some use of drugs, he was sure they already knew about Sal's contacts. If he completely lied here, they would be very suspicious about everything else. Even Eve's corroboration.

"I have—experimented—with marijuana."

"Cocaine?"

"Only on very few occasions."

"Heroin?" Phil Crow scrutinized Marc closely.

"Never!" Marc had no doubt he passed that test.

Cassandra was staring at this suddenly strange man. Dismayed by his revelations, relieved only a little they hadn't included heroin.

Detective Phil Crow put away his notebook. "That should do it for now. Forgive my intrusion. A young girl, Gigi Gereau, was found dead in Sal Tracy's living room—"

Cassandra gasped, "Oh, no—!"

Marc went over to support her.

Crow continued. "Obvious cause of death was an overdose of heroin. We just don't know if it was an accident, or if she was 'helped.'"

Cassandra's voice was almost inaudible. "You—you mean someone deliberately—"

"Not likely, Mrs. Saville," the detective said calmly. "But we have to examine everything and everyone. Time of death was between five-fifteen and five-thirty. Mr. Tracy is in the clear, he was seen at a nearby bar during that time. We will be talking with whoever was in that apartment today."

He rose to leave, and Marc walked him to the door. "If Miss Handel's story agrees with yours, we probably won't be bothering you again."

A few steps later he said quietly, "Sorry if I upset the applecart in there. I could tell the wife didn't know much about your friend's gatherings. A word of advice—put a lid on it!"

Eve and Marc's alibi invention did work. Luckily the press could only mention the names of the guests who frequented Sal Tracy's home. There were no speculations, however, because the police ruled "an accidental overdose." No one was held accountable.

The rumor mill did however churn up some interesting tidbits about the wild and torrid "happenings" surrounding Sal's apartment. He found himself quite in demand. But the new thrill-seekers were disappointed, because Sal had shut down his operation. In fact, he moved and just laid low. This had been too close a call. He needed time.

Marc succeeded in pacifying Cassandra's qualms. She had missed any possible sexual innuendoes, but had been disturbed at the drug implications. He painstakingly explained how this was a hang-over from his deprived years in New York. He was not addicted, he only did it haphazardly, if he was bogged down or worried. And he wouldn't do it again. This tragedy had opened his eyes, and he wanted no part of that culture. The drinking wasn't a problem, really, he only did that so Sal wouldn't feel abandoned altogether.

Very gradually their household returned to normal. Only now Marc came home directly from the studio. Cassandra suggested having Sal come for dinner at least once a week. That way he would feel a part of his old friend's family. They all settled into a comfortable lifestyle. At least for now.

39

Los Angeles, California
Tuesday, January 30, 1962

The Hollywood community was saddened by the news that Wade Colby had died of cancer. His condition had not been a secret, but it hadn't seemed possible that someone so young, so vital and full of joy and love could be gone from their lives—just like that.

Eve sent a note to Arthur, knowing how close he and Wade had been. She felt doubly bad for him, since she also heard of his pending divorce. Abe kept her informed on how Arthur was doing. Actually, he got the impression Arthur wasn't too upset about Gwen; the loss of Wade of course was another matter.

Douglas mentioned that he had run in to Gwen Clarke Burdsey a few times and reported she seemed very upbeat. She told him she had decided to keep a penthouse apartment in Los Angeles and buy a town house in Washington D.C. That way she wouldn't miss any action on either coast. "She does know how to live!" Douglas said that night at dinner.

"Depends how you define *live!*" Eve had retorted. "I don't know her well, but it sounds like such a shallow and superficial existence. But in all fairness, it could just be her way of working through the pain of the failed marriage."

"I don't know about that," Joseph Hassal joined in. "Artie's father, Randall, told me this Gwen had always been very social, liked to be on the 'inside.' You know, the newest club or the most exclusive shop or restaurant. Or the latest 'star' attraction. He said thank God she had money and Artie had plenty or they wouldn't have lasted as long as they did!"

"That's so unlike Artie," Eve said, more hotly than she intended. She imagined all eyes were staring at her, surprised by her intensity. "I mean, from what I've observed, I—it doesn't seem to fit his personality."

Her face felt hot and flushed, but in fact there was no need. No one else had noticed anything odd.

Eve couldn't sleep. Her mind wouldn't let go of the preparations for *In Shining Armor*. There were some scenes between Cassandra and Marc that weren't exactly right and she wanted everything perfect before filming began. Suddenly she sat up, confused. She wasn't sure if she had dreamed it—no—there it was again. A dog's howl, a woman's—what?—wail or scream. Then she identified where the sounds were coming from—the floor below! She shook Douglas awake, then bolted for the door, grabbing her robe on the way. The cries grew louder as she neared her in-laws' bedroom.

Eve flung open their door and saw Esther cradling her husband's upper body and shrieking, "Wake up! Wake up!"

Lucy was beside their bed, baying and barking. Molly had followed Eve and joined in the uproar.

"Doug call Emergency! Get the dogs out of here." Eve was shouting orders that Douglas obeyed almost in a robot mode.

Gently, Eve pried Esther loose and realized what she had feared was indeed true. Joseph Hassal was dead.

The next few weeks were horrendous. Esther was inconsolable, barely able to attend the services. And Douglas wasn't much help, he was wrestling with his own demons. The burden fell on Eve and her assistant plus the Hassal office. Utopia couldn't shut down operations, although they did close the afternoon of the funeral. Eve was beside herself as *In Shining Armor* was set to roll on March 5, less than two weeks away. She hadn't had as much time with the actors as she would have liked, but she could manage that as they went along. The writer and Eve had fixed the weak spots in the script that Eve had worried about, even with all the turmoil.

Randall and Alicia Burdsey flew out and stayed with Arthur. In the crowd at the Hassal home, Arthur spotted his soon to be ex-wife.

"What are you doing here?" he asked in disbelief.

"I came to pay my respects to the family," Gwen answered haughtily.

"But you didn't even—I mean—"

Douglas came up, interrupting, "Gwen, how good of you to come!" Then he noticed Arthur. "Ah, good of you both—"

Arthur explained. "I'm here with my parents. Gwen and I just happened to bump in to each other. My condolences, Doug. If you'll excuse me?" He backed off, wondering what the hell that was all about. He knew Gwen couldn't have cared less about Joseph or Esther Hassal. But Douglas and she must have become friends at some point. Obviously he had invited her.

Arthur was still engrossed when he felt a tap on his shoulder. Abe smiled. "Penny for your thoughts!"

Arthur laughed softly. "Not sure they're worth that much. How's everybody doing?"

"Not too bad, except for Esther. Your mom and dad are with her now. Come say hi to Eve."

Abe and Arthur approached Eve, who was just leaving Peter Padon and Nick Larrington.

"Oh, it's nice to see you, Artie. Thank you for being here. Your parents are a godsend for Esther, poor dear. She's comforted by them."

"I appreciated your note," Arthur said quietly.

"This year hasn't started off very well, has it," Eve said woefully.

"Well, let's hope that means 'Bad beginning, good ending.'"

"Artie, you're still our wonderful optimist. Don't ever change!" Eve sounded wistful. "Forgive me, I see some new arrivals, I'd better go. I don't know where Doug is."

Later in the evening, Eve, Ruth and Harvey, Abe and Nick were gathered in the small study. Esther had retired; Eve had hired a nurse to stay with her. Douglas was upstairs in their apartment, resting, she supposed.

"The drink tastes good," Eve sighed. "I like this, just us, together. I wish Mama and Papa had felt well enough to come, then it would have been really complete." She looked at her menage, feeling very grateful.

Ruth had pulled her life together after a shattering experience. And Abe had handled what could have been a real gauntlet with grace and nobility. Abe and Nick maintained their separate lives, separate homes. Their discreetness and behavior offered no openings for criticism or speculation. They gave unconditional friendship and caring to each other, and to those who were fortunate to also be called friends.

With a sharp pang Eve understood clearly what was missing. Arthur should have been in this circle. Not because of their earlier relationship but because he was part of the family, had been since that first day almost twenty-eight years ago. She exhaled sadly, knowing she had made that an impossibility. It would be too awkward in the Hassal home.

"What are you writing?" Douglas asked Eve, unexpectedly coming into her dressing room on a quiet Saturday morning in June.

"Oh, just jotting down some notes in my day-by-bay book before I forget."

"What kind of notes?" He was curious. "Let me see!"

She pulled back. "Really, Doug, it's nothing important, except to me. For instance, Friday, Cassie told me she wanted to take time off when *Shining Armor* is finished to be with the children more. I like to remember those little happenings in my loved ones' lives."

"God, how boring!"

"I told you it would be insignificant to anyone else." Eve was relieved it hadn't become an issue. The book demanded privacy, where she could visit times and people and thoughts in her life.

Douglas sat down on the cushioned stool opposite her chaise

lounge. "You know the picture goes on location next week to San Francisco. I want you to come."

Eve was surprised. "But, dear, that would be difficult. My appointment calendar is full, and your mother is really not doing—"

"Yes, yes," he cut in. "You can postpone the office and there's a nurse here for Mom."

She hesitated, so he continued.

"You know I like to fall asleep with you holding me against your breasts." Douglas put on his most appealing "lost little boy" look. "And you can make sure Cassie and Marc and the others are prepped for the next day."

Eve smiled indulgently. It was gratifying to feel needed, as a woman and as a professional. "We'll compromise. I'll take an afternoon five o'clock flight to San Francisco during the week, work with the cast—I don't think they'll need very much as we've been putting in a lot of time these past three months, spend the night, and come back to Los Angeles on an eight o'clock morning plane. That way I can check up on Esther and not have to cancel the studio, maybe only the last hour. I'll send my luggage up with you. How's that sound?"

He showed her right then and there how good it sounded.

The shooting in San Francisco went smoothly, except for one day. When Eve arrived on Wednesday, June 20, Douglas was pacing the floor of their suite at the Fairmont Hotel on top of Nob Hill.

"Oh, Eve, I'm glad you're here! We have a terrible problem. Cassie couldn't do the—"

"Calm down!" Eve said soothingly. "Now, what problem are we talking about?"

The company was filming in pastoral Muir Woods, located in beautiful Golden Gate Park, which was substituting for a forest in medieval England. Lady Anne, played by Cassandra, had been rescued from her evil abductors by Sir Lawrence, played by Marc, and his men. Douglas had explained that the scene in question had Lady Anne attempting to help prepare a meal where the group had stopped for the night, and at the same time parrying Sir Lawrence's increasingly amorous innuendoes.

"Cassie knew that scene perfectly and was very effective in rehearsal, capturing every nuance," Eve said.

"She sure didn't show it this afternoon!"

"What did you have her doing that was so different? We had staged it. Naturally we had to imagine the actual setting and props—ah—"

"What?" Douglas asked impatiently.

"How much rehearsing did you do?" Eve demanded.

"We were losing light, so not much. I told the director she was ready!"

"Emotionally ready, yes! But not with the actual terrain and props, which would be completely foreign to a woman of today. Lady Anne could be a bit clumsy because one of her stature would not be doing scullery chores."

Eve thought for a minute. "Call the prop man and have him bring over every single thing Cassie has to handle, and right away. Call the cinematographer, ask him to mark out the moves of the camera in our living room, and distance them accurately. The director should be here, too. I'll call Cassie and ask her if she would come up when everything is ready, and I'll tell Marc to stand by, we'll let him know when we need him!"

Cassie arrived, tearfully apologetic. "I feel so bad. I've let everyone down."

"Nonsense!" Eve assured her nervous ward. "I'm going to tell you all a story which I think will be informative and I hope useful. You've heard of Maria Ouspenskaya, the Russian actress who came from the Moscow Art Theater and studied with Stanislavsky?"

Her audience responded with decisive affirmatives. "Brilliant performer!" "Nominated at least twice in the late 1930s, I believe!" "Read about how wonderful she was!"

"Good!" Eve continued, knowing she had everyone's full attention. "About a year after I started to work for both Pad-Dar Pictures and Status Films, Peter Padon asked me to a small dinner party at his home. The guest list included some pretty big guns in Hollywood, like the producer Joe Mankiewicz, Charles Boyer, Mary Astor. I was seated next to the well-known director Frank Borzage, and I was like a kid in a candy store being in the midst of all this talent.

"Mr. Borzage politely asked about my position. I explained I worked with actors, trying to help them find the core of a role and build the character around that center, while still maintaining their own personality.

"He looked at me—I remember he had piercing dark eyes—and said, 'I'm going to share with you a lesson I just recently learned myself because I feel it will be valuable.' Believe me, I was all ears.

"He told me he'd been directing Maria Ouspenskaya in a busy scene—she was cooking, going back and forth from stove to sink, and listening to what was going on between Jimmy Stewart and Margaret Sullavan. When Mr. Borzage saw the dailies, the scene just wasn't right, Maria wasn't involved with Jimmy and Margaret as she should have been. He was terribly disappointed and knew they had to redo it, but he wasn't sure how to make it better.

"As luck would have it, Mr. Borzage lunched with Paul Muni the next day and mentioned his dilemma. He asked if he could see the dailies and of course Borzage said yes. The minute they were finished Muni told him what was wrong. He painstakingly defined how an actor must have the moves and actions rehearsed so their mind doesn't even think about them, because then the mind is free to concentrate on the important stuff, such as the intent of the scene. Muni told Borzage that if he took Maria to the set and let her practice the routine for an hour, he would have what he needed."

"It's a lesson I haven't forgotten," Eve concluded. "Cassie will go over each piece of business, each move until they become secondary, and then Marc will come down and they'll play the scene. I guarantee the performances will be right on the money."

Los Angeles, California
Sunday, August 5, 1962

Eve and Douglas sat in shock. Lucy and Molly were curled up by Eve's feet, not asleep, their big, forlorn eyes looking at her for some sign that everything was going to be all right. Their world seemed very confused and shaky at this point.

Dr. Gaitworth was speaking. "There was nothing any of us could have done differently."

Eve stifled a sob. "Believe me, Mrs. Hassal, no daughter could have been more attentive or caring. Esther loved you deeply. And Douglas, you know her universe always revolved around you. But after her husband left us, I believe she just gave up and waited to join him."

"May—maybe if I could have given her a grandchild she..." Eve couldn't go on.

"Come, now! You know better than that. Both of you, just be grateful the Lord was merciful and took her peacefully in her sleep."

Ruth and Harvey were ushered in. "Oh, are we interrupting? We came as soon as we got Eve's call!" Ruth said.

"No, no, I was just leaving," the doctor explained. "My work is done. Do you need a sedative or anything before I go?"

Eve shook her head. "Thank you for your help, Dr. Gaitworth. Harv, would you see the doctor out, please?"

"Call me—whenever—if you have any questions. I will take care of all the details, papers, et cetera."

Abe walked back in with Harvey and immediately hugged Eve and gave Douglas's shoulder a touch of support. He seemed edgy, unsure, and finally motioned for Ruth to follow him to the other room.

Ruth and Abe returned in a few minutes. "Abe heard some disturbing news on the car radio when he was driving over. No sense to try to spare you. Believe me, this will be headlines in every country." She hesitated. "Marilyn Monroe was found dead early this morning, apparently a suicide."

Eve's and Douglas's heads jerked upright. "Are you serious?" Eve was incredulous. "What am I saying? Of course you are! You couldn't joke about—my God in heaven, what is going on?"

Douglas was spluttering to himself, to everyone, "How could this happen? To me?" He seemed abnormally bewildered. "She had—the Kennedys were going—I was hoping to produce her next..."

Abe and Harvey went over and helped him out of the chair. "Maybe you should take it easy, lie down for a bit." Harvey whispered to Eve and Ruth, "He's not making much sense, babbling away. It's been too much all at once, I guess. We'll bring him to his room, hopefully he can relax some."

The two sisters sat dejectedly until Abe and Harvey rejoined them. The phone rang incessantly, the butler took all of the messages.

Abe asked Eve, "Do you know anything about a project Doug had going with Marilyn Monroe? He kept repeating what he had started to mumble down here."

"Not really," she answered. "He mentioned once or twice that Gwen, Artie's ex, had close ties to the Kennedys and subsequently to Marilyn, but I never heard of anything concrete. He was probably just reacting to the fact that now—there is no way anything could ever come of this possible connection.''

Eve rose and went to get a glass of water. ''I don't know, this kind of day, these random deaths, makes one feel so helpless—so mixed up. I barely knew Marilyn Monroe, but I feel such sadness for the loss of this young—what was she, thirty-five, thirty-six?— woman. She was obviously a troubled soul. And on the other hand, Esther, with whom I lived in the same house for twenty years, naturally I have a heavy heart from her death, but not one filled with the same sense of doom and gloom.''

Ruth crossed to Eve. ''You're not the only one having blurred emotions. I don't think it's an unsolvable enigma. Dear Esther had lived a rich, full life. She had been loved and appreciated her blessings, which included you, my sweet Eve. She was loving to everyone but she was frail, and missed Joe. I think she was weary. Thank God she didn't suffer.''

Eve nodded in understanding. Ruth went on. ''But Marilyn Monroe, we'll never know what her life might have become, what heights she might have reached. Maybe it's just as well we won't know what depths she might have endured.''

Ruth walked restlessly around the room. ''My gut says there is much more to this story. I wonder if any of us will know the truth in our lifetime. Or ever?''

Once again, Eve's journal for the day would be filled.

Los Angeles, California
Tuesday, January 1, 1963

Douglas stood up and clinked his glass for attention. "A toast to two of the 'beautiful people' on their third anniversary. Cassie and Marc were married in my house and I'm proud to honor them again on their special day. Congratulations!"

Eve didn't look directly at her husband, she fiddled with her napkin, trying to camouflage her feelings.

Was she being overly sensitive? Why hadn't he said "our" home? She might as well face it, he had been acting strange lately. Like a lieutenant who suddenly became king and reigned supreme, relishing the role. When had she first noticed this change? Could he be going through a midlife crisis?

One incident really stood out in her mind. When Douglas had seen Sal Tracy's name on Cassandra and Marc's guest list for tonight's dinner, he had a fit.

"Isn't that the schnook who had a drug-overdose murder at his place?"

"It wasn't a murder, it was an accident," Eve had carefully explained.

"I don't care, I won't have him in my house!"

''But it's Cassie and Marc's party, not ours, and Sal is their friend.''

''Doesn't matter! You tell them no drug dealer is welcome here!'' He had stamped out in a huff.

Eve hadn't wanted to push the issue—she was still uneasy about the position Marc had put her in. So with as much tact as possible she had suggested to Cassandra and Marc that perhaps it might be awkward if Marc's stand-in was invited and not Cassandra's stand-in, which could open up a whole can of peas about the rest of the people they worked with in their pictures, and the number could get out of hand.

Marc caught on immediately and recognized that Eve was uncomfortable about having to bring the subject up at all. So Douglas had to be the one who objected. What a prick! But he certainly owed Eve, and he let her off the hook quickly.

''Ah, sure, never thought about that. Sal will understand—not his bag, anyway—too fancy!''

Eve decided that Douglas's ''attitude'' had begun a month after his mother's and Marilyn Monroe's deaths. Without his parents, he had become the sole possessor of the family estate. Except for Eve. California was a community-property state, so what would be the reason to separate their holdings?

When Eve had casually asked him about his vague allusion to some Monroe film deal, he had curtly denied making any such reference, suggesting they had all misunderstood him in their agitated states.

But Eve knew that wasn't the case and wondered what the mystery was all about. Something was definitely not right.

Cassandra was very happy. She was relishing the time with her children, who were simply adorable. K.C. was a precocious two-year-old who kept her hopping and Dianne was a one-year-old cuddle-bug. She had done only a handful of interviews and gallery photo sessions since *Shining Armor* wrapped in July. Cassandra was gloriously free, at least until closer to the release time of the picture.

Marc had just started a new film in December 1962. This one

had a Korean War background, a mostly male cast with only a few small roles for women. It was a departure from the norm because the studio thought it would be smart to broaden Marc's base. And he was delighted at the opportunity to expand his range as an actor. He also liked the regimen of keeping himself in tip-top shape and doing "guy" things. So both Cassandra and Marc were in a fairly good place on their third anniversary

Around the first of April, the baby developed eczema in her ear and was teething badly. Cassandra was by her side, holding her, caring for her night and day. Unfortunately K.C. caught the flu from one of his playmates at the same time, and Cassandra had two sick, cranky little ones on her hands.

Everything returned to almost normal in about ten days. But when Cassandra let down a bit, she was so tired she went to pieces. She became sick to her stomach, she was cold, hot, dizzy, and cried for no reason. Luckily with treatment and medication she recouped enough to go to the three big openings of *In Shining Armor*—New York, Chicago and Los Angeles. The studio had arranged time away from Marc's current shooting schedule. It was important for the distributors that the picture had blockbuster premieres to launch the movie's early summer release. The tour was a whirlwind of print interviews, television and radio appearances, receptions, plus the gala evening in each city.

For a woman these were grueling trips—change of wardrobe at least three times a day so as not to duplicate her look for competing media, and her hair and makeup always had to be kept in perfect condition. Both men and women were faced with answering the same questions in interview after interview, while trying to make those answers sound fresh and energetic. Cassandra and Marc were naturally enthusiastic so they met these challenges well. But it was exhausting!

The morning after she arrived home, Cassandra collapsed. She suffered violent pains in her stomach and felt weak and feverish. The doctor determined that the flu had settled in her liver and that if she wasn't careful it would evolve into jaundice.

When the children were down, Cassandra had slept in their

rooms so Marc wouldn't be disturbed in the night. Then when she fell ill the first time around, Marc had stayed at his studio dressing room so she had some peace and quiet. And so that he wasn't exposed to anything contagious. Utopia had to pay heavy insurance rates to protect its budget if a star's health problem shut down a production.

Now with the latest development, Marc went back to his dressing room during the week. Cassandra needed absolute rest in calm surroundings, so another nanny was hired. She now had no worries about the care of her little ones, she just enjoyed them whenever she was up to it.

Slowly, way too slowly for Cassandra, who was champing at the bit, the penicillin and vitamin shots began to take effect and she regained her strength.

Marc was feeling a mite sorry for himself. He had been on the job since last December. His home life had been turned topsy-turvy for more than two months now. Sal could see his boss was becoming restless and suggested Marc come and crash at his pad for a day or so.

"We been on our good behavior fer a long time. Mebbe we need to cut loose."

"You could be right!" Marc was definitely in need of something. "But no crack! Don't want that scene again! Little pot would taste pretty good, though."

Sal added the dessert—he invited a couple of the girls who played nurses in the picture to come for a drink and a bite of dinner.

"You're right, Sal, this is good," Marc said, thanking his friend. "I gotta let go once in a while, I was starting to think I'd lost my touch. What was that old song? 'Now, this is number one and I've got her on the run, lay her down, roll her over, do it again. Roll her over, in the clover, lay her down, roll her over, do it again. Now this is number two—' I do believe, Sal ol' buddy, it's time to switch partners and I'll get me number two—"

Cassandra was humming to herself as she drove toward Utopia. She was one hundred percent better, the doctor had just given her the go-ahead to resume all regular activities, and she was on her way to tell Marc to come home, she wasn't "off limits" anymore. She would let the second nanny go and life would return to normal. Thank goodness!

She knew his movie was supposed to finish tomorrow, Friday June 7, so she thought it would be fun to pop in and say goodbye to the crew on the set and tell her husband the good news.

First Cassandra went by Eve's office to give her a hug. Eve was relieved to see her looking so well, it had been a nerve-racking time. Eve had tried to fill in for Cassandra with the children as much as she was able.

When Cassandra walked onto the set, Marc was not in sight. The assistant director said he was probably in his dressing room because there had been a couple of shots where he wasn't needed.

"Shall I call and check?" the A.D. asked.

"No, no! I'll go over and if he isn't there he's probably in the commissary. I'll see you all later!" she waved gaily.

She was almost at Marc's when she spotted Sal coming toward her carrying a large paper bag.

"Hi!" she called out.

Sal looked up and turned white.

"Wh-what are ya—doin'—*here?*" He was completely non-plussed. "I mean—how are ya?"

"Fine, thank you Sal," she said as she moved to the door.

"Where ya goin'?" He was panicked.

"Well, I am about to go into my husband's dressing room and give him a big fat kiss. Is that okay with you?" Sal seemed to be goofier than usual, poor guy.

"No! I mean—natch!" He thought quickly. And then yelled, "Or course, Cassie, you can go into your husband's dressing room!"

"Thanks for the approval!" Cassandra swung open the door, took two steps and then stopped dead in her tracks.

The tableau before her was unfolding in slow motion. She saw the nude rear view of a female going into another room. Then she focused on a male figure desperately pulling up a pair of pants over his naked torso. Her eyes traveled around the room—clothes scattered willy-nilly, half-filled glasses on a table, an ashtray with the remnants of some kind of cigarettes—ending on Sal, openmouthed and foolishly still holding his paper bag of goodies.

A strangled cry escaped from Cassandra before she turned and ran. She kept on running, threw herself into her car and tore out of the studio parking lot. Tears were streaming down her face, wrenching sobs tore at her insides. She drove without looking, without knowing where she was—speeding dangerously along the twisting and precipitous Mulholland Drive on the top of the Santa Monica Mountain Range. She didn't care if she made the turns or not, subconsciously she wished she would miss and put an end to this pit of hell that was her soul.

Suddenly, from the silent screaming in her head, a small voice cut through the uproar. "Where's Mommy? I want Mommy!" It was Kent.

Weeping came from another source. "Ma-ma!" Dianne blurted out.

A masculine tone. "Mommy had to go away—for a long, long time. But Daddy's here."

Oh, no! She pulled herself together. Oh, no! She wasn't going to give him her children. Desperate, she barely hung on for the next curve and struggled to get the car and herself under control.

Cassandra sped down Benedict Canyon and pulled into the driveway of the closest familiar house, which happened to be the Hassals'. The butler was obviously surprised to see Cassandra Hollister at this hour and in this state, but with his typical deadpan expression led her to the telephone in the study.

Cassandra first called the Bel-Air Hotel, where luckily they had a bungalow available. Then she called her house.

"No, Mr. Saville is not at home, ma'am," her housekeeper, Margaret, said.

"All right. Here's what I would like you to do..."

Cassandra outlined what she wanted: thank the temporary nurse for her assistance and ask her to please leave the bill, and ask the regular nanny, Anne, to pack whatever the children and Cassandra might need for a few days away and meet her at the Bel-Air Hotel.

"And, Margaret, please don't mention to anyone where we are. I'm afraid Mr. Saville and I are—oh, Maggie—it's a mess. We're—we're—I have to leave him." Cassandra started to cry. "I—can't do this. Anyway, I hope you'll hold the house together until—until—"

"Don't you worry about a thing, Mrs. Saville. I'll be right here, and no one's going to give me no trouble. Or find out anything from me."

The following call was to Eve to see if she could come by the hotel after work.

"Yes! I'm in between appointments, so I'll be right there. Matilda will cancel the rest of the day. I think it would be wise for you to get in touch with your lawyer and find out the next steps. I'll call Harvey Hill, he'll know how to handle the press. See you soon, honey." Eve hung up, very upset. Had she contributed to this in some way? By giving Marc his alibi that horrible night? Damn him, why couldn't he keep his zipper closed? Once again, she agonized over her reasoning and finally concluded she had reacted correctly. Having Marc connected to a murder, and hard drugs to boot, would have been more difficult for Cassandra to bear than simply facing the fact she had a weak, womanizing husband. Eve believed this was an inevitable happening.

Harvey Hill had his hands full. The media was all over him. Was there another woman? Another man? Where are they?

The newshounds called every hotel. But the Bel-Air had already been sworn to secrecy, plus there were extra plainclothed security people stationed throughout the spacious grounds to ward off any snooping eyes.

Marc had been warned by James Carpenter—originally the couple's lawyer, but now Cassandra's—to quickly go to the house and retrieve some things and hide out somewhere, because once the news was released their home would be haunted by photographers, reporters, TV cameramen, the curious and on and on.

Harvey echoed the same message—he had the unenviable job of

protecting Utopia's hot properties as well as having a personal friendship with the young couple. He waited until he knew Marc had left his home with his belongings before informing the press of the separation.

Sal's new place was not common knowledge, so Harvey thought that would be a safe haven for now. Harvey arranged to meet Marc the next morning at Harry Lewis's Hamburger Hamlet on Sunset Boulevard, a popular hangout for celebrities—informal and burgers with a bit of the "bard."

Then he would drive Marc through the onslaught surrounding the entrance to Utopia Studios for his last day of filming.

Everyone agreed that no details would be discussed, no accusations made regarding the split. It was simply a matter of "irreconcilable differences" between the two. Any hint of real scandal would be damaging to both careers and to the children.

Marc didn't protest or fight any of the proceedings, what could he say? He was very depressed, he knew he had really botched up. Cassandra did mean a great deal to him, and the little ones, too, but there was a bug or gene or something inside of him that seemed to crave—what, exactly? Variety in women? The power of a new conquest? A sense of living dangerously? Self-destruction? Whatever, he didn't fit into the mold of "the marrying kind." There was no question he wanted to and would take care of his family. If he couldn't do it personally or emotionally, he could do it financially.

Money to Marc had only meant he could buy whatever he desired—cars, clothes, fun, women. Jewelry didn't interest him. He had started gambling before Cassandra but let up during the marriage. Now that he was a free man he thought he might visit Las Vegas more often. When he'd first come to Hollywood before Ernie Kovacs was killed in a car crash, he had sat in on some of those poker games. They had been wild times—Frank Sinatra and his group, Dean Martin, Irving "Swifty" Lazar, the players read like the "Who's Who" of Hollywood! Pretty rich for his blood then, but he had held his own!

So although he was distraught, as Sal said, "There's always a bright side. Now ya don't have t'sneak around. Ya can have all the poontang ya want, whenever ya want.''

Eve helped Cassandra find another house during the summer. The old one was too large and held too many memories—it was the only home she and Marc ever had together.

Eve had also gone with Cassandra when she met with Peter Padon and Mo Jeddu.

''I'm sorry, you've all been like family to me, but it would be so hard—unbearable—for me to be working at the same place and at the same time as my...''

''We understand, Cassie, you don't have to say any more.'' Eve had laid the groundwork so Peter and Mo were already briefed. ''Our yearly option is due in August and naturally we planned to renew. But under the circumstances, we won't. There are a couple of choices you have, however. We could just allow the time to expire and you would be a free agent. Or, Colvas Studios is interested in buying your contract from us. It's your call, Cassie, we won't force you either way. There is one consideration you might think of. With Colvas, you'd be more secure financially, you'd have your salary guaranteed just like here.''

Cassandra thought for just a minute. ''You mean Colvas would pay you? That's good—at least you'd get something back for taking a chance on me. I like that.''

She hesitated again. ''I barely know Mr. Abavas. Would I have to work every day, one picture right after another? Not that I'm afraid of work, it's just that I think my babies need me a lot right now. I guess I'm spoiled, maybe scared, you're so caring—''

''You can stop right there, Cassie!'' Peter interrupted emphatically. ''Don't bother your pretty head! Jude Abavas is probably the kindest, fairest person in this town. That we know! He wouldn't force anyone to do nothin' they didn't feel comfortable about.''

''Would you mind—if I still worked with Eve?'' Cassandra asked timidly.

''I can answer that, honey,'' Eve broke in. ''Of course they wouldn't mind. And if we don't have time during the day, I'll come by in the evening, give me a chance to see my K.C. and Di.''

Cassandra stood up. ''Well, that seems to be the best solution for everyone! I'll miss you—and—and being here. I better go before I make a fool of myself....'' She ran over and hugged the two surprised studio heads, then quickly left the room.

Eve saluted her bosses and friends. ''Thanks! You are, always have been, always will be first-rate stand-up guys!'' And she followed Cassandra.

Los Angeles, California
Friday, November 22, 1963

Walter Cronkite, looking stricken, came into view on the CBS-TV news bulletin. "President Kennedy died at 1:00 p.m. Central Standard Time in Dallas, Texas."

Someone had called Matilda in Eve's office, alerting her to the fact something momentous had occurred. She'd quickly turned on the television set, and now the two of them sat stupefied, unable or unwilling to grasp what had just been said. The station then reviewed the events that led to this cursed announcement, at least the fragments of information they had. Reports kept filtering in at an alarming rate, but instead of the pieces of the gathering data filling in the holes, each new input seemed to widen the scope of the puzzle.

Eve numbly reached for the telephone. "I must call Doug."

"Mr. Hassal isn't in, Mrs. Hassal," his secretary, Nell Brewster, said. "He received a call and rushed out without a word. Isn't this a terrible thing?"

Eve mumbled some words and hung up. Her phone rang, it was Cassandra. Then Ruth. Then Abe. It was decided they would all meet at Eve's since she had the most room. No one wanted to be by themselves. Eve made arrangements so the house was prepared for the crowd. Cassandra brought the nanny to help watch K.C. and Dianne.

There was comfort being in the midst of loved ones. As each new scrap of info was recounted they could discuss it, dissect it, torment over it. And not be alone.

"Oh, my God," screamed Cassandra suddenly. A picture of the policeman, Officer J. D. Tippit, who was killed near a theater while attempting to capture the suspected assassin, Lee Harvey Oswald, flashed across the screen.

"Look how young...his poor family...the children...all these babies without their daddies. It's too awful...."

Eve was sitting closest. She held Cassandra and spoke soothingly. "There, there Cassie. Nothing we can do right now except send our prayers to them. If and when we can help, that's what we'll do."

Each person's reaction to the chain of happenings reflected their own personal agenda as well as the general attitude of misery and horror and hopelessness.

"I called Artie to see if he wanted to join us. I don't believe anyone should go through something like this without their friends. I hope you don't mind." Abe looked toward Eve, who nodded in agreement. "But I forgot he had left to see his folks, evidently his dad isn't very well. I did get hold of him in Chicago, and he was devastated like everyone."

Douglas staggered in around 7:30 p.m., taken aback by the number of people lodged in the house. "What's going on?" he asked Eve.

She walked up to him, pecked his cheek. "Hello to you, too!" It was apparent she was miffed. "I was concerned about you, you might have phoned."

His eyes glazed over. "Someone—called. Needed to see me. This tragedy—was more than—this person could handle. I'm going upstairs." And he did!

"Maybe we should leave," Nick Larrington offered.

"Nonsense!" Eve said strongly. "You are all welcome for as

long as you want. The whole second floor is empty and we have
the guest rooms downstairs here. If you are more comfortable going
home to sleep, fine! But come back tomorrow. Abe is absolutely
right. We should be together.''

Cassandra elected to stay, Margaret drove to their house to pick
up some things. About ten, the rest decided to go and promised to
return Saturday. And Sunday. No one was anxious to break up
their small support group.

After Cassandra's entourage was securely anchored on the second floor, Eve slipped quietly up to their level. She didn't go into
the bedroom, she laid down on her chaise lounge with a throw.

The day itself had been draining, she ached from all the suffering
being endured. And she was distressed by this tumor of doubt that
gnawed at her insides.

*What is wrong with the man I married? Where is he? Could
it be my fault, could he feel neglected because I've been with
Cassie too much? No—I've noticed something odd since last
August.*

*Or is nothing the matter? Maybe the calamities of the past
two years have finally caught up with both of us and caused
a pall on our relationship. Does that sound right? I don't
know.*

*I'll try anything. I'll be more understanding and patient—
deal with his pain and not center on mine so much.*

Saturday and Sunday Douglas said he needed to go to his
friend's aid again. Even though Eve thought it very odd he didn't
identify this person, she didn't say a word other than she hoped
his friend—whoever it was—would be better soon.

Jenine Jasmine called Eve on that Sunday and wistfully asked if
she could come over. She was ''between'' romances and felt very
blue and cut off, this whole thing was getting to her.

Jenine and Eve had had a minor falling-out a while back. When
Douglas's mother was gravely ill, Jenine had made one of her early
morning calls to Eve.

"I'm sad and you have to help me!" she had said, sounding a bit like a spoiled child, a looped spoiled child.

Eve was exhausted but tried to stay calm. "What do you want?"

Jenine had blurted out, "I want a man. I want Paul Newman. I want you to give me his telephone number or I'll die!"

Eve had been so exasperated she said, "Then die!" And hung up!

Jenine had not known Eve's mother-in-law was sick and went around in a pout. Until a few days later, when she heard Esther had died. Then of course she was quite contrite and felt like a complete idiot.

Jenine did apologize and the two did patch it up, but she hadn't called Eve much after that. Until today.

"Of course you can come," Eve told her warmly, glad to put that silliness behind them.

Jenine arrived, clearly happy to see the whole troop. "Where's Doug?"

When Eve explained, she got this cryptic, knowing look on her face. "Really!" But she didn't go on.

Eve thought to question Jenine but decided against it. Anything seemed so petty and unimportant compared to what was happening now.

The drama kept unfolding. Theories blossomed like mushrooms after a rain: conspiracy; Cubans; CIA; bullets from several sources; inside job; outside job.

And the images kept all eyes riveted to the small screen. A traumatized Jacqueline Kennedy watching while Lyndon B. Johnson was sworn in as president aboard Air Force One. Air Force One landing in Washington D.C., surrounded by dazed, unbelieving officials and family and friends. The close-ups of the sixth-floor window from where the fatal shots were fired. The waving, smiling John Fitzgerald Kennedy minutes before the end—the end of this generation's idealism.

Everyone thought there could be no more histrionics, they had been exposed to enough for a lifetime. But fate had one more ace up its sleeve, like the practiced magician it was!

On Sunday, November 24, as Lee Harvey Oswald was being transferred to the Dallas county jail, shown on live television, a nightclub operator known as Jack Ruby shot and killed him. In front of the police, the news media, the world.

The people huddled in Eve's study stared at the mayhem erupting before them. Then they looked at one another, questioning their own vision, needing reassurance or verification that they actually saw what they thought they had seen. The revulsion mirrored in every face confirmed their fears. They had all just witnessed an actual murder.

No one could talk. They sat or stood frozen in whatever position, hypnotized. Finally, Cassandra in a weak whisper said, "Thank God the children were napping." Then, after a slight pause she added, "What kind of a world did I bring them into?"

Each day brought its own set of effects. The Kennedy family walking in a procession of grief, following the slain president to St. Matthew's Cathedral in Washington, D.C. The burial in Arlington National Cemetery. The weird outpouring of sympathy toward Oswald's wife, which made one wonder about people's values and allegiances.

But what would haunt them forever, what would be etched in their memories for their lifetimes, would be the photo of John Fitzgerald Kennedy Jr. on his third birthday saluting his father's coffin in the way he had seen soldiers salute his dad.

Los Angeles, California
Friday, May 15, 1964

"Can you believe it?" Marc Saville was thrashing around Eve's office. "I got a traffic ticket for *ogling! Ogling* for Christ's sake! I thought it was a joke!"

Eve couldn't help herself, she had to giggle, it was pretty funny.

"The cop said I was looking at the people too much and not the street. I think I'll fight it!"

Eve buzzed the intercom. "Matilda dear, would you check with research, please, see if they have a DMV booklet, the handbook you're supposed to know before you get your license?"

She turned to Marc. "Better find out the facts first. Now, you okay with this new film?"

"Yeah, piece a cake! If I run into a snag I'll give a holler!" Even though Eve and Marc didn't see each other socially any longer, he still was one of Utopia's biggest stars and therefore still Eve's responsibility.

"Uh, how's Cassie?" He had wanted to ask before, but had to muster up the courage first.

"She's doing well. I think Colvas found a script everyone likes, so she'll start working in a few months. Have you seen the children?''

"I've, ah, been pretty busy—couple a times. Cute as hell!'' He couldn't admit he missed them and that it just hurt too much when he saw them.

Matilda knocked and saved him. "Here's the DMV pamphlet, Ms. Handel. And this letter was delivered for you.''

Eve and Marc thumbed through the pages. "I'll be a son of a bitch!'' he exclaimed. "Here it is—law against excessive ogling! That's plain bull—that guy is a sack of shit in a uniform!''

"Marc, take my advice, just pay the fine!''

Eve didn't get to the note that had come until after her next appointment.

Please meet me at 134 Gayle Drive, between Wilshire and Charleville, penthouse apartment, around 5:30 p.m. Important. Key enclosed. Don't knock!

JENINE

"Now what is she up to?'' Eve muttered. She knew it wasn't work-related, Jenine wasn't on a picture at the moment. Eve speculated that maybe another studio had offered her a script. Or perhaps Jenine had bought a new place? "Well, I guess I'll find out this afternoon!''

Eve parked on the street once she had found the building. It looked like a small luxury hotel, the exterior landscaped in subdued artistry. The key allowed her to enter. Inside, there was a small lobby, beautifully and tastefully appointed. She pressed PH after the key let her in the elevator.

In a way it was really eerie, no doorman, no concierge, no names on a directory. She surmised, correctly, there must be an underground garage for tenants, again accessed by some code. Obviously people living here desired total anonymity.

The elevator opened into a short corridor leading to the sole door. She looked for a doorbell to ring, but there wasn't one. She lifted her hand to knock and then remembered the instructions in the note—*don't knock!* Evidently one was only supposed to use the "magic key." What an oddball idea! This whole place was weird!

Hesitantly she opened the door slightly. Immediately she heard music. So each apartment must be soundproof as well. As her eyes adjusted to the light change she made her way along an entrance hall toward the sound of voices, or more accurately, one voice— Jenine's.

She reached an archway, beyond which appeared to be the living room. Unlike Lot's wife, whose fate was determined by looking *back,* the view *before* Eve turned her to stone.

Douglas Hassal reclined on an oversize sofa, a silk Sulka robe draped casually over his bare body, a champagne goblet in one hand, and when he spotted Eve, his mouth froze in the position of forming a word.

Jenine Jasmine sat curled up in a deep armchair, a glass tumbler in her hand, clad in the new fad, a see-through bodice and panties. She, however, was not speechless when she saw Eve.

Jumping up she exclaimed, "Thank God you got here in time. I thought I might have to actually screw this CPA. Oh—I forget— sometimes you need a translation, Eve—this Constant Pain in the Ass!"

Eve had not moved. Nor had Douglas.

Jenine approached Eve and said in a softer tone, "I wanted you to see what a real bastard you married. When he asked me to meet him at his 'apartment'—the nerve to think I would be attracted to him—anyway, I thought it was a way to expose him. I duplicated the key he gave me—he's so full of it, acted like he was giving me the stairway to paradise—and sent it to you."

Jenine walked around. "I found out he's had this pad since the beginning of '62. Where do you think he went after he heard Marilyn Monroe died? And then when Kennedy was killed? Here! Probably with that Gwen bitch, that lady's so tough she could rip *my* tits off! The laugh around town is that those two actually thought they could finagle the Kennedys into financing some flick with Monroe. Not a chance in hell. Don't look so surprised, Doug, I know the right people who know *everything!* God knows how many keys are out there, unless he asks the one-timers to give it back. Or maybe he just brings some of his girl toys with him, along with his rubber duckies.'' She laughed derisively. ''You should see the bathroom!''

Jenine took the key out of Eve's bloodless hand, retrieved hers near her clothes and tossed them at Douglas. ''We won't be needing these, you low-life scumbag.'' Quickly she slipped on her sweat suit and loafers, picked up her purse and started to lead Eve away. ''You are too good for him, he should kiss the ground you walk on!''

Jenine took charge, guiding Eve as one would a sightless person, talking to her as if she were a child, for indeed, at this moment Eve was both. ''Where are your car keys? I took a cab, hoping I could hitch a ride with you.''

She had no way of foreseeing Eve's reaction, but she was glad she'd planned it this way, obviously Eve was not fit to drive.

At the house she put Eve to bed, worried now because Eve had not responded in any manner to anything, she seemed cataleptic. Jenine phoned Ruth, who gave her the doctor's number and also Yvonne Birshgeld's. ''I'm on my way, you make those calls. Yvonne is retired but she'll come for Eve. Also tell Abe to hurry over!''

Ruth ordered the butler to pack an assortment of Mr. Hassal's wardrobe and put them in Abe's car.

''I don't know where to take them!'' Abe said, troubled.

''Don't worry,'' Ruth assured him. ''Dapper Dan will want his fancy duds to impress his 'friends.' Damn it to hell, how could we all have been so blind?''

''I think Eve has been disturbed about Doug for some time,'' Harvey said, giving his wife a supportive hug. ''We can't know what goes on behind closed doors, honey. I'm grateful Jenine had the know-how and the guts to bring him out into the open.''

''Yeah,'' Jenine answered gloomily, ''but I may have really hurt her with my good intentions!''

Yvonne came into the den. "Eve didn't acknowledge me," she said somberly. "But there was a flicker when Molly and Lucy jumped on her bed. My, I forgot how big fully grown Labradors can get, barely room for Eve. But they'll keep her nice and cozy, cuddled right up close, one on each side." She sighed. "The important fact is, Eve reached out to them. She probably feels her animals are the only ones making any sense right now."

Ruth was correct. Douglas telephoned to say he planned to come home soon and expected Eve to be out as quickly as possible.

Ruth thought she was going to explode. "You'd better put your hand in your pocket and get a grip on reality!"

Harvey and Abe looked at Ruth and gave her the thumbs-up sign.

"You don't come near here! Do you understand me? I'll call the police if you do, *after* I get the restraining order our lawyer is preparing at this very moment." She crossed her fingers, knowing that was a lie, then scribbled on a notepad, "Get hold of Jim Carpenter!" Abe ran to obey.

She went on talking to Douglas. "Just tell us where you want your clothes sent, they're all ready to go."

Douglas was still ranting and raving. Ruth held the phone away from her ear, everyone else in the room could easily hear. "That bitch lied—propositioned *me!* Who do you think they'll believe— me—or some broad who's had more men than—"

Jenine was about to attack the telephone, but Ruth mouthed "No, no!"

The tirade continued, "Obviously my wife is trying to take control of my beloved parents' house and belongings. I won't let her steal their valuables—things they worked for years to accumulate, memories…"

Nick Larrington mimed sticking his finger down his throat and up-chucking.

Harvey gave his opinion. "An Academy Award performance!"

Finally, Douglas dwindled down and gave an address, the apartment, for his things. His new manservant would be outside to collect them. "Temporarily!" he warned.

Dr. Gaitworth met with everyone after he had visited with Eve. The group had expanded to also include Cassandra and the lawyer James Carpenter.

"Physically Eve will be fine, providing she takes nourishment. I can supplement the diet with vitamin shots, that sort of thing. I am prescribing a sedative so she gets rest, but I want one of you... Mrs. Birshgeld, I believe, is staying with her, is that correct?"

"Yes, I am," Yvonne answered.

"Good! Then you will keep the bottle with you and give her one pill at night. It's evident she is in a depressed state, perhaps in shock, and—not to alarm you—but it is a wise precaution not to have narcotic substances too available."

Cassandra was indignant. "Eve would never—"

"I'm not saying Eve would knowingly do anything," the doctor explained. "But until we determine the extent of her depression we can't take any chances. This has been a severe blow to just about everything she holds dear—love, family, trust, self-worth, judgment, and yes, even to life itself!"

Dr. Gaitworth let this bit of information sink in for a minute.

"I am recommending that she begin therapy sessions with Dr. Dwight Gaard, a highly regarded psychiatrist, as soon as she is able."

The room was silent.

"May I ask a question?" James Carpenter spoke finally.

"Of course!"

"Would it be harmful for her to leave this house?"

"I don't quite understand," Dr. Gaitworth said.

"Well, Mr. Hassal has threatened to take Eve to court, in what could be a nasty exploitive lawsuit, which would allow the press to have a field day. It isn't that he will win more than what is community property, anyway, but in the process he warns he'll paint Eve as a woman plotting to rob him of his family heritage. And her only collaborating witness will be described as a seductress, a liar, a drunk and a tramp. All of this is to obscure or redefine his own contemptible course of actions."

A chorus of voices arose. "He can't do that!" "How dare he!"

"The studio will fight!" "I'd like to get him in a dark alley, just for ten minutes!"

"Stop!" yelled James. "Forget what we think of him! He has the legal right to claim what he wants. Is he truthful? No! Will he benefit? No! Except—and this is the biggie, folks—except he will have succeeded in blemishing Eve and Jenine's reputations and, perhaps, completely destroying Eve's psyche. And don't forget, people tend to remember, even believe, what they read, no matter how ridiculous it may be."

Again, a hush fell.

Calmly, he continued. "My thought is this—if it wouldn't be injurious to Eve, we find a pleasant, cheerful house so she can have her dogs; move whatever pieces of furniture she feels belong to her along with her choice of china, crystal, art, et cetera, and let the bastard live in this mausoleum. Monetarily the value will be split, it doesn't matter who is actually in it. But it stops his proposed, albeit preposterous case!"

He saw their wheels turning. "I discovered, and I don't believe Mr. Hassal is aware of this, that his mother and father included Eve by name in their will. So it's no longer just a community-property dispute, Eve is entitled to her share whatever their marital status was at the time of his parents' deaths. I bet the old man knew about his son's, ah, quirks."

Dr. Gaitworth spoke. "What—is it, Mr. Carpenter?"

"Jim—Jim Carpenter," he quickly replied.

"What Jim suggests is very sensible. The resulting publicity from such a reckless legal maneuver could cause irreparable damage to Eve. Actually, getting away from here would probably be a healthy move. I don't know how much help she can give any of you, however, regarding her preferences of things."

"No sweat!" Ruth declared. "Between us we should be able to sort out what she really likes. We know her tastes and what she gravitates to. And I know what she brought with her and what she bought when she redid their apartment. What had been here is stored—we'll just put it back close to what it was!"

"Operation Eve" was put into motion: Abe and Nick were in

charge of real estate; Ruth, Cassandra, Jenine were the set decorators; Yvonne kept guard over Eve.

James Carpenter handled all of the legal business. He had taken the wind out of Douglas's sails once he gave notice that Eve was indeed leaving *their* house. Douglas was still reeling from the blow of discovering the content of his family's will. He had instructed his lawyers to break it at any cost, but so far they had not found a loophole. Mr. and Mrs. Hassal had been sane, the witnesses were of good standing…. "Keep looking!" Douglas had ordered.

James had also worked out an agreement with Utopia Studios. Peter Padon and Mo Jeddu had been flabbergasted.

"Of all people—why our Eve?" they both moaned. "What can we do? Anything at all!"

"I really don't know how long before Eve could conceivably return to work. If ever!" James was trying to be realistic, not alarming. "I'm afraid I don't know the contractual obligations either."

"Contract, schmontract—we don't give a donkey's ass about that! We care about her! Would it help if we got rid of that pissant Douglas?"

James smiled. "Not at the moment. In any case you can't deplete your business all at once."

"He probably ain't worth a damn without her, anyway," muttered Mo.

"Yeah, right!" agreed Peter. "So, what do we do? Tell us!"

"You are being so considerate, it's very gratifying. And your actions speak volumes about the kind of people you are, and your beliefs in and caring for Eve. Also of her character for deserving this kind of loyalty." James was speaking from the heart. "Right now, I guess the best way to go would be to have her take a sabbatical leave, for an unspecified length of time. This would allow everyone to sit back and evaluate the situation in their own mind-set and time frame."

"Done!"

"Operation Eve" went smoothly and quickly. A lovely house with a gated yard was found on Medio Drive in Brentwood, a nice area between Bel-Air and Santa Monica, not too close to and not too far from anything and anyone. The sellers also preferred a short escrow, so the arrangements were convenient for all parties.

The style was a cross of country French and New England quaint, Eve's favorite antiques and accumulated eclectic pieces fit in well. Fortunately the carpeting, flooring and window coverings were acceptable, no structural changes were necessary, so the move could be expedited. The property had a good-size pool and pool house, which eventually could become a projection room. The interior was spacious but not cavernous, having the usual rooms plus an oversize study that could serve as an office, two master suites upstairs, as well as guest quarters, and accommodations over the three-car garage for live-in employees.

The heartbreak for everyone was to see Eve's reaction, which was no reaction, to all of this activity. Nothing registered or made a dent in her floating sphere of existence. There was not a personal response; she was watching a play evolve on her stage. The characters were changing the decor of the set, placing costumes in cardboard wardrobes, packing the china and crystal props in big boxes, crating the collection of tasteful artworks that had been displayed. Eve, Molly and Lucy sat as extras, or the audience, allowing the players to manipulate them, even to driving them to a new backdrop where the set decorators had relocated all of the furnishings and effects. She approved of their choice of locale, it was a more inviting environment. Obediently the three of them, when asked, participated in the presentation by following the cast on a tour. Again, Eve endorsed their judgment, quite a talented group, she thought.

"When will she come back?" Ruth cried when talking to Dr. Gaitworth. "We're going mad, looking at someone we love so dearly and not being able to make contact, she's like a nonperson."

"I realize how difficult this has been. Please be patient for just a while longer," the doctor said gently. "I deliberately waited until you had physically positioned Eve in the new home before starting her with Dr. Gaard. I don't believe any of you, or Eve, could have handled the move otherwise. When Eve's protective shield begins to crumble and reality starts oozing inside, the pain and anguish will be excruciating—almost unbearable for her to endure and her loved ones to witness. She will go through her own private hell and all we can do is stand aside and let her *feel* our support. Not vocally, not until she is ready to open up and let us in." He patted Ruth's hand. "It's going to be an ordeal, for everyone."

Los Angeles, California
Friday, July 31, 1964

"Aaah—" the scream echoed in every nook and cranny of the Medio Drive house.

Yvonne Birshgeld jerked upright in her bed and ran quickly toward the sound. She bounded into Eve's room and found Eve crouched in a corner, her arms flailing above her head as if to ward off invisible attackers.

Yvonne sat down next to Eve and gathered her close in her still-strong arms. Eve clutched Yvonne, crying helplessly. "It's—it's the questions—the *questions!* They keep coming at me like—like diving hawks...."

The daily meetings with the psychiatrist had begun three weeks ago, and soon after, so had the nightly outbursts. First Eve had to acknowledge what had actually occurred, she had to break through the denial. And then she'd begun to deal with the anger, bitterness, guilt, the self-doubt, the doubt of judgement. And the *questions!*

I'm writing—almost as a last resort. Through the haze I remembered that this is where I used to sort things out. Where I could stand aside and try to make sense out of the happen-

stances of life. I guess, I guess, I put this behind the barriers—along with everything else.

I'm still afraid—afraid the questions will come and keep possession of me, that these mere pieces of paper can't shield me.

But I knew that when I pulled my journal out. Where is my head? Maybe, maybe I was hoping that here somehow answers would come for these abominable pounding questions. The same questions day after day—night after night—over and over... Why did I marry him? Did we say "I love you" to each other? Did he ever love me? Did I ever love him? What attracted me? Was it his dependency on me? Did that make me feel powerful or superior? Did I see his weaknesses? Did I encourage them and in that way remain the stronger? Was it his "little boy" behavior? Did he become the child I couldn't have? Was there a sign I missed that he was losing interest? Yes, yes—but I didn't miss it. I felt a strangeness but I dismissed it! How can I be so-called "intelligent" and be so stupid? Was I fearful of confronting him, fearful I'd find out something I didn't want to know, fearful that after all these years I'd have to admit I made a mistake? Was I lulled into the comfortableness of our union? I liked his parents, we both had the same work interests, both had compatible sexual appetites—

Did I cripple my emotional life by pursuing my ambitions? Did Grandpa's omen prove correct in the end?

Was I upset about the failure of a marriage as much as I was outraged at being betrayed? Did the humiliation outweigh an actual sense of loss? Can I trust anyone again? Can I trust myself again?

Los Angeles, California
Wednesday, August 5, 1964

Cassandra read the telegram in disbelief. It was from the family doctor in San Jose.

> Dear Cassie,
>   I'm afraid I have bad news. Your parents were in an automobile accident. Your dad, I'm sorry, was killed instantly. Your mom is in intensive care, and not doing well. I think you should come right away. Your telephone number is unlisted, I only had your address. I regret to be the person who sends this message to you.
>
>   Dr. Thomas Barren

In a daze she called James Carpenter's office. She had come to rely heavily on Jim and his staff since the divorce. Mr. Carpenter was not in, but his secretary immediately took charge of the travel plans. The ever-dependable Margaret packed a few things, assuaged her concern about the children and ordered a car.

Cassandra asked the driver to go to Eve's house first. She had called, but Yvonne said Eve was in the shower. She also had whispered that Eve was having a bad day.

Cassandra hurried upstairs and knocked on Eve's door. "Please open the door, Eve, I need you so much!" She began to cry, pleading through the tears. "I can't lose you, too! I have no one—oh, God I have no one—if you're lost to me. Please! Please! Hear me, Eve!"

No sound came from the other side of the door. Only Cassandra's grief was audible. Cassandra slumped against the wall, defeated. Her one remaining pillar of strength had seemingly collapsed. For most of the past three months, she had steadfastly clung to the belief that Eve—her mentor and friend and leader, the woman who could match wits with the titans of Hollywood and then in the next moment melt your heart with a reading of a scene—would come through this trying period and conquer the demons who had claimed control of her.

And now, for the first time, she was forced to give up that hope. And she felt alone, defenseless, abandoned. Slowly she retreated down the stairs, barely able to acknowledge Yvonne. Despair weighed her every step, burdened her every breath, clouded her every thought.

Eve's phone rang before Cassandra reached the door. "It's for you, Cassie," Yvonne said, handing the instrument to a surprised Cassandra.

"Hi, Cassie, it's Jim."

Cassandra made an attempt to disguise her overwrought state but didn't entirely succeed. "Oh—hello. Th-thank you for helping out. I must be, I mean, I'm becoming a, I'm sorry, I'm not making much sense—"

"Don't worry about talking." He paused, then blurted out, "I—I would like to come with you, so you have someone there."

Cassandra was not prepared for that proposal, the first good thing that had happened the whole day. He was clearly telepathic since that was definitely on her mind. She really would have liked James to accompany her, the last thing she wanted was to be alone. But somehow, it hadn't seemed right to ask.

She sighed sadly. "That is so nice of you and the fact you even asked means a lot to me. But, but I think it might be awkward. It's time for me to—to grow up. Some things you just have to face by yourself.''

The intensive-care section was not what Cassandra had imagined. She pictured darkness, profound quiet, uniformed figures moving surrealistically between shrouded corridors.

On the contrary, the hub of the unit where desks and equipment were gathered was brightly lit, a loud hum of activity was quite pronounced, and doctors and nurses walked briskly. There were roughly ten cubicles on the perimeters of the room, all facing the center with most of their doors open. Several times Cassandra heard a voice sharply bark out information, ''Number four, pulse fluctuating!'' Then scurrying footsteps would answer the summons.

Dr. Barren led the trembling Cassandra to the last of the partitions. This door was closed.

''Cassie, brace yourself! Your mother isn't going to look the same as you remember. She had massive head and internal injuries, she's covered in bandages, her face is black and blue, she's hooked up to monitoring machines. And I can't promise that any of this will save her. But she keeps calling your name, so I do know seeing you will make her very happy. Are you okay with this?''

Cassandra nodded her head weakly. She prayed for help, prayed for the strength to see only the essence or spirit of her mother. She readied herself and entered the small room. Light came from fixtures on two side walls. The machines attached to various parts of her mother's anatomy spewed out data, flashing in brilliant hues of green and yellow and blue and red.

Cassandra faltered, horrified when she saw the figure on the hospital bed. It looked like a mummy, except it had a face, a battered, bruised, swollen rainbow-colored face that was unrecognizable.

Cassandra willed herself not to see—not to look—to pretend it was like the last time they were together. She thought of how happy and beautiful her mother had been, holding the baby and laughing at K.C. and Spartacus goofing around. She was supposed to be an actress—this would be the performance of a lifetime!

''Mama,'' she said softly. ''Mama, it's me, Cassie.'' Carefully she placed her hand on her mother's arm. "Can you hear me, Mama? It's Cassie and I'm home."

Kathleen Hollister stirred slightly. "Ca-Cassie?" The broken ribs made breathing painful and difficult, she could only speak in short gasps. "It's...really...you?"

"Yes, Mama, it's me." Cassandra found Kathleen's hand under the covers and squeezed it ever so gently. There was a feeble response.

"So...glad..." The older woman opened her puffy eyes and tried to focus on her daughter. "We...did...it...this time...." She studied Cassandra's face and saw the sorrow under the facade. "Daddy's dead, isn't he...?"

Cassandra couldn't mask the reply, she sensed her mother knew already. "Yes, Mama."

Tears escaped and rolled down Kathleen's cheeks. Cassandra tenderly wiped them away, trying to hold back her own.

"Shouldn't drink...and...drive. Remember that..."

"I will, I promise. You should rest now, I'll be right here."

They sat silently, hand in hand. Kathleen didn't close her eyes—it was clear she didn't want to miss one second of looking at her lovely child. Cassie understood her mother knew these moments, these memories, would have to last her for a long time, for eternity. It was as if she understood her body's messages—as if she knew she was dying.

"Cassie...?"

"Yes, Mama? Do you need anything? Should I call the nurse?"

"No, my darling. Come...closer. I...want...to...explain... something...."

Cassandra lowered her head and listened intently as Kathleen began to talk.

Finally, Kathleen Hollister relaxed, perhaps more at peace with herself than she had been for many years. "I...think...I... can...sleep...now. I love you..." Cassandra kissed her good-night and whispered, "I love you, too, Mama."

Cassandra didn't know how long she sat in the chair, her mind filled to capacity, brimming over with thoughts and notions too

confusing to organize. Suddenly she was jarred from her thoughts.
A doctor came charging through the door, motioning for her to go
outside. She heard snatches of sentences. "Start defibrillat-
ing...again...*again*—" Through the window she could see frantic
movements, faces fraught with concern.

Dr. Barren arrived, out of breath. "I was in the last wing when,
whew, I got the page. Came as fast as I could! Let me see what's
happening!"

He approached the opening, talked briefly with the attendants,
then gravely returned to her side. "Come with me, Cassie, we'll
go to another—"

"No!" she screamed. "I want to stay with my mama!"

"You can't do anything, Cassie, none of us can anymore."

She glared at him, unwilling to accept what he was saying. "I
won't leave. I want to see her—" Cassandra broke away and
rushed toward the bed as the attending doctor was pulling the white
sheet over her mother's head.

"Mama, Mama, come back to me. I love you. I love you...."
Cassandra sobbed, holding on to the lifeless form.

Kind but firm hands pried her loose. Still hysterical, she was half
carried to a private room where Dr. Barren gave Cassie a shot to
relax her.

Cassandra opened her eyes slowly, hazily scanning her strange
surroundings. Where was she? As the fog cleared somewhat, she
remembered, and quickly closed them again in a vain attempt to
shut out the recollections.

A familiar voice called to her. "Cassie?"

She didn't believe her ears so she warily peeked through her
lashes. She saw Eve bending over her and immediately thought she
must be in very bad shape and hallucinating because she knew it
couldn't be Eve.

"Cassie dear, it's Eve. Please forgive me. I failed you when you
needed me, and I have no excuse, other than I was a selfish, self-
centered fool. Can you forgive me, my darling Cassie?"

This time Cassandra looked, and believed. She spread her arms and the two women embraced. And cried. And hugged. And wept. Finally, they talked. And they talked. And they talked.

"I heard you outside the door," Eve told her, ashamed. "But I was so hell-bent on my own troubles, I blocked out what you were saying because it had nothing to do with *me!*" She shook her head, disgusted with herself.

"Don't do that," Cassandra said. "I understand."

"I have to, because it's true," Eve interrupted. "And saying it helps me realize how I've been hiding and resenting and wallowing! Yvonne came up and scathingly read me the riot act. She reminded me that everyone rallied around me in my crisis and accused me of not having room in my heart for anything else besides self-pity."

Eve lowered her head. "I have a long way to go yet, but today was a huge step. I wish I hadn't had to disappoint you to come to my senses."

She drew Cassandra closer. "I'll try so hard to make it up to you, and to everyone who has been by my side. I realize for some, like you, caring is a natural response. But it was quite unexpected in others. Like, in my mixed-up mind I thought James Carpenter was merely an acquaintance. Now I'm beginning to see the kind of person he really is. When Yvonne jarred me into a degree of reality, I didn't know what to do or where to turn. And then Jim called and said he would arrange for a plane to fly us up here if I wanted to come to you. He offered to come with me since he didn't think I was ready to travel alone. Isn't that something?"

"You mean he's here?"

"Downstairs at the entrance."

"Oh, dear. I—I need to think. I can't see..."

Eve assured her quickly, "He isn't expecting you to do anything. He's waiting for me to tell him my plans, then he'll or we'll go back to Los Angeles."

She paused. "If it's all right with you, I'd like to stay, help you through this time, and when you're ready, Jim said he'll send a plane for the two of us. Yvonne packed some things for me, but—

but this is only if you want me here.'' Eve was still visibly insecure about Cassandra's feelings toward her.

''Oh, please, please stay, Eve. You're all I have!'' She started to panic again.

''Of course I will, my darling Cassie. Thank God! Thank you for allowing me back.''

The next days were difficult ones. Eve tried to relieve Cassandra of as many decisions as she could, but most were her call. But as difficult as the situation was for Cassandra to endure, it was eased by Eve's presence.

Both Kathleen and Jim Hollister had instructed cremation and a very simple memorial at their home. The Hollisters hadn't moved when their daughter went to Hollywood, and it hadn't been a big house to start with. But they no longer rented the home, Cassandra had managed to buy it for them after her first film and salary hike.

Cassandra desperately hung on to Eve when they walked through the front door. They had gone to a hotel from the hospital, because Cassie had known it would be too painful to attempt to stay at the house. Then they had braved the inevitable.

It was as if her parents had just stepped outside. Four cocktail glasses were still on the coffee table, cigarette butts filled a large ashtray, a few cracker crumbs and cheese bits were scattered on an hors d'oeuvre platter. A scrapbook was opened at the latest pictures of Cassandra and K.C. and Dianne and Spartacus. The accident had happened after cocktails, after the Hollisters and their friends had gone out for dinner. The two couples had had a night-cap, and then separated, each making their way home.

In the kitchen, a small amount of Scotch was left at the bottom of the bottle, melted ice languished in the ice bucket. Music from the forgotten radio softly filled the room with the mournful song, ''Who Can I Turn To?''

Cassandra began to lose control. She picked up something shiny off the counter. ''Oh—this is the animal pin I sent Mama on Mother's Day. You know, the newest thing—it's supposed to be

Sp-Spartacus. Oh, Eve!'' She sat down and buried her head and arms on the table. ''It's—so—so hard!''

''I know, honey. Let it out, let it all out!''

The basic arrangements were over. Legally it was quite simple, the few assets were left to Cassandra. She just wasn't sure what to do next.

''My advice is this, Cassie,'' Eve suggested. ''Show me what you want to keep—photos, mementos, furniture, whatever. I'll tag them, have them crated and sent to you. I would say to donate the clothes and such, and leave the rest as is. I asked around and one of your parents' friends gave me the name of a reliable real estate broker. Unless you have other ideas, I think you should put the house up for sale.''

Cassandra nodded her agreement. And she began the task of deciding what to save. Again, Eve was there with advice. ''Try to think of the things that will mean something not just to you, but to K.C. and Dianne, too. Something they might have shared with Grandma and Grandpa and would remember. Photos of times together, a toy picked up at the school fair or Disneyland or at the beach or here. Maybe a piece of jewelry, not for its value, but because they might have seen your mother wearing it, or perhaps a baseball hat your dad always had on.''

Eve walked to where Cassandra was standing. ''And for me and everyone who loves you, send every piece of you—so that we can know all about your childhood and your past before you came to us.''

Eve was not even aware that something remarkable had happened. She hadn't thought of herself or her situation since she had completely focused on Cassandra's needs.

Once the labeling in the living room was finished, Eve went to see what was next on the agenda. Cassandra was in her old room, sitting on the floor, staring at a framed picture. Tears silently flowed down her cheeks. Eve glanced over Cassandra's shoulder to see a beaming Jim and Kathleen Hollister holding the month-old infant. Cassandra sensed Eve's presence.

"This must have been when they were able to bring me home from the hospital. Look how happy they were!"

Tenderly holding the photo, Cassandra hesitantly said, "I haven't told you quite everything yet. So much happened in so short a time. I guess I could only deal with each circumstance in turn."

Cassandra rose and wandered around, fondling her childhood treasures. "Before Mama died—it's still hard to say—she told me something."

She faced Eve. "Mama told me I was adopted. She said she didn't tell me before because, because she and Daddy were afraid I wouldn't love them as much, or that I would leave to try to find my birth mother, or some nonsense like that!"

Cassandra looked at the photo of the three of them again, and with a little anger and a lot of frustration scolded, "You silly-nillies! How could you think any of those thoughts? You raised me, you were my mom and dad, I loved you and I'll always love you. You had to know that!"

Eve put her arms around the young woman. "Dear Cassie, you've had the whole shebang thrown at you, haven't you, sweetheart. But you know what, you've landed on your feet every time! And you even managed to take time out and teach this old dog new tricks! And all before your twenty-third birthday—let me think—yes, next Saturday! See, I'm functioning again. My mama used to quote this when I would doubt someone or something, which I have to admit, was often.

"He who loses money, loses a little.
He who loses a friend, loses a lot.
He who loses faith, loses all."

"It's important you understand your parents' fear. It isn't that they didn't trust you or your devotion. They just adored you so, so much they couldn't bear the thought of you loving them less. You must believe, they were fully conscious of and grateful for your love."

Los Angeles, California
Saturday, September, 12, 1964

"Hold it a minute, Abe!" Arthur was huffing and puffing. "Jesus, don't you ever give a guy a break? Can't we sit down and, and talk about anything? Who's screwing who? Something!"

Abe laughed, "Just trying to keep you in shape, Artie." He added dryly, "And maybe saving your life. You're getting up there, you know!"

"That's a low blow! I'm only going to be forty-seven."

"And I want to keep you looking like you're thirty-something so you can still appeal to all those young chicks!"

"You do know how to pull my chains!" Arthur moaned in resignation.

After the workout and a quick swim, they lounged around and shot the bull. Arthur was always Abe's last appointment for just that reason, a chance to catch up on each other's activities and lives.

"How's Eve doing?" Arthur asked guardedly.

"So much better, it's almost a miracle!" Abe was enthusiastic. "Like I told you, we were really worried. I can't give you the medical mumbo-jumbo, but in layman's terms, Eve suffered traumatic anxiety, caused by a sudden catastrophe for which a person is wholly unprepared. God knows she had that.''

''I can't believe that bastard!'' Arthur muttered.

''Me, neither! I'd have beat him to a mushy pulp if it would have helped. Anyway, the response to such trauma can be panic and flight, even a violent kind of assault. Or, as with Eve, a sudden trancelike state in which one wanders aimlessly, becomes paralyzed and mute. She was a mess!''

''I didn't know it was that bad. You were all so involved and occupied I didn't want to bother you with too many questions.''

''Sorry I had to be in such a hurry all the time,'' Abe apologized. ''Those of us who could, just dropped everything. Thank gosh my clients were sympathetic and patient. I didn't lose one account, which is really amazing.''

''I toyed with the idea of switching to—what's his name?—Thad Thornton. He would like to talk more and work less,'' Arthur teased. ''But I decided to be a loyal friend!''

''Yeah, you could see a middle-age paunch rearing its ugly round fat head!'' Abe retorted.

''Got me!'' Arthur was intent on learning more about Eve. ''So, how did this condition get, would one say, cured?''

''I don't know what to call it! She started therapy with a psychiatrist, which probably laid some groundwork inwardly, but we couldn't see much of a change. Then, wham! You know Cassandra Hollister?''

''We've met and I certainly know who she is,'' Arthur replied.

''Well, Cassie was working for Eve right along with us. Then in August—about the seventh—she got word her parents were in an accident, father killed, mother dying. Poor thing rushed to Eve, her guru, for some T.L.C. and advice, and was absolutely destroyed when Eve didn't respond, didn't acknowledge her.''

''That's just not Eve!'' Arthur said in bewilderment.

''Of course not! But she hadn't been Eve since May. Yvonne— you remember Yvonne Birshgeld?''

Arthur nodded.

''Yvonne stayed with Eve the whole time. Well, she didn't know it but she actually saved the day. She was so upset for Cassie that she told Eve what she thought of Eve's behavior. And I'll be damned if Yvonne's outburst didn't shock Eve back into the real world.''

''And she was all right? Just like that?''

''Yes and no.'' Abe explained. ''Yes, she immediately was able to go and see Cassie through her tragedy. No, she's still in a somewhat delicate state. But she's working with the psychiatrist in a positive manner, admitting the hurt and dealing openly with the depression, and really doing well.''

''I don't suppose she would like company?'' Arthur asked wistfully.

''Honestly? I think it's a little early. Hopefully she'll be ready for socializing soon, though.''

Abe tried to steer the conversation in a new direction. ''Didn't I hear you say once you knew James Carpenter?''

''Sure!'' Arthur was content to move on to another subject; he had learned what he wanted to know about Eve's situation. ''Nice person! His law firm represents Studio Services Inc., which is owned by my friends Vince Franks and Matthew Abavas. The Abavas family was very close to my—my buddy Wade Colby. As a matter of fact, Wade's widow, Penelope, and Jude Abavas, Wade's partner, are going to get married. You might recall that Jude and Madge divorced some time ago. And Jude's sister, Revel, is married to Vince. So in a long-winded answer, yes, I know Jim. Why?''

''Because he was instrumental in helping Eve. Not just with legal matters, but it was his idea to get her out of that house, an idea the doctors totally endorsed. And then he chartered a plane to bring Eve to Cassie in San Jose and another one for both to come back to Los Angeles. My take is that he may be hankering after Cassie!''

''Bully for him! Maybe one of these weeks we'll all get together. I know your group met Wade and Penelope, and Jude, too, and I think you'd like the rest of the clan. We'll do that, at the right time.'' Somehow, Eve ended up being in their discussion, regardless of the topic.

They were quiet for a moment. ''How's Nick, by the way?'' Arthur asked.

A small cloud crossed Abe's face. ''He's fine. I think maybe he's working too hard. He's taken on more responsibility since Eve's been away. And I've been so wrapped up—we all have, Nick, too, with Eve's problem....''

He speculated aloud. ''But, I get innuendoes that something is up at Utopia. Maybe Mr. Padon and Mr. Jeddu are getting ready to retire, maybe there's some kind of power play going on, I'm not sure. That's probably what's distracting Nick, besides the fact he's overworked. Eve could find out, but I don't know when she'll go back to the studio. Or if—especially if Doug is in evidence. I guess we'll just have to wait and see.''

Los Angeles, California
Monday, March 1, 1965

"Eve, you look wonderful!" Peter Padon and Mo Jeddu exclaimed in unison.

"You flatterers!" Eve laughed. "But true or not, I'll take it anytime."

They settled in their booth at the Beverly Hills Hotel's plush and famous Polo Lounge for lunch. It was good to be together again, theirs was a true friendship. There was business to discuss, yes, but first the threesome simply wanted to catch up and do what everyone else at the Polo Lounge did—dish about who was there.

"See that dark-haired broad over there in the white suit holdin' court?" Mo asked. "She's thin and trim now, but wasn't always!"

Eve unobtrusively caught a glimpse of the lady in question and nodded.

"She's married to a successful producer and is one of the 'elite people.' What's funny is a lot of us old-timers knew her when she was hooked up with one of those—" Mo pushed his nose sideways to indicate the Mob-type "—guys and was pumping a rich playboy who lived in the apartment above her at the same time. Busy gal!"

"I wonder," Eve mused, "if she's doing what I heard is the

newest fad now. The chic society women in Paris are swallowing tapeworms so they can eat whatever they want and still remain fashionably thin.''

Peter and Mo both made faces.

''I agree,'' Eve laughed. ''It's disgusting! Evidently when they begin to lose too much weight, they take some pill that purges the little bugger. Can you imagine, deliberately putting a worm in your mouth! Not me!''

After a while they ordered and sat back, enjoying their camaraderie. Peter exhaled slowly. ''It hasn't been the same without you, Eve. We've missed you!''

''Nothin' goes the way it should. Just ain't right!'' Mo concurred. '''Course, the business itself is changing, the world is changing. Ever since Kennedy was killed and CBS bought the New York Yankees, the sh—the stuff hit the fan!''

Eve put her hands on theirs. ''I'm so sorry I ran out on you. I would never have purposefully put extra burdens on you, the two special men who made a career possible for me and who are my dearest friends. But, but, was powerless—''

Peter and Mo hastened to explain and Peter said it for both. ''No, no, we're not blaming you! In our blundering way we were just tryin' to tell you what you mean to us now, and what you've meant to us over the past years. What you've brought to the company. That we never coulda been as successful without your input, your talent. We wanted you…''

Peter and Mo traded looks. Peter went on, ''Mo and me, well, we've decided to sell Utopia. We're not comfortable with the new ways. And we're too old to fight the good fight any longer!''

Eve surprised them with her reaction to the news. ''I'm glad! I'm glad you're retiring at the pinnacle of your profession. The two of you built an empire with dedication, excellence and dignity. This will be your legacy and I'm so proud I was one small part of the process.'' She leaned over and hugged each of them, all eyes glistened with moisture.

The men blinked back the tears, cleared their throats and tried to get back on track. ''Now, when the bidding starts, the shares will go up in price, maybe double what they're at now, which is—what did we close at—fifty dollars a share. Do you still have your original six thousand shares?''

''Oh absolutely.''

''Well, hold on to them for now. Whatever they are worth after the sale is completed, we will double that amount in cash as your bonus.''

Eve was flabbergasted and started to sputter, ''That's—oh no—you can't...''

''We can and we will! Believe us, Eve, you have earned every one of those dollars, so shush! We were thinkin' of givin' you shares, but it gets so complicated we decided cash was cleaner.'' Peter was adamant.

''I don't know what to say!''

''Nothin'!'' Mo exclaimed. ''We—it's none of our business, except when it's about you we kinda think it is our business. We heard rumors that Doug was tryin to f—screw you out of your half of the Hassals' estate.''

She lowered her head. ''I don't know very much about all the details. When I was—sick—no one mentioned anything about, well, anything. Even though I'm practically back to normal, I guess they're still protecting me. I have a good lawyer, James Carpenter, who has been very helpful. He has assured me that all is in order, so I have to believe him.''

Mo continued emphatically, ''He better be right! Or we'll do a little spoiling for Mr. Douglas Hassal ourselves. You see, he's trying to put together a group to buy Utopia. We could put the kibosh on that in a second. But if you get what's yours, we'll let him and his dumb investors bid as high as they want. If it should turn out that they get it, sell your shares the minute the deal is announced, 'cause sure as shit, they'll fuck up the company. Excuse my language, but I don't know how else to say it.''

Eve smiled. ''After all this time you're still apologizing!''

Mo looked sheepish. ''I still think of you as that young naive little girl I first met.''

"Have you given any thoughts to the future, Eve?" Peter asked considerately.

"Well it's odd you told me about your decision today because I've been tormented about when to return to Utopia. If you had remained in charge there was no doubt I would have resumed what I have been doing all along, because I could not leave you. I must admit that I've been concerned that if I ran into Doug, I would be thrown for a loop. But I would have taken that chance."

She gazed at them and then into nowhere. "It will seem so unreal, not to be there, that none of us will be there. We have to tell everyone that they can come to me for help at any time, wherever I am, and of course, at no expense to them. It has always given me such a good feeling when I see one of my—what are they?—let's just say when one of my actors gives a great performance or makes an exciting choice in interpretation."

Eve was lost in her own thoughts for a beat. "But we must move forward, mustn't we? Reconstruct, remodel, reorganize!"

Mo and Peter were listening to Eve, and realizing they would also be faced with the same ultimatums very soon.

She saw worry creep into their attitudes and mustered up all the determination she could manufacture. "But we can do this, can't we? Of course we can! And we will! And we will prevail!"

CHAPTER

48

Los Angeles, California
Wednesday, September 8, 1965

Eve Handel was nervous, had been ever since she received the call from Jude Abavas's office, asking if she would attend a meeting with the president of Colvas Studios. She naturally agreed, and today was the day.

Eve had started working with Cassandra once Colvas had decided on the first film she would star in under their banner. It was a charming romantic comedy titled *Are You Anybody?* which had been a hit on Broadway. Her co-star was the actor who had become the toast of the town when the play opened in New York, Rick Revere. This was his first feature and a big coup for Colvas.

Eve was worried about the meeting on several levels. Maybe the studio wasn't pleased with Cassandra's performance and had discovered that she was seeing Eve. Or, perhaps it wasn't the performance, perhaps they just objected to Eve's influence. Perhaps they saw it as interference with their star. In any case, her knees were wobbly as they had been on that first interview so many years ago with Peter Padon. Funny, some things never change no matter what one's age!

A secretary ushered Eve into the inner office. The tall and ruggedly handsome Jude Abavas immediately jumped up and came to greet her.

"How nice to see you again, Mrs. Hassal!"

"Please, call me Eve." She was flustered, not sure if she should say anything further and then decided she had nothing to lose. "Also, I'm using my professional name now, which is actually my maiden name, Handel."

"I apologize. I'm never quite sure how to address women in business," Jude admitted honestly.

Eve had always liked what she'd seen in Jude, even though their encounters had been brief and rare. Obviously he was intelligent and shrewd, but she sensed these traits were encased in openness, integrity, kindness.

"I understand congratulations are in order," she said.

"Yes, thank you." Jude blushed shyly. "Penelope and I have been married for almost a year."

He slapped his forehead, "What's the matter with me? Please, sit down! What would you like to drink? My manners seem to have gone AWOL!"

Eve laughed and chose a small armchair, "Some water would be nice, thank you."

Jude busied himself at the wet bar, brought her Evian with a twist and then sat in a similar chair facing Eve.

"Cassie tells me the two of you are very close."

Oh-oh, Eve thought, here it comes!

"That's true, I'm happy to say. I treasure our friendship."

"She also says," Jude continued, "that you are responsible for the success she has achieved."

"I'm flattered, but that is *not* true," Eve declared earnestly. "No one can teach or give talent, except God. One can guide a gifted person, or provide some tools, but the person has to absorb this guidance and is solely responsible for what emerges."

"So you know, Eve, Cassie is brilliant in the picture. She holds her own with a very experienced and accomplished actor who has had a year to perfect his character."

"I'm so thrilled for her. I do appreciate you sharing that with me!"

Jude hesitated a beat. "I also want you to know, Peter Padon and Mo Jeddu are good friends of mine. And we've been talking. About many things, including you."

Eve was surprised, and curious, but waited for him to go on.

"I don't think it will come as any great shock to you, they speak of you in glowing terms. Not only of your capability, but of you in general."

Now Eve was embarrassed. "We—they—well, they gave me my first opportunity, took a chance on a complete unknown. It's been a very rewarding alliance."

"As you know, Utopia has been sold." Jude chuckled, "Evidently the last two parties bid back and forth, upping the ante to unbelievable highs, which ended on a scale that made both Peter and Mo happy and very wealthy. I believe your ex-husband's conglomerate won out."

"Time will tell!" Eve smiled. She had sold her shares when the deal was finalized at a tremendous profit. "The winner sometimes becomes the loser."

Eve and Jude exchanged a look, but said no more.

"Peter and Mo may take offices here at Colvas and make independent pictures."

She gasped. "How perfectly wonderful! They won't have the headaches of a big company and yet will be able to do what they love! I'm overjoyed!"

"And I would be overjoyed if you came to work for me and be a part of Colvas also!"

Eve was caught completely off guard.

"I didn't mean to be so blunt. I'm not a good smoothie, I'm afraid, I tend to blurt out what's on my mind," Jude explained ruefully. "My partner Wade always said I had a direct line from my brain to my mouth—no stops, no detours!"

"No, no, you were—I mean—I think it was just so unexpected," she managed to say.

"I realize this is a small operation compared to Utopia, and we don't have a long contract list—yet! But we may be expanding in that direction, and Nick Larrington was suggested as a possible head of the department. We understand he is not staying at Utopia under the new management. You know him, I presume?''

''Very well, and for many years. You would be acquiring a valuable asset, he is tops!'' Eve found her voice again.

''That's what I heard.'' Jude nodded. ''Television has been and still is our strength, we only make a few movies a year. And TV is a monster, it gobbles up product faster than all the producers combined can grind out. So we need to find more talent, both in front of and behind the cameras. And more stories and situations!''

''Why would you need me?''

''First and foremost, you would work with the actors on all of our projects. Unfortunately, in TV there isn't the luxury of a lengthy production schedule as in features, and often quality suffers. If the players had the benefit of your counsel before going on the set, especially the inexperienced ones, the performances would be so much better, which obviously would elevate the quality of the whole show. We want to present the best that is possible under the conditions—no one tries to turn out crap.''

Eve saw his eagerness.

''And then—'' Jude grinned impishly ''—if you had any time or energy left, I would greatly appreciate your opinion, your feedback, your grasp of the material—script, book, play, whatever— we are considering. I keep saying *we,* but sadly it is just me. I have to have another pair of eyes, another mind-set to assure that the choices are right ones. Peter and Mo said emphatically you were the only person who could fill the void. And even in this time together, my gut tells me they were right!''

Eve tried to take charge of her thoughts. There was no doubt she was intrigued. Working with Cassandra again had stimulated her appetite; she missed the flashes of excitement that happened when she was involved, she missed feeling alive, she missed contributing.

But, was she ready to brave the world again? Was she strong

enough? And could she be effective in this different climate? She was secure in films, but she would be a neophyte in television!

Yet she knew drama and how to portray characters in drama. Just as she knew comedy or satire, or any milieu, for that matter. She understood continuity in a performance and in a story line. She had the ability to communicate with people—actors, writers, directors, producers—and argue her point. What was the difference if she prepared someone for a large screen or a small screen?

And how could she allow one mistaken judgment to dominate her life, intimidate her existence? If she faltered now, if she backed down now, then Douglas would have the victory! Is that what she wanted?

Hell no!

Jude waited patiently. He had been briefed by Peter and Mo about Eve's personal side and he knew she was still in a sensitive state. He hoped his gusto hadn't put her off, but he couldn't not be himself, that wouldn't be the way to start an association.

Eve stood, determined. At this moment, she seemed very tall and in complete command. "It looks like you have inherited Utopia's deserters. I would very much like to become a member of Colvas. I look forward to the challenge."

"I am so glad." Jude's big hands closed over Eve's. "I have such a good feeling, this is going to be a plus for us all!"

Jude's exuberance overflowed. "You know what—it just hit me—you should have Wade's office."

"No, I couldn't, shouldn't—" Eve interrupted.

"Listen to me, Eve! I knew Wade Colby better than any man on this earth. We loved each other, even more than brothers. And I can say with certainty, he would want this, he would insist on this because it's *right*. You'll find out that I'm a hands-on kind of producer. If you want me to hear the way an actor is doing a scene or if you think someone has the potential for a role, I'll be in your office in ten seconds. And if I have a problem with the dailies or the way the editing was done, you can be here in ten seconds. I want a team, and I'm positive you're the missing member. It's coming together like pieces of a puzzle."

Jude walked over and lovingly picked up a silver frame from his bookcase. He raised his eyes to Eve. "I understand this has all been sudden, and we're new allies. Even so, I'm going to tell you something very private because I want you to learn about me and trust me."

Eve was spellbound. She had flinched when Jude said "Trust me," those were the most difficult words to hear. But she sensed a presence, a power....

"Before I could marry Penelope I had to recognize and believe in Wade's approval. It wouldn't have been possible otherwise. And he sent a sign."

Jude replaced the photo of Wade Colby, Penelope Colby and Jude Abavas. "I hope you don't think I'm batty, but I'm saying what is the truth for me. I am convinced Wade sent me the thought that you should be in his office. He's still watching out for me, helping me—and he knows your closeness is what I need."

Jude's sincerity carried Eve along with him. She couldn't doubt a faith of such force. So be it! The course was set!

I am so humbled. Ever since Cassie's family tragedy galvanized my brain into acknowledging this wasn't a one-person universe, that there were other people on the planet who also had needs, I feel as if, as if I'm slowly recapturing...me.

Today someone once again felt secure enough with me to reveal something private. And today someone once again showed complete confidence in my abilities. And today, once again, I was able to hear the words "trust me" and actually begin to trust.

I am so happy!

Eve settled in her new quarters the next Monday. She didn't want to rearrange the decor in any way, even though Jude had given her carte blanche to redecorate. Actually, she was comfortable with the way it was. She brought some personal belongings, familiar gadgets, a favorite chair, and that was it.

Jude had located Eve's former secretary, Matilda Carliss, and the two had a happy reunion. He was so excited, buzzing around her like a mother hen, making sure everything was in order, despite the fact Eve was actually a year older than he.

"I should be clucking over you!" she kidded.

On day two there were five scripts, one book, two outlines on her desk. With a note.

> I hope these aren't too much to begin with, I don't want to scare you away. The talent won't come your way until the next new casting. Which, of course, could be any day now. Welcome!
>
> Jude

On the end table by a small cluster of chairs was an exquisite spray of white orchids. That note read:

> Even the flowers are smiling brighter because you are here.

Nick Larrington moved in on the floor below two weeks later. "There is such good karma coming from this lot. I could feel it the minute I walked through the gate, the day I talked with Jude. Very positive!"

Nick hugged Eve. "I think we're going to be quite happy here, old girl! And hopefully, productive!"

The protective, inner circle that had been shielding Eve for the past sixteen months breathed easier. Their vigil was over, their mission accomplished. She was almost like her old self again— bright, saucy, quick, assured. She walked with a spring, a purpose. True, she was alone when she turned her reading light off at night. But the darkness was no longer filled with thoughts of anger, betrayal, hatred or revenge! She had progressed, she had left those words far behind her!

The roster at Utopia had changed radically by the end of September 1965. Cassandra Hollister had already left in '63, followed a year later by Eve Handel. Then Peter Padon and Mo Jeddu. Nick Larrington made a hasty exit once the buy-out was definite.

Harvey Hill gave notice he was resigning at the end of the year.

He and Ruth had been talking for a while about opening a public relations firm along the lines of the respected and successful Rogers and Cowan Company. It seemed the opportune time.

Jenine Jasmine was now a freelance agent. Douglas Hassal had been so infuriated with the actress after she exposed his double life to Eve, that his first line of business was to terminate her contract, much to the consternation of his colleagues. She still reigned at the box office and they saw dollar signs disappearing when she walked out the front gate.

"Don't worry," Douglas had assured them, "there are a hundred broads out there who can put her away. I'll deliver!"

It was a wonderful opportunity for Jenine. Mo Jeddu had explained that she could get three times as much money per picture as an independent than she was getting under her studio guarantee. Plus she could pick and choose her scripts.

"Only with Eve's approval, she knows what's best for me," Jenine warned.

"Well it's a good thing you're out of there because no way would she get a say at that place!" Mo retorted.

Marc Saville was Utopia's leading male star. He didn't care who ran the studio as long as they kept those movies and paychecks coming. So he remained the head honcho.

Heidi Graham's marriage of "convenience" to Rodney Powers had blossomed with time. They were considered one of Hollywood's happiest couples. With Harvey Hill leaving, it seemed inevitable that Rodney would assume the role of leadership of the publicity department. Heidi did very well for the studio playing the "second" or even "third" banana roles and she was happy. The salary by now was excellent and she was doing what she loved to do—perform. She would stay as long as they exercised her options, after that—who knew? Maybe television!

Michael Flanders had asked for and received his release from Utopia soon after Eve left. At fifty-one he really hadn't aged and his acting ability had only become more polished. He was in great demand for movies made for television, MOWs they were called, especially the dramatic ones, and for distinguished character parts in features. He only had one problem, he was still drinking!

So the "alumni" of Utopia Studios had all sailed to various ports.

CHAPTER

49

Los Angeles, California
Monday, October 18, 1965

"I agree with you. I think this kid is right for the part," Jude told Eve.

Eve had asked Jude to come and hear a young girl, whom Nick had discovered, read for a role in a new series pilot, *Remember Ruby.*

"There's some film on her, let's look at that to see how she photographs and then make the final decision."

"Good!" Jude said. "Oh, by the way, are you free a week from Saturday, the thirtieth? Penelope thought of having a few people for dinner. She didn't want to rush you, but she's anxious to know you better. So's my whole family."

Eve hesitated. The decision to plunge back into the entertainment community had turned out so well. It surprised her how easily her reentry had been. Of course, she had returned to familiar territory.

But this was venturing into society, with strangers or near strangers. They had to know or at least have heard about the warts in her private life. Would there be stares, or whispers? Could she stand up under the scrutiny?

Once again, she had to ask herself if she wanted to live in a shell the rest of her life. Was she going to give Douglas half a victory?

Hell no!

"Why, thank you. Yes I'm open and—and equally eager to spend time with Penelope and to meet the rest of the clan."

"About seven? We're not a late-night group, if that's okay."

Eve laughed, "That's perfect, neither am I!"

"And casual, we're beach folk, you know. Could I send a car for you?"

"No, no, I'll be fine."

Cassandra and James Carpenter had been invited to Jude's as well, so James offered to pick up both women.

The settlement with Douglas Hassal had finally come to a conclusion. His lawyers couldn't break the will of the elder Hassals, but they did present the argument that Eve had come into their lives much later than their son, obviously, so half of the estate should be Douglas's alone, and then the other half would be fifty-fifty. What Eve and Douglas had earned since the marriage would be evenly split. James had wanted to debate the issue, but Eve had said no—she just wanted to get it over with. She had had enough and now just wanted to be completely free of Douglas Hassal. James realized the wisdom of this from a psychological standpoint, so he allowed their assessment to stand unchallenged.

But privately he told Douglas's lawyers that he was sending his bill to them. "You know as well as I that your scenario is nebulous and could easily be thrown out of court. Tell Mr. Hassal to pay my bill and be glad he's dealing with an honorable woman. Personally, I would have enjoyed the fight, but my client's wishes come first." James had received a check without a questioning word.

Penelope and Jude greeted the new arrivals warmly. Eve's first thought was that Penelope was even more radiant then she remembered.

Revel Abavas Franks was the biggest surprise for Eve. Matthew, the brother, was a younger version of Jude, handsome with the same dark eyes and dark hair. And Polly, his wife, was a petite, blond, blue-eyed firecracker, cute as all get out. But Revel looked as if she'd come from another family—long auburn hair, fair complexion and hazel eyes. Eve had a hunch she was a free spirit. Vincent, her husband of just over a year, was tall and slim with sandy-colored hair and brown eyes. James had mentioned him at one time, commenting on how brilliant—and pleasant—he was.

Eve recalled some vague references about Jude: poor immigrant parents who worked their way into prominence; invaluable assistant and then partner of Wade Colby; something about tragedies with a wife and child, or wives. She was reflecting on what a remarkable family they were, and only caught the last part of what Jude was saying, "—and I'm sure you've met Arthur Burdsey."

Eve suddenly found herself face-to-face with Arthur. It was totally unpredicted. But of course! Arthur and Wade had been quite close, and naturally Arthur would know Jude. She just hadn't thought about it.

"Oh, yes! So good to see you again, Artie." There was no cause to be nervous, she didn't have to worry about Douglas anymore, not that it would have mattered to him, anyway. Maybe that was why she had butterflies, no barriers to shield her. There was no reason why Arthur couldn't be a friend again.

Arthur's eyes were bright with anticipation. "You look lovely, Eve."

Jude was intuitive and instantly recognized there was something more between them than appeared on the surface. "Let me scare you up a drink. Would you like champagne, or is there anything else you might prefer?"

"Ah, champagne, please!"

"Artie, look after Eve while I play host for a second."

There was an awkward silence. Then both spoke at once. "Ar—" "Eve—"

"I'm sorry," Eve said. "You were about to say?"

"No, I'm sorry," Arthur replied. "I guess I'm a little flustered."

"Me, too!" Eve admitted.

Another pause.

"I, I have to confess," Arthur said, "I've been pestering Abe. I—he was worried about you and I made him tell me how you were. I didn't mean to pry, but I had to know. That's why I was so happy to see you tonight, glowing with health and beauty."

"I guessed as much." She lowered her eyes. "I think I was embarrassed and, and ashamed. I haven't seen anyone else but the family and the few who were there, since a year ago May."

Eve looked up, misty, but unfaltering. "The first time is over, I've been baptized. Now I can move forward!"

She heaved a long sigh of relief, then breathed in deeply as if replenishing her body, refueling her determination. "Forgive my strangeness, Artie. I've really been struggling, striving to get back to normalcy."

Eve smiled sadly. "I had no idea how difficult each step would be. First in the business arena. And now, tonight, in a social situation. Can you imagine? Going through hell over everyday things I always took for granted?"

Arthur wanted to gather her in his arms and protect her from the world. His wonderful Eve, why had she been put through this?

On one hand he would have gladly strangled Douglas Hassal for his cruelty! On the other, he almost wanted to thank him for being such an ass in desecrating a treasure and thus allowing that work of art to be appreciated and loved by others. He had no doubt now, just as he'd known all of his life, he would watch over Eve forever. He knew they had always been friends, even in the years of complete separation, and tonight he sensed she had opened the door to revitalizing that rapport. Not that he had illusions of any deeper emotions from her. He was content that he would no longer be shut out of her life. If someone should come along to claim her at a later time, he would damn well make sure that guy was worthy.

Jude returned with Eve's champagne and a refill for Arthur. "Sorry it took so long, ran into a traffic jam at the bar, naturally."

He had the feeling it was safe to leave Eve and Arthur to mingle now. "Hope it's okay with you, Eve—Artie has experienced the ritual already—but the collective children always have to have the spotlight before bedtime, so prepare yourself."

Four boisterous children burst into the large, comfortable living room. "Can we watch TV for a while? The boys won't let us see what we want—can we go into your room?"

"Whoa!" cried out Jude and Matthew. Jude continued, "First you will say hello to our guests, and then we'll sort out the rest. Ladies first!"

Dewana and Prissy stepped forward. Polly said, "This is our Dewana, who is nine." Penelope added, "And here we have six-year-old Prissy." The girls curtsied and met Eve and Cassandra and then said hello to the familiar faces in the crowd. The rest were family.

Then came cousins Dewayne and Buzz. "Dewayne is Dewana's twin," Matthew explained. Jude then introduced his nine-year-old son. "Buzz will forever be one month younger than Dewayne, a fact he finds difficult to understand." Both boys shook hands with everyone.

"Now, why don't you ask Bob at the bar for your favorite juice and then your fathers will decide how to handle the television dilemma." Penelope was loving, but firm. The four said good-night, hugged their mothers and went to collect their treats.

Matthew took Dewayne and Buzz to the playroom to see their program, and Jude took Dewana and Prissy to the master bedroom. "I think our room is safer with the two of you in there," Jude whispered confidentially. The girls giggled and then kissed Jude good-night.

None of this escaped Eve. Her "coming out" choices had tested positive! These were good people!

"So how did last night go?" Ruth asked. The family had gathered at Ruth and Harvey's for Sunday dinner.

"Actually, quite well," Eve answered, almost surprising herself. "No one looked at me as if I were some kind of freak, or oddball or sickie. They seemed to accept me as they would, well, anyone, I guess."

"For God's sake, what did you expect? That a booth would be set up with you as the star attraction of a sideshow?" Ruth was being deliberately funny and outright, to clear Eve's mind of her predetermined fear of being ''someone different now.''

Everyone laughed, albeit a little skittishly.

''Frankly, I didn't know what to expect,'' Eve said honestly. ''But this group, well, they are interested in everything. And interesting themselves! Very outspoken, independent, free-thinking! No topic appears to be taboo, but the conversations aren't petty or gossipy, or mean-spirited. But they're not Goody Two-shoes, either, they just say it like it is!''

''You mean, they're like you and all of us!'' Ruth said, summing it up and making her point.

Eve looked around the table and then directly at Ruth, sanctioning her purpose. ''Yes, that's exactly what I mean!''

Abe decided to be bold, too. ''Artie told me he was going to Jude's for dinner this week. Was last night the night?''

With only a slight beat of delay, Eve replied levelly, ''Yes, he was there. And, and we had a nice talk.''

There were audible sounds of relief from around the room. This had been the last roadblock to Eve's recovery.

Los Angeles, California
Friday, December 24, 1965

Marc Saville paced anxiously in front of Cassandra's front door. He had a sack slung over one shoulder that was crammed with gaily wrapped packages. But he wasn't in a very gay mood at the moment. He had called earlier to see if he could come by with some presents for the children and Cassandra had been very gracious about the visit, as always.

He had the heebie-jeebies for a number of reasons. The guilt factor loomed as the largest. He hadn't seen his little ones or been in their lives as much as he would have liked, and it was his fault and his fault alone. Cassandra had never denied him access, actually she had encouraged more involvement from Marc for their sake.

But when he was around K.C. and D.E.—Dianne's nickname had come about in the past year because she wanted to be more like her big brother—Cassandra was naturally close by, too. Those moments made him aware of what he had lost: seeing the tots develop; being a family; loving a woman. Sex was not the issue, he had all he could handle, but he felt nostalgia for the specialness of a certain kind of shared passion.

So he hadn't always taken advantage of the opportunity to be in contact when he had the time between pictures or on off days. Now he wondered if he could ever catch up.

Finally he found the nerve to ring the doorbell. He heard steps and then Cassandra's voice, "I'll get it, Margaret!"

The door swung open and Marc could only stare. Cassandra was wearing a forest-green velvet skirt and matching turtleneck top, with a two-strand pearl necklace and pearl-drop earrings. Her hair hung loosely, framing her perfect bone structure, and her eyes, ah, those lustrous hazel eyes, had picked up hints of the deep green. She was a beautiful sight to behold.

"Hi, Marc," Cassandra said pleasantly. "Come in. We're just about to finish the decorating."

He followed this glorious creature inside like a little puppy dog.

"K.C., D.E.—your daddy's here!"

Five-year-old K.C. didn't run to say hello. He sort of grunted his greeting. D.E., on the other hand, at four, was somewhat more enthusiastic.

"Daddy, see owa twee? F'r me?" D.E. pointed toward the big bag where colored paper and bows peeked out.

"I'm sorry," Cassandra apologized. "Let me relieve you of your bundles and take your coat."

Marc pulled himself together. "Hi, princess! Well, some are for you and some are for K.C. You wouldn't want Santa to forget your brother, now, would you?"

He picked up his daughter and waltzed her around the room. What a delicious feeling to hold her, to have her soft arms around his neck, to hear her giggle with delight. He had forgotten how good it was!

"Ain't no Santa Claus!" K.C. grumbled, spraying canned "snow" on the branches.

"Hey there, young man," Cassandra called, returning from hanging up Marc's coat in time to hear the comment. "What kind of sass is that? First, we don't say 'ain't,' and second, we talked about Santa Claus being an idea, an expression of love toward others, a way of giving a gift to show your love. So, there is a

Santa Claus—each and every one of us can be Santa Claus. And whose birthday are we celebrating? We give presents to honor…?''

''Baby Jesus!'' D.E. yelled.

''Yes. K.C., who?'' Cassandra pursued.

''Baby Jesus,'' K.C. admitted reluctantly.

Cassandra bent over and gave him a hug and a kiss. ''That's my man.''

Marc put D.E. down and went over to K.C. ''Your mom's right, you know, I believe that. Need some help?'' He picked up another can and sprayed some higher branches.

''You know what you could do,'' Cassandra suggested. ''I mean, only if you have the time—''

Marc quickly interrupted, ''I have plenty of time—for anything!''

''Well, it's kind of hard for me to put the star on the top of the tree. If—''

''Say no more! Us guys'll take it from here. Show me where the ladder is, K.C.''

The two came back with the big ladder. ''Now, you go first, K.C.,'' Marc said, explaining his plan. ''I'll be right behind you with the goods. When we get high enough, I'll give you the star and hold you for balance while you reach and crown the tree!''

K.C.'s eyes glowed with excitement. *He* was going to climb tall, just like the big boys!

''Ta-da!'' Marc announced grandly. ''Mission accomplished!''

D.E. clapped her hands, ''It's pwetty!''

Cassandra smiled. ''Would you like some wine as a reward?''

''As a matter of fact, yes!'' he replied.

Within minutes the children were arranging the packages around the tree, and Cassandra and Marc were on the sofa sipping their wine. Marc felt a sense of contentment, of peace, creeping through his person. This was right, this was the way it should be, this was what he wanted.

He put a hand over hers. ''I've longed for this, Cassie. You and me, watching our kids around a Christmas tree, holding hands. Cassie, I love you! I miss you! I want to come back, have everything the way it was. I know we could be good together again. The kids need a man around the house. And I can change, I have changed. Please take me back!''

Marc had inched closer and closer, now their faces were almost touching.

The doorbell clanged. They listened, glued in position, Marc's plea suspended in the air, as Margaret opened the door, exchanged words with someone and shuffled around, obviously taking a coat. Then they waited as one pair of footsteps approached the room.

''Merry Christmas!'' James Carpenter called out as he entered through the archway. He stopped dead in his tracks at the blissful family scene before him. His arms were laden with brightly wrapped boxes and his face quickly matched the color of the shiny paper. James was tall, well-groomed, edging toward a Wall Street look, and secure. Now, however, he appeared frazzled and unsure of himself.

''I, ah, these are, didn't mean to barge— Well, I'll be go—''

Cassandra jumped up and saved him from further embarrassment. ''Jim, how sweet of you to come by. Marc just dropped in to play Santa, too!''

She fluttered around, ''My goodness, do you think we have room under the tree? You two must have been very good this year, look how you are loved! How about a drink, Jim? Wine or...?''

James's eyes were still glazed. ''I think I could use one. Scotch, please. I'll only stay a minute....''

There was an awkward silence while Cassandra left to fix James's cocktail. The little ones acted as mediators unknowingly.

''Uncle Jim?'' K.C. said.

James forced himself to focus. ''Yes, K.C.?''

''''Member the movie at Mr. Jude's?''

''Of course!'' He was so grateful for K.C. at that moment. ''It was called *The Sound of Music*.''

K.C. cheered triumphantly. ''I told you, D.E! She said name was 'Do'!''

''Well, she is partly correct. There was a wonderful song, 'Do,

Re, Mi!' A favorite of mine. Julie Andrews and all of the children sang it.''

''Didja see movie, Daddy?'' D.E. asked.

''I'm afraid not, honey. But now I think I better.''

Both men welcomed Cassandra's reappearance. James took two healthy swigs as soon as she handed him his glass. She could understand James's shock to find Marc here, and his surprise at her apparent calmness. After all, he had handled the divorce and been privy to her emotional chaos.

Marc had sized up the situation immediately. ''Uncle Jim'' was it! He wondered how long they had been dating and if he had scored yet. The guy had the hots for Cassandra and was thrown for a loop to find her ex not only at the house but sitting nice and cozy next to her. James would be in the loony bin if he knew where Marc hoped to end up tonight and for many nights to come. Because he was serious, he wanted to marry her again.

James finished his drink quickly and said his goodbyes. Cassandra saw him to the door. ''I apologize. I—I—should have called first,'' he stammered. He was afraid to let her see him too clearly, she might see what his eyes were saying. ''Merry Christmas, Cassie,'' he whispered huskily, and made a hasty retreat.

Cassandra watched until his car drove off, then slowly walked back to the den.

''All right, the tree is done and our deal was bedtime afterward,'' she called out.

''Aw, Mom,'' K.C. started to protest.

''A deal is a deal!'' she said quietly but with authority. ''Look at Spartacus, it's been a full day, he's already out. And think of tomorrow morning, we have to be wide awake.''

K.C. and D.E. kissed Marc, and Cassandra was on her way upstairs with them when she stopped suddenly. ''How could I forget? The milk and cookies for Santa—we have to put out the milk and cookies!''

''Come on, Daddy, you, too!'' yelled the two as they raced for the kitchen. Even Spartacus woke up and ran with them, barking, but not sure what at!

They went through the ritual, carefully pouring the milk and organizing the cookies just so on the plate until everyone was satisfied, then placed the treat near the fireplace.

"Okay, now we're ready!"

Marc brushed by Cassandra, "I'll be waiting."

She helped them change into their pajamas, watched as they brushed their teeth and heard their prayers. Silently she said her own. When she tucked each one in she gave them an extra squeeze and hug, more for her reassurance than theirs.

Only the glowing fragments from the fireplace, the tree lights and one small lamp lit the room. Marc had turned off the rest of the lights. Christmas carols were still playing on the stereo.

He rose to meet her. "That was fun tonight, they're great kids, thanks to you. But I want to help now!" He started to pull her toward him, but she eluded his hold.

"I need to talk to you, Marc. Please, sit down."

She stared long and hard at him. Then spoke softly. "There were times in the last two and a half years when I would have given anything to hear the words I heard tonight. I missed you—a lot. I missed having someone to share the children with, I never liked being alone. I did still love you—for a while. I don't love you anymore Marc. I don't know when I stopped loving you. But I did. I don't hate you, either. I can be friends—I want to be friends— for the children's sake and for ours, too. You can see them, play with them, have outings with them anytime. We can even do it together, the four of us, if you want. But we can't be anything more than friends. We can only be—friends."

Now she understood why she had been so serene this whole night!

Eve settled herself comfortably in her seat. The first-class section of the American Airlines flight to Chicago was not even half filled, actually the entire plane was rather empty. Most people had probably already left for their Christmas Eve destination. Good, it would be a nice, uneventful trip; she was happy that she'd chosen the late departure time.

"Champagne, Miss Handel?" the steward asked as he checked his passenger list. "Or juice?"

"I think I'll have champagne." Why not? It was the beginning of her week's vacation. There was no shortage of material she had to read, work followed her even on a holiday. But she had plenty of time to do it leisurely and it never seemed like work, anyway—reading was a tonic to her.

The family had figured out an efficient plan, compatible for everyone. Abe, Ruth and Harvey left on Saturday, December 18 to spend the week with Mama and Papa Handelstein. Nick went to see his relatives in New York. Eve would arrive on the twenty-fourth, and everyone would have Christmas together on the twenty-fifth. The first three to arrive would leave Sunday the twenty-sixth for Los Angeles and Eve would stay until the following Sunday.

Time had just flown by. She forgot where she'd heard it, but the saying was so true—the older one gets, the faster the time goes. It didn't seem possible she had been at Colvas for three and a half months. On the other hand, because the union had been so effortless and fruitful she almost felt that she had been there forever. How out-of-the-world lucky she had been to land first at Pad-Dar, then Status, Utopia and now Colvas. She had had the crème de la crème from the very beginning of her career.

Her thoughts were disrupted by an arriving passenger. She picked up a script and buried her face in it, pretending to be very occupied. Oh, no, the person had stopped in the aisle beside her row.

"Seat 2AB, this is it! Eve? It *is* you!"

Eve recognized the voice immediately, before she looked up into the smiling face of Arthur Burdsey.

"I'm afraid you're stuck with me," he said contritely. "Unless there's an empty seat somewhere else. You look busy, I don't want to bother you."

Eve laughed, "That was my defense pose in case it was some bore. But not for your benefit. Please, sit! What a pleasant surprise."

Arthur put his carry-on in the overhead compartment and buckled up. He accepted a glass of champagne and turned to Eve. ''A toast to what has started out to be a very merry Christmas Eve.''

They saluted and drank. ''I assume you are visiting your parents for the holidays?'' he asked.

She nodded. ''Until the second of January. I haven't seen Mama and Papa since, well, for a while. They don't know all the—they just know about the divorce.''

''Same here,'' Arthur cut in quickly. ''No reason or need for them—or anyone—to have the details. They simply need to know that the dastardly deeds are done!'' He twirled an imaginary menacing mustache, and spoke in a dark, evil voice.

''Exactly!'' Eve answered conspiratorially, grateful for his ability to pull her away from a possible pitfall.

''I'm afraid I have to whisk these away for takeoff,'' the attendant announced, taking their glasses. ''But I'll bring a refill as soon as we're airborne.''

''Did you say you were coming home the second?'' Arthur asked.

''Yes, on the noon flight.''

''I'll be damned, this is my lucky day. Me, too!''

Arthur leaned back, very pleased with himself. He had known her precise travel reservations—Jude's secretary had found the information on the sly. And he had booked the seat next to her both ways. He felt meeting ''accidentally'' like this wouldn't be intimidating, that it would provide a safety net. Whereas calling and suggesting dinner could challenge her into making a decision she wasn't ready to make, committing or agreeing to an actual date.

They did have more champagne and enjoyed an uncommonly tasty dinner. The conversation was kept uncomplicated and objective.

''Our compliments to the chef!'' Arthur joked when they removed his tray.

''You should leave a very large tip, Artie.'' Eve leaned over confidentially. ''The service was excellent. We will be sure to recommend this fly-through restaurant to our friends.''

Arthur gazed at her, so happy to see traces of *his* Eve shining through. He knew at work she was in top form—Jude never stopped raving. And he was confident he could eventually strip away the remaining layers of scar tissue to discover the lady he had always known.

Arthur had thought this through carefully. He had deliberately not ordered a car to pick him up in Chicago, correctly assuming Abe would meet Eve and offer Arthur a ride, too.

"How great you were on the same plane!" Abe exclaimed. "How are you getting home?"

"Oh, I'll just hop a cab. I didn't want Dad driving at night, that worries me!"

"Gotcha! Feel the same way about ours," Abe agreed. "But the only cab you'll get in is 'Abe's Curb to Curb Service,' it's a new company."

Arthur laughed, "Okay! But only if 'Artie's Artful Dodger Limousine' gets the job of taking Miss Eve to the airport on the second. It so happens we're on the same flight back to Los Angeles, too."

"Deal! It's perfect, neither set of parents have to make the haul out here!"

Arthur just smiled. Everything was going according to Hoyle.

CHAPTER
51

Chicago, Illinois
Saturday, December 25, 1965

"I can't believe we're all together, it's been so long." Mama Mildred was beside herself with joy.

"Now, Millie, don't get yourself all emotionally worked up," Papa Samuel warned.

Everyone seated at the heavy old oak dining table traded amused glances, for each had seen Samuel's teary eyes last night when Eve had arrived and finally the whole family was gathered under the same roof.

"Even Artie!" Mildred continued, oblivious to what was going on. "It was like the old days. Alicia and Randall were thrilled their boy was coming. Randall hasn't been too well, you know."

As usual, and just like "the old days," the conversation was lively and far-flung, covering topics from the neighboring Burdseys to Vietnam.

"I know you weren't hurt or anything, but were any of you in danger during those terrible riots in Watts?" Mildred asked.

"Fortunately the damage didn't get close to our homes, but some business structures in Hollywood had a few dents and bullet holes," Harvey said, answering for all.

"A nice thing that came out of the mess was a desire from both sides to try to make relations better," Abe explained. "A client of mine, Michael Klein, whose father, Gene Klein, owns National General, met with some of the gang leaders. There hadn't even been a movie theater in the area, which could have provided the young people a place to go without inviting trouble. So Michael contacted some people, arranged for a movie projector and big screen to be set up in a school auditorium, persuaded the major studios to alternate showing first-run releases there, and only charge a quarter admission. And best of all, the gang members acted as ushers, so believe me, no one—but no one—misbehaved."

"There was even a grand opening, like a premiere, that attracted a lot of press," Ruth added. "And quite a few celebrities showed up. Jenine Jasmine made a huge hit. She got out of her limo, looking great, saw this adorable toddler, picked the little tyke up, grabbed the mom's hand and walked into the crowd. Everyone *loved* her! The picture made the front page in almost every newspaper in the country, if not the world."

"I saw that! It was in our paper," Samuel said.

"And Cassandra Hollister was supposed to make a little welcome speech, sort of a dedication," Eve added, sharing another anecdote. "It was so crowded, even in the aisles, she was helped to the stage by walking on the arms of the seats, everyone holding her and propelling her along. She made it to the front row and was just lifted up by two strong guys. She said it was an experience of a lifetime."

There was a slight lull, while they mulled over those images.

"I hope good can come out of every bad experience," Samuel stated somberly. "We were supposed to fight the war to end all wars in World War I. Then, once again, we were supposed to fight the war to end all wars in World War II. Now we send U.S. troops to the Dominican Republic in their civil war. We send thirty-five hundred marines to Da Nang in a war between North and South Vietnam. India and Pakistan are at war. I don't understand! Didn't we learn anything from two World Wars? And Korea!"

"Sam, calm down, remember your blood pressure!" Mildred scolded.

Abe attempted to ease his father's concern. "Maybe we have learned something, Papa. Maybe we realize we can't have World War III because of the A-bomb, so we try to keep the squabbles between countries in their locales so it doesn't become global. But what I *don't* get is why the U.S. has to get in the middle of every disagreement?"

"Especially when these differences—take India and Pakistan, the Israelis and Arabs—have been going on for years, even centuries," Harvey added.

Mildred put her hands to her ears. "Enough! I don't want to hear any more! Can't we talk about something pleasant?"

"What? Like the murder of Malcom X? Or Winston Churchill's funeral?" Ruth asked with a wicked grin.

"Don't pay any attention, Mama," Eve, the peacemaker, said. "There are many wonderful and interesting subjects to kick around. The advances made in medicine, for example. I read an issue of *Life* magazine that carried a report about the possibilities of artificial body parts and transplant organs opening whole new frontiers. One photograph showed a calf fitted with the most futuristic device of them all—a mechanical heart!"

"We could really get hot and heavy on the pros and cons of pop art, like Rauschenberg's paintings." Ruth was eager to debate that one.

And so the evening continued!

Discussions were going on in the Burdseys' dining room, as well. The normal amount of catching up, comments about current issues, Vietnam again in the forefront.

"Mark my words," Randall said ominously, "this involvement is going to have longer-lasting negative effects than we anticipate."

"I don't know if I share your complete doom-and-gloom prognosis," Arthur ventured. "But I agree, it isn't a situation I'm pleased about."

Alicia wanted to shift gears. "How does Eve look, Artie? I mean, is she all right?"

"She looks absolutely wonderful! And of course she's all right," Arthur added rather sharply.

"Well, I was, we were, concerned. There are rumors that she had a nervous breakdown and is in terrible shape."

Arthur was seething inside! Damn these small-minded people in this dim-witted circle of society. He was sure the source of this information had come from Gwen's mother, who had obviously heard it from Gwen. Had they nothing better to gossip about?

Ignoring the fact Eve had had a breakdown, he said, "Eve took some time off after the divorce to settle her affairs, of course. But then the head of Colvas, Jude Abavas—you remember Wade's partner—begged her to be his second-in-command at the studio. And he calls me every day wondering how he ever managed without her!"

"I'm glad, I always liked Eve," Randall said. He thought about that for a minute, and Arthur could see him starting to get riled up.

"My friend, Joe Hassal, told me that marrying Eve was the best thing his son ever did. He really thought a lot of her, and said he was going to name her as an heir in her own right, not just as Doug's wife. I remember he added, 'In case Doug screws up.'"

Randall turned to his wife. "Goddamn it, every time you come home from one of those highfalutin biddy gatherings, you tell me a lot of crap about people, all bullshit!"

"Randall!" Alicia cried, shocked.

"I don't care! That's what it is! And next time you see them you can tell them I said so!" Randall yelled.

Arthur had not intended to turn tonight into a brawl. "Tell you what, Mom. The others are heading home, but Eve is staying until the second. As a matter of fact we're both leaving on the same plane. Why don't you invite Mr. and Mrs. Handel and Eve for dinner this week, and you will see for yourself. Then you can report your opinion back to your—friends! How's that?"

"Perfect!" interjected a more composed Randall.

"Fine!" a rattled Alicia replied.

Mildred, Samuel and Eve arrived for dinner at seven sharp. Arthur hurried to the door to greet them. When he took Eve's coat he accidentally touched her neck and almost jumped back. His reaction to her was as electric as it had ever been.

It was a casual evening, but Eve had taken particular pains in choosing her wardrobe. She decided on a long black velvet skirt, a tight velvet belt decorated with a gold-and-ebony buckle, and a white long-sleeved organdy blouse with a high Elizabethan collar in back and plunging neckline in front. Extremely feminine and appealing.

She had learned from Jenine Jasmine's beauty tips. Her black hair was pulled into a twist, exposing more of her creamy skin. Her dark eyes were emphasized with a soft shadow, and she wore an earthy tone of lipstick. The years had been kind to Eve. Her bone structure protected her from early sagging, and her few lines didn't seem to define aging, only added a look of mature beauty. At forty-seven her figure was intact: the belt accentuated her small waist and the low-cut shirt allowed a hint of the full breasts it covered.

Arthur had always marveled at the way Eve entered a room. Although diminutive, she carried herself like a giant. One immediately recognized a presence. He enjoyed his mother's reaction to no end—Alicia had forgotten how impressive Eve was. His father was totally captivated. Arthur knew Randall still thought of Eve as the "little girl next door," despite the fact he had seen her a few times over the years. Arthur was positive Randall hadn't really paid attention. But he sure was tonight!

Of course Eve wasn't aware she was being graded. There was no pressure, she was just very comfortable with old friends and her family. She felt extremely relaxed and radiated warmth and charm. They were interested in her work and the people around her, and she held center stage willingly and graciously.

"And besides his flair for the business, Jude is a doting husband and stepfather. As you know he married Wade Colby's widow. Anyway, he's always telling us what the kids are up to. Buzz, he's nine, came home with his first joke. 'Jude, why does a dog cross the road? To get to the barking lot!'"

"How sweet!" Mildred said, and Alicia nodded in accord.

"Then, Jude said one night they were all watching some television show and he leaned over and kissed Penelope. Prissy, who's about six, I think, asked, 'Daddy Jude, why are you tasting Mommy?'"

"Out of the mouths of babes," Alicia remarked, and Mildred indicated her agreement.

It couldn't have been a more harmonious night. When the Handels left, Arthur looked at his mother. "Well?"

Alicia was chagrined. "I can't imagine what those ladies were thinking. I wonder if they—well, you and Gwen divorced, and you were engaged to Eve once—could they have been trying to discredit Eve because of that?"

"Who cares?" Randall said.

"The important thing, Mom, is that you saw her and can quell any future remarks."

"Alicia, it was an excellent dinner," Randall interjected. "But now I want to talk to Artie about some office matters, and I know you don't have the stomach for that. Why don't you go on up to bed?"

"I am tired and I certainly do not care to hear about business. Good night, Randall, good night, Artie." Alicia gave Arthur a hug and made her exit.

"Fix us a nightcap please, Artie, a snifter of brandy would hit the spot about now."

Arthur busied himself at the bar. Randall chuckled to himself. "Eve didn't even know it, but she scored a knockout in the first round!"

"There you are, Dad! A nice brandy to sip before the fire!"

"I imagine you don't use the fireplace much in California?"

"No, not very often."

Randall studied his son. "I've been thinking of retiring, Artie."

Arthur showed his surprise.

"Well, I haven't been feeling up to snuff lately. Maybe I should ease off, take your mother on some of those trips I always promised and seldom followed through on."

Arthur leaned forward earnestly. ''Dad, if that is what you want, then you must do it! Thank God we have enough money, you should be reaping the rewards of all you have put into the firm.''

''I'll probably be bored shitless. I always thought I'd just keel over at my desk one day. I really like what I do.''

Randall sipped his brandy. After a beat, he startled Arthur by asking, ''What would you think about moving back to Chicago and taking over the whole company?''

It was Arthur's turn to sip and think. Finally he faced his father and spoke. ''It means a great deal that you have that kind of trust in me and my ability. Thank you, Dad.''

Arthur rose and put his hand on Randall's shoulder in a gesture of affection. He walked around, groping for the right words, the right approach.

''I want to help you as much as I possibly can in the restructuring of your chain of command, if that is what you decide to do. I would come and fill in for a while until you found a qualified replacement. But Dad, I don't want to live here again. My life is in California now, my roots are too deep to pull up at this stage.''

''Eve being in California wouldn't factor in, would it?''

Arthur felt his father was teasing him, in his own conservative way. ''Possibly! I'm leveling with you, Dad. It makes me very happy that Eve and I are on an even course again. I want to protect her and be able to watch over her, as my friend. And if that is all it ever is, I'll settle for that.''

''Forgive me, son. I didn't mean to make light of something, or someone, so important to you. I should have known.''

''No, no reason! Don't misinterpret, I haven't been pining or in misery all these years since Eve went to Hollywood. I've had a great life—ups and downs just like everyone else. But fate put us in contact again and I don't want to let it go.''

''I understand, Artie.'' Randall was a little misty-eyed. He was very proud of the person Arthur had become.

''But also, Dad, all of my friends and associates are out there. I'm too old to try to reestablish myself in Chicago.''

''Nor should you have to! Give us a refill—haven't enjoyed a talk so much in a long time!'' Randall handed his glass to Arthur. ''You know, it just dawned on me. Why does the main office have to be here? Your branch does as much volume as we do. Why couldn't you be CEO with the headquarters of Burdsey & Co. situated in Los Angeles? You need to enlarge the space and staff, of course, and you'd leave a smaller office here in Chicago. You would carry most of the responsibility, I could still be involved in a minority position—that way I wouldn't go altogether crazy—but I could spend more time away from the grind!''

The two men digested the concept that had just been put forward. Arthur broke the silence first.

''Naturally, for me, that would be an ideal plan. I would do my damnedest not to disappoint you or discredit our enterprise. But this really has to be your call. Would the people you've personally handled be willing to accept me if you should happen to be away and I had to make a judgment decision? And I'm in Los Angeles, not Chicago!''

''I'll have to find that out. My gut tells me yes! Everyone I deal with knows you've represented us on the West Coast and done an excellent job. Certainly you have the background, and have continued the same high degree of service we pride ourselves on. And don't forget, my contemporaries are probably starting to relegate duties to their younger executives, too. More than likely you would bond better with them than I.''

''Also if need be, I could always hop on a plane and be here in a matter of hours.''

''Exactly!'' Randall was beaming. ''I think we may have made a giant step for the Burdsey family tonight. I salute—the new Burdsey & Co.

Eve and Arthur traded notes about their visits on the way home.

''It was one of the most pleasant holiday weeks in some years,'' Eve observed. ''Everyone seemed to be on the same wavelength. What about you?''

''Ditto! Must have been something in the air! It was particularly special I think because the Handelsteins and Burdseys congregated like—like old times." Arthur watched Eve's reaction very carefully.

With no hesitation, Eve replied, "Yes, I agree. Our dinner and the time we all spent together did make it nicer."

Arthur heaved a sigh of relief. That was a good response.

"Artie, you were very considerate to take me to a film New Year's Eve. I'm sure you had a fistful of party invitations."

"Know what?" Arthur leaned over. "Maybe some, but I didn't even recognize who the people were! I've lost touch, I really don't *know* anyone here anymore, at least on a personal basis. Some business friends, that's about it! And besides, it was fun, I've never gone to a movie theater on New Year's Eve before. The audience really gets wound up."

"Neither had I! And I felt the exhilaration too! *The Sandpiper* was fine, but it was really secondary. The celebration was the star!"

They sat back savoring their thoughts. The attendant kept refilling their wine goblets, and without being aware, both were on their way to getting looped.

"Something—something major may take place, Eve," Arthur said gravely. "I—the playboy son—may become chief executive officer of Burdsey & Co." He made a grand sweep with his hand, indicating how big.

"How wonderful, Artie! A toast!" The two drained their glasses.

All of a sudden, the plane made a sickening lurch and dropped dramatically in altitude. One of the attendants who had a bottle in her hand lost her balance near their seats and fell. Arthur quickly grabbed the bottle before it could fall and break, freed himself from his seat belt and was able to help her to her feet. The steward rushed forward and took over.

The captain's voice came from the loudspeaker. "Cabin crews take your landing positions. Ladies and gentlemen, be sure your buckles are securely fastened. Do not move from your seats. We are encountering unexpected air pockets and sudden turbulence. Don't be alarmed, we'll tell you when it is safe to resume normal activities."

Eve and Arthur hadn't realized it, but instinctively their hands had reached out for each other's.

Arthur didn't want their minds to dwell on what was happening. "What do I have here? Aha! It's wine! I don't know about you, but I intend to have some, in fact I intend to have a lot."

Eve was still clutching her glass in her other hand. Arthur poured for her. "My glass seems to have been lost in the shuffle, so with your permission I'll just guzzle from the bottle. I don't have any cooties, so here goes!"

She giggled, her face having regained some color. The plane was still being jerked about, but Arthur was succeeding in diverting her attention. He kept the flow of spirits coming, and his sense of humor turned even hazardous subjects into comedy.

Arthur beckoned her to move closer. "You do know," he whispered collaboratively, "that our ex's are an *item!*" He glanced to see if the whole Douglas debacle would raise its ugly head. So far, so good! Even in his slightly inebriated state, he knew it would be a major victory if he could get Eve to *laugh* about something connected to Douglas.

"Word has it that they are behaving so ridiculously they have become the laughingstock of the Hollywood community. And now I hear Doug had a face-lift and Gwen had her boobs enlarged—a definite necessity, I might add." Arthur burst out laughing at that disclosure, and Eve found herself joining him. Somehow the image of these two cavorting publicly and grasping at youth did present a ludicrous mental picture.

As abruptly as the turbulence had hit the aircraft, it abated. This had been a flight of enormous significance, in more ways than one!

CHAPTER

52

Los Angeles, California
Monday, February 14, 1966

Cassandra Hollister burst through the door from the garage, her arms full of packages.

"Quick," she called to Margaret, who was in the kitchen, "hide these before the kids hear I'm home!"

Margaret grabbed the gifts and put them in the pantry in the nick of time as the thundering herd hurtled down the stairs. Spartacus beat everyone, barking and jumping.

"Don't jump! Good boy! Yes, I love you, too." Cassandra threw his latest treasure for him to fetch.

"Mommy!" D.E. yelled. "I did good—Miss T. liked my color book. See!"

"That's wonderful, honey," Cassandra said, picking her up. "How was your day, K.C.?"

The boy seemed subdued. "Okay."

Margaret caught Cassandra's eye and mimed a punch and pointed to the side of her cheek. Cassandra looked closer and saw a bruise on K.C.'s turned-away face. She put D.E. down and knelt beside her son.

"What's that, K.C.?"

"Got in a fight!" He seemed close to tears.

She sat on the floor and drew him close so he was next to her. "Can you tell me about it?"

"You're a girl!"

Margaret led D.E. away. "Come help me fix Spartacus's dinner, sweetheart."

"I'll try to understand, K.C.," Cassandra said gently.

"Well, this one guy thinks he's so tough. Well, we both reached for the ball at the same time. I said I got it first. He said no you dint. He jumped me and hit me. I hit him back and the teacher came and we both got in trouble—"

"Does it hurt?"

"Little," he sniffled.

"I'm no expert, but I do believe the best remedy is an ice pack. Why don't I get one?"

"Okay."

Cassandra filled a Ziploc bag with ice cubes. "What did your teacher do?"

"Made us 'pologize. No playtime for two days. Ain't fair—he hit first!"

"I can see your point," she said, applying the bag just below his left eye. "Hold it there as long as you can stand it. Then do it again about ten times."

She sat on a kitchen stool. "Even though he struck the first blow, the teacher—was it Mr. Smith?"

K.C. nodded.

"Mr. Smith didn't know that, and he had to stop the fighting. Did you tell him the other boy started it?"

"I ain't no squealer!"

Cassandra hid a smile. Their conversation sounded like it had been lifted from a James Cagney gangster movie. "Well, that's fine. What did we learn from this?"

"Don't know!"

"For starters, would you say that hitting isn't the best way to settle an argument?"

"Guess so!"

"What would the next choice be?"

"Don't know."

Cassandra sighed. Boys were definitely more difficult to raise. "Sometimes it's all right to give someone the benefit of the doubt. Maybe he did touch it a second ahead of you, or maybe you were a second ahead of him. So it takes a wise man to be able to say, 'Okay, I'll give it to you this time. But next time we're close, it's my turn to take it.' How does that sound?"

"Guess okay."

Cassandra had the feeling that solution didn't sit too well. What would a guy think? She had an idea!

"We could make sure you always have a nickel or a dime handy, say, in your pocket, then you could say 'Flip you for it, your call!' How's that?"

She could tell right away, he liked that better.

Margaret and D.E. and Spartacus returned, and Margaret announced it was time for the children to clean up for dinner.

"Auntie Eve is coming to eat with us," Cassandra told them.

Supper was over, the Valentine presents had been exchanged. Since Margaret had prepared heart-shaped chocolate tarts for dessert, Cassandra and Eve had conferred and decided to steer clear of sweets and remembered the youngsters with alternative gifts: a heart bracelet and a little apron covered with Cupids for D.E.; marbles and a catcher's mitt for K.C.; rawhide bones for Spartacus. Margaret received a heart-shaped key ring and a silver purse mirror. Eve brought Cassandra beautiful red roses.

Cassandra laughed when Eve opened her box. It was a small silver notepad. "I thought it was perfect for your pocketbook. You're always jotting things down."

D.E. and K.C. had gone up to bed. He'd asked for another ice pack for his injury—he was playing the "big man" for Auntie Eve.

"I guess a boy's first fight is some kind of milestone," Cassandra said, discussing the day's events with Eve. "I don't understand the male mentality. Damn, it's hard not having a man here to help me out. I squeezed by today because I remembered Marc was always betting—on anything. Everything had to be decided by heads or tails—not words dealing with right or wrong—just the luck of the draw.''

''What about asking Jim?'' Eve suggested.

Cassandra seemed eager to talk. ''I've been wanting to hash out some thoughts with you, we've both been so busy we never get the chance.''

''I know, Cassie dear. But here we are now, and we can go all night if you want.''

Cassandra told her about Marc's visit on Christmas Eve and how she had discovered she was truly free of him and had been for some time. ''He was right about one thing, the children do need a man in the house.''

Cassandra fidgeted nervously. ''Rick Revere, the New York actor who was in *Are You Anybody?* well, he asked me out. I did go to dinner a couple of times, and he was nice enough, I guess. But when he kissed me good-night and hinted about going further, I just didn't feel anything. He's so wrapped up in himself and his career, I don't think he's capable of caring deeply for someone else.''

She sighed and wandered around the room. ''Same thing happened when I dated a few other guys. No one aroused anything. It was like a limp handshake. I was beginning to wonder if I had dried up or something.''

Eve understood what Cassandra was saying only too well.

''And then, Christmas Eve, when Jim came by unexpectedly and didn't stay long when he saw Marc—at the door when he said 'Merry Christmas, Cassie,' he appeared so vulnerable and hurt that I wanted to take him in my arms and tell him to stay and hold me and kiss me. I wanted him to make love to me.

''Suddenly it all made sense. D.E. and K.C. and I have had someone to turn to in the last few years, someone who was only a phone call away. Jim! James Carpenter!''

She looked at Eve shyly. ''I might be in love with him! Is that all right? Am I crazy to love again? I think he cares for me, but I don't know for sure. What should I do?''

Eve went to her and led her back to the sofa. "Cassie, sweet Cassie, I'm not positive you're turning to the right person for advice. But maybe between us we can figure out our lives, because we both have had to come to grips with infidelity and betrayal. At least your husband didn't try to cheat you as well."

Cassandra half smiled, "That's true! You're one ahead of me in complaints."

"I am certain of one thing," Eve continued. "Yes, it is all right to feel emotion, love, passion again. It's not only all right, it's healthy and advantageous and normal. It's also quite wonderful to confront the infection and know you're cured. Good girl!" Eve gave her a congratulatory hug.

"Now, are you crazy to love again? I take that to mean, trust again? Let's think about that. Is it possible to have insurance that the man you love will never be unfaithful? Love insurance—might be a hell of a business! But seriously, I doubt there is any guarantee on that. So how can we protect ourselves when we open our hearts to exposure again? Maybe we have to provide as much preventative medicine as we can."

"You mean, like look at his past track record?" Cassandra asked.

"Absolutely! See what his pattern has been." Eve paused, hoping to come up with some more remedies.

"You realize, Cassie, this is all conjecture!"

"Of course, but it's making sense. Don't you think so?"

"Actually I do. Okay, what else? Oh—check his lasting power—"

Cassandra burst out laughing, then Eve caught on and joined in. "You are a devil! I didn't mean it that way—sexually—I meant—"

Everytime Eve began, Cassandra got the giggles and that would send Eve off.

Finally they settled down. "That felt good! Jenine would be proud of me. Whoever would have imagined we could find something amusing while discussing this subject? Anyway, as I was saying, watch how long he stays interested in something. Does he become bored easily? Is he always in a hurry to move on to something new? Those responses could transfer to a relationship as well.''

Eve sighed, ''In the long run, I guess after all the questions, it boils down to the fact we need the courage to have faith and patience. We know now that no one is perfect, and that includes us. We have to take the time and make the effort to work out the minor things. The major problems—well, we have to hope we won't have any. We have to believe in something!''

''Always remember the motto One Day at a Time.'' Cassandra was pensive. ''If we do the homework, then all we can do is try to survive one day at time. We could lock ourselves in a room, no one could hurt us there. But we'd never have anything to laugh about or, or cry about, or feel about. We'd never have anything to share with anyone.''

Eve was relieved, Cassandra had worked through the process well. ''And in regards to Jim, I am convinced that if you give him an opportunity, he will follow through if he's interested. I'm not a gambler, but I would put up money that says he's not merely interested, but intensely interested.''

Cassandra bolted upright. ''I just realized what day this is—I mean its significance.'' Cassandra surprised herself with her boldness. ''This was the date you were married, your anniversary. Are you upset? Can we talk about it? I'll tell you why I'm asking as soon as you answer!''

Eve was startled by the abrupt shift in the conversation. She had thought about the date, impossible not to identify with it, but had pushed it aside to deal with later. She had been busy at the studio, rushed to pick up the few gifts she had ordered, and then had focused completely on the evening and Cassandra's revelations.

Now she had to examine her feelings. Was she troubled? Did this day relight the fire of despair? She must be honest. What was her inner self saying?

Much to her amazement, she wasn't freaked out. She was saddened that twenty-two years had ended so ignobly, but ended they had! And she had weathered the storm, was a contributing citizen again. Yes, she was even having some good times!

"Cassie, no one is more flabbergasted than I am to hear me say, Yes we can talk about it, and no, I'm not in dire straits."

Cassandra threw her arms around Eve joyfully. "That makes me so glad! And makes you a free woman again!"

"I'm not quite sure I follow you, Cassie."

"I understood I was over Marc when our anniversary date didn't send me into a fit. Before, I would rant and rave, but a year ago this past January—that would be January 1, 1965—I was unhappy we had failed, but I wasn't wholly bummed out! Your answer told me, and you, the same thing. Don't you see?"

Eve did see. She was rationalizing her own experience the entire time she was attempting to help Cassie find her way tonight. Together they had found the glimmer of the light at the end of the tunnel.

Los Angeles, California
March 18, 1966

The telephone at Eve's house rang one Friday night in March.

"I'll get it, Hilda," Eve called out. Hilda and Ted Swenson had left Douglas Hassal's employ and moved to Eve's home once she'd been well enough for Yvonne to leave. Molly Montail came with them as maid and laundress. Without going into detail they had explained the Hassal residence was no longer a place they wanted to work.

"Hello?"

"Eve, it's Artie!"

"Well hello!" She was a bit surprised; they hadn't talked since the plane ride from Chicago.

"I wanted to know if you had any lasting ill effects after our harrowing flight?"

Eve laughed. "Only a slight hangover the next day. We must have gone through more than a couple of bottles of that bubbly stuff."

He groaned. "You, too? My head felt like a ton of lead was sitting on top of it. And wouldn't you know, Dad called that very day and wanted me to come right back."

"Oh, no!"

"Oh, yes! Remember I told you, I think I did, anyway, about the possible change in the Burdsey company?"

"Yes, but I don't recall many details," she admitted ruefully.

"So much has happened. Are you free any night soon? I'd really like to tell you about it—I mean, if you have the time."

"Well, I guess, yes, I would love to hear what's going on. Uh, tomorrow—Saturday—is good. But you probably have plans—"

Arthur broke in hurriedly, "No, I don't! Tomorrow would be perfect, I'm glad you weren't booked! Is seven all right?" He was very excited; he was actually going out with his Eve. Not an accidental meeting, not a manipulated encounter, but an honest-to-God arranged get-together.

Arthur reserved a back booth at Chasen's where it was quieter, but where one could still enjoy the restaurant's excellent cuisine and tasteful atmosphere. Walking into Chasen's was always a special experience. It was almost as if you were entering a private club because you always saw so many people you knew. It was, of course, completely open to the public, and an intriguing aspect of the restaurant was its diverse clientele. A Rockefeller might be in one booth, Mr. and Mrs. Kirk Douglas and Mr. and Mrs. Gregory Peck in another, Mr. and Mrs. Alfred Hitchcock next to them with Mr. and Mrs. Lew Wasserman. It boasted an olio of the rich and famous.

Eve and Arthur were ushered to their table by everyone's friend, Ron, the maître d'. They ordered a cocktail and relaxed in the deep, soft leather seats. Arthur could barely conceal his delight at being with Eve.

"Now, tell me all about what's happening, Artie. Before I have too much of something and forget things again," Eve joked.

He was so caught up in Eve, he almost didn't remember why they were there. "Oh, yes! Well..." He explained how Randall was gung-ho on the idea of Arthur taking over and wanted to get the ball rolling immediately. The details were manifold: getting the necessary papers in order, talking to all of the regular customers, hiring qualified people for the new home base in Los Angeles;

renting and equipping an entire floor in the building where Arthur was already located; and downsizing the Chicago office.

"Would you care to order, Mr. Burdsey?" the captain finally interrupted.

"Why don't you bring us another cocktail, and we'll peruse the menu, even though I almost know it by heart. I'm afraid I haven't allowed Miss Handel time to make up her mind."

Eve decided on her usual, the restaurant's famous chili and one of its signature dishes, the Hamburger Chasen. "I'm not very original, but no one makes it like you do!"

Arthur chose the chili as well, and the butterfly steak. And then he continued, "I think I've made six round trips since I saw you."

"That's a lot of effort and travel! But it seems to agree with you, no signs of fatigue or worry! You must be very proud, Artie. And your father must be pleased as punch to have his son represent his life's work. Congratulations!" Eve reached over and squeezed his hand, a natural gesture to show her appreciation for his happy news.

But for Arthur, the gesture meant more. He knew she wouldn't have had the freedom to offer that touch a few months ago. Instinctively he felt a difference in her, an openness that had not been there, a possible accessibility. He cautioned himself to be careful not to frighten her away, to nurture this rebirth. For the first time in many years, his heart had hope.

"Let's see, the date is Thursday, September 15, 1967. You were born in 1917, ah, that would make you fifty today. Right? What are you doing for your birthday, old man?" Abe teased Arthur during a break in their exercise regimen.

Arthur hurled his sopping towel, catching Abe in the middle. "You're not that far behind me, shithead!" He laughed, "If I weren't so damned happy, I'd probably be wallowing in frustration over the aging process. But I just can't get into that right now!" His eyes were bright. "For your information, smart-ass, I'm going to pick up your beautiful sister at 7:30 p.m. and then we are going to Jude and Penelope's for a quiet dinner. That is, unless you work the 'old man' so hard he can't make it!"

"In that case, I'll take it easy on you. I wouldn't want you to be too tired to enjoy your half-century celebration." Abe ran before Arthur could throw anything else.

When the session was over, Abe stayed for a little while just to shoot the breeze. "It's such a kick to see us all together again, like when we were kids!"

Arthur sighed deeply. "I wish I could voice what the past eighteen months have meant to me. And I'm not referring to the business, although that is very gratifying, too. But to see Eve blossom, to see her know she can believe in and trust a man's friendship again—it just is, well, everything to me."

"I know. We all know!" Abe said solemnly. "It's been that way for us, too—everyone feels so good!"

Arthur pushed the doorbell at 7:31 p.m., humming his new favorite tune, "On a Clear Day You Can See Forever."

"Good evening, Mr. Burdsey," Ted Swenson said in greeting. "Miss Handel is expecting you in the parlor."

He preceded Arthur and grandly opened the double doors. Lights suddenly blazed and fifty voices yelled out "Surprise," and from somewhere a band played and the voices sang "Happy birthday to You."

Arthur was stupefied, completely discombobulated. "Wh-wh-what'n the hell?"

Eve appeared from the midst of the throng. "Don't look so frightened," she laughed, "it's only your birthday party!"

She gave him a welcoming embrace and then allowed room for the other guests to swarm around and offer their congratulations. It was an inclusive gathering: all of the Handel clan, the Abavas tribe, Burdsey & Company people; Cassandra and James; even Jenine Jasmine with her latest conquest, a department store magnate.

"Look at this rock!" Jenine showed off a huge diamond ring on her engagement finger. "He says he'll give me a million every year we stay married. I don't know how long I'll last, but it's worth a try. He doesn't care if I keep working, so with my salary plus the mil, I could stash some real moola!"

At forty-five, Jenine still turned heads all over the world. And on this night, she was making a big splash wearing a black silk miniskirt—the latest fashion. Jenine, as Mo Jeddu had said years earlier, might be a "good broad," but she was not a "dumb broad." Perhaps not a Rhodes scholar, but smart enough to invest in her assets. She knew her body was an added resource to her God-given and Eve-guided talent, and she spent a lot of time at the gym keeping that endowment in good standing.

It was a fun evening—everyone thoroughly enjoyed the fact the "surprise" was a success. Abe hooted at Arthur, "Gotcha, old man!"

Arthur retorted, "I'm amazed you could keep it a secret when you're such a blabbermouth."

Eve had tented the backyard, the top of which was draped in black, with twinkling lights as stars and a crescent-shaped globe for the moon. Potted palm trees filled three sides while shimmering tinsel created the illusion of a sea on the fourth wall. A gentle breeze from hidden fans rustled the leaves of the trees and agitated the "water." It seemed as if they were on a tropical island with the soothing wind rushing lightly through their hair and against their faces.

Eve had booked a band that specialized in music from the big-band era of the thirties and forties for this special evening. All the guests really got into the swing dancing, even those who hadn't known that beat before. And no one could resist the dreamy, romantic songs from the forties. The music transcended ages; young and old swayed closely, captivated by the haunting melodies and soulful lyrics.

Arthur held Eve tightly. "I can't help thinking of the Christmas prom my first year in college. The same tunes, the same beautiful girl—"

Eve leaned her head against his chest. "I remember that night so well. The tunes are the same, but I'm afraid the girl isn't."

"She is to me," he said softly, drawing her near. Bodies responded to the spell of the music and molded one to the other.

Abruptly, the band switched to "In the Mood." "Gotta wake

you guys up—too early to go to sleep on me!'' Tex Beneke, the bandleader, called out.

Ruth and Harvey gamely gave it their all until "String of Pearls" ended the set. "Thank God it's over," Harvey gasped. "I'm getting too old for this jazz!"

"Ditto!" Ruth panted, a remark echoed by many huffing and puffing guests.

With a slight hint from the ever-observant Eve, Beneke returned to the slower rhythm for the next and final set. Arthur claimed Eve for his partner. "It's my birthday," he said to Peter Padon, "and I wished for this when I blew out the candles. Sorry!"

Reluctantly the guests departed. No one really wanted to leave, but it was a Thursday—a "school" night—and tomorrow was still a workday. Finally Arthur and Eve were alone.

"Dance with me again," Arthur requested.

"But the band, they're packing up...."

"We can go inside and play our own music."

Eve inhaled deeply, aware of a fluttering in her nerve endings, then resolutely led him to the dimly lit, private den. He poured two goblets of wine from the wet bar as she turned on the stereo. Frank Sinatra began to serenade them, as only he could.

"I toast my hostess!"

"Happy birthday, Artie."

They clinked their glasses and sipped. Then drinks were set aside, and she went into his open arms. Slowly they moved, undulating to the pulse, skin tingling as each step bonded new parts of their bodies.

"This is what I really wished for." His voice was so hoarse, he could barely talk.

Eve was floating, her senses reliving those innocent, unexplored tremors of long ago. But now she could identify the signals they were sending, could allow them to register and become stronger, and could relish the adventure they promised. Both were powerless in their voracious yearning. Arthur lowered his hands and cupped them around her buttocks, pressing her pelvis snugly against him. She answered him by massaging her breasts against his chest. Their demand was desperate now. Quickly they slipped out of their clothes and stood before each other. He gathered her in his arms and knelt, placing her gently on the thick carpet.

And then they were flesh upon flesh, enveloped in a fury of touching and kissing, and finally the supreme contact. Both shuddered with sheer pleasure, this was so right, so ideal. Nothing could curb the frenetic avalanche of emotion that drove them—and drove them—and drove them. They clung to each other, gasping for air, laughing and crying, in awe of their own passion.

"It's going to take me a long time to kiss every inch of your body, you know. Probably a lifetime," Arthur told her when they could speak. "Marry me, Eve!"

"My darling Artie, we were one years ago, we don't need a piece of paper to tell us what we already know. I've always loved you, I just had to prove something to myself before I could acknowledge that love. Then life sort of got away from us. I don't know why God gave me another chance, but I'm grateful, and I won't let anything get in the way this time."

Eve touched his cheek tenderly. "I can't believe what I'm about to say. Maybe Grandpa Handelstein was right—I *am* a hussy." She got her courage together, swallowed and said, "My bed has been patiently waiting for you for thirty years. I think it's time!"

Santa Monica, California
Sunday, December 24, 1967

"**I** now pronounce you man and wife. You may kiss the bride!"

James Carpenter lifted the veil covering Cassandra Hollister Carpenter's shining upturned face and tenderly touched her lips.

"You have made me the happiest man on earth," he whispered.

Eve had been right, of course. When James had sensed Cassandra's interest he had found the courage to ask her out. And the two had come together beautifully. They'd taken things slowly so that the children would become comfortable with the idea of James becoming a permanent part of their lives. But it hadn't taken long to realize both K.C. and Dianne adored him.

Cassandra took his arm and the couple made the return walk down the aisle. They were followed by their attendants: Eve Handel and Vincent Franks; Revel and Matthew Abavas; and ring bearer, Kent C. Saville, and flower girls, Dianne Eve Saville and Priscilla Helena Prickler Colby.

Arthur leaned over to capture Eve's left hand. They were sitting at their table alone for the moment; their dinner companions were either table-hopping or dancing. Cassandra and James had already performed the obligatory first dance and could now relax and enjoy friends and families.

Arthur slipped something on Eve's finger and then covered her hand with his. "I had hoped to give this to you yesterday, but Cassie's wedding rehearsal took priority—understandably. But it was an important day for us, too. Happy one hundredth anniversary, Eve!"

He released her hand, and she stared at an exquisite black pearl ring. Glimmering diamonds acted as a shield around the magnificent gem.

"Artie, it's, it's unbelievably beautiful, but—"

"Sh—sh! Yesterday was our one hundredth day together, September 15 to December 23, and I will never forget one minute of those days, ever!"

Eve gazed at him lovingly, her eyes glistening with tears.

"I knew it—I knew it!" Arthur exclaimed in excitement. "When I saw the black pearl I felt I was looking into your eyes—those dark, lustrous, deep eyes that bewitched me the moment I saw you. It's perfect!"

"I don't know what to say, Artie, except I love you. And I thank God every day that you are in my life."

55

Los Angeles, California
Thursday, January 1, 1970

"Ruthie! Abe! Mama and Papa are on the phone!" Eve called out.

"I'll say goodbye for now. Ruth and Abe want to wish you a happy New Year, too. Take care of yourselves—you promised! Artie sends his love—and big hugs from everyone."

Eve relinquished the phone and joined the rest of the group clustered in the den. The guys were watching the Rose Bowl game and the gals were mainly focusing on nineteen-month-old James Timothy Carpenter II and chatting. K.C. was with the men, and his assignment for the day was to keep an eye on the animal kingdom. Ruth and Harvey had brought Jay, and Cassandra and James hadn't been able to leave Spartacus behind, so Eve's Molly and Lucy had company and K.C. was to keep the peace. Dianne was the self-appointed nanny to Little Jim.

Abe had nicknamed the baby Little Jim, but he had cautioned them to think about the "Little Jim" versus "Big Jim" issue. "I didn't mind at first," he'd explained, "but when I grew taller than my grandpa I felt kinda silly being 'Little Abe'!"

"Good point!" James agreed. "Cassie, we'll have to do something about that."

"Fortunately we have some time," Cassandra had laughed. "He won't catch up for a while."

At halftime the two factions merged, and as with every New Year the group looked back and to the future.

"I hadn't believed it would be possible to top 1968 in historic significance," Nick commented. "After all, Martin Luther King Jr. and Robert Kennedy were assassinated, Lyndon B. Johnson stepped down, ten thousand antiwar protesters rioted at the Democratic convention in Chicago—"

"Jacqueline Kennedy married Aristotle Onassis that year," Ruth volunteered.

"And there were the love-ins, the naked-ins, the Poor People's March on Washington," Harvey added.

"Then along came 1969! A man on the moon—difficult to even believe possible at one time," Arthur marveled.

"What about Woodstock?" Abe said. "And don't forget Senator Ted Kennedy's fiasco at Chappaquiddick."

"And we can't ignore the massacre at Mylai," Eve reminded them. "Vietnam has divided our country almost as much as the Civil War. That song 'I've Gotta Be Me' is a beautiful piece of music, but I'm afraid some of our people have stretched the outer limits of what it implies. Once in a while it's necessary to think *we,* not just me!"

"Well said, Eve!" James became pensive. "I feel so guilty. I was too young to do anything in World War II. And now here I am sitting comfortable and happy watching a football game while those poor bastards over there are lying in rice paddies. And dying!"

"You can't put that on your shoulders. It's not your fault when you were born," Abe said.

"I wish the people at home would be more supportive of the kids that are over there. I get a sense the ones here almost blame those who are in combat—there isn't that pride and patriotism of country and for the men who are fighting in the name of our country.'' Arthur was visibly upset.

"It's a difficult time, Artie,'' Nick tried to explain. "I know what Jim means—I was too old before and now I'm even older. It's the inability to *do* something—to help fix what's wrong—that's what's so damn maddening!''

The room became quiet—everyone was in thoughtful silence. Then Ruth mused aloud, "Now what, I wonder? Have we gone about as far as we can go? Or is there more to come?''

Halftime was over and attention returned to the Rose Bowl. Cassandra and Eve took the opportunity to straighten up, to take the empty cans and bottles and used glasses to the kitchen and restock the fridge in the wet bar. Hilda and Ted were off, but they had prepared hors d'oeuvres the day before. All Eve had to do was arrange the cold cut vegetables and heat the cheese puffs and cocktail-size hot dogs. An avocado dip was already made; Eve only needed to scatter chips on the platter.

"I'm glad Hilda left reserves of everything, our troops are probably starved. I doubt anyone had a proper lunch, more than likely just a late breakfast or brunch.''

Cassandra walked to where Eve was working. "I love watching you lately, you—you glow! You know that?''

Eve turned. "I guess that's what happens when you're happy. I see that when I look at you, as well.''

"We're so very lucky!'' Cassandra began decorating a tray with some parsley, trying to decide if she should broach a certain subject. "I've been, I've wanted, to ask you about something. I need your advice.''

Eve immediately became concerned. "What is it, Cassie? What's wrong?''

"No, no, nothing is wrong!'' Cassandra was quick to reassure Eve. "It's, well, when I had Little Jim I pictured Mom and Dad playing with him, enjoying him, boasting about him to their pals, and also what it would mean to him to have another set of grandparents.''

"Oh, honey, I know. It's a shame!''

"I'm okay about that now." Cassandra hesitated, then blurted it out. "But I thought about my birth mother. Is she alive? Would she like to see her grandchild? Is she alone? Should I try to find her?"

She saw Eve's surprise. "I don't mean that she would take the place of my mom and dad, that's who they always will be in my heart, my mom and dad. But they aren't here. And what if she is lonely and she doesn't have anybody? Maybe I could bring her some pleasure in her old age. I feel I should share my good times."

Eve took Cassandra's hands. "What a treasure you are! I know exactly what you mean and of course you're absolutely right, it would be a boon for everyone concerned. I have a friend who might be able to help us find some answers. I'll call him next week."

They heard some loud noises coming from the den. "Oops, game must be nearly over. Would you grab that dish and I'll take these— we don't want those yells directed at us!"

"Ya-hoo! USC beat Michigan ten to three!" Pleased faces looked expectantly toward Eve and Cassandra. Ruth hurried to help unload as Eve announced, "This will have to hold you until the pizza comes in an hour. I have more, so don't be bashful!"

Eve got in touch with Sam Gershe, the adoption lawyer who had taken care of Ruth's situation. She gave him as much information as she had on Cassandra's parents.

"It's a little bit like looking for a needle in a haystack," he explained. "I'll check my files and contact some colleagues. Can't tell, maybe we'll get lucky! I'll let you know when I have any news."

Hollywood, California
Friday, February 6, 1970

"I still can't believe I saw what I saw—on stage—live." Abe shook his head in denial.

Nick laughed, "Better get used to it! *Hair* has been so successful across the country—the world actually—producers will be standing in line for the next play that goes further than *Hair* did. The show will look tame in comparison to what will come, trust me!"

Abe and Nick had gone into Hollywood to see one of the six United States touring companies of the off-Broadway, on-Broadway smash hit *Hair*. It was still playing on Broadway and had been performed in fourteen other countries. Nick had seen it in New York on a scouting trip, and when the appearance dates for the Los Angeles area were announced, he had quickly ordered tickets. He couldn't wait to take Abe and watch his reaction. Abe was really rather naive and old-fashioned when it came to public displays of sex or violence. He didn't believe they belonged on the movie screen or television screen or onstage. Obviously nudity was the alluring bait for audiences seeing *Hair,* overshadowing the music and lyrics. Nick wasn't disappointed, Abe had responded exactly as anticipated.

"Oh, I want to get the new *Sports Illustrated,*" Abe said as they passed a newsstand.

"Okay! I'll mosey on toward the car. We parked on the next street, right?"

"Yeah—about halfway down the block. I won't be long." Abe was scanning the magazine rack.

He found the issue, waited for his change and sauntered down the sidewalk. They had luckily found a spot on a side street just three blocks from the theater. Parking in the lot adjacent to the theater always resulted in sitting in a traffic jam at the end of a play.

Abe turned the corner, glanced in the direction of the car and froze. He made out three or four figures moving around and heard some muffled cries and thumping sounds. He dropped the magazine and bolted toward the scene.

Nick was bound by two guys while another pummeled him mercilessly.

"Give us the fuckin' keys, man!"

"Go to hell," Nick gasped.

"Git his wallet 'fore he gits gook all over it!"

"Nice watch, ol' man!"

Nick was no match for these hoodlums, even though he tried. "You cheap scum!" he wheezed.

"You hit me, ol' man, now you gonna pay fer touchin' me, git that?" one said, swinging hard, and Abe heard the sickening thud of a breaking bone.

With a blood-curdling scream, Abe hurled his body forward and bowled into the two goons holding Nick, who collapsed once he was freed.

"Get away from him, you bastards! I'll kill ya—"

The thieves were surprised and Abe got in some powerful blows before they knew what hit them. Then all three turned their attention to the wild intruder. Abe was strong and skilled and fought hard. Finally, one of them picked up the crowbar from where it had dropped and started for Abe.

Nick came to in time to see him, struggled to his knees and

lungcd for the man with the weapon. He grabbed the ankles and pulled the guy off balance, yelling, "Abe—watch out—"

The crowbar missed Abe but swung around in an arc and connected to Nick's skull.

Abe went crazy and furiously continued his attack, sobbing, shrieking, cursing, hitting, kicking, whirling, using every trick and karate move he had ever learned—and the crowbar flew out of the thug's hand.

"Shit man, no good—" one goon hollered

"Yeah, I'm hurtin'—"

"People gonna hear—"

"Yeah, finish this asshole. I got the keys from de ol' fart. Let's move it—"

Collectively they focused on crushing Abe with a barrage of savage punches and finally they beat him into unconsciousness.

"Fuckin' prick! Made me bleed!" One was so mad he had to give Abe a last kick before hc jumped in Nick's car and they sped off.

Eve wasn't sure if she was dreaming or if the telephone was actually ringing. Through her fog she heard the answering machine rattling off her recorded message. Then an unfamiliar gruff male voice came on. "This is Sergeant Roger Marcus of the Los Angeles Police Department. If this is the residence of Miss Eve Handel, please return my call at—"

Jerked into reality, Eve grabbed the receiver in a panic. "Hello, hello! This is Eve Handel. Can you hear me?"

"Yes, ma'am, I hear you. Sorry to bother you at this hour, but it's important."

"Please, it's no problem, what's wrong?"

The intensity in Eve's voice made Arthur sit up.

"Do you know Abraham Handel?" the sergeant inquired.

"Yes, yes, he's my brother! My God, what is it, what's happened?" She was trying to keep herself under control, but her body began to tremble. Arthur took her free hand and squeezed in support.

"Miss Handel, there was a robbery and—an assault—"

"Where is he, I'll, we'll be right there—" She handed Arthur the phone to take directions and ran to throw on some clothes.

Arthur drove like a madman to the emergency room at USC County Hospital. He hoped a policeman would stop him for speeding and then give him an escort, but he barreled through without a problem.

They screeched to a halt and ran to the entrance. As soon as she was inside the door, she yelled, "Abe! Abe Handel! Where is Abe Handel?"

A doctor, nurse and two policemen moved toward her.

"Miss Handel? Easy now, we have to talk for a minute."

Arthur addressed one of the uniformed men. "Are either of you Sergeant—" he glanced at the scrap of paper in his hand "—Roger Marcus?"

The older of the two uniformed men stepped forward. "That would be me."

"I'm Arthur Burdsey, a friend of the family's. Perhaps if Miss Handel can see her brother, I could help you with any questions, or information, or whatever."

Sergeant Marcus hesitated and then said, "Okay! But maybe you better come with her at first." He pulled Arthur aside, "He's pretty smashed up, might be hard for her to see him."

Arthur understood and whispered, "Is he—is he going to be all right?"

The policeman answered, "Looks like he'll make it, but it will take a while. But the other one..." he just shook his head.

Before Arthur could ask anything else or what that statement meant, Eve called. "Artie, where's Abe?"

Arthur guided Eve and followed the lead group. They stopped at a curtained partition. The nurse pulled the drape aside so they could enter the tiny space. Abe was on the bed, swathed in bandages. But the face that was exposed caused Eve to faint in Arthur's arms, and even Arthur gagged: angry-looking open wounds; eyes almost swollen shut; lips puffed to twice their size. It couldn't be Abe!

The doctor waved smelling salts under Eve's nose to revive her. "You need something?" he asked Arthur.

"No, I'll be fine," Arthur said weakly. "What in the hell happened, Sergeant?"

"No witnesses. A car happened to drive up as a car took off. They saw two men on the ground. The couple couldn't get a license number but described the vehicle—dark blue, club coupe, BMW, maybe a '67 or '68."

Arthur nodded in recognition. "That's Nick Larrington's car."

Sergeant Marcus wrote in his notebook, "L-A-R-R-I-N-G-T-O-N?"

"Correct!"

The policeman tore off the page and handed it to his partner, who immediately disappeared. "The other—person..."

Arthur's head snapped up, eyes questioning, "You mean...?"

He spoke softly. "The second victim was DOA. No identification was found on him. Miss Handell's brother must have arrived after the robbery was in progress and caused them to flee before they could get his stuff. That's how we knew who to call."

"He's a professional body trainer," Arthur explained, "in exceptional physical condition. I hope he beat the crap out of them."

"I'm sure he did some damage that'll help us identify the suspects if we can get a lead on the car."

The doctor tapped Arthur's shoulder. "She's okay now."

Arthur helped a wobbly Eve back into the cubicle. She still desperately clutched his arm, but she did manage to somewhat pull herself together. "Have, have you been able to determine the extent of his injuries?"

"We haven't the results of all the X-rays as yet. We know two ribs are cracked, I'm afraid his nose is broken. We don't think there are serious internal problems, but no doubt he'll be pretty sore. He has a slight concussion. Even though I admit his face looks a little like ground meat, we don't anticipate much scarring."

Arthur interrupted. "Is it possible to transfer him to a private hospital? I'd like our plastic surgeon to take a look and see if he can prevent any permanent trauma."

The doctor peered at Arthur. "Burdsey, you say? Are you connected to the Randall Burdsey Hospital?"

"Yes, I'm his son—it was built to honor my father. And we certainly appreciate your excellent care of Mr. Handel. But we do have some specialists who may be able to help him as well."

"Of course. I'll make the arrangements, and we'll send along duplicates of everything we have so far." The doctor started to go, then turned back to Arthur. "I've heard only wonderful comments about your facility. Thank you, the community needed what you were able to provide."

CHAPTER

57

Los Angeles, California
Friday, February 13, 1970

Eve sat alone now in Abe's room at Randall Burdsey Hospital. Arthur, Ruth, Harvey—everyone had taken turns so Abe would never be without a loved one nearby. There had been times during the past week when he had struggled to awareness, but he had never arrived at full consciousness for any length of time; the sedatives kindly kept him groggy.

Often his body would jerk and his arms and legs would thrash about, as if he were still fending off the assailants. A team of physicians had set the broken bones—once some of the swelling had gone down, further X-rays had confirmed a broken collarbone and broken bones in his arm and hand. There wouldn't be any visible reminders after a while. It wasn't the visible scars of that disastrous night that worried everyone, however. It was what couldn't be seen, the emotional scars—could they ever be healed?

The attackers had been apprehended early the next morning just outside of Baker, California, going northeast, obviously heading for the Nevada state line. They had stopped for gas. The serviceman had admired the car and tried to start a conversation, but the occupants hadn't responded and had appeared quite agitated. Then when he went to check under the hood, none knew how to open it. Intuitively he noted the license number. They had each paid a visit to the rest room, and after they pulled out from the station, the attendant checked the place. He found blood on paper towels in the trash can. Suspicious about their whole behavior, he decided to alert the authorities.

A bulletin had gone out over the wire statewide identifying the stolen car and plates. This new information perfectly matched the existing descriptions and data, including the number of men involved and their possible injuries. Two squad cars located the vehicle about twenty miles from Baker. It wasn't speeding then, but when the police turned on the siren for them to pull over, the driver pushed the pedal to the floor and the auto shot forward at a dizzying pace.

The chase lasted for about thirty miles, where a roadblock had been set up. By the time the men in the fleeing car spotted the obstruction it was too late. The driver tried to swerve but there was no place to go. The car sideswiped the barriers and plowed into a tree, landing in a ditch on its side, wheels still turning.

Two of the guys attempted to escape but only managed to go a few steps. Officers hurriedly removed the remaining man from the car in case the gas exploded.

There was no question these were the culprits. All had injuries, and Nick's wallet and watch were found on their persons. And the car was Nick's. They would be charged with murder, armed robbery and assault with a deadly weapon.

Nick Larrington was survived by a sister and nephew, the rest of his family had passed on. Evelyn Larrington Hopper knew her brother wished to be cremated and that he had already contracted with the Neptune Society a few years ago. Eve and Arthur volunteered to take the responsibility of overseeing the arrangements. The sister would plan a memorial for Nick out east, the West Coast commemorative was to be delayed until Abe could attend.

Eve and Arthur had stood on the bow of a private yacht to say goodbye to their dear friend. The pall of sadness was made more onerous because this was such a senseless, unnecessary waste of a life. A life that had brought hope and opportunity to so many young people. A life that had enriched the lives of those he loved beyond measure. Brimming eyes overflowed as they thought of the years that had been shared, the joys and the sorrows that had penetrated all their hearts. There was some comfort knowing those experiences, those times could never be lost, those riches would be stored within—always.

Abe opened his eyes slowly.

He wondered why it was so hard to stay awake. Why did everything hurt? He had never felt like this before. Where was he—what was this place?

Eve saw him stir and quickly rose to his side. "Abe, darling—it's Eve. Do you need anything? Something to drink, maybe?"

Abe knew it was Eve, but why was she talking so silly? Why were his legs and arms so heavy? What was all this white stuff? And then he remembered—Nick, the brawl, then what?

Eve was still leaning over him, and she saw he was able to focus on her. "Hi there! Little water?"

Abe nodded slightly. She put the straw to his lips and gently raised his head. "Only sip a little at a time, sweetheart."

He gazed into her face, searching for an answer or answers to the giant puzzle that lodged in his head.

Eve recognized his need and sighed, praying for the ability and wisdom to tell him what he had to know in the least hurtful way. Maybe she wouldn't have to disclose the ultimate horror just yet.

"You are in a hospital—Artie's hospital! There was an attack—three men—"

Abe talked with difficulty. "They get away?"

"These monsters evidently were trying to rob Nick when you arrived on the scene. They did escape, but not before you walloped them good and hard."

A hint of a smile crossed Abe's mouth.

"But later that night—really, early the next morning –the police caught them and they are now in jail," she continued. "And they won't be out for a very long time, if ever."

Abe seemed satisfied for the moment and was quiet. Some minutes later, he indicated the bed and the bandages. ''How long?''

''Well, now that you are coming out of the initial shock and we can wean you from the medication, you should be able to get out of here in a few days. Of course, this is only me talking, the experts will be more specific and accurate.'' Eve smiled, hoping to keep this in a light vein.

''What—about Nick? When can he go?''

Eve's heart sank. The time had come and it was up to her. She felt a surge of panic rise in her throat. Forcefully she swallowed, pushing down the swelling, suffocating tide of emotion. Blinking hard to hold back the tears, she began, ''Abe dear, Nick has already gone—''

''You mean—he's already home?'' Abe interrupted.

''I mean he, he left to go to another home....'' Eve's voice trailed off, seeing Abe was completely confused. She realized she just had to say the truth, simply but straightforwardly.

''Abe, God took Nick to live in heaven. He was hurt so badly God didn't want him to suffer anymore. Nick is resting now and— and at peace.'' She cradled his one free hand.

Abe lay motionless, barely breathing. A tear leaked out, and then another, and another, until a stream rolled down his face. What seemed like hours elapsed. Eve didn't invade his private mourning with a word or distracting movement, she merely wiped away the evidence of his despair.

At long last, Abe spoke. ''I remember now, I remember, oh God...'' He couldn't stifle the wretching sobs. ''They were hitting Nick—I tried to stop them, then—''

Eve wasn't sure if she should attempt to prevent him from re-hashing the torturous scene or let him go on. She recalled her own devastation, and in retrospect, knew she would have recovered sooner had she not stashed away the misery inside her soul. It was better Abe should let it out whenever he could, so she kept silent.

''—then one of them had some, something in his hands. He started at me and Nick somehow got him off-kilter so—so when he went at me the thing hit Nick instead. I, I don't, I don't know any more...."

She patted Abe's hand. "They say you fought hard!"

He lay there, shaking his head as if to loosen and then lose the haunting images. Bitterly he mumbled to himself, "Not hard enough! Or, or Nick would still be here. Why, why, why? Why him?"

Abe's voice had become louder and louder. A nurse came in. "Are you all right, Mr. Handel? Can I get you anything?"

"No, no thank you, I don't want any more pills or shots," Abe answered.

When she left, Abe spoke softly and somberly to Eve. "Nick saved my life. You realize that? He died trying to save my life!"

Abe was released from the hospital on Thursday, February 19, and the memorial for Nick was held on Friday, February 27. Jude Abavas opened one of the stages on the Colvas Studio lot and made all the arrangements. His staff worked with Eve and Abe on the invitation list. Rentals, parking, catering—everything was taken care of and in order.

Abe chose a wonderful photo of a laughing, happy Nick to go on the cover of the program. On the dedication page was a simple two-line quote:

You make a living by what you get.
You make a life by what you give.

Author Unknown

Inside was a short biography, identification of the music to be played, and the names of the speakers.

Jude's assistants had researched Nick's records from his time at Status Films and Pad-Dar Pictures to his years at Utopia Studios and at Colvas. They found a photo of every single person he had brought to the various studios as head of casting and talent. The vastly enlarged stills were suspended on brass chains from the overhead catwalks, almost acting as walls enclosing the seating area. Studio stages were cavernous and tended to be barren and uninviting until a set was constructed. These photographs made the surroundings very personal and warm and reminded the guests of the extraordinary contribution Nick had made to the industry.

Prominently displayed were pictures of the English actress Cynthia Cellac, Heidi Graham, Michael Flanders, Marc Saville and Cassandra Hollister among others.

To further illustrate the effect and benefit of Nick's eye for talent, two giant screens were installed on either side of the raised platform and brief clips of footage on all the stars featured were run consecutively until the ceremony began. The array was very impressive.

The congregation represented a cross section of Nick's life, from studio executives to performers to gaffers to the guys on his softball team. The speakers were from all categories and included Jude Abavas, Peter Padon, Heidi Graham and Eve Handel. Abraham Handel's remarks were last on the agenda.

Abe still had casts on his arm and hand and he had to move carefully because of his ribs and collarbone. His face showed residual wounds from the beatings but had healed enough for him to be out in public.

It might have been a pathetic figure who made the walk to the microphone, but Abe's voice was strong, filled with fierce passion.

"'You make a living by what you get. You make a life by what you give.' What a life Nick Larrington made! Because he gave everything, the supreme, the maximum. He gave his life! He gave his life to save a friend! He gave his life to save me!"

Abe's eyes roamed around the crowd. "Each of you are here to honor him because Nick gave you something, too. Maybe it was the creative way he fulfilled his responsibilities. Maybe it was the beginning of a new and different career. Maybe it was advice. Maybe it was an encouraging smile. Maybe it was just—time—he gave you. Friendship he always gave. And loyalty. And enjoyment."

Abe stopped for a second to collect his thoughts, to fight for control of his emotions. He was walking a high wire, and he couldn't let himself fall off.

"I have been racking my brain to find a reason—any reason—why Nick was taken from us. Here was a man who did no harm, only good. Who didn't have a malicious or selfish or spiteful bone in his body. So why?

"The only clues I came up with were questions! Is it because his job was done here? And if so, by his example, is the challenge for us to carry forward his belief in giving? Three weeks ago I lost the best friend in the world. We all lost! And for the loss to make any sense at all or have any kind of meaning—for me—the only way I can cope with this emptiness is to devote my life to continuing his gift of giving. Somehow I believe that will keep his spirit here and still working."

Abe looked toward Eve, Ruth, Arthur.

"With the help of many exceptional people, I am establishing the Nick Larrington Foundation in his memory. Its purpose will be to aid and guide young people who aspire to be in the entertainment or communications business but have limited means. Training in all the fields of these industries is costly, and there are only a handful of facilities that people can turn to. It's fitting that Nick Larrington's legacy will endure through this foundation."

He paused and directed his focus somewhere far beyond the confines of the stage. "I won't say goodbye, Nick—that's too final. Just, till we meet again. And until that time, you live in our hearts."

Los Angeles, California
Monday, July 3, 1972

"Miss Handel, Mr. Sam Gershe is on line one," Eleanor Rose announced over the intercom. Matilda Carliss, Eve's former secretary, had retired last year.

"Hello, Sam, how are you?" Eve leaned back casually in her desk chair and idly doodled on her scratch pad. Suddenly her body shot upright.

"Are you sure, Sam?" She listened intently and then answered, "Of course I can come to your office, just tell me when!"

Eve canceled her remaining appointments and hurried to her car. Driving east toward downtown Los Angeles, she tried to keep her excitement in check.

She cautioned herself not to let her imagination work overtime, which God knew she could do! But this could be so miraculous! Please let it be true, she entreated over and over!

Eve diverted her speculations about today by concentrating and reflecting on what the past year or so had brought to everyone's life. It had been an uphill climb ever since Nick's death to get Abe, and themselves, back on an even keel. But they had all kept going, a few slips backward every so often, then like the lyrics from a song they would "pick themselves up, dust themselves off, and start all over again."

The Nick Larrington Foundation had made great strides. Abe had found a two-story office building for sale on Ventura Boulevard in Studio City. Arthur, Peter Padon and Jude Abavas had each pledged a million dollars to launch the project. All of the contributions were put in an interest-bearing account until the funds were actually utilized. The renovations were now almost completed. Many specialists had been interviewed and the staff was nearly at full strength. There would be classes and instruction offered in singing, dancing— both classical and modern—diction, drama, writing, journalism, broadcasting, even counseling for advice.

Later, if allowed to expand, directing and producing could be included in the curriculum.

Once the system was operational, volunteers would handle special courses and projects. Eve, for example, would direct scenes, perhaps plays, and showcase new talent to the casting directors at the various studios in the little theater that had been built. Ruth and Harvey would supervise the journalism and writing divisions. Using their contacts, promising material could conceivably be seen by publishers or editors or producers. Abe would conduct fitness classes—so necessary for everyone's health and appearance.

Professional players, when possible, would perform with the inexperienced beginners. The businessmen involved, like Arthur and James, would take care of the foundation's finances and keep everything solvent.

This was not a commercial enterprise. Students would be charged a nominal fee of admission, as opposed to the astronomical sums private instructors commanded. If the entrant was unable to pay anything, limited scholarships would be available to qualifiers.

The word had gone out and the applications had poured in. The biggest problem would be selecting the students.

Abe's broken body had totally healed. Because of his profession, he knew how to reap the most benefit from the physical therapy exercises and had applied himself diligently.

Mentally he was also progressing. The planning, the construction, the forming of the foundation had filled every available hour left after his work was done, so he was very positive.

However, when Eve's dogs, Molly and Lucy, died from old age, Abe had more difficulty accepting their deaths than Eve. And she was totally distraught. Those four-legged members of the family had seen Eve through major traumas in her life.

But Abe was simply excessively vulnerable to any loss—it struck an exposed nerve. Obviously his psyche was still exceedingly tender. So when he was confronted with potential disaster, he would feverishly work out in the gym until he didn't have any energy left to think. It seemed each episode took a mite less effort—a small step forward, hopefully.

Eve walked out of Sam Gershe's office—no—she floated out of his office on cloud nine.

She couldn't believe it! Oh, thank God, thank God, thank God! Her prayers had been answered—Sam's news had been even more than she had hoped for. She couldn't wait to set this day down in her journal. There had been so many black-letter days to put in, and then there had been the wonderful red-letter days—like the days Artie had come back into her life! And wow—this was a red-letter day! A landmark day! A glorious day! Come on, traffic, get out of the way, she silently yelled. She wanted to get home. She needed to get to a telephone.

Eve barely waited to turn the car engine off before dashing into the house. She threw her pocketbook and briefcase on the foyer table, ran to the den and dialed furiously.

"Damn!" she muttered aloud. "Damn, damn, damn! No one's home!"

She thought for a moment, and then smiled. A better idea had come to her! This news shouldn't be told over the telephone, anyway. There should be a celebration, a party, with a grand announcement, much more exciting!

Eve made some calls, left messages for everyone to meet at her place at seven. Happily she started for the kitchen to tell Hilda and Ted to prepare for guests this evening. She felt like skipping—the way she had when she was a child—or dancing.... In the middle of a turn she cried out in pain. What seemed like a bolt of lightning traveled up one arm, across her chest and down the other arm. Her figure slumped to the floor. Eve fought to regain mastery of her body, but the battle was lost. The darkness had won.

Epilogue

Los Angeles, California
July 4, 1972

The news of Eve Handel's collapse had resulted in much soul-searching during the night.

Arthur Randall Burdsey had to face the truth—if his love was to be taken from him again, he would thank God he had had the last five glorious years with her.

Cassandra Hollister Carpenter had come to a conclusion. If the woman who had been like a mother to her was to leave her, she would survive, because that is what Eve would have expected from her. She had to be here and strong for her family.

Ruth Lena Handel Hill realized only God could determine if her sister was meant to die. And if Ruth's secret should get out, who was left to care? Harvey already knew, and her daughter would never know.

Abraham Vanja Handel decided it didn't matter if Eve's journal revealed he was gay—people would have to like him for who he was, not what he was. He had had to cope with the death of someone he loved. If he had to go through that agonizing bereavement again now, he would—well—he would survive. He had to survive if that was God's will.

Marc Saville had paced all through the night. It was almost eleven years ago that Eve had given him an alibi. She had believed him, why wouldn't the police? He hadn't killed the girl, and he was tired of living in fear. He had blown away the real love of his life. After two other failed marriages, he had said enough. Now he just "went with" the girls. His career was still strong, even at forty-two. If Eve died, to hell with it, he'd go to the police and tell them the truth—before her journal exposed him.

Michael Flanders, the New York stage actor, wondered if Eve had ever mentioned the "Matthias Sigismeir" episode to anyone? Or his drinking problem?

Heidi Graham Levine only felt grief at the prospect of losing Eve. She had nothing to hide. The man she had married "for safety" had turned out to be her Prince Charming, after all.

Jenine Jasmine now lived in Europe. Older women were more appreciated there, and she still had quite a "full life." She hoped Eve had forgiven her, because she had always liked Eve and had been grateful for her guidance. And who cared if she had had an abortion or two and had bedded every eligible bachelor worth having! Everyone probably knew it already, anyway!

And Douglas Hassal? Too bad about the old girl! He hoped she never mentioned anything in her diary about the rubber duckies in the bathtub. But who would believe the ramblings of a disappointed, love-starved woman above the presence of a man such as he?

Los Angeles, California
Friday, July 21, 1972, 5:00 p.m.

There was a knock on the door of Eve Handel's bedroom.

"It's open," she said softly.

Arthur Randall Burdsey entered and quickly walked to her bed, where he leaned over and gently kissed her lips. "How's my bride?"

"You never made me legitimate, remember?"

"You wouldn't let me!" he chided.

Eve laughed, "I'm teasing, you sweet soul. But I think I'm ready now. Living in sin is so commonplace today, I would rather marry and be unique. And I guess I like the old-fashioned approach better, anyway."

Arthur's heart was overflowing with happiness. He hadn't lost his one true love and he'd gained a wife.

The emergency room doctor and Eve's own physician had been correct—the cardiograph, blood tests and X-rays all confirmed Eve hadn't had a coronary despite the symptoms. But the doctors had glimpsed stones in one X-ray plate. They did a gallbladder series, and confirmed the diagnosis. The characteristics of a heart attack and gallstones were strikingly similar.

Eve had gone into surgery immediately and came through very well. Weak and tired, but all right. No visitors, except for Arthur, had been allowed at the hospital. But she had been released two days ago and was now resting at home, ready to see loved ones.

"There are some people very anxious to visit you, three in particular," Arthur informed her. He was bursting with joy and just wanted to hold her and be alone with her, but he knew he had to share her with the others. His comfort was the recognition they would now be together for always.

Cassandra and Ruth and Abe tiptoed in, looking apprehensive and worried.

"Oh, for heaven's sake! Cassie, Ruth and Abe—run over here and give me a hug," Eve scolded. "I'm not dying. In fact, I just became engaged."

The three rushed toward her, laughing and crying, grateful their prayers had been answered.

Arthur started to inch away, thinking perhaps they didn't want him around.

"Oh, no, you don't!" Eve stopped him. "I have a lot to say, and I want you to be a part of it. Now, everyone sit down on the bed around me and listen carefully. Are Jim and Harvey here?"

Ruth answered, "They'll be here after work."

"I can't wait." Eve settled herself, looked at them tenderly. There was an indefinable aura about her as she started to speak. "If you remember, I had called everyone to come to the house for cocktails. I had a reason, but those damn stones got in my way.

Well, they are *out* of my way and I thank my Lord I am here to continue today.''

She paused for a moment, as if gathering strength. ''Ruth, I am going to betray a confidence, but only to the ones in this room.''

She turned to Cassandra and Arthur and Abe. ''You see, many years ago, Ruth fell in love. And out of that love came a child.''

Ruth started to cry and Eve took her hand. ''But because the father was not an honorable man, she was forced to allow the baby to go for adoption so she—yes, it was a girl—would have a proper mother *and* father.''

Cassandra stood up and went to comfort Ruth.

Eve continued, ''It was not easy for her then, and it hasn't been easy since. She didn't trust enough to love again until much later— too late to have a family. I thought it would be helpful if Ruth knew something about her daughter, not to sabotage, just to be aware of the kind of life she had. Was she happy? Did she have children? Things like that.

''Ruth, through our lawyer, who fortunately is still alive, we found your daughter.''

There was a collective gasp. Ruth lifted her head and stared at Eve, tears streaming, eyes wide in wonder and uncertainty. ''Can— can—you tell me about her?''

''I've seen her, my dear sister, and she is beautiful, inside and out. She is blissfully married, with three adorable children—''

Ruth hung on every word, filling her empty heart with the images Eve described.

''—she's healthy. She worked, did extremely well, but she has tapered off to spend more time at home.''

Cassandra and Arthur and Abe were deeply moved, and showed their love and support, wanting to participate in Ruth's happiness. Eve was pleased, but she had more. ''I'm not quite finished yet.'' They shifted their attention again to Eve. What else could there be?

''This seems to be my day for breaking promises of secrecy, but sometimes one has to break a promise to keep a promise.''

The four faces were a study in bewilderment.

''Before Cassie's mother died, she revealed that Cassie had been adopted. Cassie expressed a desire to know who her birth parents were, not to usurp Kathleen and Jim's positions, just to know, especially now that both her mother and father were gone.''

Cassandra drew in her breath sharply, holding it expectedly.

"I didn't uncover anything about your father, Cassie. But through the same lawyer, I did locate your mother.''

Tears filled Cassandra's eyes. "Do you think I might meet her sometime?''

Eve's body radiated her excitement. "I am positive you will meet her." She hesitated, hoping to explain so the shock wouldn't produce harmful reactions. "You must understand, the reason this lawyer was able to help me so successfully is because he handled both cases. He could not breach his confidentiality agreement before, because Cassie's parents were still living. I first saw him regarding Ruth, but it wasn't until I approached him concerning Cassie that he could piece everything together and give me the information.''

Eve took hold of Ruth's and Cassandra's hands. "Cassie, here is your birth mother. Ruth, this is your daughter.''

There was complete silence. The breathing was barely audible. Incredulousness filled the air. Faintly, realization stirred, trying to find its way. Acceptance joined the fray, and finally the two broke through and prevailed. Oh, happy day! Oh, awesome day!

Much, much later, after Ruth and Harvey and Abe and Cassie and Jim had gone home, saturated in joy, Eve and Arthur lay side by side, savoring the wonders this day had brought.

"Artie dear, would you start a fire, please?'' Eve asked quietly.

"In July?'' Arthur was immediately concerned. "Are you all right? Do you have a chill? Maybe I should call the doctor, today might have been too much for you.''

"No, no! I'm fine! I couldn't feel any better, my darling. Indulge me.''

Arthur, although a bit confused, did as she requested.

Eve walked slowly to the fireplace. "Now, don't fuss over me, the doctor said I could move around as long as I didn't overdo it. But I would appreciate it if you would bring that box by my night-stand to me.''

She sat down on one of the two armchairs facing the mantel-piece and patted the other, indicating Arthur should join her.

"When I was a girl and first learned how to write, I developed a habit of jotting down thoughts about, well, almost anything—life, me, people, events, places. This...whatever you want to call it—journal or diary—became my confidant.

"I think my purpose was to be able to look back one day on the pages and relive the whys, the whens, the whos, the wheres. I've done that now, and they accomplished exactly what they were meant to do."

Eve reached into the carton and opened one of the oversize envelopes inside and began feeding notebooks into the fire.

"But I'm ready to start fresh chapters. I'm not ignoring or forgetting what was, but rather, letting go. And I'm commencing brand-new segments, authored and created by—Mrs. Arthur Randall Burdsey.''